Dukes *in* Disguise

Grace Burrowes
Susanna Ives
Emily Greenwood

Published as a three-novella compilation, Dukes In Disguise, by Grace Burrowes Publishing, 21 Summit Avenue, Hagerstown, MD 21740.

Cover design by Wax Creative, Inc.

ISBN: 1941419275
ISBN-13: 978-1941419274

TABLE OF CONTENTS

THE DUKE OF LESSER PUDDLEBURY

GRACE BURROWES

CHAPTER ONE

Over the clip-clop of the coach horses' hooves and the incessant throbbing of his arse, Coinneach Callum Amadour Ives St. Bellan, ninth Duke of Mowne, endured that form of affection which—among grown men at least—traveled under the sobriquet of *teasing*.

More honest company would call it making sport of a fellow in a misguided attempt to cheer him up.

"Mowed down, they'll say, like so much wheat," Starlingham quipped. "One stray bullet and the great duke is *hors de combat.*"

Lucere was not to be outdone. "The moon sets, as it were."

They went off into whoops, endlessly entertained, as always, by a play on the title Mowne, which was an old Scottish term for the lunar satellite... and thus a cognate for a reference to the human fundament.

"If the Sun and Stars had not tarried with a pair of tavern maids, we would have reached the dueling ground sooner," Con groused. "This whole imbroglio is your fault, you two."

There was simply no getting comfortable in a coach after being shot in the arse. No getting comfortable *anywhere*.

"I would be spared my present indignity," Con went on, "but for the flirtatious excesses of my oldest and dearest friends. Bear in mind, if the wound festers, the pair of you will be consoling my mother on the loss of her darling baby boy, and Freddy will become the next Duke of Mowne."

Mention of Mama sobered the Duke of Starlingham and the Duke of Lucere faster than a ballroom full of unbetrothed debutantes in the last week of the Season. Faced with such a prospect, the Sun, Moon, and Stars, as Con and his friends were collectively known, would have closed ranks. They'd often stood figuratively shoulder to shoulder, defending their bachelor freedoms against all perils, most especially the artillery fire of the matchmakers.

In the present situation, Con and his friends would have to split up.

"Where did you say we were going?" Lucere asked.

"Outer Perdition," Starlingham muttered. "We're in Yorkshire. Nothing civilized goes on in Yorkshire, where the winters are long and the sheep are notoriously friendly."

"Starlingham, you will take up residence at your hunting box," Con said, assuming that handy dwelling yet stood. "Lucere, you and your manservant, should you refuse to part with that worthy, will have to bide at a local inn or boarding house. Send word to either me or Starlingham regarding your choice of accommodations. I can stay with my third cousin, Jules St. Bellan."

Dear old cousin Jules was one of Mama's many faithful correspondents, though the relationship was so attenuated as to be more nominal than biological. Nominal and fiscal, for Con had been sending a stipend north to Lesser Puddlebury for years.

"Maybe we're doing this all a bit too brown," Lucere said. "Your Uncle Leo might never get word of the duel."

"Maybe you're still cup-shot," Starlingham countered, grabbing for the strap dangling above his head as the coach lumbered through a curve. "If Leo learns we're taking a week's repairing lease in Greater Goosepuddle, he'll suspect Freddy got into another scrape, and then Mowne won't be allowed so much as a spare farthing."

Freddy, next in line for the Mowne ducal title, was *always* getting into scrapes, as were Quinton and Hector, and—not to be outdone by her older brothers—Antigone.

Uncle Leo had decided that Freddy must be taken in hand—*by Con*—or Con would lose control of the family finances, of which Leo was trustee.

"Which of you will marry Antigone if Leo cuts off my funds?" Con asked, for somebody would have to marry her if she was to be kept in reasonable style. Leo's views of a wardrobe allowance were parsimonious on a good day.

Only two paths circumnavigated Leo's threatened penny-pinching when it came to the family finances. The first was for Con to turn five-and-thirty, which fate would not befall him for another six years—assuming he could avoid further incidents of bloodshed. The second means of prying Leo's fingers off the St. Bellan money pots was to marry. If the Deity were merciful, that duty lay at least a decade in the future.

Con shifted on his pillow. The laudanum was wearing off, and the dilemma caused by Freddy's dueling loomed ever larger.

"Hearing no volunteers for the honor of marrying my darling sister," Con said, "we must deceive Uncle Leo in hopes he never learns of Freddy's latest mis-step. In the alternative, I could take a vow of poverty, which would lead perforce to the cheering vistas of unmitigated chastity and limitless sobriety."

"It might not be so bad," Lucere said, an odd comment for a man whom rumor suggested was facing an engagement to a German princess.

"Poverty, chastity, and sobriety?" Starlingham asked.

"No, spending a week in Lower Dingleberry. How many times have these people seen three dukes in the neighborhood at once?"

"They must *never* see three dukes in the neighborhood at once," Con retorted. "I shall be Mr. Connor Amadour and swear my cousin to eternal secrecy. He's a mercenary old soul, and his silence can be bought. You two will not trade on your ducal consequence whatsoever. Be wealthy, be charming, be handsome, but keep your titles to yourselves. The greatest commodity traded up and down the Great North Road is gossip, and three dukes dropping coin and consequence all over some rural bog would reach Leo's notice by the next full moon, as it were."

Three young, healthy, *single* dukes could do nothing without observation and comment by all of society. Freddy enjoyed a little more privacy, but Leo somehow learned of the boy's every stupid wager and bungled prank nonetheless.

"So… we're not to be dukes," Lucere said.

"We're not to have even a country manor for our accommodations," Starlingham added.

"But if we can pull this off," Con said, "I'll retain control over my portion of the family money, which means nobody need marry Antigone, and I won't have to call either of you out for landing me in this contretemps. All we're missing are cold Scottish mornings spent tramping about the grouse moors."

And the gorgeous scenery, and the fresh air, and a chance to get the stink and noise of London out of a man's soul.

"Two weeks, then, but we're also missing good Scottish whisky," Lucere noted.

"And the Scottish lasses," Starlingham said, saluting with an imaginary glass.

Con would miss both of those comforts, but in truth, his allowance also paid for Mama's occasional gambling debt, Antigone's excesses at the milliner's, Hector's charities, Quinton's experiments, and Freddy's scrapes.

Con financed it all out of his own allotment, a delicately balanced enterprise that Uncle Leo could easily upset. Leo never interfered with Con's decisions affecting the ducal finances, but with the personal finances, only Con's funds stood between his immediate family and utter mortification.

Though what could be more mortifying than getting shot in the arse?

"When you do see the Scottish lasses again," Lucere said, "you'll have a fetching scar."

"Would you like one of your own?" Con drawled. "All you need do is attempt to interrupt Freddy's next duel, for he's sure to have another. Stand well clear of the opponents, but position yourself such that Freddy's bullet bounces just so off a rock and grazes your ducal assets. Along with your fetching scar, you'll enjoy a significant mess and no little discomfort. I was wearing my favorite riding breeches, for which Freddy will pay."

"Hurts, does it?" Starlingham asked quietly.

These were Con's friends. He dared not answer honestly, or they'd pound Freddy to flinders when the poor lad had been trying to delope.

"I did fancy those breeches. Their destruction pains me." The truth, when Bond Street tailors could beggar a man in a single season.

Lucere passed Con a silver flask. "We'll drink a toast then, to two weeks of happy ruralizing in Upper Lesser Middle Bog-dingle-shire."

Con took a swallow of mellow comfort and passed the flask to Starlingham, who did likewise.

"To being a plain mister, and not Your Perishing Grace every moment of the infernal day," Starlingham said, raising the flask.

Lucere accepted the silver vessel back and studied the unicorn embossed amid the laurel leaves on the side.

"Good-bye to the Sun, Moon, and Stars, and for the next two weeks, here's to the dukes in disguise." He tipped up the flask, then tipped it higher, shaking the last drops into his open mouth.

Con's arse hurt, but to have such friends, well, that made a man's heart ache a little too. He raised his arm, as they'd been doing since one of them had suffered an adolescent infatuation with the paintings of Jacques-Louis David.

His friends did likewise—the most inane rituals never died—and bumping fists, as one they chanted, "To the dukes in disguise!"

* * *

"This is not a tumbledown cottage," Con muttered as the groom and coachman wrestled his trunks from the boot. "I could swear Her Grace said Cousin Jules resides in a tumbledown cottage, barely more than a shack."

The dwelling was pretty, in a rural sort of way. Three stories of soft gray fieldstone topped with standing seam tin, the whole flanked with stately oaks and fronted with a wide, covered terrace the width of the house. Red and white roses vined from trellises up onto the terrace roof.

The place gave off a disconcerting air of bucolic welcome, such as a duke in demand by every London hostess ought not to find appealing.

"Will that be all, *sir?*" John Coachman asked with an exaggerated wink.

"Thank you, yes. I'll expect to see you again in two weeks, and until then, I expect utmost discretion from you and the grooms. Ut. Most."

John wasn't prone to drunkenness, but his groom was young and new to a duke's service.

"Right, Your Worship. Mind that injury, or Her—*your mama* will have me out on me *arse*."

More winking, and then the coach creaked down the drive, kicking up a plume of dust as Starlingham's gloved hand fluttered a farewell from the window. Nobody came forth from the cottage to carry in bags, greet the visitor, or otherwise acknowledge company.

"I'm not a stupid man," Con said, gaze on the bright red front door.

But what did one do without a footman about to knock on the door, pass over a card, and ensure the civilities were observed? How did luggage find its way above stairs before the next rain shower? The knocker was the sort that never came down, so how did one tell if the family was receiving?

Mysteries upon puzzles. How would... Mr. Connor Amadour *go on?*

Insight struck as thunder rumbled off to the south. This was Yorkshire, and thunder rumbled about a good deal, even when the sun shone brightly.

Also five minutes before a downpour turned the shire to mud.

Con marched—unevenly, given the increasing pain of his wound—up the steps and *rapped on the door.*

Nothing happened. Why hadn't Con asked John Coachman and the grooms to pile the luggage under the terrace roof? The roses grew in such profusion as to make the porch cozy. A wide swing hung near one end, a worn rug beneath it, embroidered pillows in each corner of the swing.

Con had recently become an ardent if silent admirer of the comfy pillow.

He banged the knocker again, rather louder than gentility allowed. Perhaps the help was hard of hearing. Perhaps they were all down in the kitchen, scrambling to tuck in their livery because it was half day. Even the legendarily hardworking denizens of Yorkshire would observe the custom of half day.

More thunder, more rapping. Life as Mr. Amadour looked decidedly unappealing. A wind began to tease at the surrounding oaks, while Con's trunks sat several yards from the foot of the steps, apparently incapable of levitating into the house.

Mr. Amadour was a resourceful fellow, Con decided, and fit, despite his injuries. He fenced, he boxed, he rode great distances in the normal course. He gave a good account of himself on any cricket pitch and was a reputable oarsman.

Apparently, he had latent skills as a porter too, for it took Con a mere fifteen minutes to wrestle three trunks up the steps and pile them beside the door. Even wearing gloves, though, he acquired a scraped knuckle, two bruised fingers, and a squashed toe.

And he'd started the wound on his backside to throbbing. He couldn't very well check to see if it was bleeding again, though he suspected it was. The surgeon had told him to apply pressure directly to the injury to stop any renewed bleeding.

Applying pressure to a bullet wound amounted to self-torture.

Con reconnoitered. He was a duke, a single, wealthy-on-paper, not-bad-looking duke—not that single, wealthy dukes could be bad-looking in the eyes of most. He'd bested matchmakers, debutantes, card sharps, and Uncle Leo. He'd learned the knack of looking pious while napping through a Sunday sermon.

Cousin Jules would come home, for Cousin Jules never traveled to speak of. He was too busy writing to Mama in an endless correspondence of gossip, gratitude for the last bank draft, and importuning for the next one. Perhaps Jules was on a constitutional out among the lovely scenery.

Con determined that he would admire the scenery too, from the comfort of the pillowed swing at the end of the porch. All would remain cozy and dry on the porch despite the fickle weather, Cousin Jules would ramble home, and within the hour, Con would be tucked up before a fire, a glass of brandy in hand. He'd be a welcome, if unexpected, guest whose worst problem would be all the fussing and cooing from the help.

As it should be.

* * *

"I am growing to hate market days," Julianna said.

"You hate that Maurice Warren is becoming bolder," MacTavish replied, casting a scowl at the lowering sky. If anybody's scowl could have chased off the clouds, it should have been his.

"I hate that my coin doesn't go as far as it used to," Julianna said. "You can take the cart straight around back, Mac. I'll help you unload."

That magnificent scowl swung in Julianna's direction. "You'll do no such thing, miss. Bad enough you must haggle with the thieves and rogues at the market. Bad enough that lazy bag-of-sass housekeeper had to take herself off visiting. Bad enough—somebody has come to call, or driven a coach up our lane by misdirection."

MacTavish would have brought the cart to a halt, but Julianna appropriated the whip and brushed it over the mule's quarters.

"You can study the tracks later. We need to unload the goods before the heavens open up, and if you let Hortensia stop now, we might not get her moving until Yuletide."

Because Hortensia, like Julianna, was mortally tired. Unlike Julianna, the mule could make her wishes known, and frequently did. As mules went, she was a good sort. Worked hard, lived on nothing but decent pasture much of the year, and asked for little besides the occasional carrot from the children. But she was the last young mule on the property, and ploughing heavy Yorkshire soil was best undertaken with four stout draft horses, not one overworked mule.

Mr. Warren owned a literal herd of mules, of course.

The cart rattled along to the back of the cottage, and Hortensia halted at the door without any prompting from Mac.

"Good mule," Mac said, climbing down. He came around to assist Julianna, but she hopped down on her own.

"Let's hurry. If the rain doesn't start in the next two minutes, the children will come pelting up the lane, and their help isn't to be endured."

"Children, bah. Locusts, sent from the devil to plague adults and innocent mules. Horty agrees with me."

Julianna grabbed a pair of coarse sacks from the back of the cart. "Sometimes, I agree with you, but we'll let that be our little secret."

In the course of "assisting" to bring in the weekly haul from market, the children could drop, misplace, sample, hide, and damage half the goods Julianna had haggled away her morning procuring. Thank the gods of Yorkshire weather, or the charms of Mr. Hucklebee's summer natural sciences academy, Julianna managed to get the produce properly stored in the pantries and larders before any little feet thundered through the back doorway.

The rain was almost as accommodating, though on the last trip to the cart, Julianna felt the cold slap of an impending downpour against her nape. She paused for a moment, face turned to the sky. If the children were out of doors, downpours could mean colds, colds meant sitting up with a sick child, and sitting up with a sick child meant...

"Please take Hortensia around to the stable," Julianna told Mac. "She's earned a few oats for her efforts."

"Oats, in summer? You're daft Julianna Marie MacKinnon St. Bellan." Then, more gently as he grabbed the mule's bridle, "C'mon along, princess. The mule, I'm allowed to spoil. The lady of the house must work herself to exhaustion."

As must the man of all work, muttering all the while.

"You can cut some fresh roses when you're done with Horty," Julianna said, for Mac was getting on, and Julianna had to find ways to make him rest occasionally. He'd been getting on for as long as Julianna could recall, but like the sturdy stones that formed her home, his looks never changed. He and Hortensia were the twin pillars of Julianna's independence, and without them...

Maurice Warren's self-satisfied smile rose in Julianna's imagination.

So she sent Mac to pluck roses rather than let him work all afternoon in the barn. Instead of sitting down herself, she started on the stew that would have to do for dinner that night. The meat—a brace of lean hares Mac had caught the previous day—was sizzling in the pan, vegetables chopped and ready for the pot, when Mac tromped into the kitchen, a bouquet of thorny roses in his hand.

His expression promised that, as usual, he had bad news. "Miss, there's a set of fancy travelin' trunks on the front porch. Doubtless, they're full of goods we can sell over in York. Every cloud always has a silver lining, my ma used to say."

Trunks? "We're not expecting guests."

They never expected guests, thank God. Guests ate, they required bed linens, they interfered with household routines. How many times had dear Cousin Marie threatened to visit, and how many times had Julianna put her off?

"The trunks are mighty fine, miss. Shiny brass hinges, stout locks, though a bullet or two judiciously aimed at the——"

"You will not assassinate trunks belonging to somebody else," Julianna said, trading her apron for a plain brown wool shawl. "Nor will you sell goods we cannot claim as ours, lest the king's man take you up and my entire property fall into ruin."

"Not stolen," MacTavish said, crowding after Julianna as she mounted the stairs. "More like inherited, miss. Anybody can inherit or find abandoned goods."

"Mac, have you been at the whisky again?"

"I'm never far from my flask, but that's the rest of it, ye see. The good news is we have trunks on the porch, fancy trunks such as a nob might stash out of the rain. The bad news is..."

Julianna marched to the front door, Mac on her heels.

"Out with it, Mac. If the duchess has finally made good on her threats to visit, we'll simply have to endure the expense."

And the shame. Julianna hated taking charity, and for her wealthy relation, Julianna had painted a rosy picture of life in Yorkshire. According to her letters, she thrived on embroidery, she went for long walks in the beautiful countryside, enjoyed the regular company of friends, and was sliding into the cheerful embrace of spinsterhood amid a cloud of contentment and genteel, well-read solitude.

"The trunks are right lovely," MacTavish said, darting around to stop Julianna from passing through the front doorway. Mac could move faster than a guilty eight-year-old boy when motivated. "Did I mention there's bad news too?"

Julianna put both hands on her hips. "There's always bad news too."

Mac peered at the bouquet he still held. "As to that, seems that in addition to a set of fancy trunks on your porch, somebody came by and left a dead man on your swing."

* * *

"He's good-sized," a man growled in a Border Scots accent. "His clothing will fetch a pretty penny, though bloodstains are the very devil to get out."

Con's brain refused to function. Impressions came to him in a disjointed and curiously pleasant mosaic. The fragrance of roses in the rain, the sensation of embroidery pressed against his cheek, the scent of hearty fare simmering over a nearby fire.

"He's not dead, MacTavish. Shame on you, and I'll hear no talk of selling his clothing."

"Likes of him won't miss the occasional waistcoat, miss."

A gentle hand brushed the hair back from Con's brow, though the fingers were callused. "Please return to the kitchen, MacTavish. The children are due back any moment, and I'll want them at the table, cramming their bellies with bread and butter while I deal with this... this gentleman."

The vowels were broad and lilting, the register feminine.

Heavy boots stomped off. A door closed.

Another gentle caress to his brow. "Sir, can you open your eyes?"

Con wasn't a sir, he was a Your Grace, though something told him that wasn't important right now. His eyes did not want to open. For the lady with the soft voice and the soothing touch, he made the effort.

She was pretty and her face was near his. Hair a lustrous red—not carroty, not quite auburn. Eyes the blue of a summer sky on a still, sunny day. Features... strong, sharp-drawn, a few years past the dimples and softness of girlhood.

Mouth... Con was not exactly a candles-out, bayonet-at-the-ready sort of fellow between the sheets, and yet, a young, single duke consorted only with women who knew what they were about. They didn't expect much bedroom flummery from him, but this woman's mouth was... flummerous in the extreme. Full, rosy, eminently kissable.

He'd linger over the pleasure of acquainting himself with those lips, though at present the mouth they belonged to was also... worried.

"Are you ill?" she asked, ruffling Con's hair.

He shook off the pleasure of that touch and the longing for more of it.

"Flummerous is not a word." Con's mouth was dry, which reminded him that he'd been dosed with the poppy. "A mouth cannot look worried."

She withdrew her hand. "Perhaps you've suffered a blow to the head? Can you sit up?"

Her question alerted Con to the fact that he was toppled over on his side, on a porch swing, in the wilds of York-Godsaveme-shire. Reality came galloping at him from several sides, though, of course, he could sit up.

"Almighty, perishing, bloody devils," he said as fire lanced up from his wounded buttock. "I have not been struck on the head."

"It's only your manners that have been injured?" the lady asked, sitting back on her heels. "Then explain the bloodstain at your hip."

Not his hip, his arse, though in this position... the pain was substantial, which hardly signified. What did signify was that a duke did not offer explanations, much less produce them on demand for housekeepers or servants of any stripe.

"I'm looking for Jules MacKinnon. I'd appreciate it if you would please alert him to the arrival of a kinsman."

The woman—who might herself be slightly deficient in the brainbox—

plunked herself down beside Con.

"What business have you with Jules MacKinnon?" she asked.

Servants could be more protective than siblings. Con had had occasion to appreciate this very quality. Moreover, he was in the countryside—deep in the countryside—where households were a good deal less formal.

"I am a cousin," Con said. "MacKinnon and I have never met that I can recall, but our households have corresponded for years. I was in the area, my coach developed a problem, and I am at my cousin's mercy for hospitality over the next two weeks."

That was rather good, if Con did say so himself. Having the coachman kicking his heels elsewhere qualified as a problem, and the rest was pure fact.

"You're lying," the woman said, though she sounded as if she often heard lies. Weary, half-amused, half-disappointed. "Polite lies, probably well intended even, but you have no direct acquaintance with Jules MacKinnon, even by letter."

"What I am, madam, is in pain from an injury that could well become infected, and unless you want me expiring on your porch, you will inform Mr. MacKinnon that a relative needs the favor of the household's hospitality for the next fortnight. Tell him… tell him Connor Amadour has come to call."

The name apparently meant little to her. That full, rosy mouth firmed.

"What is the nature of your injury? Were you set upon by highwaymen?"

"Yes."

"You're lying again. I cannot have you—"

An aging kilted giant stepped onto the porch from the front door.

"Beg pardon, miss. Children are home and at their bread and butter. Where shall I put the trunks?"

The fellow struck Con as a specimen of human geology, all craggy jaw, white eyebrows like flying rowans on a cliff face of a profile, a raptor's gaze peering from faded blue eyes. That face was inhospitable country, with plenty of muscle and meanness as well.

Con rose, though moving after inactivity made his injury scream. The courtesy of offering his hand to the lady was instinctive—to him.

Not to her.

His gloves had come off at some point and lay on the worn carpet. She gazed at his hand, then peered at his face.

"The trunks go in the blue bedroom, Mac. Thank you, and tell the children I'll be along shortly. They are to fold the towels before they come upstairs."

With no more effort than if the trunk had been a sack of feathers, the old fellow hoisted the largest of the three to his shoulder and disappeared into the house.

The lady rose without taking Con's hand. "I cannot abide dishonesty, mendacity, prevarication, or any of their *cousins*. Every member of this household eschews mendacity, or he's not welcome. Tell me the truth: Why are you here, and how were you injured, *Your Grace?*"

CHAPTER TWO

If Cousin Marie's sketches hadn't given him away, if the signet ring fitted to his smallest finger hadn't give him away, his choice of pseudonym would have. No less person than Coinneach Callum Amadour Ives St. Bellan, ninth Duke of Mowne, stood in wrinkled finery on Julianna's porch.

Bloody, wrinkled finery.

"I was injured when the highwaymen fired upon my party," he said, looking exactly like Harold when the boy told a great bouncer. All bravery about the posture, but uncertainty in his green eyes.

"Do dukes typically flee the scene when set upon by brigands, such that injury is suffered to the posterior? Your mother claims you never travel with fewer than two armed grooms, two footmen, a coachman, and two outriders."

Julianna could not imagine this arrogant beast fleeing anything, except perhaps an honest day's work. His very bearing shouted privilege, while his features invited lingering study. Dark red hair—a coincidence, for he and Julianna were not blood kin—height, military bearing, and features that could define male beauty for the angels of portraiture.

His looks made Julianna both angry and unaccountably sad. She wanted to sketch him. She must get rid of him.

The rain intensified, and thunder shattered the heavens immediately overhead.

"Come inside," Julianna said, for Roberta was terrified of storms, and the boys teased her when on their bad behavior. Folding laundry often provoked bad behavior.

"That is how you greet a guest? *Come inside?*"

Julianna marched to the door and held it open. "Come inside, Your Grace. *Now*, before you develop a lung fever to go with your injured nether parts."

He was probably trying to strut, but his injury—he'd bled a narrow, dark streak through his breeches—doubtless accounted for an uneven stride. Handsome breeches they were too. Mac could tell Julianna to the penny what they were worth.

The duke—for this was Mowne, no mistake about it—paused before the open door and peered down at Julianna. Most men other than Mac were not tall enough to peer down at her. She met their gazes eye to eye and made sure the fellow was the first to look way.

"How is it you know of the title?" He had the effrontery to even smell like a duke, all sandalwood and spice, clean soap, and fresh laundered linen. His lashes were as long as a new calf's, and Julianna knew how soft that dark hair was.

"Your mother is ever so proud of you. She's sent dozens of sketches, described the longing glances of hundreds of debutantes and legions of their scheming mamas. Artists beg for the favor of your annual portrait, and any self-respecting rose drops its petals in your path."

He glanced around at the roses embowering the porch, as if botany had abruptly become his true calling.

"You are Cousin Jules."

This revelation did not please him, and in that moment, Julianna hated all those debutantes. "Those are my roses, Your Grace. You will note each rose petal remaining affixed to its blossom, despite your uninvited presence." That the duke, the nominal head of Julianna's family, should see what a once gracious country manor had become in her care stung bitterly.

He plucked a white blossom poised to fade and shook it before Julianna, so the petals fell on the dusty toes of her half boots.

"I need a place to convalesce in peace and quiet, *cousin*, a place where nobody will hear of His Grace of Mowne being shot in the backside, and bruit the news about in every ballroom and men's club in the realm. Will you allow me that sanctuary under your roof?"

Several of the rose petals had fallen on his lace-edged cravat. Nobody but a duke could get away with that much delicacy about his dress. Julianna brushed the petals away.

"I cannot afford to turn you away. Your mother's pin money provides necessary cash to support my household, though her charity—"

Another crash of thunder sounded, suggesting God himself was trying to blast the farmhouse to pebbles.

"Let's take our squabbling inside," Mowne said, gesturing as if the premises belonged to him, which they nearly did. "You may scold me for my mother's charity at length, and while you are, of course, impervious to the elements and disease both, I am not dealing well with the ruin of another pair of my breeches."

That wet, dark streak on his flank had grown longer. Something in his gaze had shifted too. Julianna could read little boys as accurately as she could recite her Book of Common Prayer, but she could not read the man bleeding on her porch.

He'd find neither peace nor quiet under this roof, though Julianna refused to be ashamed of the racket healthy children made. She swept into the house and let the duke close the door.

"We need to get you out of those breeches." A fresh stain had a prayer of coming out, even from soft leather. A dried stain was a more difficult proposition, though little Roberta had a miraculous way with a gum eraser.

"Have you any idea how imperious you sound?" the duke asked, limping after Julianna. "My mother would envy you the angle you achieve with those marvelous eyebrows. The headmaster at Eton needed your skill with an eyebrow."

"Don't flatter my eyebrows," Julianna snapped at the foot of the steps. "You are indirectly family, and one cannot turn away family. Even if you are not family to me by blood, you are kin to the duchess, and her generosity is all that stands between the children and the poorhouse. We'll provide this sanctuary from gossip that your pride requires, but don't expect London hospitality."

He braced himself against the newel post, which came off in his hand because too many small children had slid down the banister, their little bums smacking into the polished maple orb with gleeful velocity.

Julianna snatched it from him and set it on the sideboard, though it rolled right off and hit the faded carpet with a thud.

"All I need," Mowne said, "is discretion from you, dry sheets, and a bit of toast with my morning tea. In two weeks, I'll be on my way, and you can forget I ever darkened your door. You will please introduce me as Mr. Connor Amadour, distant cousin on the St. Bellan side of the family, if you must introduce me at all. My coach has suffered a mishap, and I'm biding here while the repairs are made, also catching up with my kinfolk and enjoying the fresh country air."

"Such a busy fellow." While he would, in fact, do nothing but stand about ruining his breeches and flattering Julianna's eyebrows. "As it happens, we have a spare bedroom, and I'm competent with minor wounds. Your tea will be weak, and you'll come downstairs to dine in the morning. I simply haven't the help to accommodate a duke."

"Not a duke," he said, following Julianna up the stairs. "A distant cousin, late of… Kent, on the way north to do some shooting. Who is your pet Highlander?"

"MacTavish is our man of all work, and you cross him at your peril. He's the reason this farm hasn't fallen to wrack and ruin, and I treasure him beyond words. Between him and Hortensia, we have a crop, we have gardens, we have stout walls to keep in the sheep and shelter our fruit trees. You malign

MacTavish—"

"Yes, yes," the duke said, twirling a lace-cuffed wrist. A hint of lace, a peek of lace, a mere gesture of lace. "Death by eyebrow at thirty paces. This house is lovely."

Julianna almost snapped at him not to admire the house, except… he wasn't wrong, and she was exhausted. Market days had become increasingly fraught, with Maurice trying to escort her everywhere while, to a person, the merchants and tinkers charged her daylight robbery prices for every necessity.

"The house used to be lovely," she said. "The place has grown weary in recent years, faded and worn. The winters are long and bitter, the summers endless work."

They'd reached the blue bedroom, the only other furnished room in Julianna's wing of the house. His Grace's lips had acquired a whitish cast, even in the gloom of the corridor. The streak on his breeches had grown another alarming inch.

"I'll fetch water, clean bandages, and my medicinals," Julianna said, opening the door to the bedroom. "You will get out of those breeches, and I'll deal with them as soon as I've seen to your wound."

"You are a woman," the duke replied, this time bracing himself on the doorjamb in an elegant, casual pose. "Can't this MacWondrous fellow do a bit of doctoring? A surgeon has already seen to the injury once. I'm sure all it wants is a change of dressing."

In the kitchen, the children were probably begging second and third helpings of bread and butter from MacTavish, or even inveigling him into breaking out the jam. Mrs. Periwinkle would have stood firm against such maneuvers, but she was off visiting her sister in York.

"I have seen more bare male hindquarters than you can imagine," Julianna said. "They all conform to a common design, and yours is no different. Your pride is the greater affliction, would be my guess. If it's any consolation, I can likely salvage your breeches, which MacTavish claims are worth a pretty penny."

The duke tried for a smile and came up… short.

Oh, the expression was engaging, a practiced blend of charming, arrogant, handsome, and self-deprecating. He'd likely had that one well in hand by the age of three, and his old nanny was still recalling it fondly from some snug pensioner's cottage.

And yet, the angle of Mowne's lean body against the doorjamb suggested not a casual pose, but a desperate facsimile of one. He was injured, bleeding, and… in pain. Worse, he wanted nobody to see his suffering.

Pride was not the exclusive province of dukes.

"The breeches are ruined," His Grace said, shoving away from the door and sauntering—crookedly—into the room. MacTavish had cracked a window, so the air was fresh, if a bit chilly. "You may toss them in the rag bin."

"They are far from ruined. The stain is still wet, and a good blotting cloth will get out most of the blood. Once it dries, we can take a gum erasure at just the right angle—"

Lace fluttered as he waved his hand. "The breeches are ruined, I say. I never want to see them again, but tell me, where does a fellow sit when he's a hazard to the upholstery and must get his boots off?"

"On the raised hearth," Julianna said, following him into the bedroom and closing the door. "I'll get your boots off. You'll only tear the wound worse if you try, and you're making enough of a mess as it is."

He sat, gingerly, and Julianna resisted the urge to help him. He was pale, and the only thing worse than a duke expecting free hospitality without notice was a duke expiring from loss of blood on Julianna's very hearth.

Though maybe having Mowne underfoot wouldn't be all bad. MacTavish would take the discarded ducal breeches to the shops in York and come back with nothing less than Sunday roast, a laundry tub that didn't leak, new shoes for Horty, and heaven knew what other necessities.

Julianna took the heel of the duke's right boot in her hand and tugged as gently as she could, for she had the suspicion His lacy, drawling, arrogant Grace knew exactly what the fate of his fine breeches would be.

* * *

Revelation followed upon insight crowded closely by surprise, very little of it good as far as Con was concerned.

One truly could see spots before one's eyes, for example. When dear Cousin Jules tugged upon the heel of Con's boot, the protest from his backside was painful enough that, in addition to black spots, his vision contracted, and the lady's murmured apology seemed to come from across the surf of an angry invisible ocean.

The second boot wasn't as bad, though Con could feel his life's blood soaking into the wound's dressing.

"Why does nobody warn a fellow that most activities involve the fundament in some way? I dread to sneeze, for example, and rising right now…" He was babbling. Worse, he was whining and babbling. A tanned, callused female hand appeared in his line of sight as the pain in his arse faded to a roar.

"You can remain there until autumn remarking the wonders of your anatomical functions, or I'll help you to the dressing screen," said his angel of dubious mercy. She waggled her fingers. "I haven't all day, Mr. Amadour."

Perhaps she had other arses to insult elsewhere in the house, but—give the woman credit—she pulled Con, fifteen stone of fit adult male, to his feet easily, then kept hold of his hand while another shower of spots faded.

"When did you last eat?" she asked, as if inquiring of a suspect regarding his whereabouts on the night of the triple murder.

"Yesterday."

"You drank your sustenance," she said, leading him to a dressing screen painted the same shade of blue as her eyes.

Quite pretty, that blue, and yes, now that she'd graciously reminded him, Con had passed famished hours ago.

"And you likely got no rest because of your injury," she went on. "What would your mother say?"

Ah, delightful. A compassionate Deity had placed a sturdy washstand behind the privacy screen. A great mercy, that, because Con's body chose then to recall that laudanum often gave him the dry heaves.

"My mother would tell me a duke does not bleed in public. If you'll excuse me, I will see about disrobing while you fetch your medicinals."

Being sick might figure on the agenda somewhere as well, but so would being… grateful. The room was pleasant and airy, with roses climbing about the windowsills. The storm was rumbling on its way, leaving the scent of cool rain and lavender sachets in its wake. The herbal fragrance soothed Con's belly, the pattering rain on the roses eased his soul.

Cousin Jules was a tartar, though apparently, she'd had to be. Con had been remiss not to investigate her circumstances himself—Cousin Jules, indeed— even if she'd welcome his prying about as much he welcomed the thought of her probing at his wound.

The wound on his arse, which hurt like nineteen devils were applying their pitchforks in unison. Con waited for the lady to go scowling and muttering on her way before bracing himself against the washstand and forcing the pain down to ignorable proportions.

The pain refused his ducal command. Another revelation.

By slow degrees, he peeled himself out of his clothing. Contrary to his valet's conceits, Con was capable of dressing and undressing himself. The valet was a bequest from Con's father, and Con simply hadn't the heart to pension off a fellow whose greatest joy in life was a perfectly starched length of linen.

The dressing was affixed to his flank by long strips wound about his hips and thigh. He was loath to dislodge his bandages, for the wound was indeed bleeding. One did not, however, want to unnecessarily offend a lady's modesty, regardless of how many arses she claimed to have inspected—nor to affront a duke's already tattered, hungry, weary, and thirsty (come to think of it) dignity either.

From his trunk, Con unearthed a dressing gown. Blue silk, not his favorite, but sufficient unto the present need. By the time Cousin Jules returned, he'd helped himself to a glass of water and was affecting a lounge against the window frame, studying green countryside that seemed to go on forever.

"How shall we do this?" he asked.

"Carefully," she retorted, setting down a basin and a sack on the night table. "And quickly. I've a stew on the stove, and if MacTavish gets distracted, dinner will burn and the pot will be ruined. Can you lie facedown on the bed?"

Facedown was an excellent notion, for another revelation had befallen Con: His cock was in excellent working order, despite fatigue, hunger, humiliation, pain, and volition to the contrary. The notion of Julianna ogling his nearly naked self, her hands on him in highly personal locations, and those hands being no stranger to the male anatomy, had worked a dark alchemy on his male imagination.

Con got himself onto the bed and managed to stretch out without revealing anything untoward. Mere stirrings, but bothersome, highly ungentlemanly stirrings.

He moved pillows aside and got as comfortable as he could. "Tell me about all these naked fellows you've seen. Are you a widow?"

"I am a widow, and there haven't been that many fellows. Modesty in the male of the species is rare in my—oh, you poor man."

She'd twitched his dressing gown aside and peeled away bandages far enough to expose only what needed exposing, a flank more than a cheek, as it were. Her compassion did what Con's conscience could not, and un-stirred the mischief his cock had been brewing.

He said what pain-crazed men had likely been saying since the first spear had creased the first male behind.

"It's only a flesh wound."

A cool cloth was laid over the wound, not shoved at it, as the surgeon had done, but gently pressed against Con's skin.

"Did some half-sober barber-surgeon tell you that? Superficial wounds hurt awfully because they tear through flesh and muscle. You won't bleed to death as you might if an artery were pierced, but this is…"

She wrung out the cloth and brought more relief. This went on for some minutes, until Con was nearly asleep and prepared to sign over his entire wardrobe for MacMiraculous to pawn in York.

"The wound looks clean," Cousin Jules said after a final, careful dabbing at the injury. "Infection can strike any time, though, so we'll want to change the dressing regularly."

Four times a day at least. Considering the article at risk was a duke, and the next in line for the title was Freddy, tending to the wound six times a day might be—

Shame upon me.

"How long have you lived here?" Con had been sending bank drafts for at least… five years?

"Since I married Mr. St. Bellan when I turned eighteen. This might sting a bit."

Whatever minty decoction she'd applied to the wound stung far more than a bit. Then the stinging faded, and for the first time in more than a day, the pain subsided without recourse to the poppy.

"I gather Mr. St. Bellan was not well-fixed?" Con asked.

"John worked very hard. Had he lived, the farm would doubtless have thrived, but as it is, we struggle. Your mother's generosity is necessary, and even with that—" Cloth was torn smartly asunder.

Who was this *we*? Cousin and her pet Highlander, a maid of all work, and a few obese cats? The sheep and goats? But, no.

She had mentioned children.

"As it is, you are the one left working very hard," Con said. "I can re-bandage myself, if you'll leave me the supplies."

"Some fresh air wouldn't hurt the wound," she said. "Fresh air will help it heal more quickly, in fact. I have a bit of laudanum, though we try to save it for when it's truly needed."

We again, and hoarding the medical supplies.

"See to your stew," Con said, remaining on the bed, breathing lavender and relief. "Thank you, for your kindness and for your hospitality. You will be careful not to mention my identity below stairs?"

She gave Con's silk-clad bum a little pat, or maybe she'd accidentally touched him in passing—on his aching backside. So gently.

"We don't have a below stairs or an above stairs, Mr. Amadour. We have only hard work, liberal affection, fresh air, and good, simple fare. I'll bring you a tray now, though don't expect me to make a habit of it. The bandages are on the night table."

Fatigue was crashing down on Con like an overturned coach. "You needn't bring a tray. I'll find my way to your kitchen easily enough. Don't forget to take the ruined breeches."

Con had been in perhaps six kitchens in his life, and none in recent years, but he knew they were typically ground-floor establishments at the back of the house, where tradesmen could come and go without disturbing anybody.... Without disturbing *him*, rather.

"Rest," she said. "Your wound will appreciate a day or two of complete rest."

An hour, perhaps. An hour to nap would be a novel departure from Con's unceasing schedule of responsibilities and recreations. He ought to write to Starlingham and Lucere, make sure they were comfortably ensconced in their temporary identities.

He should also write to his mother, asking what in blazes she was about, expecting a St. Bellan widow's household *with children* to eke by on a pittance. Write to his solicitors, and… Paper would also be hoarded in this household. Quill pens, ink, everything would be hoarded, except hard work, which would be available in endless quantities.

Con pulled his thoughts back from a near drowse. "Do you go by Jules?"

"Julianna."

"Then in a household without an above stairs or a below stairs, Julianna, you must call me Connor." Though the notion was odd. How could anybody function without a proper sense of where they fit in and where they were unwelcome?

She withdrew soundlessly, leaving Con to wonder, as sleep stole over him, and his injured parts were soothed by fresh Yorkshire air, about all those naked backsides Julianna St. Bellan had seen, and how his would have compared to the others if she'd been less considerate of his modesty.

* * *

Julianna gave herself two minutes to lean on the bedroom door and worry.

Also to miss her husband. "Honest John" St. Bellan had been well-liked, good-humored, a tireless worker, and shrewd. When everybody in the neighborhood had been succumbing to the coal developer's promises of riches, John had smiled and kept his hand on the figurative plough.

Old John, Julianna's father-in-law, had accurately predicted that England would become a wheat-importing country in his son's lifetime, and John had bet his livelihood on that prediction. The gamble should have paid off. For others who'd not died of a virulent flu, it had paid off handsomely.

Coal was important, at least part of the year.

Bread was necessary nearly every day. That thought had Julianna heading for the stairs, because when it came to bread and butter, the children put biblical plagues to shame.

"Seconds, MacTavish?" Julianna asked as she put the medicinals on a high shelf. "And did we wash our hands before we sat down?"

Four little pairs of legs stopped kicking at the worktable bench, four pairs of eyes found anywhere to look but at Julianna. Three blond heads and one brunette—Roberta was their changeling—all bent as if bread and butter required relentless study. John would have known how to remind them without scolding, but Julianna had lost the knack of a cheerful reminder a year ago, when the last plough horse had come up lame.

"I should be flattered," she said, tousling each blond mop and winking at Roberta. "My bread is so delicious, my butter so wonderful, you cannot resist a second serving. I might have to have some myself."

Relief shone from the children's eyes, while MacTavish gave the stew a stir. "How's the patient?"

"Resting," Julianna said, cutting herself a thin slice of bread. How she longed to slather jam on it, to eat sitting down, and ask the children how their studies had gone that morning. "Children, I have some news. Harold, please stop crossing your eyes."

He'd been crossing them at Roberta, which was better than when he took a notion to tease her.

"Yes, missus," they chorused.

Julianna took out her handkerchief and wiped a spot of jam—jam?—from Ralph's chin. "This is good news, for we have a visitor. Mr. Connor Amadour, a distant cousin, is paying a call. He'll bide with us for a short time."

"Can he fold towels?" Ralph asked.

"Guests don't work," Harold shot back. As the oldest, he was often obnoxious, but he was also a hard worker. In the Yorkshire countryside, much—almost everything—was forgiven a hard worker of either gender and any species.

"A guest can grow bored," Julianna said, "and if he'd like to help fold towels to pass the time, as Cousin Connor's hosts, we'll allow him to help." Though how the poor man would sit still for long was a mystery. The wound he'd suffered was no mere scratch.

"I hope he's bored all the time," Ralph said. "I hope he's so bored, he'll like to churn the butter, shell the peas—"

"Beat the rugs," Harold sang out.

"Get the eggs *and* wash the chicken poo off them," Lucas shouted.

"And read to us," Roberta whispered.

Her brothers rolled their eyes, and Ralph shoved at her little shoulder. "We don't need anybody to read to us. We're not babies."

Not any longer they weren't. John had gone off to York one day to buy seed and come back with four children collected from the poorhouse.

We have love to give and none of our own to give it to. They'll die there, or soon wish they were dead. Fresh air, family, a sense of belonging, and an opportunity to make a contribution commensurate with their abilities... A farm needs children, and the children need the farm.

He had loved them, and they'd loved him, and that winter, he'd died with the children gathered about his bed and worry in his eyes.

"You are my babies," Julianna said. "And I love reading to you."

"So why don't you do it anymore?" Lucas was blessed with a logical mind, according to the curate, Mr. Hucklebee. The boy had not yet learned that logic could sound disrespectful.

MacTavish wrapped up the bread in a towel and put the lid on the butter crock. "Summer is the busy time. Come winter, the evenings will be so long we'll read every book in the house."

Which was fewer and fewer. Julianna passed the last of her bread to

MacTavish and gave the stew another stir.

"I will make a trade with you, children. While you fold the towels, I'll read to you. First, I must bring our guest some bread and butter."

"Has he washed his hands?" Ralph asked.

"Why can't he eat with us?" Harold chorused. "There's room at the table."

"He's quite tired from his travels," Julianna said—not a lie. "I'm being hospitable, but you'll get to meet Cousin Connor soon. For now, you will sweep your crumbs for the chickens, wash your hands, and start on the towels, please."

Groans, sighs, the sound of the bench scraping back, but for all that, compliance with Julianna's directions. For now. The boys listened to MacTavish for now too, but they also teased Roberta without mercy some days, tested Julianna's authority, and lately had taken to using their fists with each other.

"MacTavish, if you'd start the children on the laundry and regale them with some of Mr. Burns's offerings, I'll be along shortly to take over."

Over the last of his slice of bread, Mac sent her a look worthy of Ralph in a rebellious mood. The rain was still coming down though, and for Mac to spend the afternoon repairing harness in the carriage house, mucking Horty's stall, and otherwise out in the damp would not do.

Or perhaps Julianna simply wanted Mac to keep an eye on the children while she tended to Connor.

As the children jostled each other at the wash basin and fought over the hand towel, Mac put the bread in the bread box along with the butter.

"So who is this *cousin*, Julianna, and why must you be his Samaritan? He can well afford to stay at an inn."

"Why must you sneak the children jam, Rory MacTavish? You undermine my authority and waste our supplies. Come February, you'll wish you'd saved a bit more of the jam."

Mac had the grace to look sheepish, for about two seconds, then he took up a rag and began scrubbing at the counter.

"I'll bring up the other two trunks, but I know what I saw, miss. You've welcomed trouble to this household."

Julianna had had nearly the same thought when John had come home with a squirming lot of dirty, hungry, unruly children. She'd been right, but she'd also been wrong too. John had loved the children, and the children were growing to love the farm.

"Mr. Amadour honestly is a cousin, of sorts. His coach has suffered a mishap, and he was injured in the process. There's a pair of fine gentleman's breeches in the laundry that you're welcome to take to the pawnbroker's as soon as I work the stain out."

Which Julianna ought to be doing that instant.

"Roberta can get out the stain. The wee girl's a wonder in the laundry. My granddam had the same knack. That doesn't change the fact that this cousin of yours will meddle, upset the children, and cause talk. Mr. Warren will not approve of talk."

"Who was the first Baptist?!" Harold yelled, flicking water in Ralph's face. "John the Baptist!"

"I'll baptize you, you runt," Ralph shouted back, elbowing Roberta aside. Ralph cuffed the water in the basin so it slapped over the side and splashed on Lucas's and Harold's sleeves. Roberta shrank back, looking worried, while Lucas snatched up the basin.

"Enough!" Julianna snapped before Lucas could dash the remaining water in the other boys' faces. "You will please clean up the mess you've made and meet MacTavish in the laundry. One more such outburst and no dessert for whoever's involved."

Now she'd have to make a dessert, of course. But the riot subsided, and the children did a credible job of mopping at the floor.

"Mr. Warren has caused talk," Julianna said, keeping her voice down. A raspberry cobbler would do, but she'd promised her guest some bread and butter first. "He was glued to my side all morning and blathering about how well his mines are doing."

John and Maurice Warren had been friends, of a sort, but Maurice was convinced coal was the salvation of Yorkshire, when in fact, coal had been the salvation of the Warren family fortunes and the ruin of their tenants' dreams. The men who went down into the mines were a rough lot, not particularly prone to showing up at Sunday services, or to seeing their children educated when those same children could earn coin beside their fathers.

"Maurice Warren is the answer to your troubles," MacTavish muttered. "Honest John would agree with me."

Honest John was dead, God rest his soul. "Please start Roberta on blotting the stained breeches. Read the children a bit of Tam o' Shanter, and I'll be along shortly."

Tam o' Shanter was a sop to the males of the household. Drunkenness, lurking devils, mad storms, beautiful witches, wild dancing, all rendered in Mac's best broad Scots.

"Julianna…" Mac hung the drying towel just so over the back of a chair. "The trunks bear a crest. The Mowne crest. It's a Scottish dukedom, but a dukedom nonetheless. Is this fellow related to your duchess cousin?"

"Yes."

Mac was angling toward some point, one Julianna would not like. She got out the bread and butter again and cut two slices about twice the thickness she normally served herself. She buttered both slices, then she carved off a strip of ham from the joint hanging by the larder.

"How close a relation?" Mac asked.

He probably already knew, though how he knew, Julianna could not have said.

"We have the Duke of Mowne himself under our roof. He is injured in a delicate location and seeks to convalesce quietly rather than be an object of gossip. I've promised him hospitality and discretion in equal measure. For the duration of his visit, he's Cousin Connor Amadour, late of Kent, waiting for his coach to be repaired."

MacTavish swore in Gaelic. Something about when a mule gave birth, which was all but impossible, mules being sterile.

"Language, Mac. Connor is family, and he's hurt."

"He's trouble. If I noticed the ducal crest on his luggage, Mr. Warren will notice a great deal more than that. Then too, dukes have a way of sticking their noses into anybody's business, particularly the business of their family members."

Some cheese wouldn't go amiss, and Yorkshire cheddars were excellent. "This duke has been happy to ignore us for years. His mother's charitable impulses are no business of his. Have you been consorting with many dukes, Mac, that you can vouch for their habits?"

The cheese wheel was heavy, and Julianna couldn't resist a nibble for herself. She passed Mac a bite, which he did not decline.

"You've got it all wrong, lass. Now that Mowne has realized he has a poor relation whose household is going threadbare, his pride will require him to take matters in hand."

Unease joined the cheese in Julianna's belly. "He'll be on his way and forget he ever tarried here. He nearly promised me that."

And Julianna had been both relieved and resentful to have those assurances.

"You've never told the duchess about the children, or about how bare the larder has grown trying to feed them. Yon duke will soon realize you could not have had three boys who look nothing like you within the space of a year, much less well before you married John St. Bellan. His Grace will meddle, all right. He'll send the boys to public school if they're lucky, or send them to the parish if they're not."

Maurice had hinted that Julianna ought to do the latter. Reduce the number of mouths she had to feed and enjoy herself as a "lady of the manor" ought.

"I was arguably gentry when I married John," she said, ladling stew into a bowl. "I'm barely a landowner now. You will cease conjuring worries from simple hospitality. Cousin Connor will not bother with the situation of a rural nobody to whom he's not even related by blood."

Mac spared a glance for the plate before Julianna: bread and butter, cheese, ham, a steamy bowl of stew. Closer to a feast than a snack, by the standards of the household.

"He's trouble," Mac said again. "Expensive, meddling, titled trouble, and you've nothing with which to combat the mischief he'll cause. Go carefully, miss, and don't let his stew get cold."

CHAPTER THREE

The stew was cold. Con ate it anyway, and contrary to the dire predictions of every nanny, mother, and governess in the realm, he did not expire as a result. Who knew? The bread, butter, ham, and cheese met the same fate, as did a glass of cold milk.

He could not recall the last time he'd drunk milk as a beverage, but consuming every drop and crumb on the tray seemed only polite. The stew had lacked delicacy—no hint of tarragon, suggestion of oregano, or trace of pepper, but had been adequately salted.

A stout knock sounded on the door, followed by the Scotsman hauling the second of Con's trunks into the room. Clan MacTavish was an impecunious lot by reputation, but they'd not turned on their own when clearing the land to make way for sheep had become popular, and they'd played their politics adroitly through the whole Jacobite mess.

"My thanks," Con said. "I have the sense if I offered you a vail, you'd scowl me to perdition."

MacTavish dusted enormous hands. "You'd not be worth the bother. Make trouble for Julianna St. Bellan, though, and I'll kill you properly dead."

Con remained seated rather than stand and reveal that he'd added a pillow to the padding on his armchair.

"Nothing like Highland hospitality to make a traveler feel welcome, MacTavish."

"Nothing like deception, added expense, and imposing relations to make an old man feel out of charity with the Quality."

Lucere and Starlingham would like this fellow quite well, as did Con. "How bad are things?"

MacTavish lumbered into the corridor and returned with the final trunk.

"What business are the doings of this household of yours, Your Grace?"

"I have a responsibility to every member of my family," Con said, shoving to his feet. "If Julianna St. Bellan is in difficulties, she need only apply to me, and the matter will be taken in hand." How it would be taken in hand, Con did not know, because every penny—every damned farthing—was spoken for.

"She did apply to you," MacTavish said, hands on kilted hips. "Three months later, your mother answered, with a small bank draft. Very small. Four children can eat a lot in three months. They can outgrow shoes, destroy clothing, require a blessed lot of coal to keep warm too. You did nothing in those months, while Julianna grieved a husband gone too soon, and dealt with a spring crop that wouldn't plant itself."

Con added a letter to Mama among the correspondence he'd draft—by his own hand. His secretary would be leaving London for Scotland any day.

"I'm here now," he said, rather than explain himself to that patron saint of mental intransigence, a Scotsman who'd made up his mind. "I'll not shirk responsibility when it stares me in the face, MacTavish."

MacTavish took a step closer. He smelled of wool, equine, and, oddly, of fresh bread. "You'll not meddle, *Cousin Connor*. Maurice Warren will offer for Julianna the instant she looks favorably on his suit, and he'll take adequate care of her."

Con felt an immediate dislike for this Warren fellow. A man didn't wait for optimal market conditions before making a commitment of resources to a cause he believed in. Even Uncle Leo, whose grasp on a found penny rivaled John Coachman's grip on his flask, admitted that investment should be guided by principles other than unfettered greed.

"Spare me the household's petty dramas," Con said, "and I'll spare you my meddling. My thanks again for bringing up the trunks."

The thanks—which were sincere—caused bushy brows to lower. "Can you get your backside properly trussed up, or must I help you with that too?"

"I've managed for now," Con said. "I will bring my tray down as soon as I've finished dressing. I'm not your enemy, MacTavish."

"You're not Julianna's friend." He stalked out, closing the door quietly.

Con managed to shove his feet into his boots without reopening his wound, piled his dirty dishes on his tray, and set out to find the kitchen. The tray was heavier than it looked, the kitchen farther away. Servants' stairs would probably have shortened the journey, but Con had no idea how to locate them, for a well-built servants' stair was usually well disguised too.

As he opened yet another wrong door, insight struck. The Duke of Mowne expected his staff to know how to get him where he needed to be. He also expected them to ascertain the route, reserve accommodations, see to the horses, and otherwise handle the details that, upon reflection, weren't details at all.

The duke himself would never, ever ask for directions. Connor Amadour, though, was just a lowly fellow having a spot of difficulty and biding with family for the nonce. He might have asked directions of MacTavish and been ensconced in the kitchen before a hot cup of tea by now.

Asking directions, dressing himself in half the time his valet took, napping when he was exhausted… life as a distant relation to the duke had much to recommend it. *Much.*

* * *

From the corner of her eye, Julianna saw the duke march past in the corridor beyond the laundry. He was having a good look around, apparently, though he'd remembered to bring his tray with him to the kitchen. She wanted to chase after him and make sure the door to every empty larder and pantry was closed, and that folded linen sat on shelves bare of provisions.

"Then what happened?" Roberta asked, leaning all her weight on the blotting cloth pressed to the bloodstain on His Grace's breeches.

"You know what happens," Harold said, snapping a towel within inches of Ralph's arm. "The evil witch snatches up the stupid children, because the little girl can't travel as fast as the little boy, who'd find his way home in no time, except his stupid sister is tagging along, as usual, and—"

"Am I interrupting?"

The duke, minus his tray, stood in the doorway, looking somewhat rested, if a bit wrinkled. The children fell silent at the sight of a fine gentleman in country attire, or perhaps simply because a stranger had intruded into their very laundry.

"Cousin Connor," Juliana said, closing her book of fairy tales around her finger. "Welcome. Children, please greet Mr. Connor Amador as I introduce you."

Please recall the manners Julianna hadn't drilled them on in too long, in other words. She started with Roberta, the best bet when decorum and civility were wanted. Harold, Ralph, and Lucas managed floppy, boyish bows, and His Grace returned each child's gesture with a bow of his own.

Elegant, correct, deferential bows that nonetheless trumpeted good breeding and consequence.

"I'm almost done," Roberta said, holding up the breeches. "It's nearly gone, but the rest must be brushed free of the cloth after it completely dries."

The duke appropriated the breeches before Julianna could intervene. The stain was still visible, but Roberta had the right of it. Blotting damp fabric was only a first step. A duke couldn't know that, of course, but Roberta had tried her best, and for her brothers to hear her being chided—

"You have worked a miracle," the duke said, brushing his fingers over the stain. "A miracle, I tell you. I have despaired of these breeches, and they were my favorite pair. Miss Roberta, I am in awe."

The child had very likely never been called Miss Roberta before, nor had she smiled quite that smile. Sweet, bashful, and brimming with the suppressed glee of a girl complimented before her usual tormenters.

Roberta would be made to pay, of course. When Julianna's back was turned, Lucas would taunt, Harold would deride. Ralph might try to distract the other two, but he wouldn't take on both of them at the same time. They weren't bad boys, but they were approaching a bad age.

"Was that the story of the clever children who bested the old witch?" the duke asked. "I haven't heard it since I was a boy myself. Might I join you for the rest of the tale?"

He gathered up a clean, folded towel and arranged it on a stool, then arranged himself on top of the towel.

The children looked to Julianna, for one didn't sit on clean laundry. "Cousin was in a coaching mishap," Julianna said. "He's injured."

"Too injured to fold towels?" Ralph asked.

"Perhaps Miss Roberta could show me how it's done?" Connor asked, hoisting the girl onto his lap. "Or perhaps I might take over the job of reading the story. Anybody who's nasty to a pair of orphaned children deserves to come to a bad end, don't you think?"

More glances were exchanged, and Julianna felt the currents of the children's bewilderment swirling about her. In his manners, his conversation, his cordial demeanor, the duke was turning the laundry room into something of a family parlor.

"Please do read to us," Julianna said, passing over the book and reaching for a towel from the mountain on the worktable.

"Miss Roberta, where shall I start?"

Roberta pointed to the page.

"Roberta isn't very good at folding towels," Lucas said. "Her arms are too short."

"She's just a girl," Harold added, for once charitably.

His Grace lowered the book slowly. "*Just* a girl? You're Master Harold, correct?"

"Yes, sir."

"Master Harold, if you'd oblige me by closing the door? We're family, indirectly, and some discussions are meant only for the ears of our trusted relations."

This was nonsense, but Harold was off the bench and across the laundry without a word of protest. When the boy was back between his brothers, Connor brushed a hand over Roberta's crown.

"I ask you fellows," Connor began, "who makes the best biscuits? Is it the butler? The steward? The haughty duke? No, it's the cook, who began life as a girl paying attention to her elders in the kitchen. What would life be without the occasional biscuit?"

Julianna would have a lot less to bribe the boys with if she gave up baking biscuits.

"Who's the most important sailor on the ship?" Connor asked. "The navigator? Bah, he's only reading charts and maps, or the stars God put overhead for all to see. The captain struts about giving orders any swabbie could anticipate, the bosun is always tweeting on some infernally stupid whistle that knows only two notes."

"Then who's the most important sailor?" Lucas asked. "They don't let ladies onto sailing ships."

Oh yes, they did. Julianna kept her peace, though, because most of the women who sailed with the Royal Navy were not considered at all respectable.

"What's the first thing you notice about a great ship of the line?" Connor asked. "Those enormous billowing sails, am I right? They rise up over the horizon, and everyone stops to look. Another ship coming into port, one laden with exotic silks, grain, cotton, wondrous goods from all over the world. A ship bringing more sailors home safely to hug their loved ones once again—because of those magnificent sails. Who keeps those sails in good repair?"

"A sailor," Ralph said.

"A sailor who sat among his sisters as a mere lad and paid attention to how carefully they stitched. When all the other louts at his dame school were ignoring the ladies, the sailmaker was learning a valuable skill from them. Nobody's ship comes safely to harbor on tattered sails, but how many of you can sew as well as Roberta?"

Roberta was sitting quite tall on Connor's lap, and positively... *preening.*

"This girl, this mere girl," Connor said, dropping his voice to an awed quiet, "is the secret to your success in life. I'm sure you've noticed that Roberta has preserved me from the indignity of going about in stained breeches, and she's not done working her magic. A fellow can get into worse scrapes, though, let me tell you."

What followed was a tale worthy of the brothers Grimm, about a young boy feigning sick to dodge lessons and meet friends for a day spent stealing pie, fishing, napping, and enjoying the summer weather.

All went awry, of course, and not a stain but, instead, a great tear in the hapless boy's trousers resulted.

"What was I to do?" Connor lamented when the pile of unfolded towels had been significantly reduced. "I'm not much of a tailor, more fool I, and right upon my person was the proof that I'd disobeyed, told falsehoods, led my friends into mischief, and ruined a new set of trousers. My dignity was flapping in the wind, as it were. I was in for it, and my tutors were not shy with the birch rod."

"I don't care for the birch rod," Harold said, to the assent of his brothers.

"All appeared lost," Connor went on, lowering his voice. "My fate sealed, my future dire, when my younger sister stuck her head out of the window and whispered to me to meet her in the gardener's shed. She'd seen me sneaking out and had watched for my return."

"Was she about to peach on you?" Ralph asked, reaching for another towel.

"My *sister*? My own *younger sister*? Peach on me? How could you think that? I'd let her have a turn on my pony from the time she could walk, routinely saved her a biscuit off my own tray, and always chose her for my archery team. She is *my younger sister*, after all."

"You can shoot arrows?" Harold marveled.

"Not as well as Antigone can," Connor said. "She's a little bit of a thing, but a right terror with a bow. She's handy with a needle too, and that's how she rescued me. Sewed up the torn seam so nobody detected a thing.

"I ask you," Connor said, "who but a sister could have saved the day like that, and never once breathed a word of my stupidity to anybody? It's the ladies of the family who often have the best solutions to our difficulties, witness my situation now—tossed into the ditch, far from home, breeches a wreck. Cousin Julianna and Miss Roberta are putting me to rights, aren't they? I don't know when I've filled up on such a hearty stew, or had such a nice nap, and now my favorite breeches have been rescued too."

Awful, horrible man. He was thanking Julianna in public, before the boys. He was praising Roberta's cleverness, he was… getting the towels folded without an hour of grumbling and bother from the boys.

Or folding a single towel himself. Julianna would have hated him for his charm, except she was too grateful.

She rose when she ought to have been thanking him. "Cousin Connor, perhaps you could finish reading to the children, while I make us a cobbler for tonight's dessert?"

"I would be happy to," he said, opening the book. "Though I'll have to read quickly. You have the fastest towel-folding crew I've ever seen, and they do such a tidy, careful job too."

Oh bother. He'd never seen a towel folded before in his pampered, ducal life.

"The children are a marvel," Julianna said, "when they put their minds to something."

Julianna endured another marvel: Connor Amadour, duke of the most perilous ditch in Yorkshire, smiling at her. His smile held the conspiratorial pleasure of an adult who'd managed children without generating ill will, but also the glee of a man who'd shown himself to good advantage before a lady. Worse yet, his devilment was simply that—not flirtation, not innuendo, for all his eyes conveyed warmth and merriment shared exclusively with Julianna.

Hunger—or something—went skipping around in Julianna's middle. According to the duchess's letters, the duke did have a younger sister named Antigone, and she was a noted markswoman with her arrows.

Julianna resolved to make a double batch of cobbler. Convalescing required strength, and His Grace could doubtless put away a deal of sweets. The sooner he was on his way, the better for her ledgers and her larders.

* * *

That somebody would read to Con had been a foregone conclusion in his childhood. Read to him, fold his towels, make his meals, pat him on the head for being a good boy, chide him for being naughty.

He did not much recall the towels or the meals, though some of the stories had stuck with him, and the rare missed meals had been enormous inspiration for martyrdom, despite that he'd doubtless deserved the discipline.

He recalled his parents' disappointment in him keenly, and the pats on his head too. Also the rare hugs and the sense of conspiracy shared with his siblings on occasions such as Antigone's daring rescue by needle and thread. She'd sewn a terrible seam, but spared Con the horror of being marched through the house with his underlinen on display.

For two whole days thereafter, he and Tiger hadn't fought.

"I adore cobbler," Lucas said. "MacTavish says he'd kiss Horty's nose for a bite of Miss Julianna's cobbler. Papa loved her cobbler too."

"MacTavish gets two servings," the boy named Harold explained. "He works the hardest, though sometimes he can't finish his second portion, so we each get an extra bite if we're good about helping to clean up."

"Cobbler does that," Con said. "You think you could eat the whole business yourself, and then your belly contradicts you when it's too late." Starlingham had a tale of woe involving a cobbler made with whisky, though Con suspected the story was part fairy tale.

"Miss Julianna says she doesn't care for cobbler," Lucas observed.

The children referred to the lady of the house as Miss Julianna, but to her late husband as *Papa*. Interesting.

"Do you suspect she's being diplomatic?" Con asked.

"She's telling a fib," Roberta replied from her perch in Con's lap. "She wants to leave more for us."

Three boys became fascinated with the fine art of towel folding.

Con hugged the girl, who was the perfect size for hugging, though maybe all children were.

"You're probably right, Miss Roberta, but we needn't let Miss Julianna get away with her falsehoods. Nor MacTavish, if you catch him being less than truthful."

"How do you catch a grown-up in a lie and not come out the worse for it?" Lucas muttered, setting one frayed seam to another. "Miss Julianna works too hard, she never eats much, and she hardly ever sits down. Even now, we can get her to read to us only when we're doing chores, and except for Bertie, we're too old for anybody to read to us."

"*Miss* Bertie," the girl said, sticking out her tongue.

"You're our sister," Harold said. "Our secret weapon against torn breeches. We don't have to call you miss."

"You have to share your biscuits with me," Roberta countered. "Cousin said."

The wonders of the sibling barter economy were likely pondered behind youthful brows, while Con considered the problem the children had so carefully confided in him.

"The next time you must fold laundry," Con said, "you declare a contest. Roberta will referee, and you three boys set the rules. *No adults allowed.* The boy with the largest pile of neatly folded laundry wins."

Ralph smiled, a diabolically angelic grin. "We can declare contests in anything, right?"

"You must first decide the rules," Con said, which had been the best training his tutor could have devised for dealing with the idiots in the House of Lords. By the time he, Lucere, Starlingham, and their friends had determined the rules for their impromptu games and challenges, half the day had gone by, and the occasional nose had been bloodied.

"You can have a race to see who brings in the peat the most quickly," Roberta suggested. "I can keep count."

"I'll bring two buckets at once." Harold was a good-sized lad, maybe a year older than the other two.

"If I use a stout pole across my shoulders, I could bring in four," Ralph countered, "and get it done in half the time."

"You'd have sore shoulders," Lucas said. "Peat is beastly heavy."

"He'd have sore shoulders," Con said, tousling Ralph's hair, "until the exercise had built up his muscles to the point where he could do it easily. Like racing into the village to pick up the post. The first few days, you'll not make the whole way at even a trot. By the end of the summer, you'll be quick as the wind and barely breaking a sweat."

The last of the towels were folded as Con delivered the evil witch to her well-deserved fate. Roberta scrambled off his lap and went to inspect the stained breeches, and Con's backside began to throb.

"What's your first contest?" Con asked the boys across a sea of folded linen.

"We'll bring in the peat, though we rarely have fires in summer," Harold said. "Miss Julianna has asked us to see to it."

She'd probably threatened them within an inch of their little lives for putting it off so long. "Bringing in the peat makes the cobbler taste sweeter, I always say."

"You can't bring in peat, Cousin Connor," Harold said. "You hurt your arse, and Miss Julianna says you're to rest."

"Best do as she says," Lucas added. "She gets to looking at a fellow like he doesn't smell very good when you don't do as she says once too often."

"Then she crosses her arms and taps her foot," Ralph said. "Three times. It's awful."

"I can imagine." Or she'd lift that russet eyebrow and make a man want to trace its arch with his thumb. "What comes after bringing in the peat?"

"We could make a list," Ralph said. "Three things, three contests, a chance for everybody to win at least once. A list and a schedule."

"Spoken like a born man of business, Master Ralph."

Lucas's gaze went to Roberta. "What about Bertie?"

Harold stood and pushed a mop of blond hair from his eyes. "She already won at getting out stains and sewing. She wins at turning pages. She wins at staying out of trouble. I'd say Bertie's way ahead already." The very grudging nature of the admission probably echoed its sincerity.

"Off to the peat pile with you," Con said. "Don't forget to wash your hands when you're done. Dirty business, hauling in the peat."

"I like the smell of it burning," Harold said, refolding a towel given haphazard treatment. "Better than that stinky old coal."

On this the children seemed agreed, as was Connor. "Miss Bertie, perhaps you can teach me how to put the towels away?"

"I'll put them away," Roberta said. "Then I'll finish with the stain. You're to *rest*."

She folded her arms, and damned if the little minx didn't lift an eyebrow.

"I will heed your guidance," Con said as the children filed out the door, Bertie with a load of towels in her arms.

Con brought up the rear, but unlike the children, who turned left in the corridor, Con went to the right. No rule, law, list, or schedule prevented a fellow from resting in the kitchen, or learning how to help a busy woman make a fresh cobbler.

* * *

The weeps hit as Julianna cut the butter into the flour. The milch cow, Henrietta, had freshened in May, but already her output had dropped considerably. Winter without butter was an awful prospect, but buying a late heifer would be entirely beyond—

"The boys are bringing in the peat. Roberta is putting away the towels," said a voice at Julianna's right elbow. Connor peered into her crockery bowl, bringing with him a hint of sandalwood. "So this is how cobbler is made? I confess I am amazed. That doesn't look anything like a cobbler."

"It won't look much like cobbler when I'm done either," Julianna said, mashing the butter with two forks. "A proper cobbler, according to my grandmother's recipe, has preserves on the bottom and in the middle, not simply dabbed about to add a dash of color."

Connor leaned across Julianna and dipped a finger in the raspberry jam sitting to her left. When she would have chided him for snitching, he touched that finger to her lips.

"So whose children are they?" he asked. "Was John St. Bellan married previously?"

In a fit of optimism, Julianna had liberally sugared the last batch of raspberry preserves. The flavor was exquisite, all summery abundance and tart luxury. Connor's touch on her mouth was casual and incendiary at the same time.

"I was Mr. St. Bellan's only wife. We took the children in shortly before he died. This is their home. Don't do that again."

This time, Connor helped himself to a dab of jam, his expression suggesting he was tasting the first sip of a suggested vintage at some gentleman's club.

"Took them in from where? You're in the middle of nowhere, barely eking by."

Gone was the spinner of fairy tales and in his place a man who'd probably eat far too much. "How I eke is none of your affair, sir. John fetched them from a poorhouse in York. They say they're siblings, but I have my doubts. The boys wouldn't come without Roberta. Here, they can *be* siblings."

Connor turned and leaned his hips against the counter. A slight bunching beneath the fabric of his breeches gave away the location of the bandages, but other than that, he appeared hale.

"You told me that you wrote to me when your husband died, and then several months later, my mother returned your letter. Are you quite sure your letter was addressed to me?"

Julianna left off hacking the butter into smaller bits, for Connor would not leave her in peace until he'd got whatever he'd come for.

"Yes, I am certain. It's the only letter I've ever sent to a duke, and I did not enjoy writing it."

"Because you asked for help?" Connor apparently grasped the difficulty of swallowing pride, of admitting fear.

"Because I asked for *your* help," Julianna said, staring at the jumble of ingredients in the bowl. The recipe called for a dash of orange juice, though she hadn't had that ingredient on hand for several years. "I had never met you, and to presume…"

"You comprehend some of my dilemma," Connor said. "Here I am, a duke, a peer of the realm, seventy-third in line for the throne, or some such rot, and I must rely on a struggling widow to keep my secrets."

True enough. "You are concerned with your pride. I'm concerned with what will happen to my children. I did write to you. You did not write back." He was a duke, and thus his pride would be no small feature.

He studied her, though Julianna refused to give him more than her profile. He took the towel from her shoulder and dabbed at her chin.

"You've a dash of flour," he said. "Or batter, or whatever one calls a cobbler in its un-cobbled state. You can't blame me for… Julianna?"

One tear, one damned, hot, miserable tear, trickled down Julianna's cheek and splashed onto the towel.

"Go away," Julianna said, sounding very much like Bertie in a taking. "Please go away, I mean. You don't have to leave the house, but if you'd just get out of my—"

Oh hell and damnation, Connor took her in his arms. His embrace was gentle but implacable, and worse, it was the embrace of an adult male who knew how to hold a woman. No fumbling, no awkward distance, nervous patting or brushing.

A snug, lovely embrace such as Julianna hadn't enjoyed for years.

"They are wonderful children," he said. "I suspect most children are wonderful, though one can't know. I was certainly wonderful. I'm sure you were too. MacTavish might not have been."

What came out of Julianna's mouth? What brave, dignified pronouncement did she offer from the depths of a wrinkly, lavender-scented cravat?

"The cow will go dry too s-soon. I haven't the juice of an orange. I'm skimping on the sugar. I hate to skimp, and you'll eat too much, and I'm so tired of being ashamed."

And afraid.

Connor shifted so he leaned against the counter between Julianna and her cobbler, and she leaned against… him.

"You have nothing to be ashamed of," he said. "Not one damned thing."

"I can barely feed the children. If Horty goes lame, I'll not be able to bring in my crops. If the cow dies, we'll not even have cheese. If the blight comes through again, the potatoes are a loss. Each year, I'm planting more potatoes, and that is not what my husband worked his entire life to see happen with this farm."

Potatoes were the crop of the nearly destitute, capable of being tended by children and producing more food per acre than corn, but humble fare it was.

Especially without butter.

"My mother has apparently been reading my mail," Connor said. "For years, she has surreptitiously been reading my mail. Your story confirms it and makes sense of many odd looks, contradictions, and strange coincidences. I don't know why I didn't see it sooner."

The pleasure of his embrace was heartrending, inviting Julianna to rest, to be still and sheltered, to repose in the emotional safety created when somebody cared enough to offer physical comfort.

"I miss my husband."

"I know, love. I'm sure John St. Bellan was a man well worth missing. He chose you, after all, and all of his efforts, all of his resources were devoted to creating a home for you and the children. Of course you miss him and probably always will."

Julianna sniffled, but did not step back. "I'm furious with him too. After five years, you'd think I'd get over that part." She'd never get over the sheer loveliness of a husband's physical company. John had been a quiet fellow, but affectionate.

And lusty. She very much feared Maurice would be lusty too, and that… that would not be lovely.

Connor's fingers made slow, sweet circles against her nape. "Perhaps if you had an orange in the house, or my mother weren't snooping through my mail, we wouldn't be so angry."

Julianna ought to get back to her cobbler, but a certain duke stood between her and the counter. When she rested her cheek against his chest, she could feel the anger in him, now that he'd mentioned it. Hear that edge in his voice, sense it in his posture. A woman who'd been married apparently never lost the ability to read a man.

"What will you do?" she asked.

He was quiet for a few interesting moments. In those moments, fatigue dragged at Julianna, made her eyes heavy, her breathing slow.

"You need to sleep at the club," Connor said.

"You're not making sense." Neither was he sliding away, shooting his lacy cuffs, and snitching more jam.

"When a fellow has stayed too late, drunk too much, lost too much, instead of stumbling home and ending up in the gutter, or worse, he gets a room at the club for the night. Often he keeps rooms there, for a fee. Will you take a nap while I finish making this cobbler?"

Julianna pulled back to peer at him—a mistake. He still had lashes worthy of a newborn calf, was still tall enough that she had to look up at him, but now she knew what his smile looked like and exactly how warm his embrace could be.

She pushed dark hair back from his brow. "You'll ruin my cobbler, and it's a double batch. The children would be so disappointed I'd never live it down."

He might have kissed her—she was certainly tarrying in kissing range for no discernible reason.

"I wish I had an orange to give you, Mrs. St. Bellan. An entire basket, in fact. I'd like to help."

Now she stepped aside. "You're in my way, sir."

He moved not one inch. "Here's the problem. If I let on to my ducal solicitors where I am, they'll tell Uncle Leo, who will effectively shut the purse strings for years and cause the equivalent of riot and mayhem in the Mowne dukedom. At least fourteen scandals will follow, and I'll have no peace. I have a very limited budget myself, despite being the head of your family. Nonetheless, but for my mother's meddling, your circumstances might admit of an orange or two."

"You feel guilty," Julianna said, her anger directing itself at him, not at a husband long dead.

"I feel *responsible*, and you will chastise me for it. How do I make this cobbler?"

She pushed him one step to the left, and after resisting for a moment, he obliged. "How is your backside, sir?"

"A mild throb that threatens to descend to an undignified itch. Can you spare me some paper?"

"Yes. Without paper, I could not write to your mother, so I'm careful not to run out. If you're truly intent on learning some culinary skills, then I'll brew a pot of tea."

Because at the rate she was going, Julianna would never remain standing until the children were tucked in for the night. She explained where the writing supplies were as she made tea, allowing herself to use fresh leaves for the first time in three days.

While Julianna sat at the worktable and swilled a lovely, strong, hot, sweet cup of tea, she instructed the duke on how to make a creditable cobbler, even without the dash of orange juice. He took direction surprisingly well, though Julianna spent her entire tea break wondering what sort of kisser he'd be.

CHAPTER FOUR

Dear Tiger,

I have need of some coin for reasons I'm not at liberty to disclose. Please post what you can comfortably spare to the Yorkshire inn named below. UDR. Enforce same on Her Grace BAMS. Freddy is well but has taxed my resources. Uncle threatening utter ruin, as usual. Moon and Stars send love, as do I, to you, Hector, and Quint. Mama must bear my ire, for now. SNM. C.

The note was tiny, as befit one carried by a pigeon, but for all that, it was the most precious communication Antigone had received from her older brother in years.

"Antigone! Antigone Charlotte Dardanella Josephine Marie! Open this door or have your mother's complete collapse on your conscience."

Antigone's cat yawned, for even the pets were inured to Mama's histrionics. How Mowne stood Her Grace's daily dramas was a mystery.

"Coming, Mama!" Antigone tucked her brother's note into her skirt pocket, for Mama could read upside down in far too many languages.

"That boy!" Mama said, sweeping into the library. "That awful, mean boy. I try to help him, try to guide in him in the ways his sainted father no longer can, and what do I get? Read this!"

Another tiny note was shoved at Antigone. Pity the poor pigeon who'd carried double the load.

Your Grace,

For the remainder of the Season, your allowance has been cut in half. If you ever read my mail again, your funds will be cut off entirely. Kirkwood has been asked for his resignation by post for having accommodated your meddling. Drummond's livelihood hangs by a thread. I am very disappointed in you, madam. Complain to Uncle Leo of this development, and you will do so from the permanent comfort of the dower house. Mowne

"You must write to him," Mama said, stalking back and forth before the fire. She'd begun to apply henna to her flaming hair even before Antigone's come out, but she was still an impressive figure. "He's met some woman, and she's put him up to this, I vow it. That Culpeper girl was the determined sort."

No woman in her right mind would take on Mama for an in-law, which fact probably accounted for Mowne's continued bachelor status.

"Mama, please have a seat, and I'll ring for tea."

"Tea will not return my funds to me! Helen Gibbersley expects vowels to be paid immediately, as if we were officers on leave with nothing better to do than shoot at each other on foggy mornings. I will have my funds of that boy, or else."

UDR. The initials were a long-forgotten relic of the code developed among the ducal siblings and stood for Utmost Discretion Required.

No whining to adults allowed, no turning to sympathetic servants. Sibling bonds alone would have to resolve the difficulty. Antigone had wondered in recent years if Mowne even recalled that among his dependents and responsibilities remained a trio of siblings in addition to Feckless Freddy.

"Mama, how much do you owe and to whom?" Antigone asked.

Her Grace named an appalling figure, though Antigone suspected it was accurate to the penny.

"How much is owed to you?" Antigone asked.

Mama's hems swished to stillness around her slippers. "A duchess doesn't bother with those amounts. I can't very well ask for the sums to be paid, can I?"

Mama meant well, most of the time, but she could become invested in her own consequence to the exclusion of common sense. Antigone, on the other hand, loved puzzles, her brothers, and haggling with milliners. Freddy, Hector, and Quint all but ignored her, while Mowne paid her bills, admired her frocks, and escorted her when escort was needed.

He also never, ever let her help with anything.

"Mama, you will bring me your vowels, both those owed and those owing. You will not breathe a word of this to Uncle Leo, or he'll applaud Mowne for cutting you off, and then where will you be? You recall how Leo was with Aunt Lillian?"

Mama seated herself on a delicate gilt armchair, though for a woman of her statuesque proportions, the effect was not to enthrone a duchess so much as to put the penitent on the sinner's stool.

"Lillian was a flighty, nonsensical, interfering woman," Mama said, twitching back her skirts the better to reveal intricate embroidery about the underskirt. "Leo chose poorly."

According to Con, Leo had married the love of his life and lost her too soon. An excess of concern for remaining family members had turned Leo penny-pinching and sour.

"Mama, have you been reading Mowne's mail?"

Much sniffing ensued, and twitching of skirts, and shifting about on the chair. "A mother worries."

This mother worried mostly about gossip, tattle, and maintaining her position as the Duchess of Mowne—a *dowager* duchess being a far less powerful and interesting creature.

The next acronyms in Con's note had been equally intriguing: BAMS—By Any Means Suitable—and SNM.

Show No Mercy, as when Lucere or Starlingham had committed some childhood offense that generated the sort of animosity of great moment to small boys. For the space of entire hours, the Sun, Moon, and Stars might stop talking to one another when in the grip of a childish pique.

"You won't read his mail again, will you?" Antigone pressed as the cat hopped onto the sofa beside her. King James was a grand specimen, all feline dignity and magnificent orange coat. "When Mowne makes up his mind, he cannot be reasoned with, and you have offended him beyond bearing."

Antigone had learned years ago not to leave her mail where Mama could even see it, coming or going. Why hadn't Antigone warned Con about Mama's snooping?

"I have tried to assist your brother to step into his papa's shoes. This is the thanks I get, when all I've done is sort through a few bits of correspondence."

Meaning Mama was reading nearly every letter to find its way to the ducal address.

"You have cost Kirkwood his post," Antigone said. "What would Papa think of that?"

Kirkwood, the Mowne town house butler, had been old when Antigone had been born. He was a relic not of the former duke, but of Antigone's grandfather—and was the duchess's familiar among the staff.

Mama withdrew an ornate double-ended scent bottle from her skirt pocket. "I'll tell Kirkwood not to resign. Mowne is being dramatic. It's a very unattractive trait in a person of high station. *Very* unattractive."

She took a significant whiff from one end of the bottle—more posturing, for lavender graced the library air, not the reviving spirits of ammonia the bottle likely also held.

"What's unattractive," Antigone said, "is a mother undermining her own son's authority under his very roof. Fortunately, the dower house at Mowne is lovely. I'm sure you'll be very comfortable there, and your friends will visit you often."

Showing no mercy was downright enjoyable, even more enjoyable than haggling with milliners.

Mama jammed her scent bottle back in its pocket. "Teasing your own mother is beneath you, Antigone Charlotte. I'll not have it."

"You're right. I shouldn't tease, and you should never have read Mowne's correspondence. Your friends won't visit you, unless they're pockets to let and need a repairing lease. Given the way your set gambles, that will be a frequent occasion for a few of them."

Mama rose to yank the bellpull. "I have raised a brood of vipers. Sharper than the serpent's tooth, and whatever the rest of that quote is." She appropriated the seat behind the estate desk in another artful rustle of skirts. "I must indulge your brother's queer start for the nonce, nonetheless. I'm not about to hare off to Scotland to argue sense into his misguided head. I'm done trying to help, do you hear me? Done exerting myself to the utmost to ease his burdens every day in every way I can. What can we do about those vowels?"

Drummond, the conscientious solicitor who handled disbursement of the family funds, would doubtless be relieved to hear of Mama's latest sacrifice.

"You'll no longer have time to meddle with Mowne's mail," Antigone said. "I'll tell you what to do about your vowels, and you will follow my directions to the letter." Lucere and Starlingham had warned Antigone years ago about the perils of the casual IOU. "If you owe Helen Gibbersley fifty pounds, you send her Penelope Framingham's note of hand for sixty, along with an apology for not being able to make an exact exchange. You thank Helen for her willingness to be a bit flexible, and trust your own note will come back from Helen by return post."

Mama left off poking through the desk drawers, closing the last with a bang. "One does this? One trades the vowels about? Are you sure? Do your brothers know how this is done?"

The cat hopped off the sofa and strutted across the library.

"One does so at a discount, so to speak, which is part of the danger of even making a note of hand. Your obligation can travel anywhere in Mayfair—or beyond—and the unscrupulous gambler can find herself owing an enormous sum to a party whom she'd rather not recognize in the street."

Mama's horror was probably entirely genuine. "*Anybody* can collect on my notes?"

Well, no. IOUs were not enforceable contracts, for they did not represent an exchange of consideration. They were a mere promise to pay, unsupported by legal weight. A debt of honor, in other words, which concept might tax Mama's tenuous grasp of personal integrity.

"Anybody can hold you accountable for the sums you owe, and Mowne has apparently already directed Drummond to reduce your pin money by half. Perhaps it's time you did enjoy some Highland scenery, Mama."

Mama was a Lowlander, her people hailing from the Borders, though she seldom acknowledged those antecedents.

"Scotland is relentlessly cold, young lady. The men are always flaunting their knees in those ridiculous kilts, and nobody sleeps properly during a Scottish summer. I'll enjoy a few weeks' respite at Mowne, and you may tell Drummond to direct my few remaining funds there."

Having ensured Mama would not inflict herself on Mowne in person, Antigone spent the next hour sorting out her mother's finances, and then penning notes to Hector and Quint. Utmost Discretion Required meant only the St. Bellan siblings were to know of an epistle's contents.

The time had come to remind Hector and Quint that their older brother was more than simply the fellow who signed bank drafts, managed Mama, placated Uncle Leo, and kept Freddy from ruining them all.

* * *

Con waited nearly a week for Antigone's reply, and during that week he felt shot in the arse all over again.

Julianna worked without ceasing, an education in itself for a man who'd thought running a dukedom demanding. The household had a cook/housekeeper, but Con could not decide if that good woman had been let go, sent on an unpaid visit to relatives in York, or had chosen to take a summer holiday.

Julianna, meanwhile, didn't merely give orders, review draft correspondence, and stay out waltzing until all hours. She swept, washed, cooked, totaled ledgers, stitched, cooked some more, beat the rugs, cooked yet more…

While Con tried to keep the children productively occupied and his hands to himself.

His wound itched, his conscience positively tormented him, and his cock… became an increasing bother as well.

"Make me a list, and I will go to market for you tomorrow," Con said when the children had been put to bed with another story of Con's misspent youth.

"You cannot," Julianna replied, drawing her needle through the hem of Harold's trousers. "MacTavish goes in to York to fetch your mail and bring Mrs. Periwinkle home to us tomorrow, and Maurice will escort me about at market. I consider that preferable to having him take me to services."

Between MacTavish's silences, Julianna's haunted gaze, and the children's declarations that peat was better than coal, Con had concluded that nobody in the household liked Maurice Warren, but they dared not say so.

"Julianna, if you don't want this fellow sniffing about your skirts, you tell him his attentions are flattering, but you cannot in good conscience encourage them. He expresses his regret that he's misread the situation, begs your pardon, and asks that you let him know if you'd ever reconsider. This is how it's done, and there's an end to it."

In the alternative, Connor could simply strut about in his ducal finery, wave the signet ring conspicuously, and let it be known Julianna was a valued relation of the Duke of Mowne. Even for a widow of independent means, Warren would be bound to reckon with her family before imposing his addresses on her.

"It's not that simple," Julianna said, drawing the thread snug against the fabric. "Mr. Warren has been a friend to me and to this farm."

While Connor had been his mother's dupe, kicking his heels two hundred miles to the south. To reveal his identity outside this household would invite Uncle Leo's worst interference, though, and then where would Antigone, Hector, and Quint be? Where would the charities be that Connor supported from his own funds? The notes of hand he'd quietly bought for his friends until their own finances came right? The small pensions, and not so small, that Uncle Leo would never have approved?

"Mr. Warren has lent you a few mules he can easily spare," Connor said. "Any neighbor should do the same for a widow trying to make a go of good land. I've wondered where your neighbors have been, in fact."

Julianna's needle paused. She sat back in her rocking chair, her eyes tired, but curious. "What do you mean?"

How to put this?

"I don't think farmers in Kent are that different from farmers in Yorkshire, and as to that, I own farms in the East Riding. Won them from Northumberland, and God knows he has land to spare."

She let her sewing fall to her lap. "You win farms in card games?"

Connor took the trousers from her and resumed stitching. He'd learned to stitch hems in the past week, make bread, sweep, scrub pots with sand and a tough rag, and more.

All manner of useful activities were within the grasp of an injured duke. He'd put the boys up on Hortensia one by one and passed along some rudimentary equitation, taught them how to groom her properly, and how to tie a simple neckcloth. They'd watched him shave, and joined him in a nightly hand of whist.

In another week he'd be gone, but while he was here, he'd make up for five years of neglect as best he could. Then too, all this activity had meant he'd slept well, when dreams of Julianna hadn't plagued him.

"Northumberland has farms coming out his... his ears," Con said. "He's a good farmer too, unlike some dukes I could name. I'm not a bad farmer, for a duke, and I know that neighbors in a district cooperate. They schedule their shearing, haying, and harvesting together. They confer about who's growing wheat and who's growing barley, whether the year will be wet or dry, and when to trade their breeding rams, and so forth. Your neighbors all but ignore you, apparently."

Julianna rose and brought the tallow candle closer to Con's elbow. They were in her parlor, which five years ago had likely been a pretty room. Now, the carpet was worn, the space over the mantel vacant, and the curtains tattered about the hems.

"When John was alive, it was different," she said, dropping back into her rocker. "You're right about that, but at first I thought the neighbors were simply respecting the privacy owed a widow during mourning, and then I was too tired to think. You sew a fine seam, Mr. Amadour."

Her smile had become Con's reward for jobs well done. To glimpse that smile, he had read a dozen fairy tales, swung the children about by their wrists until he was dizzy, and groomed the mule until she'd fallen asleep.

"Are you ashamed to be seen with me, Julianna?"

The question had cost him, but needed to be dealt with. Con hadn't left the farm in the past week. He'd healed for the most part, though sitting a horse was still out of the question, and he'd rested and pondered life in a way not possible for a duke. MacTavish had brought word of two other swells biding in the area—Lucere and Starlingham, of course—and Con hadn't wanted to add to the talk.

"I am not ashamed of you," Julianna said, "but a widow must be careful. Mr. Warren will not like to hear of me keeping company with a young single fellow under my own roof, regardless that he's a distant relation of my late husband. I cannot afford to court Mr. Warren's disfavor."

Mr. Warren could not afford to court the disfavor of Julianna's ducal relation, did he but know it.

"I have means, Julianna. I simply need time to redirect them. Once the Little Season ends in the autumn, my mother and sister leave Town, my brothers go off flirting to the house parties, and my friends often pay their vowels. I can put this farm to rights by harvest, if you'll allow it."

Her expression went from tired to bleak. "Thank you for those good intentions, Connor. Thank you from the bottom of my heart, but I hope it won't come to that."

She rose and kissed his cheek, a gentle, lingering kiss that bore more resignation than gratitude, and between one flicker of the candle and the next, Con hit the limit of his damned ducal gallantry.

He kissed her back, on the mouth. Set the sewing aside, cupped her chin, and informed the lady—lip to lip—that distant relation of a long-departed spouse or not, this was a kiss between a healthy, if arse-shot, man and a healthy, if exhausted, woman.

Julianna made a soft, yielding murmur, and Con rose to envelop her in his arms. In the past week, he'd sneaked the occasional arm around her shoulders or her waist, a half hug, a pat on the shoulder, and each time Julianna had reciprocated with a shy, bewildered smile.

Once, she'd let her head rest on his shoulder, and Con had nearly danced a jig, despite any repercussions to his wound. Twice, he'd felt a surreptitious pat to his bum that might have been his imagination or sheer accident.

"We shouldn't—" Julianna muttered, twining her arms around Con's neck. "I can't—"

"You are the most independent, selfless, hardworking woman I've met. A damned duchess of the dales, and if you want to kiss me, you should be free to kiss me. God knows, I want your kisses."

His compliment was genuine, and another testament to the degree to which Con's family situation had drifted from its proper course. A duchess should be generous and kind, gracious and dignified, while Con had allowed his mother's widowhood to lapse into—

He lost track of that thought as Julianna pressed closer. Hers was not the rounded, pampered form of a London beauty, but rather, a strong, fit, womanly shape that could match a man passion for passion.

And heaven defend him, the lady could kiss. She went a-plundering with her tongue, delicately at first, then more enthusiastically as Con returned her overtures and shaped her waist and hips with his hands.

He loved the feel of her beneath his palms. Loved all that vitality and strength, femininity and eagerness, responding to his touch. Kissing Julianna, he sorted out what had been distracting him for the past week.

At this humble farm, as Connor Amadour, he'd come alive. He'd felt what it was to work hard physically and see the immediate results. Not make investments by means of three intermediaries, but make bread and slice it still warm from the hearth.

He'd not trimmed expenses from the gardening budget for his town house, but trimmed the hair of a young fellow still in the grip of boyhood, and seen a bit of the young man emerge.

And he'd fallen in love.

Con shaped a luscious, full breast, and Julianna's hands on his back went still.

Her forehead dropped to his shoulder. "Connor, I have missed—"

She'd missed her husband. Con kissed her—a quick buss—rather than hear that sentiment, understandable though it was. He wasn't missing anything, for he was exploring completely new terrain.

"I have missed the passion," she said. "The sense of being cast away and relieved of all thought, all cares, breath even. I've missed feeling desired, and I shouldn't be telling you any of this."

Who else could she tell? From what Con had seen, not even the other widows in the neighborhood, the pastor, or the families on the nearest farms took notice of her. If they'd known she counted a duke among her allies, they would never have dared to neglect her so.

"I'm coming to market with you tomorrow," Con said. "Let them all wonder about your haughty relation, let them speculate that you have friends in high places of which they knew nothing. John St. Bellan had to have mentioned a duke on the family tree at some point."

Her arms fell away, and she stepped back. "You cannot come to market with me, Connor. My neighbors will think the worst of us both. Any mention John might have made of you will be forgotten when I flaunt your wealth and good looks before the whole village. Puddlebury *is* a village at heart. We're lucky to have a market day we're so small, and nobody will believe such as you is simply my visiting relation after all these years."

In other words, his past neglect would cost her his present consequence, even were he free to flaunt it. In the space of a morning, all her hard work and proper living, her charity to the children and hymn-singing in church would mean nothing as she fell from genteel widowed neighbor to rural disgrace.

Con took her in his arms again, but remained silent. For years he'd brushed aside the odd looks from servants and solicitors, the peculiar non sequiturs in correspondence or conversation that should have caused him to suspect his mother's meddling.

For all he knew, his brothers were reading his correspondence, and Antigone was borrowing his new stallion in Con's absence.

He'd not paid attention.

The Bible in the Mowne library included a family tree, and Con had never truly studied it to learn who Cousin Jules was.

Mama had gambling debts, and Con had never chided her for them. Hector was a soft touch for charities that Con suspected were little more than swindles.

Something about Julianna's circumstances—and Mr. Maurice Warren's role in them—wasn't adding up. Con had learned his lesson, though. He was here, he was the Duke of Mowne, however disguised, and for the next week, he would pay very close attention.

Julianna sighed, then slipped from his grasp, and when she wrapped her shawl about her and withdrew, Con let her go and resumed his mending.

* * *

John would have understood what Julianna was about to do, maybe better than she understood it herself. He'd been kind and practical, both, and had told Julianna never to deny herself happiness for the sake of his memory.

Happiness was nowhere to be found these days, but pleasure… pleasure might be as close as the bedroom across the hall.

John had been a generous man too, though not as close to perfect as Julianna had once thought. John had disdained *women's work* even through the long winter when the land was fallow and the housework unceasing, he'd dreamed too ambitiously most years, and he'd trusted Maurice Warren.

Not well done of John, that last part.

Julianna looked in on the children, changed into her nightclothes, got ready for bed, and brushed and rebraided her hair. Saying her prayers would have to wait for another time.

Julianna's tap on Connor's door met with a moment of silence, then the door opened, and there stood the Duke of Mowne, naked from the waist up, his chest and the hair at his temples damp.

"Are the children well?" He held a towel in one hand, his feet were bare, his features were etched with concern.

"The children are fast asleep. May I come in?"

His expression became unreadable, but he stepped back and held the door for her. His room was the best guest room on the premises, the only one still entirely furnished, and yet… it had become shabby.

"Are *you* well, Julianna?"

The grate held no fire, though the night was cool. Connor had brought up a single tallow candle from the parlor, and thus shadows flickered about him. The house was so profoundly quiet, Julianna could nearly hear her heart hammering against her ribs.

"Make love with me, please." She wouldn't beg, but she'd ask. Invite, something in between. "I'm a widow. I can bestow my favors where I wish, as long as I'm discreet."

Connor pulled a shirt down over his head, the muscles of his arms, belly, and chest bunching and rippling, but he didn't do up any of the buttons.

"You can't be seen with me at the market, but you invite my intimate attentions now. What am I to make of this, Julianna?"

"You are to make nothing of it," she said. "A week from now, you'll go on about your ducal business, and I'll have a farm to run. We're adults free for the present of other encumbrances. I like you. You seem favorably disposed toward me."

He folded the towel over the top of the privacy screen, seams matching precisely, no hurry at all.

"You want a dalliance of me?"

Julianna longed to give him her heart, but what a paltry offering that would be, mortgaged to a farm, four children, and very likely a future with Maurice Warren.

Though apparently, even dukes could be cash-poor.

"I want an hour with you," she said. "A special hour."

She'd asked to see his wound the previous day and confirmed it was healing well. He'd have a scar, but the bandage was more a safeguard now than a necessity. The sight of his exposed muscular flank, though, would remain emblazoned on Julianna's memory for the rest of her days.

Connor took a step closer. "You would have *one hour* of pleasure with me, and then we rise in the morning, please pass the eggs, Harold get your elbows off the table?"

"The boys no longer need reminding, thanks to you."

He grasped Julianna's braid and tugged her closer. "One hour? If that's the best St. Bellan could do with his lawfully wedded wife, I must reduce the esteem in which I hold him. A *single hour*, Julianna?"

Fifteen minutes, if she and John had been tired, but that wasn't the point Connor was making.

"I'll settle for an hour," Julianna said.

"I won't," Connor murmured, closing the distance between them. "You are warned, madam, I will not settle for an hour, when you deserve so much more."

For long minutes, he expounded on that point, kissing Julianna anywhere except her mouth and touching her only with his lips. She endured that pleasure as best as she could, vaguely aware Connor was issuing a challenge.

One hour from now, she would not be stealing out the door, ready for a night of dreamless slumber before getting up to make the bread in the morning. Perhaps she'd not leave in two hours, or even three.

She wouldn't *want* to leave ever. Julianna slid her arms around Connor's lean waist, hugging his warmth close. Connor was aroused, truly, unmistakably aroused. By *her*, in her threadbare robe, with her freckled hands, her tired eyes, and unremarkable figure.

"How I have longed…" he whispered, arms closing about her.

Julianna craved his embrace, craved the strength and caring in it, craved the fit of their bodies seamed together. She stood in the circle of Connor's arms, kissing him, nuzzling at the male contours of his neck and shoulders. He'd used the lavender soap she'd made last summer, and his flesh was still cool from his ablutions.

"Into bed with us," Connor said, patting Julianna's bum. "Before I have you against the wall."

Relief coursed through her. He was a duke. Of course he'd understand dalliance. Some helpful soul probably wrote treatises for ducal heirs about how to accommodate the intimate demands of widows without getting entangled in expectations.

Julianna turned back the bedcovers and started to climb between the sheets.

"Are you that modest?" Connor asked, undoing the buttons of his falls. "I'm not particularly modest. Hard to be when there's always a valet about who lives to fuss one into clothing."

"I usually wear my nightgown to bed because the sheets are cool."

"The sheets will soon be quite warm," Connor said, shoving his breeches down. His arousal arrowed up along his belly, a testament to desire and his lack of modesty, both.

Julianna turned away. One didn't want to compare, but joyous, heavenly days and celestial nights. The term *merry widow* abruptly made more sense to her.

Connor came up behind her. Julianna could feel his heat along her back and his breath on her shoulder.

"Last chance to change your mind, Julianna. I do not share my favors lightly, nor do I hold you in casual esteem."

He'd learned that people took advantage, in other words. "I esteem you greatly," Julianna said as he slid his arms about her waist and pulled her back against him.

She did esteem him greatly, for taking the boys in hand, for complimenting her cooking, for setting an example—of helpfulness, good manners, good humor, and cooperation—that the boys were inspired to follow.

She esteemed him for doing what Maurice Warren could have done so easily and hadn't—for simply being decent.

Connor kissed his way from the top of her shoulder to the shivery spot below her ear, gently pushing aside her nightclothes, setting a tone of leisurely seduction.

"I've never been... enticed before," Julianna said. "I like it."

"You are the impetuous sort?" Connor murmured, gently cupping a breast. "A little impetuosity can be marvelous."

A little pressure was marvelous-er. A little gentle exploration of this touch and that caress, on both breasts at once, and Julianna's nightclothes became an impediment to pleasure. Connor helped her out of them—his assistance was practiced without being presuming—and then Julianna was naked with a man for the first time in years.

Why, oh why, hadn't she told him to blow out the candle first? Summer nights in Yorkshire took forever to grow truly dark, even when the hour was late.

"I'm not... I'm not young," Julianna said. "I'm not what I once—"

Connor wore only the bandage about his waist and flank. "Thank God you're not a silly, blushing girl, unsure of herself and incapable of knowing what she wants and deserves. This might have escaped your notice, but I'm not a boy myself."

His smile was far too wicked to belong on any mere boy, and abruptly, everything inside Julianna came right. Tomorrow would be an awful day, mincing around the market with Maurice fawning at her side, while Julianna spent far too much coin for far too little merchandise. She'd come home frustrated, worried, and trying to put a good face on matters for the children and MacTavish, probably fooling none of them.

Tonight, she was desired, and her every wish was about to be indulged.

* * *

Lucere maintained that success with a new lover was all about tempo, about being able to read how aroused the lady was, and knowing when to get down to the business of pleasure, as it were. Starlingham maintained that being a good lover required lingering afterward, and that much would be forgiven a fellow who'd been too hasty or too dilatory, if he indulged the lady's whims when the fireworks had concluded.

Especially her whims where fine jewelry or good seats at the opera were concerned.

Connor might have said—before—both of his friends had valid points. Now, he knew they were both wrong.

The essence of loving a woman well was simply that—loving her. Putting her first, listening for her responses, attending to her needs and wishes. *Paying attention.*

Julianna liked having her breasts touched, for example, a happy discovery because Con enjoyed touching them. He laid her on the bed, came down over her, and took a moment to admire how candlelight created shadows of the curves and hollows of her body.

"You taste good," he said, kissing his way down the center of her chest. "Of roses and fresh bread. Maybe a hint of basil. Delicious."

Her hands landed in his hair, holding him close. "You are ridiculous."

What Con was, was determined. Determined to look after this household that he'd neglected for the past several years. Determined that the sense of usefulness and mutual caring he'd found here wouldn't be left behind when he departed from Lesser Puddlebury.

And determined that Julianna would at least consider coming with him.

She grasped intuitively something Con was only beginning to realize: Infatuation and desire were but the immature and frolicsome impersonators of love. True love got up early to make the bread, taught a little girl her letters by the light of a tallow candle, and asked an old man to sharpen the knives, simply so he'd have an excuse to sit by the warmth of the kitchen hearth.

True love was a lot like being a duke: endless helpings of duty, hard work, and honor, mostly in the name of aiding others to thrive or preserving them from folly. Con had spent days marveling at Julianna's discipline and self-restraint, and nights wondering if she was as passionate about her pleasures as she was about caring for the children.

The notion enthralled him as no mere passing encounter ever had. Ridiculous, to be nigh thirty years old and never truly have made love.

Con put his ridiculous mouth to Julianna's nipples and made her wiggle and sigh for a good five minutes, long enough to convince him that being enticed did, indeed, agree with her.

"Do you know," he murmured, "how lovely you look to me when you're sewing up Harold's breeches? How much I want to kiss you when you're kneading the hell out of the bread? How much I resent that you send MacTavish and the boys to replace your roses, but never send me?"

Julianna traced the contour of his right ear, an oddly pleasurable caress. "If MacTavish and the boys are off cutting roses, then you are in the kitchen, reciting poetry and scrubbing the pots for me, aren't you?"

"Strategy," Con whispered. "How I adore a woman with firm command of strategy, but Julianna, now isn't the time for subtlety."

She ran a toe up his calf. "It's not the time for ducal proclamations, Connor. You do know how to go on in bed?"

He retaliated by sitting back enough to ruffle the curls between her legs. "Right now, I barely know my name. I know only that I want to be inside you."

She stretched, she arched, she let him play for a few minutes, or perhaps she was learning a little bit how to play herself.

"I know your name, Connor," she said when Con had her moving restlessly against his hand. Her sex was wonderfully damp, and Con's cockstand rivaled a drover's staff. "I know I want you inside me."

"Do you want me inside you *now*?" He would expire if she said anything other than *yes*.

Julianna grasped him by the shaft, the first time she'd put her hands on that part of him, and drew him right against her.

A *yes*, by God.

Con braced himself on his arms and kissed the woman he hoped would become his duchess. The joining was easy and sweet, also profoundly tender. He knew by watching Julianna's face, that in accepting him this way, she also said yet another good-bye to her late husband and to the young woman who'd married years ago with such hopes and innocence.

He kissed her as they joined, kissed the passion and the welcome, the grief and the approaching glory. When Con was hilted inside her, he lowered himself to his forearms.

"Julianna, I will not fail you."

She undulated sumptuously, and words became superfluous. Con did not fail her. He sent her into pleasure's maelstrom easily and often, until consideration alone made him pause.

"I could love you all night," he whispered. She might be making up for lost time, appeasing years of unsatisfied desire while he was learning to love a woman, truly love her, for the first time. Fresh bread came into it, folded towels, the boys, washing the eggs with Roberta, and reading stories.

Asking his siblings for help was part of it, as was trusting that Lucere and Starlingham could manage without him too.

Loving Julianna involved all of Con, and the joy of that, the odd, unexpected passion of it, was like coming home to himself in a way that being just another duke could never accomplish.

Julianna's fingers brushed over his derriere. *Enough.*

Never enough. Con sent her over the edge one more time, then withdrew and allowed himself the consolatory bliss of spending on her belly.

The damned towel was hanging over the privacy screen across the room, but even that—even forgetting to tidily fold a handkerchief on the night table— pleased Con. A fellow in love was allowed to be a bit disorganized about his passionate encounters.

He tended to his lady, then to himself, and left the towel on the night table when he climbed back into bed.

"I do believe, Julianna St. Bellan, that recourse to a timekeeping device would suggest, more than an hour has elapsed. Come here."

She curled close, her head pillowed on Con's shoulder. "I don't want to get up. My own bed feels miles away, across an arctic plain, down miles of lonely corridor."

Her bed was probably four yards from Con's.

"I'll tuck you in when it's time to placate appearances." Con kissed her brow and started mentally composing a letter to Uncle Leo. "Sleep now."

She murmured something and did that thing with her toes that made Con's heart purr.

"What time do we leave for market?" Con would make sure she slept in. Fortunately, eggs and toast were among the fare he'd learned to cook.

Her eyes opened, the butterfly kiss of her lashes sweeping upward against Con's shoulder.

"Connor, you cannot come to market with me. We've been through this."

Perhaps Starlingham had a point. Perhaps the cuddling part mattered rather a lot.

"When you become intimate with a man, then his escort is yours to claim, Julianna. I don't indulge in an amour and then pretend a woman who has granted me the greatest liberties means nothing to me."

Connor wouldn't allow such a callous lout among his distant acquaintances.

Julianna hiked herself up on an elbow to peer at him. Con had forgotten to blow the candle out, but it would soon gutter on its own.

"Connor, I must tolerate Maurice Warren's escort at market, at the very least. He'll see me from shop to shop and merchant to merchant as he always does, ensuring I get the best bargains. Then he'll bow me on my way, if I'm lucky. Lately he's had a look in his eye I haven't found at all comforting."

Julianna brushed Connor's hair back from his brow. He'd come to love that casual touch from her, for she did it even before the children.

"What sort of look, Julianna?"

She flopped to her back so they no longer touched. "Like he's about to propose. I strongly suspect he's about to propose. Either that, or he'll call the mortgage due that John signed with him five years ago. Possibly both. Both is my worst nightmare, but it makes the most sense."

CHAPTER FIVE

Julianna had forgotten how an argument with a man could sour everything, though that probably explained why John had never told her of the mortgage he'd signed with Maurice Warren.

She would have sold her wedding ring, her dresses, her grandmother's cameo—anything to avoid relying on Maurice Warren's good offices to see the farm through a bad year.

Now, she would have sold her soul not to feel the nagging tension between her and Connor across the breakfast table. She'd wanted an hour of passion last night, a respite from her cares, an interlude of simple adult pleasure.

Not too much to ask, but so much less than Connor had offered her.

Tenderness, passion, caring, *ferocious* cherishing, such as even Julianna's late husband had never quite conveyed in years of marriage.

And then questions she could not answer: Had she ever seen this mortgage document? Was it a mortgage or a promissory note? What were its actual terms? Was forfeiture of the farm required by the note, or had Warren merely implied as much? Where had the money gone that John St. Bellan had supposedly borrowed so shortly before his death?

Julianna could answer none of it, but neither could she afford to provoke Maurice into foreclosing. Months ago, Maurice had begun implying payment was overdue, and this morning, Julianna could hardly keep her tea and toast down, she was so unsettled.

"May we have a turn on Mr. Yoder's mare before you go into York?" Harold asked MacTavish.

"Best not," MacTavish said. "When you borrow a horse, you don't go lending it around to others. You lot behave yourselves, and I'll be back from York with our Mrs. Periwinkle as soon as I can."

"I'd like to see this mare," Con said. "Perhaps you might stop back this way after you've picked her up?"

A look passed between the two men. Bertie used the moment to take another piece of toast from the plate in the middle of the table. Con plucked it from her grasp and added butter—not too much, but not skimping either.

"I'll pass by here on my way to York," MacTavish said, pushing back from the table. "My thanks for an excellent omelet, Miss Julianna."

"Take Mrs. Yoder some roses, please," Julianna said. "And thank the Yoders profusely for the loan of the mare."

Connor had asked MacTavish to fetch the mail from York, today of all days, so Julianna would take the children with her to market. Maurice was not fond of the boys, though neither was he rude to them, nor they to him—overtly.

All too soon, the boys were on the front porch, faces scrubbed, hair combed back, and Connor was leading Horty around, the cart rattling behind her.

"Where's Bertie?" Harold asked. "She's never late."

"Miss Roberta tarried arranging the flowers in my room," Connor said. "I account myself most privileged."

He was up to something, but at least he wasn't sulking. Last night, he'd argued, he'd fumed, he'd argued some more, but then he'd grown quiet, wrapped himself around Julianna, and rubbed her back until she'd fallen asleep.

"What will you do to pass the time?" Julianna asked, pulling on her driving gloves. These were gardening gloves in truth, but they protected her hands well enough.

Con scratched Horty's hairy neck. "I'll get some weeding done, beat a few rugs, maybe make a cobbler."

"Cobbler for dessert!" Lucas yelled, which caused Hortensia to startle.

"Into the gig," Connor said. "I'll hand your mother up."

Did he know he referred to Julianna as their mother? The children didn't seem to mind... and neither did Julianna, really. Con kissed her on the cheek in parting and tousled each boy's hair.

"Best behavior, gents. Spend your tuppence well."

Julianna unwrapped the reins from the brake. "What tuppence?"

"For many jobs well done," Connor said. "I've asked the boys to help Miss Roberta choose some hair ribbons. She said she'd prefer green, because it's MacTavish's favorite color."

Damn him for his thoughtfulness. Sixpence was nothing to most households, but to these boys... Julianna could not recall when she'd ever given them money of their own. She simply hadn't any money to give.

Roberta dashed onto the porch, her hair in lopsided braids courtesy of Ralph's attempt to be helpful. Practicing for if he ever had to braid up a mane or a tail, he'd said. Con tucked tuppence into Roberta's hand, and lifted her into the back with the boys, though he hugged the girl conspicuously in the process and been hugged in return too.

Julianna searched Connor's gaze for something—ire, reassurance, clues— but he was very much the duke this morning, not the lover, not the amiable relation.

"Horty, walk on," Julianna said, giving the reins a shake. Hortensia obliged with a mule's version of alacrity.

When Julianna glanced over her shoulder at the foot of the drive, Connor stood before the house, merely watching, while she drove off to meet a man she didn't like or trust, but would probably marry.

* * *

Con had purposely not cleaned his boots very well, and he'd borrowed a too-large, dusty coat from MacTavish. Because Con wouldn't put anybody to the bother of ironing his clothing, his attire was wrinkled, if presentable by village market standards.

The two-mile walk into the village set Con's wound to itching, and also gave him time to think.

He'd sent MacTavish into York's pawnshops with two trunks of London finery, including watches, cravat pins, a spare pair of brand new Hoby boots, cuff links, fobs, and assorted whatnot. More trunks had of course gone north with Freddy, and yet still more clothing hung in cedar-lined wardrobes at Mowne.

None of which Con could retrieve without risking Uncle Leo's notice, or unacceptable delay.

"Well, if it isn't yet another genteel stranger lounging about trying to look inconspicuous and mostly failing." Starlingham took up a lean next to Con outside the posting inn. Across the street, the market day merchants were doing a brisk business on the Puddlebury village green.

Con had warned the boys to ignore him and had also given them tasks more specific than that.

Starlingham blew the foam off a tankard of ale. "How's the, er, injury?"

"Healing. How do you find your accommodations?"

Con was also holding a tankard of summer ale, as were various others loitering outside the inn. The day was sunny, noisy, and not a duke's usual summer diversion.

"My accommodations are... interesting. I've never been to a village market before. Puts one in mind of a London ballroom with livestock."

Starlingham had a point. Across the green, a pair of fiddlers busked for pennies. The tavern had set up a keg to draw custom on the front terrace, much like a crystal punch bowl drew thirsty debutantes. Business was being transacted, of course—much business occurred at Mayfair's social gatherings too—but the general air was convivial.

"We're not so different," Con said as a sizable ewe darted away from the green and a small boy pelted after her.

Starlingham stuck out a booted foot, stopping the ewe for the instant the boy needed to grab two handfuls of fleece.

"Thank 'ee, sir!"

Starlingham lifted his mug and smiled. "You mean people the world over aren't so different from one another? Do you feel a poem coming on? I'm told the Lakes will bring out the poet in anybody."

The Lake District lay farther west. Perhaps Con and Julianna would honeymoon there.

"I mean dukes aren't so different from the farmers in the dales. How fares Lucere?"

"Can't say, which suggests he hasn't shot anybody—or been shot. Which one is Cousin Jules?"

Con had spotted Julianna before he'd ordered his ale. She'd worn a straw hat without so much as a ribbon to dress it up, and that very plainness made her easy to track.

"She's with the gent in green."

"Blond fellow going a bit portly amidships? Squire Lumpkin? Why isn't *she* with you? If I had a *Cousin Jules* who looked like that, she'd have my devoted escort."

She did have Con's devoted escort. "Squire Lumpkin is Maurice Warren, who has both farming and mining interests in the area. Wealthy gentry."

"Mines," Starlingham said, taking a sip of his ale and wiping his mouth on his sleeve with the practiced indelicacy of any yeoman. "Don't care for them. My papa refused to own them. He said he couldn't trust the factors not to employ children. Nasty business when children are hacking themselves to death on coal dust before they're properly grown. The gent in green is sticking quite close to your cousin."

And Julianna was tolerating Warren's presumption. Letting him lean close and attend every word of her conversations with the merchants, though Warren didn't even carry the lady's basket.

"If I asked you for all the coin you have with you, would you lend it to me, Starlingham?"

"Don't be daft. I'd give it to you if you promise not to thrash me for implying you need the charity. Pity I haven't much coin, though. My valet or coachman usually carries the purse. This is the best ale I can recall having."

Well, damn. "Fresh air and the good Yorkshire sunshine give a man an appreciation for the simpler joys. How dare that presuming buffoon?"

Warren had just doubled the amount of honey Julianna had placed in her basket. Reached right past her and dropped a second sizable jar next to the first, then stood by while Julianna parted with coin she could not spare.

"Are we still leaving next week?" Starlingham asked, a bit too casually.

"You'd rather tarry here?" Con certainly would. For the rest of his life.

"Uncle Leo would grow suspicious," Starlingham said. "Can't have him playing skittles with your pin money."

"Spoken like a true friend who occasionally owes me blunt." Con bumped his tankard against Starlingham's. "Until we do leave, I'll pass the time folding linens and stitching hems. If you see the Sun come out, pass along my best regards."

Starlingham gave a minute bow, and Con set his half-full tankard on the nearest table for some enterprising child to enjoy… or sheep, or stray duke in disguise without much coin.

Ralph came sauntering across the road, hands in his pockets, a gleam in his eye. He sidled right past Con, as if the abandoned ale were his goal, but spoke loudly enough for Con to hear.

"You were correct, sir. Mr. Warren's a right bastard, and I'm not sorry I've used bad language."

"Save it for when we get home," Con said, shading his eyes to admire the very modest church steeple. "Tell Harold and Lucas to do likewise. Good work."

Good work, but bad news. Con made his way to the vendor selling lemons, limes, and oranges, bought the best two on offer, and tucked them into his pockets. He tugged his hat brim down and found a handy patch of shade near the smithy, from which he could watch Mr. Warren work his wiles on an unsuspecting widow.

Con relished the opportunity to study an adversary he would not underestimate. A promissory note signed by a man who'd departed this earth five years ago was easy to forge, though proving the forgery would be nearly impossible.

The Duke of Mowne could have swarmed Warren with solicitors, inquiries, and intimidation. With a little time, His Grace could sell a farm in the East Riding to rescue a farm in Lesser Puddlebury.

Connor Amadour could not call upon the resources of the Duke of Mowne, and based on the increasing worry in Julianna's eyes, even if Con did reveal himself as the duke, he had no time—no time at all—to bring the duke's resources to bear on Julianna's situation.

* * *

"Please stop pacing," Antigone muttered. "You're attracting notice again."

Hector flopped down beside her with a loud sigh. Quint flipped out his tails and took a more decorous seat on her other side.

"This is one of the finest posting inns in York," Quint said, withdrawing a deck of playing cards from a pocket, "but a lady of your quality loitering about in the common can't help but earn stares."

"With such handsome escorts, the stares aren't all directed at me." Antigone was accustomed to being overshadowed by her brothers, to being teased and flirted with by their friends. She was not accustomed to harebrained journeys half the length of the realm, but Quint and Hector had both leaped at the notion.

While Mama had packed for Kent, thank heavens.

"That fellow does not belong here," Hector said, sitting up straight.

Sir Walter Scott's novels had imbued all things Highland with dashing romanticism, and kilts were not unheard of even in London ballrooms. The closer to Scotland one traveled, though, the more in evidence clan dress became. Usually, the kilts were patterned in bright plaids, neatly folded, all tucked up with jeweled pins, silver brooches, and the like.

This fellow's kilt had seen better days, and the pleats had gone soft for want of pressing.

"Big lout," Quint said, shuffling the cards. "Wouldn't want to tangle with him when he's put away a wee dram too many." Quinton always traveled with cards, a chess set, and dice, all of which had helped to pass the hours in the inn's common.

The Scot in question was tall, muscular, and into the ageless years. He might be fifty, he might be seventy. Cold blue eyes said he would not be trifled with.

For the second day in a row, Antigone and her brothers had come down from their rooms early, intent on spending the day appearing to pass the time in the common. All manner of people had come in to pick up mail.

When the Scot stepped up to the bar, the publican took the towel from his own shoulder, refolded it twice, and passed across a single letter—presumably Antigone's reply to Con.

"That's him," she said, the refolded towel being the agreed-upon signal. "Of all the urchins, footmen, dandies, and dowagers, that... that representative of Clan MacMuscle is Con's emissary. Quickly, you two, or we'll never catch him. I own I am intrigued."

"I'm alarmed," Quint said, stuffing the cards back in his pocket.

"I'm having the time of my life," Hector retorted, springing to his feet. "Haven't had this much fun since Tiger threatened to turn her archery skills on Lucere's horse."

"She would have hit the poor creature too," Quint muttered, escorting Antigone to the common's side entrance. "Quite the markswoman, is our Tiger."

Antigone loved it when her brothers used the nickname Con had given her in infancy. Nonetheless, as they gained the street, and the Scotsman climbed into a farm cart that bore two trunks bearing the Mowne ducal crest, Antigone had to admit Quint and Hector were both right.

The adventure of rescuing Con had been a lark thus far, but this development—an enormous Scottish ruffian in possession of Con's personal luggage—was purely alarming.

* * *

"Maurice wants a fortune from me," Julianna said, skirts swishing. "He tried to dodge and deceive, as you said he would, but I pressed him for answers."

She paced the length of her porch while Connor sat on the swing—on a pillow on the swing—exuding a damnable calm.

"You asked him about both the principal sum borrowed and the rate of interest on the loan?"

Connor had been very insistent last night, very clear. Whether a mortgage or a promissory note or something else entirely, whatever John had signed— Connor had had doubts that John had signed anything—the document would state a sum borrowed and terms of repayment.

"Maurice didn't want to tell me even that much. Why bother my pretty head—he used those words, my *pretty head*—when settlement discussions would obviate the need to mention such unpleasant details?"

Marriage settlement discussions, of course. Maurice had taken the gloves off, to use language the boys would understand. Julianna was to marry him, and all monies owed him would be "worked out" in the settlement discussions pertaining to "disposition of the real estate."

Stealing the farm that Julianna was determined should go to the children.

"Come sit beside me, Julianna, and tell me what he said."

Such calm, reasonable words. "Not even you, Connor, not even with such a harmless suggestion as that, should tell me what to do right now. I am in a taking. I have never been in a taking before." A taking meant Julianna wanted to throw herself into Connor's lap and weep on his shoulder, also apply her broom repeatedly to Maurice Warren's backside.

Connor stood, plucked a white rose, and passed it to her. "You should be in a taking. Shall I tell you the rest of it?"

The rose had thorns. Julianna held it carefully. "Yes. The whole of it, and then I can find apprenticeships for the boys, write MacTavish a character, give him Horty, and—"

And what? Send Roberta back to the poorhouse? Maurice had hinted that he might find an apprenticeship for Roberta, because she was such a *biddable child*.

"You will visit Maurice Warren in jail," Connor said, taking Julianna's rose from her grasp and gently batting her on the nose with it. "I asked the boys to watch you at market today, and they did."

"I saw them." All on their own, enjoying their freedom. Julianna would soon need to let down trouser hems for Lucas and Ralph too. "That rose should be in water."

Connor tucked the rose into a half-full vase Julianna had brought out. He leaned a hip against the porch railing, silhouetting himself against the rioting roses and the afternoon sun.

"Warren has apparently directed the merchants to bilk you at every turn. They are all, every one of them who can, charging you double what they charge anybody else. Warren stands beside you to enforce this behavior. Two of the merchants pulled the boys aside and told them you ought to buy your goods in York if you want better prices."

"York is half a day's journey coming and going, assuming the roads are passable."

"And Warren knows you can't leave the children that long. Did he mention that the sum you owe him is subject to late penalties, delinquent fees, anything like that?"

Everything like that, and Maurice had been so sad, so reluctant to tell Julianna the true state of her indebtedness.

"He named a total." Julianna collapsed onto the swing, muttering the amount loudly enough for Connor to hear. "I'm ashamed. I hate being ashamed. Why haven't I forced an accounting from him sooner? Now, he won't even give me until harvest to make a payment and says he owes it to John's memory to attend to matters where I'm concerned."

Attend to *matters*. Holy matrimony should mean years of shared dreams, work, laughter, loving… And Maurice Warren might as well be buying another mule at auction.

"I think the matter he wants to attend to is a fortune in coal," Connor said. "MacTavish told me a surveyor came down from Northumberland earlier in the summer, and there's talk in the village that Warren's mines are playing out. That could be why Maurice is forcing your hand. He is desperate to impress investors, and yet, he has no capital of his own. Your property is the asset he needs to lure them into turning over their coin."

The children were across the lane, playing in the apple orchard. Even Roberta was up a tree, impersonating a pirate or a highwayman. Why did children never play at being farmers, shepherds, blacksmiths, or publicans?

"He wants to turn one of the best farms in the shire into a coal pit," Julianna said. "A fitting metaphor for what my life will become. I can resign myself to such a fate, but for the children…"

For the children… Maurice would make her beg, plead, bargain, and agree to anything, and she'd do it, to keep the children playing in their trees, grumbling about their chores, squabbling over the last bite of cobbler.

Connor prowled away from the railing and drew Julianna to her feet. "I cannot resign myself to such a fate—not for you, *and not for us*. Where is your fight, Julianna St. Bellan? Do you know the family motto?"

"*Faciemus proelio*," Julianna quoted. "We make war, or battle, or something grand. All very well for dukes and coal nabobs, but I make bread. I make beds, and I make children do their sums."

His arms came around her. "Only a duke can recognize a duchess in disguise. You make a home out of hard work and love. You make children feel safe. You make a farm successful despite a knave trying to bring you down. You make me so proud of you, if I had a sword, I'd cheerfully run Maurice Warren through for you."

"You don't have a sword," Julianna said, heart breaking. "You have kindness and honor. You have patience with the children and with me. You have a fortune you cannot command as you ought. You have a scar on your backside, and you have such kisses…"

Connor gave her some of those kisses. Sweet, soft, fierce kisses that tempted Julianna to take him upstairs that instant.

"If I marry you, I gain control of my fortune shortly thereafter," Connor said, his hand going to Julianna's nape. He knew exactly how to touch her, how to squeeze and caress and muddle her…

"You cannot marry me," she said, burrowing closer. "You are a duke. I am the widow of a distant relation and even poorer than I thought I was."

"I can marry you, but not in time to keep Maurice from snatching away your farm, and this farm matters, this legacy that John St. Bellan wanted for you and the children. A ducal marriage is a complicated, drawn-out business, done properly. If we marry simply to foil Maurice, you'll be doubting forever after that I chose you for love and no other reason. Then too, Leo might prove difficult, and I'm not in the mood to humor anybody's crotchets where you're concerned."

Julianna's insides had gone from unsettled to fluttery, and her anger was slipping away on a rose-scented tide of wishes and hopes.

"What are you saying, Connor?"

"I'm saying, please marry me, Julianna. Me, your Connor, who isn't very quick with a needle, but he tries hard to keep his stitches straight. He'll put his shoulder to the plough if need be. He'll read to the children at night so you can have an extra hour of sleep. I have no confidence I'll ever be able to direct my own fortune—Leo is stubborn and contrary and tiresome. I should have told him to stop interfering years ago, regardless of my papa's damned will. I should have taken my family's excesses and my mother's meddling in hand. I was too busy being a dupe instead of a duke."

How fierce he was. Julianna spared some pity for this Uncle Leo fellow if he thought to turn up tiresome now.

"I wish my late husband had explained this loan to me," she said, pushing Connor's hair off his brow. He was proposing to her, offering her marriage, and yet, he would always be the duke too. "I know nothing of being a duchess."

"I knew nothing of being *myself*," Connor said, leading her back to the swing. "I waved a gloved hand, and a coach-and-four appeared before my mansion. I don't need that to be happy. I'd rather hitch up your mule and put her away for you when you come home. I'd rather read to four rapt children in this farmhouse than make speeches nobody listens to in the House of Lords. I'd rather love you than be a duke to the rest of the world. This farm, you, the children… that's duchy enough for me, and if Leo doesn't like it, he can spend my fortune himself. Please marry me."

Everything in Julianna wanted to say yes, of course, yes. She was a mother four times over, though. MacTavish, even Horty, depended on her to be wiser now than she had been in the past.

She took a seat, and Con came down beside her. "What about Maurice, Connor? You're willing to spend the rest of your days as the duke farming in the dales, but we might not even have a farm. Your uncle could disdain to recognize your marriage to a nobody, and then the children would have nothing. Once the mining starts here—and it could start literally overnight—the farm is gone forever."

Con took her hand and kissed her fingers.

"I asked a few questions in the village today. Maurice fancies himself quite the gentleman, even to the point of assembling a weekly card game for the gentry in the area. They lounge about the posting inn's best parlor and think they're playing for lordly sums while they over-imbibe and run the serving maids ragged. I'll win your farm back before Maurice can start crying banns on Sunday. See if I don't."

"Our future comes down to a wager? What have you to wager with?"

"A duke might not know how to stack hay, wield a scythe, or brew ale, but he can handle a deck of cards the way you knead bread, my love. He can loll about, swilling spirits, wagering, and looking useless by the hour. He can pay far better attention than most people know. I'll be a duke in disguise, and Maurice Warren will be much lighter in the pocket for my efforts."

Five years of widowhood took a toll on a woman's ability to trust anything to chance. "We could elope to Scotland."

"Which would take a good ten days of planning and travel, at least. While our backs are turned, Maurice Warren could buy himself a judgment of foreclosure from a friendly judge and dig up half your pastures."

In the middle of a summer afternoon, Julianna shivered. "I hate Maurice Warren."

Con's arm came around her shoulders. "He deserves your hatred, but I also have to wonder who else's, Julianna. If he has every merchant on the green cowed, if he's talked your neighbors into ignoring you, if he can threaten everybody in the shire… somebody needs to put him in his place. Not only for you and the children, but for all the widows and all the children. For the farms he'll go after next, the children he'll send down his mines. This shire needs a duke or two, and I know one who happens to have time on his hands."

This was not the Connor Amadour whom Julianna had found asleep on her swing last week. This was a different fellow, a different sort of duke, a different man.

The children were right across the lane, making a racket in the trees. At any moment, MacTavish could rattle up the drive in the Yoders' cart, or worse, Maurice might presume to pay a call.

Life was short. Life was sometimes tragically short, and five years of working hard and hoping had got Julianna a tired back and a powerful, unscrupulous enemy. She shifted so she was sitting in Con's lap and put her head on his shoulder as his arms came around her.

"Best Maurice Warren, Connor. Trounce him, shame him, humiliate him. Take back from him what he's stolen and make sure the entire shire knows you've done it. Put him in his place, because I have every confidence, if Maurice had to groom a mule, cook up a pot of porridge, or make a tired fairy tale exciting for good, innocent children, he'd fail miserably. See Maurice put in his place, and I'll marry you gladly."

She'd marry Connor on any terms at all, but he'd set a task for himself that went beyond her, the children, and even the farm. He'd had the title for years, but in a way Julianna didn't entirely grasp, Connor had only now decided *how* to be the Duke of Mowne.

"It shall be as my future duchess commands," he said, kissing her temple and setting the swing to rocking.

Julianna fell asleep in his embrace. She ought to have been plagued by nightmares and worries, but stealing a nap on the swing with Connor was the best, most refreshing rest she could recall in years.

* * *

Dukes might excel at playing cards, lolling about, and looking bored, but they did not excel at waiting. Con, at least, did not.

MacTavish did not come home from York on market day. He did not come home the following day either, and while Julianna made cheerful excuses in response to Mrs. Yoder's polite inquiries—the housekeeper's sister had asked her to tarry another day, perhaps—worry crowded the entire household close.

Duke or not, no stranger could join a card game without some demonstration of his ability to handle the stakes. In increasingly wrinkled finery, with a single watch chain and ring to his name, Connor would pass for gentry, or even a lord's younger son, but little more.

"MacTavish will return," Julianna said when they'd tucked the children in. "This time tomorrow, you'll have full pockets and look every inch the duke. You'll be sitting about the inn's best parlor, winning great sums, swilling excellent brandy, and looking bored."

"How can you be so calm? I've half a notion to ride Horty into York tomorrow and search through every hostelry and livery. Horse thievery is a hanging offense."

Julianna took Con by the hand. "You aren't concerned that Mac might have stolen your clothes? Your jewels? Your trunks?"

Even the feel of her hand in Con's had a rightness about it. "Of course not. But for tomorrow's card game, I wouldn't miss them. They'd be little enough recompense to MacTavish for standing by you when everybody else has fallen under Warren's sway. I'm more concerned that your only ally has lost his nerve."

Or worse, attracted the notice of thieves. Here in the country, crime was seldom an issue. In a bustling place like York... Con knew city life, knew its temptations and pitfalls. MacTavish was one man, laden with relative treasure, and no longer young.

Julianna led Con into his bedroom, then closed and locked the door.

"Rains might come tomorrow," she said, "and ruin what promises to be a good harvest of wheat. The blight can show up on the potatoes. Harold could come down with a lung fever. Roberta might step on a nail, for she does love to go barefoot in the grass. Horty could turn up lame. The roof might leak, the chickens all die."

"Hush," Con said, putting a finger to her lips. Eggs were a major staple at breakfast and a significant part of other meals as well. "You are frightening me, and I'd flattered myself that I possessed some modicum of courage. I have four siblings who test that courage regularly."

Siblings whom he... missed. Quint had surprising reserves of discretion. Hector brought good humor with him nearly everywhere. Tiger had a practical streak not often seen in a duke's daughter, and Freddy... Freddy had an enviable store of derring-do.

"Family tests our courage," Julianna said, kissing Con gently. "They die, blast them. Your papa left you too soon. John should be sitting out on the porch this instant, watching the moon rise over a lovely farm. The land tests my courage, the children test everything in me... MacTavish will come."

Nobody reassured a duke, and yet, Julianna's embrace was not only reassuring, but fortifying. Whether MacTavish came in time or not, Julianna's affection and loyalty would not waver. Her kisses said as much. Her hands, stealing little caresses as she helped Con disrobe, made the same promise.

Con provided reciprocal courtesies, unhooking this, untying that, until they were both under the covers, her head resting on his shoulder, her bare knee tucked across his thighs.

"Your wound has healed quickly," Julianna said.

Everything in Con had healed during this interlude in Lesser Puddlebury.

"I'm worried." He could say this to her, in the dark, under the covers. He could say it to her anywhere, and she'd not judge him for it.

"So am I. Let's distract each other, shall we?" She slid her hand slowly down, down, to grip Connor snugly by something much more interesting than his worries. Her touch was gentle but sure, and quite... inventive.

Inspiring, even. When Con would have retaliated, Julianna rose over him instead.

"Not tonight, Connor. Tonight you let me love you. You have exhausted yourself these past two days, doing MacTavish's work. Tonight, you enjoy your rest."

Con should protest. He should remonstrate, and review options, and think up contingencies. He should go downstairs and pen an imperious epistle to Uncle Leo and pawn the last set of fine clothes he possessed to hire a messenger to gallop to Scotland...

Though in which direction Scotland lay, Con could not have said just then.

Julianna's idea of distraction included using her mouth in ways Con, with all his London experience, would never have expected of a woman. Her attentions proceeded at a luxurious pace, as if she enjoyed driving Con to incoherent sighs.

"You excel at distraction."

"Mmmm." Followed by a swirl of her tongue, left then right, then right, right...

Con gathered her braid at her nape, though whether he was bent on encouraging her or dissuading her, even he could not have said.

"Julianna, please..."

She nuzzled him in the most lovely, indelicate location, then sat up. "I was never so daring as a younger woman, never so selfish or indulgent of my curiosity. I hope you're convinced of your own fortitude, sir."

Con hauled her over him as gently as madness allowed. "*Fiend*. Lovely, luscious, delectable, sweet—for the love of God, *Julianna*."

With no ado whatsoever, she'd swooped down on him, joining them in one glorious descent. She was ready—she was wonderfully, enthusiastically ready—and yet, a small corner of Con's awareness, the part not praying for restraint to match his supposed fortitude, was admiring more than Julianna's naked form.

To love like this in the face of possible ruin took courage. To know that tomorrow might bring more uncertainty and worse options, and yet love tonight with unfettered passion, that took... that took a degree of faith and strength that stole a man's breath.

Julianna was loving Connor with all the hope in her, all the faith she had in herself, laid before him like a feast of optimism, resilience, and loyalty. *We'll manage*, she said with every kiss and caress. *We're in this together.*

And she was right.

This was what it felt like to be loved, for himself, unconditionally, come what may.

Con returned her passion, cherishing her every curve and callus, her every sigh and whimper. He couldn't sustain nearly as much restraint as he wanted to, but that was part of loving, too—the surrendering, to passion, to hope, and to pleasure. They soon lay in a tangled, panting heap of warmth and wonder, the only sounds their breathing and the rustle of the covers.

"I love you," Con said, mustering the energy for one last, lovely kiss to the lady's lips. "I love you."

"Then I am already your duchess, and you are my duke, for I love you too. Come what may. Blow out the candle, Your Grace, and dream with me."

CHAPTER SIX

Never, ever would Julianna regret the nights she'd spent in Connor's arms. His reserves of tenderness and passion—and his displays of imagination—would keep her memories warm into great old age, even through Yorkshire winters, destitution, and the possible heartbreak of failing the children who in the past week had taken to calling her Mama.

"Where's MacTavish?" Roberta asked over the last of her cobbler.

"Probably on his way home right this instant," Julianna replied. "We gave him much to do in York, and Mrs. Periwinkle might have been reluctant to leave her sister. Would you care for another serving of dessert, Bertie? You didn't take very much to begin with."

To give away MacTavish's portion of the cobbler had been a slip. The boys exchanged looks that said they well knew Julianna was anxious.

"Let's save the last of the cobbler," Connor said. "MacTavish will be hungry after days away from home cooking. Children, if you'd help with the dishes, your mother can assist me to don my finery."

Con had called them all together on the porch after luncheon and explained exactly what was afoot. He'd used simple language, nothing alarming, and yet, the children seemed to grasp the gravity of the situation.

Without a word of protest, the boys rose and took their dishes to the slop bucket.

Roberta turned huge blue eyes on Connor. "Mr. Warren pinched me once. On my arm. I didn't do anything wrong either. I don't like him, and he's not nice."

"Where did he pinch you?" Connor asked.

Roberta pointed to the muscle near her shoulder, which Con kissed.

"I will make him pay dearly for treating one of my ladies ill, Roberta. He should not have done that. If anybody else *ever* behaves similarly, you tell your mama, your brothers, or me."

Roberta studied Connor with a seriousness that tore at Julianna's heart, while the boys silently cleared the table.

"Will you be my papa?"

Oh God. Oh God. Oh God.

Con's smile was sweet and grave. "If your mama will have me, and I hope she will, I would be honored to be a parent to all of you."

The children were safe, in other words. Whatever else happened to the farm, the children would be safe. Connor would find the coin, the determination, the way forward, regardless of his family's foolishness, or the already strained ducal exchequer.

"I'll shine your boots," Harold said, "as soon as the dishes are clean."

"I can brush your hat and jacket," Ralph added.

"I'll start pressing your shirt," Lucas chimed in. "And don't worry, I won't scorch it. Roberta will make sure I'm careful."

While Julianna would help Connor as she tried not to panic. For the sun was setting, and even a duke could not win back a farm without the means to first invite himself into the requisite game of chance.

* * *

The ducal finery felt the same—pressed, starched, exquisitely fitted—and yet, it felt different to Con too. A costume, chosen for his purposes, not simply the outfit handed to him by his fussing, fawning valet. Another exquisitely embroidered waistcoat, another perfectly starched cravat.

They were his battle dress, now.

"Will I do?" Con asked, turning slowly, arms outstretched before the children. Julianna had pronounced him ready for the evening before they'd come downstairs. She'd refused to kiss him, saying she must not wrinkle his cravat, but Con sensed the worry in her.

Four equally fretful little faces surveyed him from the sofa.

"You're very fancy," Ralph said. "Mr. Warren won't like that you're fancier than he is."

"Good." Harold passed Connor a spotless top hat. "The more Mr. Warren doesn't like it, the happier I am. He pinched Roberta, he wants to steal from Mama. He deserves to land in Horty's manure pit."

"He *has* been stealing from Mama," Lucas said. "Mr. Greenower and Mr. Plumley said as much."

"Where's MacTavish?" Roberta whispered.

Con was out of excuses for MacTavish, and Julianna had given up an hour ago. The summer sun was sinking inexorably toward the green horizon, and Con's hopes were sinking with it.

Julianna met his gaze over the children's heads, the look in her eyes resolute. "MacTavish will come. He's never let us down, never shirked, and he'll not—"

Roberta bolted to the window. "I hear wheels! He's home!"

The children thundered onto the porch, waving and yelling uproariously as a bay mare trotted up the lane, MacTavish at the reins, a plump, graying woman beside him. The trunks were gone, a good sign, and MacTavish wasn't scowling any more than usual. He pulled the gig up before the house and swung the housekeeper down.

"What's all this racket? You'll spook the poor mare, and she's had a long, tiring week."

MacTavish apparently had too, but he was back, and Julianna and the children were swarming about him, all smiles and hugs. Con came down the porch steps, waiting, because MacTavish obviously had something to report.

When the children had dragged Mrs. Periwinkle into the house with Julianna in tow, Con offered MacTavish a hand.

"Welcome home. You had me worried."

MacTavish watched the others depart, his expression hard to read. "I am sorry for going a bit off schedule. I got engaged."

Ah, hence the slight daze in MacTavish's blue eyes. "Congratulations. So did I."

"Maud said we should give you lovebirds some privacy. I told her she was daft. Never knew how much sense a daft woman could make when she's determined to celebrate her engagement. Then there were the pickpockets."

Not pickpockets, please God, not pickpockets now. Much less pickpockets, *plural.*

"How much did they get?"

"You lot, with your fancy airs… They get every groat from you every time, because you expect some grimy boy to be fumbling at your watch chain. That's not how they operate."

"MacTavish, my fist will operate on your newly engaged face if you don't get on with the telling. My family—and our mule—are depending on me to save the farm on the turn of a card tonight. For that, I need money, not a parable."

MacTavish's grin was a work of benevolence. "*And the mule?* That's the last time I argue with Maud Periwinkle MacTavish. The pickpockets got nothing, for all their trying. A good pickpocket dresses like quality and works with two accomplices. The finest of the three lifts the goods from your pocket so lightly you never feel but a bump and jostle. Quick as a wink, he hands off the goods to the second, often a lady, the prettier the better. The third fellow, looking a bit down on his luck, takes off at a conspicuous run, but has no contraband on him, while the lady slips quietly away."

Well, yes, that was how it was done. "You were followed by pickpockets for days?"

"Most tenacious and best-dressed criminals I've ever seen. I had to take some of your goods to every pawnbroker in York to get the best price. If I'd left them all with one, he wouldn't have been as inclined to bargain."

MacTavish passed over a reassuringly heavy bag of coins. "You're set, lad. I'll mind the farm, you catch a rascal. The whole shire will be in your debt, and you'll never want for cobbler again."

Julianna had come out on the porch and stood at the top of the steps, her shawl clutched about her. Con took one instant to imprint the image of her there among her vining roses, then blew her a kiss.

"I'm off to battle. Wish me luck."

"*Faciemus proelio*," Julianna said, blowing him a kiss in return. "Failing that, knock Maurice Warren into the dirtiest manure pit you can find and blacken both of his eyes. Roberta asked me to tell you that. She said manure stains never come out."

"Remind me not to cross our daughter," Con said, bowing. "MacTavish, if you could drop me outside the village before returning the mare, I'd appreciate it."

"I can do better than that," MacTavish said, passing over a silver flask. "I can tell you who plays in this card game and how they play, how much they already owe Warren, and how many daughters they have to dower."

"All the better," Con said, climbing into the cart and taking a seat on the hard bench. They were all the way to the edge of the village before he realized something else that had changed for the better.

His wound no longer pained him. Didn't even itch, in fact, not in the slightest.

* * *

Getting into the game had been the work of a moment, for apparently, every baronet's son and squire was tired of losing to Maurice Warren. Con had introduced himself as Connor Amadour, then smiled, bowed, dropped a few innuendos about needing to avoid some London matchmakers, and easily gained himself a seat at the table.

Warren sported a prosperous figure, thinning blond hair, and three gold watch chains stretching across his paunch. His manner was gracious if a bit obsequious. A sennight ago, Con would not have noticed the fawning. Warren also won steadily, which any damned fool would have noticed.

Winning streaks happened—very, very rarely. Long winning streaks tended to happen before the odds, or the machinations of a particular card sharp, were about to knock a foolish man on his arse. One by one, the others at the table dropped out, while Con's resources dwindled.

He saw Julianna losing one pasture after another. Her orchard, her crops, her home farm, her home wood…

Panic tried to take root, but Con batted it aside. Dukes did not panic, and neither did competent farmers.

"Let's order another bottle, shall we?" Warren suggested. "Celebration of my windfall, consolation for your losses. A fancy London gent like you can stand to lose a bit, eh? The evening is young, after all. You might win back a bit of your own before we call it a night."

That sop to Con's dignity, thrown across a table from which all others had departed, brought with it an alarming realization.

Warren was cheating. Sitting directly across from him, Con could observe him from only one vantage point. Had Lucere or Starlingham been on hand to take the flanking chairs, Warren's perfidy might have been checked. Con was without his allies and was not himself adept at cheating, nor did he wish to be.

"If I wanted to invest some real money," Con said as Warren signaled for yet more brandy, "are there opportunities in this area?"

Warren passed the deck over for Con to cut, but instead of cutting, Con picked up the cards and shuffled them. The markings were subtle, barely discernible unless a player was paying attention.

"Real money?" Warren echoed.

"Investment sums," Con said. "The cent-per-cents are all very well for a sister's dowry or a widow's portion, but to hold a man's attention, something more adventurous is required, don't you think?"

"A canal would be—"

Con waved a hand, his signet ring winking in the candlelight. "Canals were fine for our fathers' day, but steam will soon make the rails a viable alternative. My brother is something of an inventor, and he assures me this is so."

The markings weren't falling into a pattern Con could detect with casual handling, and Warren's gaze had gone calculating.

"Mining in this region is quite lucrative," he said. "One needs a sound grasp of the local terrain, such as a lifelong resident of the area has, and familiarity with the mining industry, which accomplishment I can also boast, Mr. Amadour. My own modest wealth owes much to a certain perspicacity where mining ventures are concerned."

Oh, right. Which was why every fellow who'd left the table had likely lost a good portion of his savings to Warren and now could not risk offending him over even a hand of cards or a jar of honey in the market.

Inspiration came to Con as the serving maid set a fresh bottle on the table along with clean glasses. The deck was marked with minute pinpricks and nicks along the edges of the cards. Con set to subtly adding to the wear and irregularity of the surfaces while Warren blathered on about the potential riches a man of vision might find if he were patient and daring, shrewd and well connected, brilliant but willing to trust those who'd trod the path to riches before him.

Warren ought to be making speeches in the Lords, so impressed was he with his own elocution.

Con kept him going with questions and with brandy, and all the while, Con worked the deck.

And yet, when play resumed, an hour went by with Con barely winning back the sum he'd brought with him.

"Are you tiring, Mr. Amadour? I confess wagering against somebody other than my neighbors is a refreshing change. Suppose we raise the stakes to something a man of your consequence might find interesting?"

In other words, enough of the markings on the cards remained that Warren was confident he could still read them.

Con felt a sense of floodwaters rising, crops withering, and fate closing a fist around Julianna's hopes and dreams.

He hadn't lost ground tonight, and he'd learned a great deal about his opponent. Retreat might be the wisest course, a chance to regroup...? Lucere and Starlingham could travel on without him, perhaps?

And have Leo sending pigeons in all directions.

"What do you have in mind?" Con asked.

"Congratulations are in order, Mr. Amadour. I'm about to announce my engagement to a certain young lady, and as it happens, the dowry she'll bring to the union is the jewel in the crown of a potential mining empire. Mineral rights are the true wealth of Yorkshire, sir, and by combining my marital good fortune with a certain—"

Con casually worked his thumbnail under the label on the brandy bottle, when he wanted to bash his opponent over the head instead. Warren hadn't even bothered to propose to Julianna. He'd simply made threats and taken advantage of her grief and lack of business acumen.

And now here was Julianna's great ducal champion, without means, without allies, without a plan—

Con had Julianna's love, though, and that was all he'd ever need. "You're seeking investors," Con said. "I need a place to invest my coin. Most interesting."

"I thought you'd agree. Let's call for a fresh deck, shall we? Our play is about to get interesting."

Their play would turn disastrous if Con allowed a "fresh" deck of Warren's choosing to be brought to the table. Calling Warren out abruptly loomed as a wonderful solution. The bastard was a cheating, lying disgrace who took advantage of widows, children, neighbors, and merchants.

Lucere and Starlingham might not approve, but they'd serve as Con's seconds. Freddy would approve, as would Hector, Tiger, Quint, and even Mama.

"Warren, I don't think a fresh deck will serve, not in the sense you mean."

Something in Con's voice, in the sheer menace of his tone, must have communicated itself to his opponent. Warren left off shuffling—or reacquainting himself with the tools of the immediate swindle.

"Perhaps we should just get on with the wagering, Mr. Amadour? I do admire a man of dispatch."

"Dispatch, excellent choice of words." For Con would love to dispatch this scoundrel.

"Or we can resume our discussions at another time," Warren said, downing his brandy all at once. "If you've been traveling, you might want to seek your bed and consider the day's developments. I could meet with you, say, Tuesday next, if you're tarrying in the area?"

By Tuesday next, Con needed to be on his way to Scotland—or announcing his engagement. "That won't serve either."

Impatience flickered across Warren's brow.

Con was reaching for his gloves, about to call a man out for the first time, when the door opened.

"Ah, exactly what a fellow hopes to find at the end of a long day's journey." Hector strutted in, followed by Quinton. "Good company, some fine spirits, and a bit of diversion over a deck of cards. Gentlemen, Lord Hector St. Bellan at your service."

Hector?

And Quinton?

Warren was on his feet faster than Harold settled to his cobbler. "Lord Hector, good evening. Mr. Maurice Warren at your service, and this is Mr. Connor Amadour. Who would your companion be?"

Quint bowed. "Quinton St. Bellan. We had distant family in the area once upon a time and, on a lark, thought we'd pass through on our way to the grouse moors. Very pretty country, but... sheep and dales and dales and sheep, you know, followed by more dales and sheep. A hand of cards can look quite attractive by comparison. May we join you gentlemen?"

"You had family in the area?" Warren inquired carefully.

"A generation or two back," Quint said, taking the seat to Warren's right. "Farmers, from the distaff side of the family. Every ducal family has a distaff side or three. What are we playing?"

They were playing... some game, but Connor had never been happier to see his siblings. Bless Tiger, bless his brothers, bless all family who came to one another's aid unasked.

"Whist," Con said, "and I'm happy to partner you, Lord Quinton or Lord Hector. I've had the advantage of several hours' play with Mr. Warren, so it seems only sporting that each pair include one of you, rather than allow familiars to side against you. I don't suppose either of you travels with a deck of cards? Mr. Warren and I were about to call for a fresh set."

For Quinton always traveled with his own cards, both to pass the time, and to prevent… mischief.

"My brother gifted me with a deck from France," Quinton said. "Freddy's the artistic sort, but it's not a deck one can display before the ladies. While Lord Hector and I wash the dust of the road from our throats, I'll have my man fetch it down to us."

And just like that, the tables turned. Left to skill rather than cheating, Maurice Warren was soon losing badly. Hector didn't help, for which Con was grateful. The cards were honest, and Con and Quint made an excellent team.

They did not cheat, they cooperated.

And they won… and won, and won… until Hector frowned at the scribblings made on a sheet of foolscap.

"I don't mind telling you, Warren, we've about exhausted my immediate cash stores. Doesn't do to keep much of the ready on one's person when traveling the provinces. What say we get serious?"

Quinton sat back. "Your credit is good with me, Mr. Warren. One hears ceaselessly about the trustworthiness of the English gentry. Backbone of the nation, lifeblood of our economy, and all that. A note of hand is common between gentlemen of means where we come from."

Con remained silent. His brothers had done a brilliant job of being themselves—young lords at loose ends, not as idle as they appeared, but hardly astute businessmen.

They were the best of brothers, though.

"As it happens," Con said, "Mr. Warren and I were discussing an interesting situation before you gentlemen joined us. He has investment opportunities, and lo and behold, I have substantially more cash before me than when I started the evening."

"Give Mr. Warren a chance to win it back," Hector said. "Only sporting thing to do. Besides, these chairs are hard on a man's backside, and the serving maids are glowering at us. I don't fancy a glowering serving maid."

More to the point, Julianna would be worrying.

"Win it back?" Quint scoffed. "Are we schoolboys playing for farthing points? My brother is a duke. I'd love to be able to tell him I won an interest in a mining venture at some rural outpost. What is the name of this town?"

This town was Connor's new home.

"Lesser Puddlebury," Warren said, eyes darting from Quinton to Hector to the calculations on Hector's paper. Warren picked up the paper and studied the column of figures thereon.

"I own a mortgage," he said slowly. "Badly overdue, ripe for collection, tenants barely scraping by. We'd be doing them a kindness to turn them out, in fact. And regardless of which of us foreclosed on this property, it would be a useful addition to my own mineral rights. Mr. Amadour and I were discussing such a venture earlier in the evening."

In other words, Warren would allow even strangers to turn Julianna and the children out in hopes of keeping his mining prospects alive.

A manure pit was too good for such a man.

"I'll wager you," Con said. "My winnings for your mortgage. If the farm is failing as you say, then you're the one being done a kindness, Warren. Nothing says there's coal to be had, and legal proceedings can take forever if the judges are feeling contrary. I daresay their lordships might charm the law into signing a judgment of foreclosure more effectively than either you or I could."

"Mining?" Hector mused, taking the sheet of figures from Warren. "I know many a younger son who's done well with mining investments. Lord Quinton, shall we?"

"Another hand, but then I must seek my bed. This brandy is not quite up to standards, and we'll want to be on our way early. I've seen enough sheep and dales to last me into my dotage."

But they hadn't seen Con's beloved, met the children, or admired the endless beauty of Julianna's farm. Con looked forward to sharing all of that wealth with his brothers, and with Tiger, assuming she lurked above stairs in the inn's best rooms.

The end of the evening was a work of ducal dispatch.

All Con needed to win the mortgage on Julianna's farm was a steady focus on the cards. Con was lying about his identity, of course. He had played both with and against his brothers, but he was also telling the truth.

He was new to the area, had no expertise with mining, and did routinely make business investments on a much larger scale than Warren envisioned. Time to point that out to Uncle Leo, among other things.

And had Warren *paid attention*, he might have noticed the evidence of Con's identity glinting on Con's smallest finger all evening.

Con sat back as Hector gathered up the cards and tidied them into a stack. "An evening well spent, Mr. Warren, I thank you. You're out one mortgage, but probably not much of a loss from where you're sitting."

"Perhaps not," Warren said, helping himself to the last of the brandy. "I still have many fine ventures in train."

Quint and Hector muttered good nights, though Hector paused at the door to wink at Con over Warren's head. Con ignored him, lest he offer applause on an excellent and well-timed performance of fraternal loyalty.

Exquisitely timed, in fact.

"And in addition to all of your fine business opportunities," Con said, "you're in anticipation of holy matrimony. A man can't contemplate a more worthy and rewarding venture than that."

Warren grimaced. "She's pretty, I'll give her that, or she used to be. Going a bit... mature around the edges, though. Might have to look elsewhere, in fact."

That grimace, even more than Warren's lying, cheating, and stealing, offended Con on Julianna's behalf. She'd worked damned hard for years, far harder than she ought, because Warren had been stealing from her.

"If you're discussing Julianna St. Bellan," Con said, gathering up his funds and Warren's note of hand, "which would be extremely ill-bred of you, then please be informed that the lady would under no circumstances accept a proposal of marriage from you, for she has already accepted my suit."

He rose, needing to put distance between him and Warren before he did violence to the man.

"Your suit?" Warren peered up at Con. "Who the devil are you to be proposing to Yorkshire farm widows?"

"I'm the man who just prevented you from making good on a despicable swindle," Con said. "Mrs. St. Bellan will anticipate receipt of any and all documents purporting to be notes, mortgages, or encumbrances on her property not later than noon tomorrow. Those documents had best withstand the closest scrutiny by the best solicitors at the command of her ducal relations, some of whom joined you at cards in this very room.

"I noticed," Con went on, "you did not call her situation to their attention when you had the chance, though the lady is much in need of her family's support. You are a disgrace, Warren, and if I were you, I'd take a repairing lease on the Continent before the mine's creditors get word you're rolled up."

Which they would as soon as Con could put pen and ducal seal to paper.

The bottle hit the table with a thunk as Warren pushed to his feet.

"You can't know my financial situation, Mr. Amadour. I'm not rolled up. I have... prospects, and my associates understand that business means risk, not like farm crops that come in year after another. Business partners will see a fellow over a bad patch, extend him a bit of credit. Nobody turns his back on Maurice Warren without regretting it."

Righteous certainty backed Warren's statement, as if seven hundred years of breeding and reputation stood behind him, or seven hundred years of arrogance, rather than fortunate birth, greed, and lack of honor.

Con picked up his hat and gloves. "I am relieved to say, Mr. Warren, and I will happily report to my fiancée, that I pity you. Miss Roberta wanted me to knock you into the manure pit, and well you deserve it. I've learned something, though."

"Begone, sir, and have the wench bring me a fresh bottle on your way out."

"I do not take orders from felons, Warren, and Horty's manure pit is pure gold compared to your company. Manure makes the crops grow, while you are a pestilence who'd best make travel plans while he still can."

Con sauntered out, tired but jubilant, only to find Hector and Quint waiting for him in the common.

"I love you," Con said before either brother could set down his drink. "Thank you from the bottom of my heart, and I love you both. I love Tiger, and Freddy too. I love Horty, MacTavish, and the children, of course—very much. Please do not leave the area without paying a call on Julianna St. Bellan. I warn you, you will be stuffed with the best cobbler you've ever eaten."

He hugged his brothers, kissed each one on the cheek, then dashed into the cool night air and half ran the entire distance back to the farm.

* * *

"Damned thing is a forgery," Lord Hector said, passing Maurice Warren's so-called promissory note over to Lord Quinton. "That's the sloppiest description of a piece of agricultural property I've ever seen."

"Uncle Hector said damned," Roberta bellowed from that same fellow's lap.

"Sometimes," Julianna replied, "the word takes on its literary meaning." Such as when the signature on the note bore no resemblance to John St. Bellan's handwriting. "Would anybody like more lemonade?"

Connor's siblings had come out to the farm bearing gifts. Lady Antigone traveled with her own stores of fresh fruit, Lord Quinton had already performed a few card tricks for the children, and Lord Hector had brought a colorful picture book of exotic birds that the boys were paging through in a rapt huddle on the porch steps.

"Stay where you are, Julianna," Lady Antigone said, rising from the chair Connor had brought out for her. "I'll fetch the pitcher."

This gathering had started in Julianna's guest parlor, a space in which she'd set foot only to dust in recent years, then moved out to the porch. The children were looking as dazed and pleased with life as MacTavish and Maud did, albeit for different reasons.

"This is a da—right pretty patch of ground." Lord Quinton sat tailor fashion on the floor, his lemonade balanced on his knee. "A pretty part of the world."

"The winters can be a challenge," Julianna said. And how odd to think she might not spend the winter here.

"I'll keep you warm," Connor murmured, but not quietly enough to escape the notice of his siblings. He sat beside Julianna on the swing, the cushions having been given up to his brothers. With his family looking on, he'd taken a firm hold of Julianna's hand.

She wore Connor's signet ring in place of another token to be chosen when they had access to Edinburgh's jewelers, though Julianna would always treasure this simple ornament the most. For several hours last evening, in the privacy of the best guest room, that ring had been all she'd worn.

And a smile too, of course.

She was still smiling, and might never stop.

"I don't understand something," she said, over the general merriment. "How did you three discern Connor's location in Lesser Puddlebury?"

"Antigone got the idea of seeing who picked up her reply to Con's letter," Hector said, brushing a hand over Roberta's crown. "We hared about Yorkshire, following MacTavish as he visited every pawnshop in the city, until Hector simply asked a shop owner if he knew the direction of the big Scot who'd parted with some lovely clothing. The shop owner knew MacTavish from some darts tournament or other, and so out to the countryside, we came."

"We asked about at the Puddlebury inn," Quinton said. "Heard there was a regular game of cards in progress in the best parlor, and the players included a swell answering to Con's description, though the fellow hadn't even taken a room at the inn. The rest was the best lark I've had in ages."

"The best timing you've had in ages," Connor said. "I cannot thank you all enough for coming to my rescue. I was ready to call Warren out."

Lords Quinton and Hector found it necessary to study the roses, which were in particularly good form on this lovely summer morning. Lady Antigone studied her oldest brother.

"You've done nothing but look after us, Connor. We've been spoiling for a chance to return the gesture, but you never ask for anything. You manage Uncle Leo, mitigate Mama's excesses, keep Freddy from jail, dance with the wallflowers… we've been remiss, not looking after you too."

Con stroked his fingers over Julianna's knuckles. "I've been remiss then too, but having seen the error of my ways, I will impose on all of you regularly. I can promise you this, too. When Leo and I are done rearranging the ducal finances, you will have your own funds, and I want neither to hear nor speak of what you do with them, unless you invite my opinion."

"Even Freddy?" Antigone asked.

"Especially Freddy," Con said. "I strongly suspect half his adventures were an effort to keep me from growing too much like Uncle Leo."

The talk wandered on, the boys getting into an argument about the plumage of peafowl, into which debate Connor's siblings entered with high spirits.

"They are pleased for you," Julianna said, beneath Lord Quinton's fanciful insults to Lord Hector's judgment.

"They are relieved, as am I. I think this is what my father would have wanted me to see to first, the protection of my family's… heart, and yet, I let it slip from my view."

"John St. Bellan would thank you for seeing to the protection of his family's heart too," Julianna said, laying her head on Connor's shoulder. Foiling Maurice Warren's greed had settled some aspect of Julianna's grief at last—the guilt perhaps, the sense of having been let down by her late husband and wanting to resent him for it. John had never borrowed a penny against the farm, Julianna was now certain of that.

"We'll visit often," Connor said. "Your first love is buried here, the children adore their farm, and somebody will need to listen to MacTavish fret about the crops and the sheep and Horty's moods."

MacTavish would have the tenancy on generous terms until the children were of age to decide what to do with their legacy. Julianna had suggested this, and Connor had been delighted with the idea.

Connor seemed delighted generally, a veritable Duke of Delight.

"I'll be sorry to leave this place," Connor said as the argument shifted from peafowl to the best route up the hill for viewing the farmstead. "I'm not at all sorry I came. In fact, I don't think that was a bullet that creased my fundament after all. I think it was Cupid's arrow."

Antigone's head came up. "You were *shot* in the… the… *nether parts* with a *bullet*, Mowne?"

Con abruptly looked very much the duke. "Did I say that? I must have misspoken, for a duke would never tolerate such an indignity. Shot in the hindquarters? Never. I was felled by the arrow of true love and intend to remain in that blessed state for all the rest of my days and night."

As it happened, he did just that, and so did his duchess of the dales.

As for his friends Lucere and Starlingham… well, those stories took somewhat different turns…

THE END

To my dear Readers,

This entire anthology grew out of a conversation between me, Susanna Ives, and Emily Greenwood at a romance writer's conference, (and yes, the bar was still open). We came up with a premise, a few plot basics, and the name of the village, and next thing you know… well, you're holding the result in your hands. I hope you enjoyed Con and Julianna's story, because this whole project has been sheer fun for the authors.

My next Regency tale is **Duke of My Dreams**, a Regency novella set a summer house party. Some of you might recall Elias, Duke of Sedgemere from **Dancing in the Duke's Arms**. His story is bundled with **Another Dream**, a novella by Mary Balogh set in the Bedwyn world, and both stories will be released in April as **Once Upon a Dream**. Over the summer, I'll publish **Jack: The Jaded Gentlemen, Book IV**. (You know Jack as Sir John Dewey Fanning, but Madeline Hennesey knows him as a very accomplished kisser!)

You can keep up with all of my releases and author events by signing up for my newsletter at graceburrowes.com/contact.php. My newsletters are infrequent—I might do six a year—and I will never, ever, no never, part with your email address.

You can also stop by my website at graceburrowes.com and get all the latest news, read excerpts, and find the occasional giveaway on the blog.

Happy reading, and before we get to Lucere's story… I tucked in a little sneak peek from **Duke of My Dreams.**

Grace Burrowes

DUKE OF MY DREAMS

"You are my oldest and dearest friend, Sedgemere. I do not ask this boon of you lightly."

Elias, Duke of Sedgemere, strolled along, damned if he'd embarrass Hardcastle with any show of sentiment in the face of Hardcastle's wheedling. Hardcastle was, after all, Sedgemere's oldest and dearest friend too.

Also Sedgemere's only friend.

They took the air beside Hyde Park's Serpentine, ignoring the stares and whispers they attracted. While Sedgemere was a blond so pale as to draw the eye, Hardcastle was dark. They were both above average in height and brawn, though Mayfair boasted any number of large, well-dressed men, particularly as the fashionable hour approached.

They were dukes, however, and to be a duke was to be afflicted with public interest on every hand. To be an *unmarried* duke was to be cursed, for in every ballroom, at the reins of every cabriolet, connected to every parasol, was a duchess-in-waiting.

Thus Sedgemere endured Hardcastle's importuning.

"You do not ask a boon," Sedgemere said, tipping his hat to a fellow walking an enormous brindle mastiff. "You demand half my summer, when summer is the best time of year to bide at Sedgemere House."

They had known each other since the casual brutality and near starvation that passed for a boy's indoctrination at Eton, and through the wenching and wagering that masqueraded as an Oxford education. Hardcastle, however, had never married, and thus knew not what horrors awaited him on the way to the altar.

Sedgemere knew, and he further knew that Hardcastle's days as a bachelor were numbered, if Hardcastle's estimable grandmama was dispatching him to summer house parties.

"If you do not come with me to this houseparty, Sedgemere, I will become a bad influence on my godson. I will teach the boy about cigars, brandy, fast women, and profligate gambling."

"The child is seven years old, Hardcastle, but feel free to corrupt him at your leisure, assuming he does not prove to be the worse influence on—good God, not these two again."

The Cheshire twins, blond, blue-eyed, smiling, and as relentless as an unmentionable disease, came twittering down the path, twirling matching parasols.

"Miss Cheshire, Miss Sharon," Hardcastle said, tipping his hat. Though Sedgemere discreetly yanked on his friend's arm, nothing would do but Hardcastle must exchange pleasantries as if these women weren't the social equivalent of Scylla and Charybdis.

"Ladies." Sedgemere bowed as well, for he was in public and the murder of a best friend was better undertaken in private.

"Your Graces! How fortunate that we should meet!" Miss Cheshire gushed. The elder by four minutes, as Sedgemere had been informed on at least a hundred occasions, she generally led the conversational charges. "I told Sharon this very morning that you could not possibly have left Town without calling upon us, and I see I was right, for here you both are!"

Exactly where Sedgemere did not want to be.

Abruptly, three weeks trudging about the hills of the Lake District loomed not as a penance owed a dear friend, but as a reprieve, even if it meant uprooting the boys.

"My plans are not yet entirely made," Sedgemere said. "Though Hardcastle and I will both be leaving Town shortly."

Miss Sharon was desolated to hear this, though everybody left the pestilential heat of a London summer if they could. She cooed and twittered and clung from one end of the Serpentine to the other, until Sedgemere was tempted to push her into the water simply to allow some blood to flow back into his lower arm.

"We bid you adieu," Hardcastle said, tipping his hat once more, fifty interminable, cooing, clutching yards later. "And we bid you farewell, for as Sedgemere says, the time has come for ruralizing. I'm sure we'll see both of you when we return to London."

Hardcastle was up to something, Sedgemere knew not what. Hardcastle was a civil fellow, though not even the Cheshire twins would accuse him of charm. Sedgemere liked that about him, liked that one man could be relied upon to be honest at all times, about all matters. Unfortunately, such guilelessness would make Hardcastle a lamb to slaughter among the house-party set.

Amid much simpering and parasol twirling, the Cheshire ladies minced back to Park Lane, there to lurk like trolls under a bridge until the next hapless title came along to enjoy the fresh air.

"Turn around now," Sedgemere said, taking Hardcastle by the arm and walking him back the way they'd come. "Before they start fluttering handkerchiefs as if the Navy were departing for Egypt. I suppose you leave me no choice but to accompany you on this infernal frolic to the Lakes."

"Because you are turning into a bore and a disgrace and must hide up north?" Hardcastle inquired pleasantly.

"Because there's safety in numbers, you dolt."

"I say, that is a handsome woman," Hardcastle muttered. Hardcastle did not notice women, but an octogenarian Puritan would have taken a closer look at the vision approaching on the path.

"Miss Anne Faraday," Sedgemere said, a comely specimen indeed. Tall, unfashionably curvaceous, unfashionably dark-haired, she was also one of few women whose company did not send Sedgemere into a foul humor. In fact, her approach occasioned something like relief.

"You're not dodging off into the rhododendrons," Hardcastle said, "and yet you seem to know her."

Would Miss Faraday acknowledge Sedgemere? She was well beyond her come out, and no respecter of dukes, single or otherwise.

"I don't know her well, but I like her very much," Sedgemere said. "She hates me, you see. Has no marital aspirations in my direction whatsoever. For that alone, she enjoys my most sincere esteem."

* * *

Effie was chattering about the great burden of having to pack up Anne's dresses in this heat, and about the dust of the road, and all the ghastly impositions on a lady's maid resulting from travel to the countryside at the end of the Season.

Anne half-listened, but mostly she was absorbed with the effort of *not* noticing. She did not notice the Cheshire twins, for example, all but cutting her in public. They literally could not afford to cut her. Neither could the Henderson heir, who merely touched his hat brim to her as if he couldn't recall that he'd seen her in Papa's formal parlor not three days ago.

"It's that dook," Effie muttered, "the ice dook, they call him."

"He's not icy, Effie. Sedgemere is simply full of his own consequence."

And why shouldn't he be? He was handsome in a rigid, frigid way, with white-gold hair that no breeze would dare ruffle. His features were an assemblage of patrician attributes—a nose well suited to being looked down, a mouth more full than expected, but no matter, for Anne had never seen that mouth smile. Sedgemere's eyes were a disturbingly pale blue, as if some Viking ancestor looked out of them, one having a grand sulk to be stranded so far from his frozen landscapes and turbulent seas.

"Your papa could buy and sell the consequence of any three dooks, miss, and well they know it."

"The problem in a nutshell," Anne murmured as Sedgemere's gaze lit on her.

He was in company with the Duke of Hardcastle, whom Anne had heard described as semi-eligible. Hardcastle had an heir, twelve estates, and a dragon for a grandmother. He was notably reserved, though Anne liked what she knew of him. He wasn't prone to staring at bosoms, for example.

Always a fine quality in a man.

Sedgemere was even wealthier than Hardcastle, had neither mama nor extant duchess, but was father to three boys. To Anne's dismay, His Grace of Sedgemere did not merely touch a gloved finger to his hat brim, he instead doffed his hat and bowed.

"Miss Faraday, hello."

She was so surprised, her curtseys lacked the proper deferential depth. "Your Graces, good day."

Then came the moment Anne dreaded most, when instead of not-noticing her, a scion of polite society *did* notice her, simply for the pleasure of brushing her aside. Sedgemere had yet to indulge in that particular sport with her, but he too, had visited in Papa's parlor more than once.

"Shall you walk with us for a moment?" Sedgemere asked. "I believe you know Hardcastle, or I'd perform the introductions."

A large ducal elbow aimed itself in Anne's direction. Such an elbow never came her way unless the duke in question owed Papa at least ten thousand pounds.

"Sedgemere's on his best behavior," Hardcastle said, taking Anne's other arm, "because if you tolerate his escort, then he'll not find other ladies plaguing him. The debutantes fancy Sedgemere violently this time of year."

"The young ladies fancy unmarried dukes any time of year," Anne replied. Nonetheless, when Sedgemere tucked her hand onto his arm, she allowed it. The gossips would say that the presuming, unfortunate Anne Faraday was after a duke. No, that she was after two dukes.

"Will you spend the summer in Town, ma'am?" Hardcastle asked.

"Likely not, Your Grace. Papa's business means he will remain here, but he prefers that I spend some time in the shires, if possible."

"You always mention your father's business as early in a conversation as possible," Sedgemere said.

Anne could not decipher Sedgemere. His expression was as unreadable as a winter sky. If he'd been insulting her, the angle of his attack was subtle.

"I merely answered His Grace of Hardcastle's question. What of Your Graces? Will you soon leave for the country?"

Miss Helen Trimble and Lady Evette Hartley strolled past, and the consternation on their faces was almost worth the beating Anne's reputation would take once they were out of earshot. The gentlemen tipped their hats, the ladies dipped quick curtseys. Hardcastle was inveigled into accompanying the ladies to the gates of the park, and then—

Like a proud debutante poised in her newest finery at the top of the ballroom stairs, Sedgemere had come to a full stop.

"Your Grace?" Anne prompted, tugging on Sedgemere's arm.

"They did not acknowledge you. Those *women* did not so much as greet you. You might have been one of Mr. Dorning's mongrel dogs."

Well, no, because Mr. Dorning's canines were famously well-mannered, and thus endured much cooing and fawning from the ladies. Abruptly, Anne wished she could scurry off across the grass, and bedamned to manners, dukes, and young women who were terrified of growing old without a husband.

"The ladies often don't acknowledge me, Your Grace. I wish you would not remark it. The agreement we have is that they don't notice me, and I don't notice their rudeness. You will please neglect to mention this to my father."

As calculating as Papa was in business, he was a tender-hearted innocent when it came to ballroom warfare. In Papa's mind, his little girl—all nearly six feet of her—was simply too intelligent, pretty, sophisticated, and lovely for the friendship of the simpering twits and lisping viscounts.

"An agreement not to notice you?" Sedgemere snapped. "Who made such an agreement? Not that pair of dowdy poseurs. They couldn't agree on how to tie their bonnet ribbons."

The park was at its best as summer advanced, while all the rest of London became malodorous and stifling. The fashionable hour was about to begin, and thus the duke's behavior would soon attract notice.

"Your Grace will please refrain from making a scene," Anne said through gritted teeth. "I am the daughter of a man who holds the vowels of half the papas, uncles, and brothers of polite society. The ladies resent that, even if they aren't privy to the specifics."

Anne wasn't privy to the specifics either, thank heavens.

Sedgemere condescended to resume sauntering, leading Anne away from the Park Lane gates, deeper into the park's quiet greenery. She at first thought he was simply obliging her request, but a muscle leapt along his jaw.

"I'm sorry," Anne said. "If you owe Papa money, I assure you I'm not aware of it. He's most discreet, and I would never pry, and it's of no moment to me whether—"

"Hush," Sedgemere growled. "I'm trying to behave. One mustn't use foul language before a lady. Those women were ridiculous."

"They were polite to you," Anne said.

"Everybody is polite to a duke. It's nauseating."

"Everybody is rude to a banker's daughter. That's not exactly pleasant either, Your Grace."

"Everybody is rude to you?"

Sedgemere carried disdain around with him like an expensive cape draped over his arm, visible at twenty paces, unlikely to be mislaid. His curiosity, as if Anne's situation were a social experiment, and she responsible for reporting its results, disappointed her.

"Must you make sport of my circumstances, Your Grace? Perhaps you'd care to take yourself off now. My maid will see me home."

He came to a leisurely halt and tucked his gloved hand over Anne's knuckles, so she could not free herself of him without drawing notice.

"You are sending me away," he said. "A duke of the realm, fifty-third in line for the throne, and you're sending me packing like a presuming, jug-eared footman who neglected to chew adequate quantities of parsley after overimbibing. Hardcastle will not believe this."

Incredulity was apparently in the air, for Anne could not believe what she beheld either. The Duke of Sedgemere, he of the icy eyes and frosty condescension, was regarding her with something approaching curiosity. Interest, at least, and not the sort of interest that involved her bosom.

"Perhaps you'd better toddle on, then," Anne said. "I'm sure there's a debutante—or twelve—who will expire of despair if she can't flaunt her wares at you before sundown."

"I'm dismissed out of hand, and now I'm to toddle. Dukes do not toddle, madam. Perhaps the heat is affecting your judgment." His tone would have frozen the Serpentine to a thickness of several inches.

Sedgemere, poor man, must owe Papa a very great deal of money.

"*Good day*, Your Grace. Have a pleasant summer."

"I must make allowances," he said, his grip on Anne's fingers snug. "You're not used to the undivided attention of so lofty a personage as I, and the day is rather warm. When next we meet, I assure you I will have the toddling well in hand. I enjoy a challenge, you see. You have a pleasant summer too, Miss Faraday, and my kindest regards to your dear papa."

Sedgemere's demeanor remained crushingly correct as he bowed with utmost graciousness over Anne's hand. When he tipped his hat to her, she could have sworn those chilly blue eyes had gained a hint of warmth.

Or more than hint?

Find out more about Once Upon a Dream at
graceburrowes.com/books/elias.php
and enjoy the rest of Duke of My Dreams!

DUCHESS OF LIGHT

SUSANNA IVES

CHAPTER ONE

"Just hang me," the Duke of Lucere declared. He stood, holding his bag and surveying the teeming metropolis that was Lesser Puddlebury.

The main thoroughfare was no more than a rambling medieval passage. On either side of the narrow lane, crumbling timbered buildings sloped against each other as if for mutual support. The muddy street was empty save for a washerwoman, who was tossing the contents of a chamber pot into the gutter, and an old man in a workman's tunic, drinking from a flask while herding pigs. He tugged at his hat as he passed and muttered an unintelligible, but happy-sounding, greeting. He had one tooth.

"And a fine morning to you, kind sir," Lucere answered, tipping his hat in return. He then muttered to Harris, his manservant, "I should have been the one shot in the arse for getting entangled in this low scheme."

It was the meanest Mowne, Starlingham, and he had befallen, which, given the men's propensity to locate and bask in trouble, was rather significant.

"That would be most unfortunate," observed Harris.

Harris had been Lucere's late father's manservant and conduit for conversation between the warring father and son. He was a tall man, possessing the powerful build of a pugilist bruiser. Yet his visage was that of a noble Roman with a prominent nose, metallic silver hair that fringed his large head, and grave gray eyes, the type that poets might describe as calm oceans.

Upon meeting Harris for the first hundred or so times, one would think he possessed a great talent for observing the obvious. However, Lucere knew a wise seer with supernatural powers lay beneath the man's placid façade.

For instance, when, after downing three bottles of fine Portuguese port with Mowne, Starlingham, and several lovely actresses, Starlingham had said, or more accurately, he had *slurred*, "Let's ride to Scotland together. Unity in battle," it had seemed like a completely rational plan given the inebriated circumstances. The words "jolly" and "congenial" had even been bandied about.

When told of this proposed travel party, Harris had said, "It will be a most exciting adventure, I'm sure," which, if translated onto a lay tongue, had meant, *There is a strong possibility you or your friends may be arrested, injured, or shot dead.*

And Harris had been right, of course.

Mowne's brother had become embroiled in an unsavory duel before they'd even managed to cross the border. And poor Mowne had received a shot in the rump as a reward for trying to stop the unpleasant business.

Now Lucere was worried, nervous, and furious.

Worried that Mowne's poor wound would fester—it would be a sad affair for a duke in the prime of his life to have his backside amputated.

Nervous that Mowne's Uncle Leo would receive word of the duel.

And furious at Mowne's brother, but mostly at himself.

What am I doing here? Hadn't he made a vow to be a better man?

A year had passed since a footman had found Lucere playing deep in a London gaming hell, a cigar in his mouth, a brandy in one hand, an ace in the other, and a dainty ballerina decorating his knee, to inform him of his father's imminent death. Lucere had dashed through the yellow fog-filled streets that evening. He hadn't been to his father's home since the old duke had told him to stay out of his sight for the remainder of his life.

"So you're going to be the duke," his father had rasped when Lucere knelt beside his deathbed. The air reeked of mucus, urine, and medicine. His father sucked for breath and then released it with a gravelly, wet rush. "Well, you're a disgrace to the ancient Primrose blood line. A stalwart English family that for hundreds of years upheld our motto of duty, honor, truth, sacrifice, and courage. You're a libertine like The Despicable Uncle, except you can't be shaken from the tree but remain to blight it. Oh, had your worthy brother lived. Had he ascended to the title. Woe, that he and I—admirable, honorable men—should die and you should be the duke." He fell into violent coughs that sounded like rocks scraping together.

The duke had been throwing these little knives of words for years at his surviving son. Lucere hadn't experienced that acute, fresh sting at their utterance as he had in disreputable youth. What had brought the shine of tears to Lucere's eyes that evening was to see his formidable father shriveled to yellow skin draped loosely over bones, everything in between eaten away. Even though his father would never have believed it, and would have scoffed at such weak sentimentality from a man, Lucere loved the duke. He wished he could have been a better son.

"Take my hand," his father growled.

Lucere had never held his father's hand in his life. It was hot and reduced to cords of tendons and hard knuckles.

His father labored for words. "Promise me before the ghosts of the old Dukes of Lucere gathered in this room tonight, coming to bring me to their great fold, that you will be a better man. Worthy of your title."

Lucere wasn't one to believe in ghosts, but that night the room felt alive with specters. His voice cracked when he said, "I promise upon the Primrose family name to be a better man."

"Tell me how you will improve yourself."

"Now?"

"No, son, in a fortnight. Of course now. What other time is there?"

"I-I suppose I'll start attending the House of Lords and help bolster several bills I've been reading about."

"No!" his father hissed, which brought more coughs. When he spoke again, his voice was a mere thread. "You will stop keeping company with low women and take a gentle wife of proper breeding and manners. She will bear you a son as soon as may be possible, who, God willing, will inherit her good sense and restore dignity to the title of Duke of Lucere." His father strained on. "Once the question of the heir is settled, what will you do?"

Lucere began making brash promises to his father. He would improve the tenants' homes, research farming techniques to increase yields, form charities for the orphans and widows, and so forth. Things the old duke hadn't done, but it hadn't been the time to further explore that subject. The duke nodded his head best as he could. Finally, in the very last hours of his father's life, Lucere had managed to please him.

The old duke released his last breath in the early morning. The new duke had walked to the empty nursery at the top of the house where Catherine, his favorite childhood nurse, and he had shared so many hours. He had squatted onto the cold, bare floor planks and imagined she was with him, embracing him and whispering that all would be well when he knew it wouldn't be.

Even as a grown man, Lucere desperately missed her abundant smiles and the way she embraced him without reserve—so different from his cold parents, or the grasping courtesans who would later decorate his adult nights. How readily Catherine praised his childish drawings and songs he made up— all created to worship her. No night of wild passion had ever surpassed the gentle, warm feeling of when she had tucked him into bed, singing a lovely song meant to lull him to sleep. He had heard enough false *I love you's* dripping from ambitious women's lips. But Catherine had truly meant it when she'd said, "I love my sweet, sweet boy."

Catherine was the only person who had ever truly cared for him.

And he had killed her.

After his father's death, Lucere had tried in vain to find the proper wife in

London Society to fulfill the vow he had made, but the Catherine problem had assailed him at every turn. He knew he would never find Catherine again, but that didn't stop his heart from yearning for her. For years, she had sent him drifting restlessly from one beautiful courtesan's arms to the next, finding no solace for very long. And now she was determined to prevent his marriage and transformation.

Lucere was a mordant caterpillar stuck in a gloomy chrysalis. In the depths of his marital despair, he had received a fateful letter from Mowne's interfering and matchmaking Uncle Leo. Leo wrote that a lovely German princess, who Leo and Lucere's late father had agreed would make an excellent Duchess of Lucere, was attending a hunting party in Scotland. Leo provided a genealogy chart— Leo consulted genealogy charts like fortune-tellers conferred with astrological tables—showing her impeccable pedigree, as well as German articles attesting to her gentle manners and acts of charity. Lucere decided to give up trying to talk sense into his adamant heart—Catherine was dead, he had killed her. Even if he found an incarnation of Catherine, he wouldn't be worthy of her. He should just surrender to the ease of an arranged, loveless marriage. After all, his friends Mowne and Starlingham were already heading to Scotland, so the entire affair seemed rather destined—the sun, moon, and stars aligning in his favor.

"*The fault, dear Brutus, is not in our stars, but in ourselves*," Lucere now muttered, quoting Shakespeare as he gazed down the narrow lanes of Lesser Puddlebury, seeking an inn that might be devoid of fleas and thieves.

"Harris, do you see that slowly collapsing building with the word 'Arm' scribbled upon the side? Do you think it houses people, such as The Royal Arms or Chauncy's Arms might? Or is it a shop of arms, say, wooden arms? Or perhaps a physician whose specialty is the arm?"

"It is a captivating mystery, Your Grace," said Harris in his unperturbed tones. "However, might I suggest the Duke of Lucere's Boarding House as your temporary home?"

"Are you attempting a joke? Because I don't feel in the mood to laugh, but would rather kick something very hard, namely myself."

"No, Your Grace. If you will kindly position your sights farther down the lane, you will see a sign advertising the Duke of Lucere's Boarding House."

Lucere turned, located said sign, and studied it with his head tilted, a brow cocked. The wood—embellished with vines and primroses, no doubt after his family name Primrose—did, indeed, read "Duke of Lucere's Boarding House." Below that, a line further expounded, "Apartments for Elegant Persons of Gentle Breeding."

What?

Intrigued by this mystery, Lucere strolled down the uneven pavement until it ended in a dirt path. Set slightly apart from the town was a crumbling manor house. It was a dreary gray stone edifice from Jacobean times. The left side of the building was higher than the right, and ugly cracks ran in slants from the roof to the foundation. The grounds, which twenty years before might have been a pleasing, manicured garden, appeared to run feral.

"Well, that's convenient," Lucere said, at length. "Exceedingly odd and rather puzzling, but terribly convenient. Ah, Harris, but do we possess the required gentle breeding demanded by this exacting Duke of Lucere? Starlingham said something about being *in* disguise—or did he say *be* disguised?"

"I do believe he was suggesting assuming false identities, not being inebriated for the duration of our time in Lesser Puddlebury."

"I could be both, for good measure. For I can hardly stomach this place sober. Very well, who is genteel and poor? We haven't regimentals or clergyman's clothes. Good God, no one would believe I was a man of the cloth for a moment—an aura of sin surrounds me."

"Perhaps we could be tutors in want of employment."

"You shock me with your fast, devious mind, Harris. Tutors we are. I shall resurrect dead and tedious languages, and no doubt, you shall want to teach philosophy, given your great esteem for Kant."

"If it pleases Your Grace."

"No, it does not please," Lucere said, gazing at the dilapidated lodging house. The dying domicile with his name on its sign seemed like a sad metaphor for his life. As if to further illustrate the point, a slate slid from the roof and thudded on the ground. "Nothing pleases, and that is entirely the problem. Since my father's death and that bloody vow, my life has become gray. London is gray, this village is gray, and everything I touch, hear, or see is as dull, relentless, and despondently gray as this sad home. And I can't chase away this feeling, no matter how much I try. I feel so doomed and trapped by life."

Harris studied his master, his heavy brows raised in alarm. Lucere felt embarrassed by his outburst.

"Damn it," Lucere muttered, feeling foolish and exposed in Harris's penetrating gaze. "Forget I spoke. I'm just frustrated that I agreed to this sad folly." He slid his identifying signet ring into his bag, which also carried Leo's letters and charts as well as a diamond ring and necklace Lucere would give his princess should he decide to ask for her hand in marriage. "I hope this Lucere cove has chambers for us. I hear tell he is a blackhearted rogue who would be well served with a good shot in the arse."

"You may find, Your Grace, that good things are often born of unfortunate circumstances."

"I assure you the only good thing that will come of this unfortunate circumstance will be that for the rest of my life, no matter what evil befalls me, I can always say, 'At least, I'm not in Lesser Puddlepiss.'"

CHAPTER TWO

Estella pondered why, at least in her case, bad news never meted itself, for example, dropping a tidbit of badness on a Monday and a little more on a Thursday. But alas, vile tidings must all fall at once. For the past few days, she had prayed for a positive reply from the Duke of Lucere before she met next with the despised banker. Out of financial desperation, she had recently tried to strike up a correspondence with the great duke, or to be more accurate, with the great duke's secretary, Mr. Fellows. Naturally, a cold letter from Mr. Fellows, denying her requests for help, and a call from the banker, Mr. Todd, occurred within the same hour.

Now the franked letter lay folded before her on the parlor table beside twenty pounds and three shillings in stacked coins—all the money she possessed. She sat on a chair, her hands clutched in her lap, her eyes focused on the stained and snagged carpet as she struggled to remain civil.

Mr. Todd tossed back his head in belly-shaking laughter, then lowered it again and studied her. The side of his thin lips rose in a boyish smile. A twinkle warmed his gray eyes that were mantled by heavy lids. She did not know whether to describe him as stout or powerfully built. He was a man of dualities. At this moment, he resembled a lovable, chubby puppy. This puppy side was the one most people saw.

But Estella wasn't fooled.

She had witnessed his visage harden to frightening menace in a flash.

"You are a lovely little darling." He leaned down until they were at eye level. "But let me help you perform a little mathematics problem." He spoke slowly, as if to a child. "You owe 3,120 pounds at four percent. Do you know what that equals per month including last month's missed payment?"

"I only owe you 3,112 pounds," she said. "Here is the correct amount for two monthly installments. I keep careful ledgers."

"Of course you do." He leaned in closer, his eyes mere inches from hers. "But, my dearest, you owed the butcher, the coal deliverer, and the apothecary for your mother's medicine. You can't leave your house without incurring more debt, can you, my silly darling?" He laughed again. "What would happen if you weren't so beautiful? If I weren't so willing to help you? My dear, you live entirely on my graces." He placed his large, hot hand on her cheek. "Now I would appreciate a little gratitude."

"You did not ask my permission to pay those creditors." She gently removed his fingers. She knew better than to anger him. "You are intentionally making me further obliged to you."

"Obliged?!" he cried. "Y-you're like a bird with a broken wing trying to fly. It's pathetic to watch you." He stepped back and swung his arm, gesturing to the room. "You can't run this house. It's falling down around you. You have no sense of economy. You're not intelligent enough to take care of yourself, let alone your sisters and a sick mother. Only I have the patience to put up with you—no one else—and yet, you give me no consequence. No respect."

Estella tried to keep his ugly words from sinking into her heart and further weakening her. That was his intention. Every week, he called to try to break her down.

"I'm the only man standing up for your honor," he continued when he didn't garner a reaction. He brushed his chin with his hand; it made a rasping sound. "What do you think the villagers think when they see a young woman running a lodging house? That you're entertaining the royal princesses? You, my dear, have made yourself the object of lurid gossip. Decency forbids me to say how the gentlemen in this town regard you."

What an insidious man! He was guilty of spreading the very rumors about her that he claimed to dispel. She wouldn't put him above suspicion in the mysterious events surrounding her chicken coop being left open overnight and all the chickens eaten by dogs, or the sudden, fatal illness of their milch cow.

Estella glanced at the letter. "I will write the Duke of Lucere again. I will scratch up the extra monies." She would beg the duke. She would sign her name in blood.

He slammed his palm hard on the table, rattling the coins and the tin candlestick holder. "Enough with this inane Duke of Lucere foolishness! Enough, I tell you, woman! You could drive a tolerant man to madness."

She came to her feet. "We are Primroses!" She kept her bearing high. "The duke is my cousin through my grandfather, Lord Maxim."

He cocked his head and raked his gaze over her body, stopping at her breasts.

She gathered her arms about her bosom, trying to conceal herself from his eyes.

"Would you care to know who my cousin is?" he asked, and didn't wait for her answer. "Lord Nelson. That's right." He slowly approached her. She backed up until she hit the bureau desk, shaking the glass cabinets. Still he came even closer to her. He kept his legs spread, his face so close she could feel his breath on her cheek. "My mother claims he's a fourth cousin. I've never met him. Therefore, I don't call my bank Lord Nelson's Bank, because I don't shamelessly live off the name of another. I rise and fall by my own merit."

She didn't mention that the lodging house had been her mother's idea before she'd had the heart spasm. Her mother had taken out the mortgage and named the business after the great duke. Now Estella shielded her mother and twin sisters from Mr. Todd and the desperation of their situation. Around her family, she upheld the pretense that their world was running merrily along. But inside, Estella was breaking under the weight of Mr. Todd's bombardment of her character and her business.

"You mock me and then wonder why I don't want to marry you," she whispered in an unsteady voice.

He studied her, slowly shaking his head. "My dear, I only become angry with you like a patient father to his child. Why must you reject my help for your own good? You willfully and incorrectly cast me as a villain, refusing to let any affection grow in your heart." He cupped her chin, raising her head. "Come, let me love you. There now, see how nice you are when you're docile?" She watched him close his eyes, his open mouth descending onto hers.

She shrank away from his touch, escaping to the corner by the sofa. She wrapped her arms about her. "I-I can have the remaining monies to you in a fortnight."

He raked his hand through his hair and began to pace, his chest rising and falling with his rapid breath. Estella's belly tightened with dread. In a sudden motion, he slammed his fist into the sofa cushion. And then again and again.

"Mr. Todd!"

He pointed his finger at her, his nostrils quivering. "You cannot keep your home. You cannot tend to your sisters and mother. You purchase her medicine on credit. What kind of daughter are you? Selfish and unthinking, that's what. You're living in some dream world. As though this were a bloody dollhouse and you're the Duchess of Lucere."

Was she truly living in some dollhouse dream world? It didn't seem like much of a dream, more the stuff of nightmares.

He snatched up his hat. "I'm taking Mama to York to visit her sister for two weeks. I shall buy her gowns of silk and sarsenet while I'm there. That's how I treat proper ladies. I could have treated you that way."

Estella bit back a nasty retort about treating ladies to silken threats and sarsenet-draped coercion. When she said nothing, he stalked to the table, scooped up her coins, and strode out the door. But a few moments later, he was back. "You *will* take my hand, Estella," he hissed. "You *will* learn to love me." He walked out again, this time with a muttered curse.

Estella pressed her hands to her face. Her heart thundered. She waited a moment more until she heard the thud of the front door and then fled to the kitchens.

She felt as though the failure of their lodging house was her own doing. Somehow, she should have done something different, something better. As much as she tried to ignore Mr. Todd's cruel words, some echoed her own fears. She couldn't take care of her mother; she couldn't raise her lovely sisters to the genteel lives they should have. It was her fault.

Don't cry, she told herself as tears blurred her eyes. *Don't you dare cry. Not if you care for your family.*

She poured a fortifying cup of pure black tea—such luxuries as milk and sugar were saved for paying lodgers—and sat at her writing desk. She had lugged it to the kitchens so she could take care of correspondences while watching whatever was simmering on the range, as well as enjoy the warmth radiating from the coals. Without the necessary funds to resupply the coal, she had rationed the precious black gold to the kitchens and her mother's room when they didn't have lodgers. And they hadn't had any for a month.

She unfolded the letter from the duke's secretary and reread it, looking for some ray of hope she might have missed upon the first perusal. He had written that His Grace thanked her for her gracious letter and for the felicitations for his happiness. Unfortunately, she could claim no ties to the great family, and thus the duke was under no obligation to offer her any assistance.

"How can you say that?" she cried. "I have repeatedly detailed how we are related through my grandfather."

Mr. Fellows closed by saying that the duke wished she and her family— although entirely unrelated to His Grace—health and happiness.

Happiness? She wasn't sure she knew what that word meant anymore. Now when she thought of happiness she remembered being a child, holding her grandfather's hand as she and the toddling twins walked through the forest paths. He would make up wondrous stories about fairies living amid the ferns. How lovely their lives had been then, filled with affection and security. Now she met every morning with fear.

She studied the secretary's missive. Had the Duke of Lucere even seen her words? She sighed, turned the letter, and began to write in very small lines across Mr. Fellows's neat scrawl. The words she kept safe from her mother and sisters now burst onto the page.

Dear Duke,

Thank you for your last letter composed by your secretary. Please thank him for inquiring after the family. I do not understand why Mr. Fellows insists that you and I are not related. I have more than once established the connection through my beloved grandfather, Lord Maxim, your great-uncle. Your Grace and I are second cousins. To this end, I beg your assistance of a mere ten pounds to meet some of my creditors. Upon my honor as a Primrose, I shall recompense every borrowed pound and with a generous three percent interest. My mother is an infirmed widow; she suffers greatly from weakening ailments. I am trying to raise my twin sisters as genteel ladies worthy of the Primrose family motto—duty, honor, truth, sacrifice, and courage. Words I have endeavored to live my life by.

As we are family, I shall open my entire situation to you. Unless I receive kind assistance soon, I shall have no other course than to make an undesired alliance with a powerful man of a harsh, brutish nature. This gentleman has used his influence to vilify my character and chase away more worthy suitors.

I beg that Mr. Fellows will pass along my letter to Your Grace's hand. I am most desperate in my plea.

Yours sincerely,

Estella signed her name to this outpouring and hurried to open the door for Lottie, who was dragging a copper kettle into the kitchens for the laundry. Dear Lottie was the only remaining servant. She was a sturdy woman of thirty-five years, but her mind remained that of a child.

Estella addressed and sealed her letter, and then gave Lottie explicit instructions to mail it and ask for a receipt.

"Yes, miss," the servant replied, happy to be tasked with the important chore. Before Lottie could leave, she had to hug Estella. "I love you, miss. I do. You are my favorite person in the whole world."

"I love you too," Estella assured her.

This pleased Lottie, and she skipped off, a huge grin lifting her face.

Estella had begun to make her way to her mother's room when the bell for the front door rang.

She panicked. The only people who called lately were Mr. Todd and creditors. But what if it was an actual customer?

She dashed into the breakfast room where her sixteen-year-old twin sisters, Cecelia and Amelia, were supposedly doing their geography studies. Instead, she found them giggling and trimming each other's gowns with garish cloth flowers cut from old, unusable drapes. The book on the customs and landscapes of the Orient, which she had begged to borrow from the circulation library, lay unopened on the table beside a sliced beet and a jar of something resembling black clay. The girls stopped giggling, as though Estella were some warden, and shoved the vegetable and jar under the cut-up drapes.

"What are you doing?" Estella cried, staring at their garments. "You are ruining your gowns!"

"We are not!" Amelia protested. "We are making them fashionable."

"That's not fashionable! That's… that's… garish! Hideous! Appalling!"

She desperately desired to treat her sisters to a smart scolding. After all, she scrubbed, cleaned, cooked, and mended so that they could be raised as proper ladies and make good establishments, escaping the prison in which Estella found herself. But she had more pressing matters to attend.

"Answer the door," she begged the twins. "If it's a creditor tell… tell him that I'm out. And then remove those repulsive flowers from your gown. And I don't want to see them put on a bonnet either."

What a terrible example I'm setting for my sisters, Estella thought as she stationed herself behind the stairs to listen. *An antithesis to the Primrose motto.* But if a creditor was calling to demand payment, she had no funds left. Mr. Todd had taken them all.

CHAPTER THREE

"It is entirely possible this structure may collapse on our heads during our stay," Lucere observed to Harris, now that he could assess how badly the foundation of the Duke of Lucere's Boarding House had shifted. "His Grace requires a better steward." If the outside was so atrocious, he could only imagine the inside of crumbling walls, falling ceilings, and frightening inhabitants—both human and rodent.

Then the door opened, and two stunning blonde twins gazed at the men with lovely, wintry blue eyes fringed with unnaturally dark lashes. Their full lips were beet red and complemented their garish gowns, which appeared to be in bloom for the season.

Lucere was rarely at a loss for words, but his jaw flapped open. Harris was rather discommoded, as well.

The ladies gave no greeting, but looked at each other and then broke into a prolonged fit of giggles.

Seeing no introduction from them in the near future, Lucere stepped up to the task. "Good day, my lovely ladies, I'm Mr. Stephens," he said, converting his first name to a last. "And this is my good friend Mr. Harris. We are seeking an interview with the Duke of Lucere regarding letting rooms in his esteemed boarding house."

The twins blushed and giggled with greater violence.

One of the girls rolled her eyes. "The Duke of Lucere doesn't live here," she said in a voice that intoned that Lucere, the real Lucere, could possibly be the stupidest man alive.

"Does he not?" Lucere feigned surprised. He was falling into his normal pattern of resorting to mordant humor to hide his disdain. Nothing set him off a lady faster than insipid giggles and eye-rolling. "Then why, my fair ladies, does he advertise his name on the sign? My companion and I are quite disappointed not to meet the man in full. Alas, we shall take our business elsewhere."

"The Duke of Lucere is our beloved second cousin," a soft soprano said. The twins parted, revealing the most ravishing female Lucere had ever beheld.

And Lucere had beheld many females.

She had all the fair coloring of the twins, but her eyes were larger and paler, her chin more delicate, her cheeks more majestic, her lips less red. A living, breathing angel, until he took in her figure. No celestial being of goodness could possess such luscious, sin-enticing breasts, further enhanced by a slim waist. And she clearly knew the allure of her body, for she wore a blue cotton gown that appeared several inches too small for how it strained across her abundant breasts. She curtseyed with the grace of a ballet dancer, giving him a good eyeful of that delicious bosom.

All Lucere could think was, *For the love of all that's right and just in the world, please don't giggle.*

Followed by, *Precisely what kind of boarding house is this?*

Had he stumbled into the Duke of Lucere's bordello? He didn't know whether to be intrigued or furious. For the moment, he would try intrigued.

"Please, do come in," the woman said.

She beckoned the men with a graceful wave of her hand to follow her to a shabby parlor. The cream paint was faded, the ceiling plaster cracked, the brass fixtures tarnished, the burgundy upholstery suspiciously hidden behind blankets and pillows. He took in all these details at once because the beautiful goddess so vividly contrasted with her surroundings.

She curtseyed again. "I'm Miss Estella Primrose, and these are my sisters, Miss Cecelia and Miss Amelia." She gave her giggling sisters a meaningful look. "Please properly curtsy for our gentleman guests."

Ah, so they were Primroses! That explained why they were trying to pass themselves off as relations to the duke.

"It's lovely to make your acquaintance," Lucere said coolly. "I'm Mr. Stephens, and this is my friend Mr. Harris. We are in want of…" He paused, uncertain. Did he say he was in want of a room or a companion?

Harris finished what Lucere had started. "We are tutors in want of agreeable apartments."

"Very good." Miss Primrose smiled. Lucere swallowed. Those delicious upturned lips and white teeth wielded a scary power. They sent a hot wave over his skin and into his blood, sending it rushing to his sex.

"Won't you please sit down?" she said and then turned to her sisters. "Bring our kind guests tea."

"With milk and sugar?" one asked.

"Of course with milk and sugar," Miss Primrose replied, a taint of exasperation beneath her soft tones. Once the twins had trailed out, Miss Primrose took the wing chair opposite the men. She kept her back ramrod straight, her hands clasped in her lap. The sunlight streaming from the window created a Madonna-like halo around her pale, fine hair.

"So, you have recently arrived in Lesser Puddlebury?" She fixed her bright gaze on Harris.

Despite the fact that Lucere had made a vow to his dying father to avoid low women such as Miss Primrose, and that he should be on his way to Scotland to meet his future wife of saintly reputation, he was annoyed that Miss Primrose didn't look at him.

"Yes, miss," Harris replied. "Our former pupils have reached their age. We were given a handsome recompense for our years of service, but we are currently in want of work. We have excellent letters from our prior services and seek a place to stay while corresponding with potential employers." Truly, the man was a dead-face magician.

Her smile widened, its power increasing exponentially. This woman was clearly skilled at her arts.

"How fortunate for you that two apartments have recently come available," she said.

"You must run a very popular boarding house, *Miss* Primrose," Lucere replied, pointing out the suggestive anomaly of a "miss" running such an establishment. He was happy to note that he was coming back to his usual cynical nature after the initial shock of her beauty.

He smirked inwardly as she shifted in her chair.

"My mother is the proprietor," she answered.

Of course, he refrained from saying. Such establishments were often family businesses.

"And many of our genteel guests are away at house parties and such for the summer, so we are rather dull for the moment."

What a honey-tongued, scheming little angel. No one of any elegance or high breeding would step foot in this hovel unless for lurid purposes.

She lifted her eyes to Harris and graced him with another devastating smile. Perhaps she thought him more gullible to her charms than Lucere. "Therefore, I'm grateful to have such conversant and learned company to enliven our evenings."

"And you chose not to journey to London to be with your cousin, the duke?" Lucere asked. "Most young ladies in your position revel in the delights of the Town." He enjoyed watching a blush creep across her cheeks.

Harris cleared his throat, a subtle warning that Lucere chose to ignore.

She shifted again and averted her beautiful eyes from Lucere's face. "My mother prefers not to travel."

"How extraordinary that you are cousins with the duke," he continued, enjoying her obvious discomfort. "As a humble tutor who must rely on the kindness of great men for his living, I'm keenly interested in learning as much as I can about elegant society. Might I kindly ask you what you know of this man?"

A little pleat appeared between her brows. "I find him to be a…" She studied the faded carpet. Her voice turned quiet and wistful. "A kind man of gentle nature. He listens with patience and compassion to others and always responds generously to those in need."

It took a great deal of restraint to keep Lucere from breaking into laughter. Someone should hint to the poor miss that she should read a London scandal rag or two before uttering such obvious fibs. Good heavens, he must remember this description and retell it to Mowne and Starlingham. "Ah, you correspond with the duke frequently," he said, feeding her more rope to hang herself.

"We correspond every week," she readily lied, keeping her eyes on the carpet. This was doing it too brown. He had never received a letter from an Estella Primrose in his life.

"And what of his sisters?" Lucere continued. "Or his mother?"

She squirmed. "The duchess is as kind and generous as her son."

At that point, Lucere couldn't contain a derisive bark of laughter. "How extraordinary! You have met her?" For if she had, Miss Primrose would know that his mother put the haughty Almack's patronesses to shame.

"A f-few times," Miss Primrose stammered. "As I said, my mother prefers not to travel."

Lucere templed his fingers beneath his chin. He felt his lips curl in a predatory smile. Why had he thought he wouldn't enjoy Lesser Puddlebury? "So it is the duke and you who share the intimate relationship."

Her head jerked back, and she blinked. "Pardon me?"

"What are your rates, Miss Primrose?" Harris broke in.

Estella didn't answer but stared at Lucere, her mouth dropped, her brows tensed. Harris repeated his question, this time in more gentle tones.

"Five shillings a week," she replied to Mr. Harris in a flustered voice. "W-would that suit you?"

Five shillings for a room and beautiful companionship was a trifle in London.

At this point, the twins returned with the tea. After setting the tray upon the table, they shamelessly ogled Lucere and quietly giggled to each other.

Miss Primrose made a show of elegantly pouring their tea. It was comical watching her feign airs amid the chipped china. How she must make her customers feel important, as if they were genteel men on par with the duke himself. How she must entice them with her smiles and gentle eyes. Lucere knew how these ladies operated. Contrary to opinion, their work was less about the actual act and more about making a lonely gentleman feel loved and desired.

But Lucere was stuck with a quandary. An honorable man would stalk from this den of dissipation and write immediately to his solicitor. Although there was no law against someone using another's name for advertisement, Lucere would think of some rule to toss at her. But that didn't give him a place to stay while Mowne healed his arse.

And every fiber of Lucere's being desired this delightful, scheming morsel. But, good God, he was on his way to Scotland to meet his bride and begin his transformation. Was it ungentlemanly to be in lust with another woman just days before his engagement? Didn't he vow to be a better man?

She passed his tea, giving him another potent smile. That smile coupled with the sunlight streaming through the window and sparkling in her pale eyes was a lethal combination to a man's virtue. A hot current rushed through Lucere's mind, silencing his thoughts, leaving only throbbing desire.

The decision was made not by his rational brain, but a part of his body located between his legs. He set his teacup upon its cracked saucer and said in a low voice, "Won't you show me to my bedchamber?"

* * *

He followed behind her through corridors and stairs. She spoke of the general rules of the house, location of the privy, and the hours of dining. Her words made no impression, his mind focused exclusively on her lovely curves, imagining them unclad. He drew in her warm sugar-and-spice scent. The despondency that had been following him for months was dissipating like the sun chasing off the rain. Again, he was struck with a core truth. Rakishness made him happy. He couldn't be a better man no matter how he tried. He was a rogue to the bone. A succulent, designing light-skirts had undone all his months of honest effort in a matter of minutes. As he mentally disparaged himself, thankfully Harris was listening and making appropriate conversation with Miss Primrose. Behind him, the twins giggled along.

Miss Primrose opened a door. "This can be your bedchamber, Mr. Stephens," she said and gestured for him to step inside. "I believe it possesses everything a learned man may desire. A writing desk and shelves for any books you may have."

The room was composed of scuffed furniture. A poster bed dominated the room. Its bedcovers were mostly white, save for the yellow stains. The walls were not adorned with paintings but pressed flowers and samplers in frames. The only architecturally pleasing feature was the arched window that afforded a view of the feral front garden and small drive.

He set down his bag and pressed upon the sloping mattress. "Yes, I do believe you have supplied me with everything I may desire," he said in a low, dusky manner. How natural flirtation came to him—as thoughtless as breathing.

That lovely blush heated her cheeks again. Her ample breasts rose with a suck of her breath.

"I am pleased," she whispered and spun around. "Mr. Harris, allow me to show you your accommodations."

"Of course," Harris said, giving way so that she might exit, and then followed behind.

Across the hall, Lucere could hear Harris complimenting his room and thanking her for her kind hospitality. Lucere waited until he heard retreating footfalls and giggles and then strolled to Harris's room.

"Good God, Harris," Lucere exclaimed. "Your apartment is much finer than mine. You even have a small sitting room. I believe Miss Primrose likes you considerably better than me."

Harris dusted the battered wardrobe with a handkerchief. "Yes, Your Grace, it would appear so."

Harris then turned quiet. Lucere read something in that heavy silence.

"I know you don't approve of how I acted," Lucere confessed. "I know I made a vow. But my God, have you ever seen such an angel? Lucifer's angel, that is. What a calculating, ruthless liar beneath her mesmerizing voice and becoming smiles. Yes, yes, I do not miss the irony that I, too, am lying. But ours is an innocent ruse. She's an ambitious schemer intent on dragging my good name in the mud. I didn't know whether to laugh or succumb to indignant rage or... or make love to her."

Lucere sank into a chair. Away from Miss Primrose's all-consuming presence, his cold reason returned, as did his conscience, what little he possessed. "Should we relocate? I can't deny my fascination for her. But I worry for any natural man *not* attracted to her. He should seek a physician. Don't deny it, she even moved you. I saw it."

Harris paused in his cleaning. "Your Grace, it is oft acknowledged among gentlemen that a bachelor might enjoy one last dalliance before beginning a lifetime of devotion to one lady."

"Harris! You still astound me after all these years. I wouldn't have expected such lurid reasoning from you." Lucere rose again, suddenly edgy. "But what of you? The twins are certainly beautiful, but their insipid—"

"There has always been but one lady for me," Harris said quietly. He opened his bag and laid a folded shirt upon the bed. He fingered its buttons, his heavy eyes narrowing as if peering into a painful memory.

A pall fell over the room except for a noisy fly buzzing in the windowsill.

Catherine, Lucere's beloved nurse, had been Harris's betrothed. Had the man remained the constant lover to her memory all these years?

Lucere felt ashamed. The depression that had lifted for a few minutes returned deeper than before. How could Lucere even contemplate a low dealing with a prostitute against such honest, abiding love as Harris and Catherine had shared?

A love that Lucere had taken away.

Without another word, he trudged back to his chamber, leaving Harris to his memories and Lucere to his self-loathing.

CHAPTER FOUR

In the kitchens, the twins were in such wild transports as to be nonsensical. Estella wanted to shake them.

"He's so handsome!" Cecelia cried.

"Such a strong, manly jaw, and his legs!" Amelia exclaimed. "La! His pantaloons were as tight as his very skin."

"His eyes were like… like chocolate," Cecelia cried. The twins were not very poetic.

"Chocolate heavens," Amelia improved. "But his lips—"

The girls devolved into inane laughter.

Estella berated herself for not better seeing to the twins' moral education. They were turning into ignorant, wild-mannered flirts.

"I assume you are speaking of Mr. Stephens," Estella said harshly.

"Good heavens, yes," replied Amelia. "Not that scary, ugly old man. Whew!"

"Ugly?" Estella cried. "Old? Well, I found Mr. Harris exceedingly handsome, but then, I judged him by his agreeable character. You are only as pretty as your character."

And by this measure, she found Mr. Stephens quite ugly indeed. His impertinent, assuming, and arrogant manners destroyed his handsome person. He seemed to enjoy baiting her, reveling in her discomfort. Many of his utterances bordered on disrespectable. She did not like him at all. He was of Mr. Todd's ilk.

Oh, had she more than a few shillings in her coffers, she would have readily turned him away.

The twins rolled their eyes. "Lord, there she goes preaching again," Amelia said.

"Well, if you find Mr. Stephens so to your liking, perhaps you will be kind enough as to keep him and his companion away from the back of the house while I work in the garden." She had to keep up her appearance of gentility and not be caught pulling up vegetables. "But first, remove yourselves from those offensive gowns. What our guests thought of you I shudder to think."

The sisters met this plan with much enthusiasm, except for the order to change their gowns. They simply ignored that part and hurried to the parlor, where they could best keep a view of the stairs, ready to accost the gentlemen should they venture down.

"Miss Estella!" Lottie burst through the scullery door, waving a receipt. "I mailed your letter! I mailed it!" Lottie tossed her arms around her mistress.

"Thank you, my love," Estella said, taking the receipt. "Now, won't you please refill the water in the white and gold rooms? We have some gentleman lodgers."

"Lodgers!" Lottie clapped her hands and dashed off to draw water.

The income Estella earned from two lodgers would hardly stop Mr. Todd but might stave him off a bit longer, giving her time to find more money.

Estella glanced at the receipt. *Please help*, she said in a silent prayer to the Duke of Lucere and then headed to her mother's room. Outside the door, she forced her face into a pleasant countenance, like an actress about to walk on stage to play the role of dutiful, cheerful daughter.

She opened the door. The smell of medicine assailed her nose. Her mother was sitting in her invalid couch. Her back was propped by pillows, and a blue wool blanket lay across her body. Estella and her sisters were mirrors of their mother. Yet, since Mrs. Primrose's heart ailments, the physician had advised "no excitement" and prescribed her draughts that sedated her boisterous spirits. In the last year, she had rapidly aged, now appearing twenty years older than her forty-five years. Her hair was almost the shade of her white cap. Her skin possessed a chalky pallor, and her pale eyes appeared to pop from their shadowed sockets. Estella remembered when her beautiful face was bright and flush, her eyes glittering with merriment.

"My dear, you look tired," her mother said.

"The wind kept me up last night." Estella fibbed to divert the conversation from unpleasantness.

"Ah, you should be in bed, then. Why did you not send a servant?"

"They are busy seeing to the broth and laundry."

The extent to which Estella had lied about the state of the family's situation was shameful. But she had to spare Mama the truth else it would bring on another heart spasm.

"I'm late giving you your draughts." Estella opened a bottle from the side table and poured the recommended amount into a spoon.

Mrs. Primrose allowed her daughter to guide the spoon to her lips. After she had swallowed, she asked, "How is our little 'pin money solution' coming along?" She meant the lodging house. Although her own father had once run an inn, she considered business vulgar upon the marriage into the Primrose family.

"It's doing wonderfully. We have two new boarders today."

"Capital. Soon we can take away our sign and put this sad episode behind us. I'm sorry that you had to take on the burden of overseeing it. I'm quite proud of my beautiful daughter." She squeezed Estella's arm. "A true Primrose, heart and soul."

Estella gave her a weak smile and placed the cork back in the bottle.

Her mother rapped her armrest. "But I fail to understand why you haven't secured a husband yet. I don't know what is the matter with these Lesser Puddlebury gentlemen. Slow dullards, to pass you up. Don't you worry, my dear. Once we no longer need the 'pin money solution,' you shall go to London and find you a fitting husband. Someone deserving of you, who will make you as happy as your father made me."

Estella remained quiet. She was no more going to London than the Prince Regent would turn Methodist. Despite her wild desires to travel to the continent, she feared the farthest she would ever go was up the lane to Mr. Todd's residence.

Her mother chattered on. "And how are Cecelia and Amelia's lessons coming along?"

"They are studying geography today."

"Such kindly, considerate ladies. How well you do with them. Please, send them up so that I might quiz them myself."

"Pray, you must rest now. I shall send the twins up before dinner."

"Very well." Her mother paused. "Estella, my dearest, I do hate to be a bother…" She paused again. "I'm perfectly happy being attended by a servant." In other words, her mother needed her chamber pot emptied but considered it too impolite to ask.

Estella took the pot to the privy and then returned it to its owner.

Then she washed up, donned her gloves and old boots, and trudged out to the garden to dig up carrots and potatoes. Their usual dinner of toast, cheese, and broth would not do. As she rooted about for potatoes, Mr. Stephens's intense, impertinent gaze filled her mind. How his eyes penetrated into her, as if he could see beneath her shift. She shivered. She pulled out a round potato, inspected it, and then tossed it in her bucket. She desperately needed the money, but at the same time, she hoped Mr. Stephens found a position very soon.

She gazed off at the woods rising behind the garden and imagined herself fleeing into their shade, running and running until she reached Italy or Holland. She knew an ocean separated her from the continent, but why worry about such trifling details in wild, liberating fantasies. As her body dug up potatoes and then removed carrots by their stems, her mind roamed quietly through the old European streets as she had read them described in books, stopping into the ateliers or listening to the lovely music in the grand old cathedrals.

* * *

Lucere renewed his vow to be a better man. He would pass the night alone in his bedchamber, provided the rickety home didn't collapse. He would remove to an inn tomorrow. Until then, he would enjoy Estella's pretty face as one enjoyed art in a gallery. At a cold distance.

Yet, at dinner, when Estella spurned him entirely to speak to Harris, an ugly claw of jealousy sank into Lucere's chest. Harris received the soft light of her eyes, all her smiles, even a beautiful silvery laugh. She asked him one question after the next, listening to his answers with an awed expression, as though he were some modern-day Plato.

Lucere received no such inquiries. No solicitations for his opinion. No admiration. He was not even worth a spare look.

Was Estella setting her sights on Harris as her evening's customer? Did she think him more pliable? Well, she would find no luck in that quarter. Harris wouldn't besmirch his love for Catherine with a tart.

Lucere stabbed a potato. Dinner at the Duke of Lucere's Boarding House was hardly up to the Duke of Lucere's standards—just potatoes, carrots, cold mutton, and stale bread. Instead of focusing on the want of food, he tried to capture Estella's attention through her sisters. He casually mentioned that he had lived in London as a tutor to a baron and had often gone to the theaters and that his employer kindly allowed him to attend some balls. Lucere knew all country ladies loved the glamorous world of London, and the twins eagerly leaped on his bait. They implored him to reveal theater and society gossip. He recounted the most scandalous tattle he knew, filled with illicit love affairs and betrayals. The blushing twins begged further lurid details to fuel their giggles.

Estella didn't grace Lucere with even one glance. But he noted that her pleasant façade turned rigid, and she kept a murderous grip on her fork as she continued conversation with Harris about such innocuous things as the weather and the growing seasons of various flowers.

Finally, Lucere could be ignored no longer and broke in. "Aside from lavender-strewn summer fields, Miss Primrose, what else do you enjoy?"

"She enjoys worrying and nagging," Amelia piped up. She and her twin laughed at her weak witticism.

How the beautiful face palls when there is no grace underneath to support it, Lucere thought. He gave the twins a glare. They should take lessons from their elder sister if they wished to succeed in their profession.

"I enjoy traveling," Estella said after a long moment's consideration. Why was knowing what she enjoyed so hard for her to determine?

"Ah!" Lucere said. "And where have you traveled?"

"London and Bath," she supplied.

"That's rather meager travel," Lucere observed.

"I guess it's more of a dream than a reality."

"In your dreams, where do you visit?" Lucere said, oiling his voice.

Her expression turned wistful. "Italy. I desire to see Rome and Venice. I even tried to teach myself Italian before... well, before Grandfather died and... this." She gestured around her. "I daresay I have forgotten every word I learned."

So her grandfather's death had sunk her family into this shameful life. A sad, yet common theme for women with no male to support them. It wasn't fair the disadvantages life dealt women.

"*Sono stato al paese dell'arte e della musica*," he said.

Her lips spread into a bright grin. It caressed him like a warm breeze. "You've been to Italy?" she cried.

"Ah yes, Rome, Venice, and Florence."

She leaned in, suddenly appearing very young. He had assumed she was in her late twenties, but perhaps he was wrong on that count.

"Would you please tell me about them?" she said. "Please. I would love to hear."

Her eyes, sparkling with admiration, fixed on his face. She waited in happy suspense for him to speak. It would take a stronger man than he to deny her anything. All he had were tales from his grand tour. He modified them, turning himself into a poor, wandering Oxford student. He told her about afternoons passed sunning himself outside of San Marco Cathedral, spending evenings in opera houses mesmerized by the voices, walking through fields lined with grapes and olives, roaming at sunset through the vastness of the Coliseum, and drifting in a lovely red-wine haze through the canals of Venice. Her features were aglow with fascination. He felt a strange, light sensation as if he were floating

London's most ravishing courtesans had danced around him for years, hoping for his patronage. This country light-skirts outshone them all. She was too good at her profession. Her pale gaze had the power to make a man think that nothing and no one else mattered in the world but him.

Damn it, he had made a deathbed vow—the most serious of vows—to his dying father to be a better man.

Harris's words echoed, *It is oft acknowledged among gentlemen that a bachelor might enjoy one last dalliance before beginning a lifetime of devotion to one lady.*

Was he truly breaking his vow? In France, they celebrated Carnival before the onset of Lent. This could be his Carnival.

Still he hesitated.

After dinner, Estella placed a bottle on the table and ushered the twins out, making a darling little lesson that proper ladies repair to the drawing room so that gentlemen could enjoy their port.

Enjoy was not a word that Lucere would use to describe drinking the watered-down vinegar. Without Estella, the room returned to its shabbiness. The table linen was stained. One chair was missing an arm. Lucere's spirit sank back into gloominess. He forced himself to empty his glass, probably killing off several vital organs in the process.

Wily Harris opened the window and dumped his poison. "Let us attend the ladies."

The men blew out the candles and hurried away.

In the drawing room, Lucere thought it odd that no other gentleman callers had arrived. Surely, Lesser Puddlebury possessed men of eyesight and natural desire.

He mentioned the dearth of callers, and Estella replied, "As I had said, the summer has left us quite lonely. You are our only lodgers this evening."

He really shouldn't complain to have such singular devotion.

But then the night took a horrendous turn when Estella suggested the twins entertain the gentlemen with songs. One twin played, or more precisely *pounded*, the pianoforte while the other sang, staying a half note and half beat behind her sister. Lucere adored music and played several instruments. He shifted in his chair and quietly tapped his fingers and feet, trying to qualm his desire to yank the music from the twins' hands and stop this sacrilege.

He glanced at Estella to see if she suffered the same agony. She watched her sisters, a glow of pride in her face. Had she no musical sense, or was she blinded by love for her sisters? He hoped it was the latter. He remembered how patiently Catherine watched with the same pride as Lucere had sung the songs he made up for her. The silly ditties of a six-year-old.

I love horses,
I love the color blue,
I love cakes with vanilla cream frosting,
And I love you.

He would have drifted into tender memories of Catherine had not the twins been mercilessly massacring Mozart. When at last they ended that torture session and were preparing to next brutalize Bach with equal vim, Lucere could take no more.

"Let's hear Miss Primrose sing," he quickly inserted, before Amelia or Cecelia could do more damage to his sensibilities. Estella could hardly do worse. And if she did, at least he could seek solace in imagining taking off her garments one by one, until he reached the yet unseen delights beneath.

"Oh, no, no, not me," Estella demurred.

"Estella has a beautiful voice," Cecelia (or Amelia) said.

"Do you sing?" Estella asked Lucere, deflecting the conversation.

Harris piped up—the man had a nasty habit of piping up at unwelcome times. "Mr. Stephens has a fine baritone. In addition to tutoring languages, he is a master of the pianoforte."

Damn it, Harris!

"Do sing," Estella implored. "Please."

The expression on her face was so beguiling that she could have asked him to cut off a finger, and he would have responded, *Which one?*

He sat at the pianoforte and thought for a moment. Outside, the rain was falling, tapping on the windows. He began to play and sing in a quiet voice that complemented the rain.

He glanced at Estella. She appeared spellbound by his voice. Her lips were parted, displaying the edge of her wet, pink tongue. She had changed gowns for the evening, and this one, as tight and worn as the first, afforded a lovely view of her creamy breasts, which rose and fell with her enraptured breath. He deepened his timbre, his desire flowing through the words. She slid forward in her chair, her gaze fixed on his face. She made him feel like a musical god.

He couldn't defeat this woman. Why did he struggle? He was a starving rogue who hadn't known a woman in weeks and who now was trapped in the lair of the most stunning light-skirts in England. His mind flew with rationales. He should just give in to her. Make love until he took her shine away. Until his thirst for her was sated. Then he would make haste to Scotland and chain himself to that saintly German princess.

He continued to sing, using his voice to seduce. He watched her nibble the edge of her lip. Sensual, yet innocent. She made the moment feel brand new, as though she hadn't known dozens of other men. Only him.

She didn't take her eyes from his face. He slowed his tempo to the one he would use when he whispered the lyrics in her ear as he slowly disrobed her, savoring every inch of her silken skin.

Harris cleared his voice, reminding him that there were people present in the room who might not prefer to see Lucere madly frolicking with Estella on the floor. Lucere glanced around, breaking the powerful invisible tie that had kept his and Estella's gazes locked together.

Even the twins weren't giggling, but staring, their jaws flapped open. Lucere quickly ended the song.

"Now I've sung for your pleasure," he said to Estella. "Now you must sing for mine." He slid from the bench and bowed before it, gesturing for her to sit.

"No, I—"

"I insist," Lucere said. Lovers should be generous and reciprocate pleasure. She approached the pianoforte and sat on the bench. "I'm afraid I don't play or sing as well as my sisters. Or you, of course. Your voice is, well, I've never heard anything so wonderful."

"Come now," Lucere said. "Let me be the judge of your talents."

She studied the keys. Lucere remained by the pianoforte, resting his hand on the top so that he might keep her face in his view.

"I do not know an Italian song," she apologized. "Or a German one."

"I assure you that I will love whatever song comes from your lips."

She colored. He enjoyed her touches of feigned modesty. They added to her allure.

She pressed her finger on the middle C and then began to sing *a cappella*. Her voice was quiet, but sweet and smooth as satin. And all his plans of spending the evening frolicking in bed with her ceased.

Dear God, why must she be a light-skirts? Why must she give her beautiful body to other men? Why must she be such a calculating liar beneath the blushes and easy smiles? Why must she sing Catherine's favorite song—the one she sang him to sleep with—in that tender soprano? He could not bear to touch her now.

He pressed his hand on the keys, creating a jarring chord. "Please," he whispered.

She gasped. "Is something wrong? What have I—"

"No, I—" He looked at Harris. The stoic man's eyes were watering. "I'm suddenly very tired," Lucere muttered. "It's been a long day." He bowed and walked from the room, his insides quaking.

CHAPTER FIVE

Did my voice really drive him away?

No doubt, Mr. Stephens, being a learned man, was unimpressed with Estella's low folk song. Alas, of the things that distressed her as she walked in the valley of the shadow of financial death, Mr. Stephens's approval of her voice was rather insignificant. He was a strange man, his moods mercurial, and his words barbed. She didn't know if he spoke in praise or ridicule most of the time.

But he told stories the way her grandfather once did. His words had a mesmerizing cadence, lulling her. He mixed drama and comedy together, grounding it all in sensual details. She could feel the eddy of the gondola on the canal waters and the hollow enormity of the Coliseum.

And when he sang, he lifted her heart from its moorings. She felt as though she drifted high above her worries.

Had not she been sinking under the weight of a mortgaged home, an ailing mother, a failing business, two sisters who needed to be established, and a ruthless suitor, she might have allowed herself the luxury of exposing her heart.

She had heard love was strong, but she doubted it was strong enough for a man to financially ruin himself and inherit three additional females with his intended. She could not conceive of marrying a man so foolish. Nor did she subscribe to the idea of rapturous love that obliterated all good sense.

And he was a poor tutor whom she had known for only a few hours, and for half of those, she hadn't liked him at all.

She gave herself leave to enjoy the fluttering of her heart when he sang. And to allow his stories to take her back to a time when her world wasn't so frightening. But she could not allow her affections to grow for this man. Her love would do neither of them any good.

With his rich, glorious voice fresh in her memory, she extinguished the lamps in the now empty parlor and hummed as she sauntered to the kitchens.

* * *

In the scullery, she found the dishes stacked precariously on the table. Still water waited in the sink, and the sounds of hiccupping sobs filled the room. Estella looked around and then under the tables. "Lottie?"

She followed the sobs to the larder. Lottie was huddled on the floor. Her face was red and swollen from crying. "Oh, Miss Estella, I'm sorry." She held up the remains of a broken plate. "Don't make me leave. I'm sorry."

Estella knelt down and hugged the distraught servant. "Oh, Lottie, I'm never going to turn you out. Ever. It's only a plate. Don't be upset."

"Plates cost money," Lottie stated, taking on Estella's tones.

How their lack of money tainted almost every aspect of their lives.

"Don't you worry about the plate," Estella soothed. "Now go to sleep."

"But the dishes—"

"Good night, Lottie. As your mistress, I'm sending you to bed."

Lottie hesitated, then hugged Estella again. "I love you."

After the servant left, Estella blew out a weary breath and gazed at the mountain of washing to be done. She felt tired down to the marrow of her bones.

Avoiding the task only prolongs the misery.

She donned her apron and picked up a towel. As she scrubbed, she listened to the rain and hummed Mr. Stephens's Italian song. Her mind flew far away from the scullery to a Venetian piazza where she and Mr. Stephens danced.

* * *

Lucere, now stripped down to his shirt, pantaloons, and stockings, sat in Harris's chamber of luxury. Both men stared at the cold grate, lost in old bittersweet memories as the rain pounded the windows. After an hour, Lucere spoke. "I don't mean to be dramatic, but what cruel god has created such ethereal perfection and placed it in a crass light-skirts?"

Lucere wanted Harris to say something like, *Perhaps there is more to Miss Primrose than can be presently known,* or *Perhaps there is a reason for her deception.*

The man just stared at the fire, broken.

Lucere could say nothing to lift the man's despair. He had been the cause of his misery, after all.

"I shall sit glumly in my own chamber now," Lucere said after an hour.

He crossed the hall and had almost passed the threshold to his chamber when he saw something white flash before him. A female giggled and then cried, "A ghost!"

In dramatic fashion, Cecelia or Amelia crumpled at his feet, wearing only a shift and dressing gown.

"What in God's name?" he muttered, kneeling down. "Are you well?" he asked, inquiring more about the state of her senses than her physical body.

"Don't ravish me, phantom," the woman cried. In a flash, her arm was around his neck, yanking him to her waiting lips.

* * *

Estella's lantern lit the dark corridors. It was a little after one, and the house was asleep. Cold wash water had soaked through her apron all the way to her shift. She only wanted to sink deep beneath her piles of quilts, listen to the rain, and drift into a sleep filled with Roman ruins, gondolas, and Mr. Stephens's beautiful voice. What had he done? Filled her head with romantic dreams that would never be realized?

She first saw the two bodies after she crested the stairs. Her initial thought was that her mother had had an accident.

Then she realized the vile truth.

She rushed forward and smashed Mr. Stephens with her foot. "Away from her, you fiend!"

"Bloody hell!" he spat, coming to sit against the wall, holding his side where she had kicked him.

Amelia, wide-eyed with terror, scurried away from her lecherous captor.

"Don't you use that contemptible language in my home, you blackguard!" Estella shouted. She should have known. How sweetly he had turned up this evening, but now she realized his true motivations. She had gardened, cooked, entertained, and cleaned for this gentleman, and he had the nerve to attack her sister?

"How dare you!" she screamed. "How dare you think you can practice your lusty appetites in my home? My genteel home! Get away. Now."

"My lusty… Wait, you are mistaken if you think—"

"I have no minute, no second, no measure of time for a lying cad who thinks he can take advantage of innocent ladies." She held up the lantern, illuminating his handsome face and those dark eyes that had enthralled her not several hours before. "For shame, Mr. Stephens. For shame. My first impression of you was correct. You are a wicked rogue of poor manners and poorer breeding. Truly, sir, you waste your fine voice and your education."

She felt a hand on her arm and whirled around to find Amelia, still traumatized from Mr. Stephens's brutish embrace, and Cecelia. "My poor darlings, you go back to bed. I'll take care of this matter directly."

"But—"

"I said I would take care of this matter. Do not trouble yourselves."

Mr. Stephens dared to speak up. "I believe you are making a hasty and incorrect assumption—"

"No one wants to hear from you, Mr. Stephens. I have caught you red-handed. And I'm not moved by your handsome face."

She strode into his chamber and, using her lantern, located his bag. Mr. Stephens was on his feet now.

"Let us try to calm down," he suggested. Oh, he sounded as patronizing as Mr. Todd. Soon he would say she didn't know her own mind.

"You're angry and not thinking correctly," he said on cue.

She snatched up his bag and jerked open the window. The cold rain blew in on her hot face.

"Put that down now," he commanded in imperial tones.

Who did he think he was to assume such consequence as to order her about?

She gave him that look she usually reserved for her sisters. He instantly softened and held up his palms, carefully approaching her. "I have my important tutor things in that bag. My... my livelihood."

"Very well," she conceded. He could never say she wasn't just, or that she destroyed his living. She gripped his bag and brushed past him out the door.

"Come now," he pleaded, following behind her in the corridor. "It was an accident. You see, she thought I was a ghost." He tried to grab at his bag, but she snatched it away.

"A ghost? Do truly think I would believe such a pathetic lie? You must think I'm an idiot. And my sisters and I are..." She couldn't utter the word prostitute or any of its synonyms. Her tongue and lips refused to form the ugly words. "... women of dubious morals."

"No, I think you are a very clever shrew. As for your morals, I can only judge by you and your sisters' actions. Dubious indeed."

She gasped. The man must have conspired with Mr. Todd, no doubt sent by him to damage her reputation further. "I will not lower myself to speak to you further! You are beneath notice, beneath contempt, beneath—"

Her mother's door opened, and her hollowed, nervous face peered around the wood. "Darling, what is the matter?"

Dear Lord, Estella would not allow Mr. Stephens to bring on one of her mother's heart episodes. Estella halted. Mr. Stephens slammed into her. She forced a pleasant smile and thrust her elbow back, happy to hit his hard rib bones. He stifled a groan.

"It's nothing, Mama," she said in the most calming voice she could muster given the circumstances. "Don't alarm yourself. The new boarder and I are merely playing a little game. I'm sorry if we woke you up. Won't you go back to sleep now and rest?"

Her mother looked at her and then Mr. Stephens.

To his credit, he remained silent.

"Estella," her mother said. "I do not approve of you wandering around the house alone with our gentleman boarders. Have Harold sent for immediately."

"Of course," Estella said, knowing that their manservant had left months ago, after Estella couldn't pay his full wages. Now he was in the happy employment of Mr. Todd.

Her mother slowly returned to her bed. Estella closed her door so her mama wouldn't hear any more of this debacle.

"There," Mr. Stephens said. "Now that we have regained some semblance of rational thought—"

Estella turned and hurried down the stairs with the bag.

"You little vixen!" he cried.

At the bottom of the stairs, she broke into a run, still gripping his bag and the lantern.

He managed to catch up as she opened the front door. She tossed his bag into the rain before he could stop her.

"No!" he protested. "You are being unfair. Will you not even listen to my version of the events?"

She gestured like a butler to the black, wet night. "Good-bye, Mr. Stephens. I regret our brief acquaintance. You may slither back to Mr. Todd now."

"Who is Mr. Todd?"

"Don't you play games with me! I know your nefarious motives. Leave. Go away."

"What in Hades…" Mr. Stephens didn't finish his thought, but ran his hand through his hair. He looked at her and then his bag being rained upon. He muttered something that sounded as if he were cursing the moon and stars. Then he stepped into the wet.

She wasted no time slamming the door, hitting his heel in the process. She snatched the key from the table and quickly locked out the devil.

"Of course," she heard him shout. "Put me out in the rain without even my shoes. How considerate."

Considerate? Considerate was not molesting your landlady's sister after she spent the night washing up from your dinner.

Yet, through her fury, a pang of terror broke through. She needed the money. More anger quickly followed. She was a Primrose, for heaven's sake. She would not compromise the moral course for the sake of vulgar money.

She stomped to the window. "This is a genteel house," she cried through the thick glass. She could see the rain pouring down his face and shoulders. "We are cousins to the fine, upstanding Duke of Lucere. You are mistaken if you think you can take advantage of my sisters or me because we've been reduced to run a lodging house. We may be poor, but we uphold the Primrose family motto of duty, honor, truth, sacrifice, and courage."

"Balderdash!" he spat.

"How dare you! You… you are the vilest man I have ever met. You put Mr.

Todd to shame." She felt positively violent and began to pace the room, the hand not holding the lantern clenching and unclenching. Oh, if she could slap his arrogant, handsome face.

"Well, my lovely dove, I happen to know the Duke of Lucere from Oxford," Mr. Stephens yelled through the window. Water ran off his nose and dripped into his mouth. He shook his head, trying to fling it off, but more fell. "He never mentioned a parcel of Primroses in godforsaken Lesser Puddlepiss. And you've no more corresponded with the duke or spoken with the duchess than I've created a bloody flying ship to the damn sun."

"I told you not to utter vile language in my presence!"

"Well, then don't bald-face lie in mine," he retorted.

She approached the window. "You can just… just… slither back to hell with your scaly brethren."

"Who's uttering the vile language now, my sweet baggage?"

She slapped the glass as if it were his face. He only smiled. "Don't become angry with me because I've guessed your pathetic game of passing yourself off as your betters. No doubt, you can fool the dull-witted inhabitants of Puddlepiss, but I've traveled the world and been in the presence of many great men, including your fine, upstanding Duke of Lucere. You may keep your Primrose motto that you've stolen. I know a conniving swindler when I see one. Albeit the most beautiful one I've ever laid eyes on. Truly, you waste your talent here. You belong in Drury Lane."

She couldn't even form words but released a deep cry born of rich fury. She hit the window with her palm.

He laughed. "You're not hurting anyone but yourself, miss," he had the nerve to say.

Nonetheless, she continued to smack the glass. "You heinous, vicious, hateful monster. You can—"

Someone tapped her shoulder. She whirled around to find Mr. Harris holding a candle, a solemn expression on his face. Her sisters waited behind him. Estella was immediately remorseful to be caught so undignified.

Mr. Stephens's muffled voice penetrated the room. "Make her see reason, Harris."

"I feel that Mr. Stephens may be correct on some small points," Harris said in calm tones. "Miss Cecelia, perhaps you would care to elucidate the situation to your sister." He stepped back, giving her sister audience.

Cecelia's guilt-filled eyes darted about, looking everywhere but at Estella's face. Dread weighted Estella's belly. What had the twins done?

"I-I dared Amelia to kiss Mr. Stephens," Cecelia confessed.

"No, you didn't," Estella replied without thinking. "You couldn't. You would never do something so vulgar and ill-mannered. This cannot be the truth. Who made you say that?"

The twins looked at each other. "I-I pretended that Mr. Stephens was a ghost and fainted before him," Amelia confessed. "And when he knelt down to assist me, I kissed him."

Estella felt like she had received a hard blow to her lungs. She staggered to a chair and grabbed its armrest. Mr. Harris hurried to take her elbow.

"How... how are you my sisters?" she stammered. She could scarce breathe, let alone make words. "How do we share the same blood? Primrose ladies do not behave this way. I—Mama—we taught you better."

"I'm sorry," Amelia muttered in a voice barely heard above the rain.

There was only one thing to be done.

Estella straightened her shoulders and raised her head. Primroses never shrank from doing their duty, no matter how much it pained them. "I do not need the apology. You will wait right here."

Estella strode to the door and opened it. "Mr. Stephens, would you please come in?" she called into the downpour.

"I don't know," he shouted back. "I'm rather afraid of you."

* * *

Lucere stepped just inside the front door. Cold rain dripped from his clothes and hair. His shirt clung to his chest, as did his pantaloons to his love pipe. He watched the ladies' eyes enlarge at the sight. Estella blushed violently. She kept her eyes trained on his face, not on his eyes exactly, but the region around his left ear.

It was her own fault if he wasn't decent to be seen.

"Miss Cecelia and Miss Amelia," she said. "I believe you have something to say to Mr. Stephens."

The twins appeared bereft of speech. They just ogled him.

"Amelia!" Estella cried.

"I'm sorry I pretended you were a ghost and kissed you, but Cecelia dared me," Amelia said, as though her twin had taken control of her body.

Estella stiffened. He realized for the first time in all the great commotion that she wore a faded, wet apron. "And I apologize for calling you vile, a heinous monster, and related to snakes," she said through tight lips.

"I apologize for calling you a 'sweet baggage,'" he conceded.

She waited with one eyebrow arched for a further apology. Unfortunately, he refused to give her satisfaction.

"Please excuse us, Mr. Harris," Estella said at some length. "Cecelia, Amelia, please go to your chambers. Or do I need to dare you to? Perhaps I should dare you to have proper manners as well?"

Lucere couldn't stop his bark of laughter. He received a vicious glower from Estella.

He had to admit, she was glorious when she was angry. His mind ventured somewhere very lurid, where she straddled his naked body and turned all that anger into desire-fueled vigor.

"Mr. Stephens, I would like to speak with you," she said. "*Alone.*"

Estella lifted a brow. She mustn't have missed Lucere's start of surprise.

"Why don't you dry yourself?" she said in saccharine, almost seductive tones, and then added, "And I'll retrieve our family Bible."

CHAPTER SIX

In Lucere's chamber, Harris dressed his master as Lucere checked on the state of his signet ring and diamond jewelry for his German princess. As he inspected the diamonds, he thought how lovely they would appear on Estella. Her pale coloring and glittery eyes—especially when she was angry—would complement them nicely. But then, Estella could make a necklace strung of pebbles and rubbish appear beautiful.

"Wasn't she stunning?" he told Harris. "And the fire in her eyes? I felt it all the way down to my, well, love apparatus."

"She is very formidable when crossed," the man conceded, straightening the shoulders on Lucere's coat. "Might I suggest a little humility when dealing with her now? Perhaps make no mention of your love apparatus."

"Good God, Harris, you must think me a simpleton indeed. I wouldn't dream of mentioning the old merrymaker at this juncture." But he couldn't leave Harris with peace of mind. "Unless, of course, she were to touch upon the subject."

Lucere found Estella sitting on the sofa in the parlor, hugging a Bible to her chest. A pile of letters rested in her lap. The burning candles on the side table cast her face in golden light. She had brushed her hair into a tight bun and removed her apron. Tension, imbued with hurt and sadness, charged the air. It made him swallow any comic, sardonic comments he would have normally made on such an occasion.

He sat carefully beside her, leaving a full three-inch gap between their bodies, which she increased to eight or so by scooting down. She brushed an errant strand of hair behind her ear, opened her Bible, and placed it in the space between them.

Nothing akin to having a Bible for a chaperone, Lucere quipped to himself.

On the page was penned a family tree. She moved her fingers along the branches. "This was my great-uncle, the eighth Duke of Lucere." Her finger ran across the page, past five of the duke's siblings. "This is my grandfather Lord Maxim."

Good God! She was The Despicable Uncle's granddaughter!

Although a great-uncle to Lucere, Lord Maxim was known to every family member as The Despicable Uncle—a libertine of such low character that he would appall the very devil. One did not bring up The Despicable Uncle to his mother or grandmother unless in close proximity to smelling salts. And one certainly did not mention Lord Maxim in polite society. The exploits of today's most-hardened London rakes (Lucere, Starlingham, and Mowne) paled to Lord Maxim's reprehensible achievements. Lucere's great-grandfather had exiled him from the family. His portrait removed from the gallery. All ties severed from the notorious rogue.

Naturally, Lucere was compared to The Despicable Uncle.

Estella, however, clearly didn't remember the man the way society did. She wore a misty smile as she spoke of him. "My father died shortly after the twins were born. We moved into this home with my grandparents. Grandpapa was the most kind, loving man. I do not know a better gentleman.

"Truly?" Lucere said, unable to hide his incredulity.

Estella waxed on. "He always hid treats for me in his pockets. For my seventh birthday, he had a miniature cart made for me, so small it could be driven by goats. I drove all around Lesser Puddlebury." She chuckled. "And how he flirted with Grandmama. He adored her."

As he gazed at her lovely profile, this revelation had a different effect than he would have anticipated. Instead of feeling shock or even disgust, a primitive possessiveness filled him: She was his forever. They shared the same blood. He could never lose her now.

Why did he feel this way? For God's sake, she ran a lodging house and traced her line back to the family villain. For an entire day, he had assumed with good reason that she was a light-skirts. He couldn't introduce her to his mother or bring her around to the respectable drawing rooms of London.

Estella continued on, unaware of the epic, earth-shifting emotions he was suffering. "Grandpapa loved a fine joke, but about the Primrose family name he was always very serious. If ever I got in trouble as a child, which was a great deal, mind you, I was rather a spirited child."

"I can well believe it," he said, remembering the fire in her face.

She turned her head to look at him. Her dreamy smile bathed him like the summer sun.

"He would say, 'You are a Primrose, young lady. Primrose Princesses—he called me a princess—do not hide pigs in their bedchamber.'"

"You hid a pig in your bedchamber?"

"To save her from slaughter. I even gave Lucie—yes, I named her after the Duke of Lucere, shhh, don't tell your acquaintance—a robe to sleep in. But she was a chubby, happy thing and didn't fit in it. So, I took one of Mama's ball gowns. It suited her quite nicely."

"Very thoughtful of you."

"So considerate." She laughed. He fought the urge to touch her small ear and let his finger travel down the line of her jaw.

"What happened to Lucie?" he asked.

"I cried and cried and then cried some more to Grandpapa. He relented and told me Lucie would be mine, but I had to take care of her else we would have Lucie for Easter dinner. I daresay he didn't think I was up to the task."

"Were you?"

She raised her chin. "Yes. Faithfully, every day. Wading in the mud to feed her. I'm happy to say that Lucie died of old age."

"You are truly awe-inspiring."

Her face fell. She must have thought he was making jest of her.

"I'm not trifling with you, Miss Primrose. You have a lovely heart."

She continued to gaze at him with suspicion and then edged farther away. She picked up one of the franked letters in her lap and held it near the candle so that he could read his name inscribed in his secretary's neat hand.

"I have recently begun to correspond with the duke." Her shoulders sloped. "Pray, in truth, I enjoy a correspondence with his secretary."

Lucere had nothing to say. He had inherited his father's secretary, Richard Fellows, and, like his father, trusted Fellows, imprudently it seemed, to alert him only to important matters.

"What—what do you write to his secretary?"

Her face darkened. "The duke is very busy. But he is a generous man, I-I'm given to understand. But you know the Duke of Lucere from Oxford. You must know of his benevolent and kind nature. You must."

She appeared to be imploring him for reassurance of the duke's character, desiring Lucere to affirm all the good qualities that she had endowed her cousin.

What had she written him about? Damn Fellows. He and his secretary would enjoy a tête-à-tête upon Lucere's return to London. From now on, every little word Estella penned would go directly to him. In fact, every incoming correspondence would pass his desk, in case other relatives were being as poorly treated as she'd been.

"My impression of the duke"—Lucere carefully chose his words—"is that he is a man of many faults—many stupid, careless, horrible faults. But, upon my last meeting with him, the duke was making strides to be worthy of his title.

I feel he wants to be a... a better man. A much better man."

His words did little to reassure his newfound cousin. In fact, she made a forlorn-sounding squeak.

"And... and you should know that I have spoken to the duchess," she said. "It was years ago. Very well, if you must know, I was six. I was visiting London with my grandparents—remember, my London travel I told you about."

"Ah yes." Why did this little admission break his heart? Had she been trapped in Puddlepiss her entire life?

"My grandpapa and I were strolling in Hyde Park when he said, 'Ho now, there is the Duchess of Lucere!' He hurried me over and presented me. I was so nervous when I performed the curtsy. I wanted to be perfect, for the duchess was the most regal, most majestic lady I had ever seen. And the duke—the current Duke of Lucere—was there. He was a boy, of course." Her face tensed as she peered into her memories. "I remember he looked rather sad, which I thought was odd. Why should a future duke be sad? He held a kite, and I asked if he wanted to fly it, hoping to cheer him up. It was a beautiful kite." She said no more, leaving the story hanging like an unfinished song, the chord sequence unresolved.

But he knew how it had ended that day in the park. Catherine had died a year before. As he'd strolled along the paths behind his mother and new nurse, he had felt lost, despondent, and, most of all, guilty. He remembered the young girl in blue frocks so clearly. How readily she had smiled, contrasting with his gloominess. He had wanted to give her his kite and run with her. But then his mother tugged his arm. "Come, my lord, we shall be late for callers," she said, refusing to acknowledge the shameless interlopers who dared to claim their acquaintance.

So that had been Estella and The Despicable Uncle all those years ago.

Estella collected her letters and her Bible. "I'm not a so-called bald-faced liar, but I did bend the facts. That is unworthy of a Primrose, and I'm very sorry. I hope you will accept my apologies." She rose.

"Wait!"

He knew he should reveal his true identity, but he hesitated. She might slap his face, for years and years of abandonment. For letters he didn't return. For the kite they never flew together. He couldn't tell her the truth in the same day he had mistakenly thought her a low prostitute and treated her as such.

He fell to his knees and seized her elbow. "I'm sorry that I questioned your morals. I'm sorry that I called you a swindler. I'm sorry that I acted like an ars—a horse's backside. I'm humbly sorry. Please forgive me."

She gazed at him, her brows lifted, lips parted. He must have appeared crazed in his desperation for mercy, because she broke into laughter.

"I admit, you were very entertaining," she said.

"I must be good for something." Then he blurted, "Why aren't you married? You're beautiful. You are the most ravishing lady I have ever seen." Humiliation and self-loathing had loosened the old tongue. If she thought him impertinent before, now she would consider him a lovesick bedlamite.

"You think I'm ravishing?" She spoke in the same voice she might have used to ask, *You think fairies exist and live in your hat?*

"Exquisite. Stunning. You should have been shackled long before now and to a very protective and jealous husband."

The laughter in her eyes vanished. She withdrew her hand from his. "It's a difficult situation."

"A secret love?" He came to his feet. "Hidden engagement?" He was being impolite, but he was curious. She was a mystery he was determined to solve.

After all, she was his second cousin. He had familial duty toward her.

"I wish it were the case." She appeared tired, her face aging years in a space of a few seconds. "Let me make you some honey and mint tea."

"That won't be necessary. Why don't you rest?"

She shook her head. "I've kept you in the rain, and I don't want you to catch a chill. It will take only a few minutes."

"Thank you, but truly I really wish to sleep now."

"Well then, please bundle yourself up tonight. There are extra blankets in the wardrobe. Do you require anything else for your health and comfort?"

Lucere stifled the reply he wanted to make, which was, *Yes, I require holding you close to me.* Instead, he said, "No, thank you."

"Good night, then."

She performed a bob-like curtsy and strolled toward the door, stifling a yawn. He didn't want to part from her. Something else needed to be said. The song hadn't reached its coda.

"Miss Primrose."

She turned.

"You truly are the most beautiful lady I have ever met. And not just your face. A gentle, warm light shines around you. Rest assured that I don't say this in any way to trifle with your affections or make you feel beholden to me. I'm very sincere when I say you are aptly named, a radiant star."

The smiles she had given him before were nothing compared to the loving thing that curved her mouth—reminiscent of Catherine's tenderness. "You are very kind." She stared at him a moment longer, then slipped from the room.

Lucere stormed into Harris's chamber. He gripped Leo's genealogical charts. Under Lord Maxim were question marks for offspring. No one had cared to learn what happened to the man.

Harris lay in bed, reading by candlelight a book of Marcus Aurelius's philosophy. He rested the tome on his chest. "Do you require my assistance, Your Grace?"

"You knew, didn't you?" Lucere held up the charts. "You knew she was related to Uncle Maxim."

"I had an inkling."

"And you suggested I seduce her!? A last dalliance before I met the princess. Good God, what were you thinking?"

"I was mistaken," was the man's unhelpful reply.

Lucere paced. Harris rarely made a mistake. Why did Lucere suddenly feel like a puppet?

"Did you tell her that you are the duke?" the manservant asked.

"No, I couldn't. Not yet. My family has been ignoring hers for years. And Fellows hasn't been forwarding her letters. I couldn't admit to being the heartless villain that, well, I am."

"You must speak to Mr. Fellows."

Harris was being unhelpfully obvious again.

"Good night, Harris." Lucere stalked toward the door. "And please let me know if you have any new inklings before I humiliate myself further," he said over his shoulder.

Harris raised his book. "Don't tell her your true identity just yet."

CHAPTER SEVEN

Estella woke with a jolt in the cold morning. She had dreamed that the small brook threading through the nearby woods had flooded. When she opened the front door, foaming swift-moving currents had engulfed everything, forming a swirling ocean around her home. A huge wave rolled above the treetops. She tried to run but couldn't move. Her scream made no sound. The wave had crashed on her, dragging her under. Swirling around her were household items such as dishes, petticoats, and candles. She looked up, seeing the sunlight breaking the surface of the water. But when she swam to the light, a gruff hand had grabbed her ankle and pulled her down, down into the black, frigid depths to drown.

Her heart hammered in her chest. She drew her knees to her chin and rocked herself, humming Mr. Stephens's lovely Italian song until her heart calmed and the break of dawn fired behind the trees.

She quickly made her toilette with cold water. She didn't bother to unbraid her hair but left it hanging long. She could pin it up in the kitchens. She donned her stays and dress, leaving them open in the back for Lottie to tie and fasten.

Then she trudged downstairs to the kitchens where the tea waited, that life-giving nectar.

Thinking herself alone, she vulgarly yawned as she opened the breakfast room door to find the wall sconces burning and Mr. Stephens holding a steaming teapot. The scents of cooked eggs, bread, and butter filled the room.

"Good morning," he said in cheerful tones as he poured a cup. "You are most beautiful."

She only stared at him in hazy confusion. Her eyes squinted as though she were peering at the bright sun. Was she still asleep? Then she remembered she was hardly dressed. "Oh heavens!" she cried. "Lottie! Help!"

Lottie hurried through the opposite door with a basket of muffins. "Miss Primrose, did you know boys could cook? Mr. Harris says that cooks in London are Frenchie men!"

"Lottie, please help me," Estella squeaked.

In the corridor, Lottie laced up her mistress, fastened her dress, and treated her to a fat hug. There was nothing to be done with Estella's hair but keep it in a braid.

When she reentered the parlor, Mr. Stephens said, "You look even more beautiful than before."

She smiled, flustered. "You and Mr. Harris need not have done this." She gestured to the table. She was embarrassed that the gentlemen realized the extent of her reduced conditions. "You're our guests."

Before Mr. Stephens could answer, Mr. Harris entered and bowed. "Good morning, Miss Primrose." He was crisply dressed and held two papers, which must have been procured in town that morning when buying the eggs. "Care to read?" he asked.

When she politely declined, he placed one paper by the chair at the center of the table and then walked around to the other side.

"Let me wake my sisters."

Mr. Stephens waved his hand. "Let them come down as they will." He pulled back the chair for her at the head of the table.

A warm shiver radiated from where their skin touched when he helped her sit. He smelled woodsy, like pine and cedar in winter. She almost came undone when he simply said, "There now," in a low, whispery voice.

Then he and Mr. Harris took their places, picking up their papers in unison. Mr. Stephens was an animated reader. His paper rattled, and he screwed his face in the most disgusted, yet comical, expression. Every few seconds, he would utter something along the lines of, "Good God, Harris, England is slipping into Hades and taking half the world with it. We are selling our souls to the devil for cheap wheat?"

To which Mr. Harris would remark, "So it would seem."

Estella hid her smile behind her teacup. How lovely to be allowed to think of something different than household accounts and village gossip.

She could no longer remain silent when Mr. Stephens remarked, "Listen to this inane speech old Bippy—er, Lord Cylesford made in the House concerning the reform of boroughs. Sheer ludicrousness."

"You are against the reform of an openly acknowledged corrupt system?" she asked.

Mr. Stephens lowered his paper and scrutinized her with a rather imperial expression, no doubt seeking to intimidate her. She would not bear it. Though her cheeks heated under his study, she kept her gaze level on his.

"Those boroughs are bought and sold at a fair price," he said in a haughty tone. "I believe you are interfering with an Englishman's rights and our market." He was ribbing her, an invitation to dance, so to speak, in the conversation.

She accepted. "Ah, rights for the rich, landowning, British *male* citizen."

"Of course, the male citizenry, who have the most stake in the British government and its policies, should have the most say."

"Ah, because poor women, reduced to workhouses with their small infants, have no stake at all in English laws," she quipped. "Nothing the government does affects her, so she should have no say in its policies or politicians."

"Precisely," he said, ignoring her sarcasm. "Our opinions are in harmony."

"They certainly are not!"

And so the conversation exploded between them. She knew from Mr. Stephens's smirk-like smile that he was enjoying baiting her, but it felt lovely to be outside her little shell of worry, to express her opinions to someone who would listen and encourage her, albeit under the guise of disapproval.

Though she didn't admit it in the midst of their mock battle, she was impressed by his detailed knowledge of politics and policy.

Their conversation was abruptly interrupted by the arrival of Amelia and Cecelia. Their eyes widened when they saw the table… and their sister merrily laughing.

Mr. Stephens refrained from further political discussion. For the remainder of breakfast, he directed questions at her sisters. A "game of knowledge" he called it, and he kept careful score. Her sisters had to list the continents, conjugate irregular French verbs, and perform increasingly hard mathematical problems. Estella wanted to sink under the table at how poorly she had neglected her sisters' education. Several times she tried to change the subject, but Mr. Stephens kept her sisters enrapt in his game, letting them try to outwit the other. No doubt, after years of being a tutor, he knew how to engage his pupils.

His being enormously handsome, and the twins being sixteen, also had its charms.

Upon finishing his breakfast, Mr. Stephens rose and set his linen on the table. "Come, Miss Amelia and Miss Cecelia, let us begin our first tutoring session."

So that was his game.

"No, Mr. Stephens." Estella shot from her chair. "You are our guest. You needn't feel you must tutor my sisters." She wanted to say that she would exchange his tutoring services for his lodging, but she desperately needed the money.

He paused for a moment to consider her. "I must do something to fend off the tedious boredom of Lesser Puddlebury," he replied in an off-putting voice.

She blinked. "Oh."

He turned, ending their conversation.

* * *

She and Lottie cleared the dishes with Mr. Harris's assistance. Lottie was enamored of the idea of French cooks, and Mr. Harris kindly regaled the simpleton with tales of pear tarts and almond cheesecakes.

Estella left Lottie to wash up and brought breakfast to her mother. As Estella helped Mama dress, she was required to tell more about last night's rowdy game, especially of their handsome guest. There was a glitter in her mother's eye as she asked the particulars of the gentleman and if he was the cause of Estella's heightened loveliness that morning.

Estella embarrassingly blushed more when she assured her mother that he was not. "He is but a tutor," she said, trying to put her mother off the idea of an establishment between them.

"But if you truly loved him, it would be no matter," was her mother's annoying reply. She was supposed to say something about him being beneath a Primrose and then not mention him again. Instead, she continued to badger her daughter about Mr. Stephens until Estella found emptying the chamber pot a relief.

After seeing to her mother's comforts, Estella picked up the sheets that required mending and repaired to the parlor, where Mr. Stephens worked with her sisters at the table.

He had devised a clever game called "Going to Almack's," which the twins played with great relish. The girls had to give him their bonnets, gloves, and cloaks. They could earn their garments back one by one if they answered his questions correctly. If one of them dare giggled, they lost their Almack's voucher and all the accessories they had earned back.

Mr. Stephens was so humorous. If a sister missed a question, he would exclaim that the Prince Regent was appalled at her ignorance and she could not make her curtsy to the queen.

The twins had lost their adolescence sullenness, although the giggling habit was difficult to overcome. Even Estella found herself giggling at Mr. Stephens's clever quips. He shook his head. "Not you too, Miss Primrose."

The twins played the game with gusto and managed to learn a great deal without realizing that they were. Estella enjoyed watching their happiness. It had been so long since joy filled this home. She felt at any moment she would look up and find her grandfather at the threshold.

How long would Mr. Stephens stay, and how hard would it be to let him go? He caught her watching him and smiled. The edges of his eyes crinkled. Her heart lifted, wanting to leave its cage of bones and fly to him.

"There now, Miss Primrose, your sisters don't know Pythagoras's theorem. Can you help them?"

"Oh, I'm afraid I can't," admitted Estella. "I think I used it once."

"Nooo!" cried Mr. Stephens. "Must I tutor you as well?" He seemed rather pleased by this prospect, and in truth, Estella would have loved to learn. She had had to drop her studies and help her mother when she had turned fifteen.

"La!" Cecelia exclaimed, happy that her bossy elder sister missed a question. "What shall happen to her, Mr. Stephens? I know, she's received an infamous set-down from our great cousin the Duke of Lucere. That will vex her." She looked at Estella. "Now, you are too ashamed to attend Almack's again. You must give Mr. Stephens your thimble, as you have no finery."

Estella colored and shifted her sewing work about, remembering Mr. Stephens's acquaintance with the duke. "Our cousin would never do something so cruel. He is a Primrose."

Mr. Stephens's head jerked up. She couldn't decipher the curious look he gave her.

"Primrose, cabbage rose," Cecelia taunted. "I think the duke is horrid. If he was such a wonderful cousin, he would acknowledge us. He would invite us to London."

"What is that old story about the troll guarding the bridge?" Amelia asked. "Well, our cousin is a troll guarding London Bridge. Never mind dull geography lessons and such, we could find husbands fast enough if we could get to London."

"My dears, Mr. Stephens is known to our cousin," Estella explained, to stop further disparagement of the man.

The twins' faces lit. The duke, who was an ogre not a half a minute ago, became the most charming and handsome man in all England.

"Is he really as satirical as the journals say?" Cecelia cried, rising from her chair. "Will one clever cut from him destroy a person's standing?"

Mr. Stephens blinked.

"Does he really have the physique and face of Adonis?" asked Amelia. "Did he truly seduce all the pretty ladies of the Theatre Royal?"

"Amelia, that is not proper discussion!" Estella cried. "Apologize, at once."

Estella's words were unheeded. "And his friends, the Moon and Stars," said Cecelia. "Do you know them?"

"Disreputable rakes, the lot," replied Mr. Stephens, his lips thinned. "I would stay away from them and their kind."

"I think rakes are captivating." Cecelia capped her words with a wistful sigh, Mr. Stephens's wise counsel ignored. She began to dance around the room, swishing her gown. "I want to marry a rake."

"Me too," agreed Amelia, joining her sister's dance.

Estella bowed her head. This was her fault. Had she more time to see to her sisters' moral improvement, the twins wouldn't dare spout such nonsense.

Before she could lecture, Mr. Stephens stepped in.

"No young lady of any sense or proper manners would want a rake. They are selfish monsters, incapable of love. They care nothing for the feelings of others and only for their own pleasure. No, you should desire a kind, rational husband who will endeavor to treat you with respect and tend to your comfort and well-being."

"Thank you, Mr. Stephens," Estella said.

"But such gentlemen are dull," protested Cecelia.

For some reason, her sister's words set Estella aflame. She jabbed her needle into the sheet. "How dare you say that?" she cried. "I very much wish I could marry a kind man who treated me with respect instead of... of..." She swallowed as all eyes turned to her.

She had gone too far.

Mr. Stephens was on his feet, coming to her. "Miss Primrose, you are distressed." He slid beside her and grasped her hand. "What is this? Tell me at once."

The pressure of his touch was so reassuring. She yearned to lean into his chest like a small child wanting to hide under the covers to protect herself from the terrors in the night. But she couldn't allow the humble man, so poor that he had to seek lodging from her, to become entangled in her staggering financial problems. She extracted herself from him and gathered her sewing. "I must see to Lottie." She walked away, her heart thundering.

Behind her, she could hear the twins begging to resume the game. One of them said something that caused them both to explode into twitters.

"Giggles!" Mr. Stephens's voice boomed. He sounded almost angry. "You are both banned from Almack's for the entire season. No rakish husbands for either of you. Now go help your worried sister and learn some gratitude."

* * *

Estella made a point to avoid Mr. Stephens for the remainder of the day, which wasn't difficult considering the amount of work that needed to be done. However, she received some unexpected assistance. The twins joined her. Mr. Stephens's admonishment had shamed them into obedience. She told her sisters to return to their studies or music, that they must be the ladies she couldn't be, but they insisted on helping. She sent them to read to their mother. Then she climbed into the attic and took down the clothes that had been hung to dry. In the kitchens, she ironed petticoats and table linens. It was hot, hard, and mindless work, and her thoughts soon flowed back to Mr. Stephens. Yesterday, as she'd cleaned dishes, she had imagined innocently dancing with him. But now she knew how an inkling of his touch felt, and she wanted more. Much more. She tried to keep her thoughts virtuous, but they kept straying to a fantasy of being nestled deep in his safe embrace, his mouth descending down, down,

down to meet her receptive lips. How would his kiss feel? How would he taste? How would his powerful chest—that she remembered so vividly under his wet shirt last night—feel against her breasts?

The acrid scent of burning cotton assailed her nose. She yanked up the iron to find an ugly brown stain on her second-best shift. And she had only three.

"You deserved that." She clicked her tongue. "Now, no more fancies or you won't have any clothes fit to wear." Yet, not a minute later, she was snuggled in his imaginary arms again as he whispered that he would make everything well. That she didn't have to be strong for everyone.

CHAPTER EIGHT

Mr. Harris excused himself to his bedchamber after dinner, explaining to Estella that he was fatigued. She asked if he required any tea or medicine to help him sleep. He declined. As she walked to the kitchens to help Lottie, Estella thought how Mr. Stephens was lucky to have such a considerate friend. She wished she had a confidant, well, aside from the Duke of Lucere's unfeeling secretary.

After helping Lottie scrape the pots and then seeing to her mother's needs, Estella headed for the drawing room. The corridors echoed with her sisters singing in harmony. She began to tiptoe and hid just outside the drawing room threshold, so she could watch the performance without disturbing it. Mr. Stephens sat at the pianoforte with her sisters standing to his right. Two candles burning on the pianoforte bathed the faces of the singers and player in gold light. The scene looked like an illustration in a journal.

"Miss Amelia, has B-flat harmed you in such a manner that you hold a grudge and refuse to acknowledge it?" Mr. Stephens said, unaware of Estella. "Listen, it's a chromatic scale." His fingers glided easily over the keys. "You are going down a half note at a time. B, B-flat, A. Become dearest friends with B-flat, Miss Amelia. Overcome your differences. Now let's try again."

The previous evening she had thought him a reprehensible blackguard, possessing a scorching caustic tongue, and now she wondered at how patiently he helped her sisters. First impressions could be so terribly wrong, and the best parts of some people waited under the surface. He gave the twins a lead note, and they sang another beautiful line of harmony. Estella clapped her hands.

"That was lovely, my dears. And Mr. Stephens, you are a brilliant tutor. A true master."

He swung quickly around. He said nothing, but studied her. His jaw worked. Dots of light glowed on the surface of his shiny dark eyes.

"I'm sorry. I didn't mean to give you a start," she said.

"Well, you did." He patted the bench beside him. "For punishment, you must sing in Italian."

"What? I don't know any Italian songs. And you don't enjoy my singing."

"You are quite mistaken." He held up a graceful finger. "I adore your voice. In fact, it reminds me of my favorite person from my boyhood, and you want to learn Italian. So we shall both be gratified if you sing."

"You are very persuasive." She sat down, and he slid closer.

"Now I'm going to sing the line, and then you repeat what I sing."

The instructions were easy, but Estella couldn't follow them. She was too distracted by his pine-and-cedar scent filling her nose and the hot quivers that rushed over her skin every time their shoulders rubbed together. And worse, all during this little electrical storm, Mr. Stephens was saying, "Round your lips when you make the O sound. Your lips are not round enough. Watch mine." But studying his lips, which she had daydreamed of kissing all day, only rendered her incapable of making any sound at all.

When he had to reach for a G in the bass clef, his arm brushed against her breasts. She felt as though an explosion happened beneath her skin. And rather than edging away to a safe distance, as a proper lady should, she strained forward, hoping for another low note, her nipples erect.

What was wrong with her? Had she lost all propriety? Yesterday she had given herself permission to innocently enjoy the gentle heart-fluttering his music aroused, but now the feelings he had awakened were dangerous and rushing up like a spring from the fertile ground.

"Miss Primrose, it's your turn to sing the line," he said.

Oh dear, what was she supposed to sing? She remembered none of his words and melody, just his lips making the kissable O shape and the wild current running between where their bodies touched. He gazed at her, waiting. His dark eyes seemed to have the power to pierce her skin. Could he see inside her to that hot throb between her legs?

She bolted up. "I-I wish to play cards now!"

He blinked, surprised, and drew his hands off the keys. "Yes, of course. I'm sorry I thought you wanted to learn Italian. I didn't mean to make you feel obliged."

"You didn't. I…" What did she say? *I want to kiss you so desperately that I'm afraid of myself.* "I enjoy cards very much."

Cards were safe. They didn't require touching or asking others to look at their lips. Her heart returned to its normal rhythm as she played. She laughed at Mr. Stephens's comic and blatant attempts to cheat because Cecelia was beating them all so soundly. Again, she felt the sensation that she might look up and see her grandfather. They played until the candles had almost burned down and the twins were falling asleep over their hands. No one wanted to leave their warm circle for the cold emptiness of their bedchambers.

But alas, she needed to put an end to the night if she was to have enough energy to face the next day. Mr. Stephens escorted Amelia to the stairs with Cecelia and Estella following behind him. Then he let the twins continue up to their rooms, while he lingered below, holding a sputtering candle. The flame reflected in those shiny, penetrating eyes that could cut through skin and bone. A gentle smile played on his mouth.

She had an urge to wrap her arms around him and cry unabashedly like Lottie, *I love you.*

What? She couldn't truly love him! That was ridiculous. No one of sense would fall in love in a matter of two days. She had been starved for laughter and happiness for so long she fancied herself in love.

She didn't know what to do. Kiss him good night? Embrace him? The air in the small space between them was saturated with crackling tension. She felt as if he wanted to say something but refrained. At length she jabbed out her hand. "Thank you, Mr. Stephens, for a perfect day. Simply perfect."

He raised her offered hand to his mouth and slowly kissed her, letting his lips linger. Estella could not contain her embarrassing gush of breath.

She needed to leave, or she would find herself in danger. Or, to be more accurate, *he* would be in danger of her roiling desire.

"Pardon me, I must check, er, something." She backed up, turned, and missed the door, instead slamming into the wall. *Ouch!*

"Estella," he whispered after her as she fled, but she dared not answer.

She dashed to the kitchens. She detested cleaning dishes, but at the moment, she desired nothing more than to vigorously scrub something, as though she could wash away her scary yearnings.

She could not fall in love with a man she couldn't marry.

No man of sense would sink his livelihood and put himself in debtor's prison for a lady. He wouldn't take a wife who carried with her an enormous load of debt, two unmarried sisters, and an ailing mother. Estella was begging for a broken heart to add to her mountain of troubles.

To her dismay, she found all the pots and dishes were put away. Lottie played with a string coiled between her fingers by the warm oven. "Mr. Harris helped me clean," she said.

That sly man! He wasn't fatigued at all.

Now Estella had nothing to do but lie in bed and torture herself with fancies of her and Mr. Stephens fondling each other's bared bodies as their gondola drifted beneath the lovely Venetian bridges and starlit night.

* * *

Lucere didn't sleep. He prowled like a nocturnal cat around his bedchamber.

His tender emotions for Estella were coming too quickly, over vaulting themselves. He and Estella would only hurt themselves if they continued this dangerous course. He needed to tell her the truth of his identity. The revelation would erect a cold wall between their unequal stations. It would destroy her unguarded, easy smiles and laughter, which made him feel as though he had woken up from years of sleeping.

He heard a quiet knock at the door. "Your Grace."

"Yes, Harris."

The man entered.

"I guess you heard me thinking," Lucere said.

"Precisely."

Lucere played silent chord progressions on the surface of his commode. "I've got to tell her tomorrow that I'm the duke. This deception cannot endure."

Harris remained quiet, the pregnant silence laden with meaning.

Lucere flung up his arms in frustration. "Just say it, Harris. Be frank. Be forthright. Bloody well try."

"Very well." He sank his huge frame in the dainty chair by the writing desk. "Miss Primrose does not need the Duke of Lucere, but Mr. Stephens. She is afraid of the future. If you reveal that you are the duke, you will distance her with your consequence. Any free interchange will be silenced. But most importantly, she will lose her true friend. If you want to help Miss Primrose, remain her confidant for a while longer and have the Duke of Lucere help from a distance."

"Some would say that what you are proposing is immoral."

"That depends entirely upon the perspective, Your Grace."

"Good God, talking to you feels like reading *Gulliver's Travels* over and over. It was trying enough the first time. So what is the perspective, the horse's or the yahoo's?"

"Are you the Duke of Lucere or Mr. Stephens? She should learn the real man beneath the superficiality of names and titles."

Lucere paced a moment and then stopped at the window, peering out at the black country night dotted with hundreds of stars. "But therein lies the problem. Mr. Stephens is finding himself rapidly succumbing to her allurements, which seem without end. I'm in danger, Harris. True danger."

"This may be a problem," Harris said, rising. He strolled to the door and paused. "Or it may not."

Lucere spun around. "I don't even want to contemplate the meaning of those words. I cannot marry a woman who maintains a lodging house, nor can I take such an honorable, kind woman as Miss Primrose as a low mistress. I made a vow to my father—" He held up his palm before Harris could point out the obvious. "Yes, Miss Primrose *is* my cousin, but also the grandchild of the most notorious rake in family, maybe even British, history. No one in polite society will acknowledge her. My mother and sisters will have no scruple cutting her."

"A brutal dilemma, indeed," Harris replied calmly. "Let us hope then that the Duke of Mowne's most unfortunate wound heals quickly, and we shall continue our sojourn to Scotland to meet your German princess, who had the great happenstance to be born to the proper parents. Perhaps you will develop such a violent passion for Her Highness that you will quickly forget your tender feelings for the worthy Miss Primrose—no doubt born of your dull entrapment in Lesser Puddlebury. Thus you are saved a decision that would otherwise characterize your courage and character." Harris opened the door and then gave another dramatic pause. Really, the man should be on stage. "But I merely state what are probably your own thoughts." With this final pronouncement, Harris made his grand exit into the wings.

Lucere stared at the now-closed door and muttered, "I need a new manservant."

CHAPTER NINE

Lucere's anxious mind turned the problem over and over through the night. When he finally succumbed to sleep in the early morning hours, he had no resolution. Nor did he possess one when he awoke three hours later.

The answer arrived as he was shaving by candlelight and nicked his jaw. He tried to contain the gushing blood on a handkerchief, but the stain spread. That was when he decided he would tell her. He was being selfish by refusing to accept the pain he would cause her.

He came downstairs with grim resolve. As he was placing the teapot and Harris's scones—really, the man seemed to revel in the kitchens, especially how he carried on about French chefs—on the breakfast table, she stepped in. The morning light glowed around her pale hair like an angel's halo. She smiled that loving, Catherine-like smile that shattered his heart into splinters and said, "Good morning, Mr. Stephens."

Thus, he spent another day as Mr. Stephens.

Then another and another, because she was the most fascinating female he had ever encountered. He knew he should tell her the truth, but she was like a wild creature nervously approaching his outstretched hand for food. Any quick or false motion, and she would scurry away.

Her presence chased off his gloom. Near her, the world became more vivid in its details. The curve of her ear as she anchored that always escaping strand of pale hair behind it, the steam rising off her tea that flushed her nose and cheeks, the gentle upturn of her lips and soft glitter of her eyes when she conversed with others.

He tried to help her around the house in his own fumbling, inexperienced ways. He tutored her sisters, he helped Harris cook, he wandered to the market and picked lovely fruit for her. The Duke of Lucere wouldn't enjoy such lowly things and stooped to perform them only if they held some promise of future mattress frolicking. But Mr. Stephens found himself enamored with the simplicity and honesty of this life.

For instance, he truly enjoyed teaching the twins about Homer, Galileo, and other things that Miss Amelia characterized as "unimportant." He relished the moment he saw the light of understanding dawn in their eyes. He knew Estella kept them from the housework so they could be educated as ladies and make successful alliances. They really weren't so insipid beneath the surface, and in a few years, they would calm to sensible beings. He just needed to point their high spirits in the proper course and guide their quick minds to worthy subjects. He wished he could be so close to his own sisters. They had followed their mother's example and become graceful, dignified women who were more like beautiful statues than blood-filled humans.

Of course, his tutoring sessions were considerably helped along when Estella brought her sewing work and eavesdropped. She was thirsty to learn. Her mind was vibrant and sharp, but she was given very little space or time to think. Her life was consumed by taking care of a decrepit home, raising her sisters to be ladies, and caring for her ailing mother.

At breakfast, he always drew her into conversation about politics, often under the guise of disagreeing with her. She enjoyed talking and thinking about the greater world. Often she would ask him questions, and he would find himself shocked that he knew the answers. Perhaps he hadn't wasted all his life, but managed to learn some useful knowledge along the way. But when he pushed her on the points that caused her anxiety, such as this Mr. Todd or her finances, she would disappear under a shell like a tiny, nervous crab.

When he asked the twins about Mr. Todd, they rolled their eyes and said that he was a banker and that their elder sister should hurry up and marry him. After all, there weren't any *real* gentlemen in Puddlebury as in London. Never mind that this logic implied that Mr. Stephens wasn't real. With unclouded, oblivious faces, they further claimed Estella had not accepted Todd because she wanted to wait until Amelia and Cecelia were ready to marry. "But we're ready now," Cecelia assured Lucere.

"Not for any *real* London gentlemen," Lucere retorted.

Of course, their explanation of Estella's reticence made no sense, but then, sense was not something the twins, or most sixteen-year-old girls for that matter, possessed in great quantity. Ladies who married men of financial or social advantage used their new station to advance their sisters' prospects. He was beginning to realize the extent that Estella had protected her family from her concerns. And she wasn't likely to let him inside her worries.

What were in those damn letters to the duke?

* * *

One morning he cornered her alone as she dusted the parlor and dining rooms. He picked up a rag from the kitchens—he had learned his way around her kitchens by now—and began to help her as best he could.

As he wiped away dust from a frame containing embroidered primroses, he related a story of being told to leave the Sistine Chapel for lying down on the floor to study the art. A true tale. "You're outrageously punishing me for a simple crime of love and admiration!" he had told the guards in those odd uniforms.

He received a lush, musical laugh for his storytelling reward. "A crime of passion, indeed," she said. "The world can be harsh to those who care to wonder."

"Who is this Mr. Todd?" he blurted. "You spoke so poorly of him the night that we"—he chose his words carefully—"had our infamous misunderstanding."

Her brows creased. The traces of laughter petered away.

"Are you a maiden in distress?" he asked, trying to keep the conversation light. "You must allow me to be chivalrous. You know my tutor imagination is chock-full of tales of King Arthur's gallant knights and such."

"You shouldn't dust," she said. "You should be reading books or writing."

He wouldn't be deterred. "Are you obliged to him?"

Her gaze shot to his face. "What do you know? Have you been talking to the townspeople?"

"Miss Primrose, let me help you." He moved to reach for her hand, knocking over a glass bowl. It broke into a dozen shards. "Oh damn, er, goodness! I'll clean this up."

"No, no, I shall."

"I want to be of help. Why won't you let me help you?" This question had nothing to do with the bloody bowl.

She caught the deeper meaning of his words and answered in kind. "Lottie is in the attics hanging sheets. It would help me if you assisted her."

So she wouldn't let him inside her worries. She kept that door shut.

He trudged up to the attics where Lottie worked. The Duke of Lucere would never mingle with a simpleton of a scullery maid. But Mr. Stephens had come to feel as protective of the vulnerable woman as Estella was. She dropped a wet linen when she saw him and rushed to give him a hug. "I love you."

If only Estella would do the same.

As they worked along, Lucere casually mentioned Mr. Todd.

"He makes Miss Primrose cry," Lottie replied. "He yells at her." The simple woman could do no more to explain these sad statements. But her words further galvanized Lucere to discover this vile man who made his lovely Estella weep. And make him pay for his heinous crimes.

Lucere helped Lottie finish stringing the laundry and then found Harris in the kitchens sprinkling powdered sugar on the French puffs he had just fried.

"I have a taste for a bit of ale at the public house," Lucere said. "Care to join me?"

Lucere knew Harris, the seer, intuited his true meaning which was, *Let's go to the public house where everyone congregates and see what we can learn about this bloody Todd cove, and if I find myself having to deal with a bit more trouble than I can manage, I may require your fists.*

"Of course," said Harris, setting down his bowl of sugar.

* * *

The public house was a sagging, timbered building devoid of any ninety-degree angles. The main chamber smelled like two hundred years of smoke, ale, and meat pies. The tables were clustered around a massive fireplace that soughed with a lulling, wood fire. The male inhabitants of Lesser Puddlebury leaned on the back legs of their chairs and conversed between puffs from their pipes and sips from their tankards.

They turned upon Lucere and Harris's entrance, their brows lifted to see what mate had rolled in. When finding two non-tribesmen, the customers' affable faces hardened with cold hostility.

An unspoken *it's them* rang in the air.

The townspeople couldn't have discovered Lucere's identity. News of that magnitude would have run like a lightning bolt through the town, sending nosy neighbors to Estella's door.

He couldn't account for the inhospitality. It severely altered his plans to befriend a local cove over a drink and discreetly ask about Todd. Now he might as well stand on a table and shout, *I'm looking for a Mr. Todd.*

Lucere sheepishly smiled in the manner of *I come in peace* and edged to a corner table outside the inner circle around the fireplace. All the while, he felt like a stalked deer. "Bloody hell, Harris," he muttered.

The barmaid, glancing nervously around, hesitated to approach. Lucere beckoned her with his hand, smiling to show he wasn't some murderous cannibal.

She slowly crossed to his table, all eyes following her, ears straining to hear.

"Good morning, miss," Lucere said pleasantly. "What a lovely locket you're wearing," he added to relax her stiff countenance. Ladies loved a compliment.

She fingered it. "It keeps a lock of my husband's hair."

"He's a lucky gentleman indeed to have such a wife," Lucere replied.

"He's been dead a year tomorrow," she said quietly.

The pain in her face pierced that place inside him where he kept Catherine's cherished memories.

"I'm sorry to hear it," he whispered. "I truly am."

She swallowed, as if trying to push down an emotion. When she spoke again, her tones had softened. "What would you like?"

"Ales for my good mate and me," Lucere replied.

"Very good." She returned to the bar.

The customers, having witnessed the exchange and their barmaid surviving unscathed, slowly returned to their previous conversations, but their untrusting eyes continued to stray to Lucere and Harris.

Then the door opened again, and in strolled a familiar face. Starlingham! Lucere knew it was unmanly, but at that moment, he desired to hug his friend and assure Starlingham of his lifelong devotion.

Starlingham glanced at Lucere and then the hostile customers. The edge of his lip hiked in amusement. He ambled over. "I'm Mr. Fitzwilliam. I don't believe we've been acquainted."

"Mr. Stephens," Lucere said and gestured to his manservant. "And this is Mr. Harris."

"How pleasant to meet you," Starlingham replied.

He sat down and leaned in, his face turning grave. "What appears to be amiss here?" he whispered. "What have you done to garner this cold reception?"

"I swear I've been a saint," Lucere hissed. "Another week in Puddlebury and I may make it to heaven yet."

"Then why is everyone staring at you?"

"A fine mystery indeed."

Lucere caught the barmaid's eye and held up three fingers. She nodded.

"I'm feeling uncomfortable," Starlingham admitted, gazing about.

"I believe we may have a mutual friend, Mr. Fitzwilliam," Lucere said, changing the subject. He had sent notes to Starlingham and Mowne by urchins, giving his whereabouts but asking them not to reply unless Mowne's condition had worsened or they were ready to leave for Scotland. The Duke of Lucere's Boarding House family was so small, any correspondence would be noted.

"A friend who suffered a most grievous injury to a delicate region?" Starlingham inquired.

"The very one. Have you heard recently from him?"

"Yes, we enjoyed some tankards on market day."

The barmaid returned with the ale. Lucere overpaid her and only waved his hand when she pointed out his error. "Then it is for the lovely lady with the sad eyes."

Then Lucere sipped from his glass, thrummed his fingers on the table, and waited until the barmaid had retreated a safe distance. "What tidings do you have of this friend?"

"It seems he has taken up sewing and folding linens in his convalescence."

"What? I thought he was shot in the arse, not in the head. We need..." Lucere caught himself. "He should repair to Scotland very quickly. This is dire, indeed."

Yet, for Lucere, the idea of going to Scotland had lost its appeal. He could not leave Estella for his princess until he knew she was safe and financially secure. Nor did Starlingham appear to harbor a great desire to gallop off. He stared at his ale, disappearing into a thought that relaxed his visage and caused a strange smile to play on his lips. Alas, he had found a woman too!

What had the Lesser Puddlepiss females done to them?

They finished their ale, and then Lucere ordered another round. Again paying a penny more. They spoke of cricket matches and horse races for the sake of appearing normal, until Lucere could take no more of being studied like the bones of some unknown and exotic creature brought before the Royal Society. When he rose, Starlingham and Harris quickly followed.

Outside the tavern, Starlingham inquired about living arrangements at the Duke of Lucere's Boarding House. Lucere had shared everything with his friends, except Catherine. And now he found himself loath to speak of Estella too. She was his precious secret for now. He was in the midst of making a deflecting, sarcastic remark about setting up his own household in accordance to the rules of the boarding house, when Harris cleared his throat.

Lucere stopped mid-sentence. What ghastly crisis had occurred to rouse Harris?

Harris discreetly glanced to his right. Several houses down from the tavern, the barmaid waited in a small alley.

Lucere broke from the other men and strolled to her. She receded several steps into the shadows of the alley.

"I'm Mr. Stephens," he said when he reached her.

She didn't introduce herself, but said, "You're the men staying at the boarding house, no? Everyone is talking. This town is so small they have nothing better to do. Pray, you seem like pleasant enough men, but you need to leave. Miss Primrose is spoken for by Mr. Todd."

"Who is Mr. Todd? Where is he?"

"He's not here for the time being. In York. But he's got spies here. And he won't like hearing about you."

Lucere protested to keep the conversation going. "We are mere boarders with no dishonorable intentions towards our landlady."

"Mr. Todd won't see things that way. He's fiercely jealous of her. You see, I'm a barmaid, and my sisters work in his house. I've heard things about the man's temper that I best not repeat. But pray, I tell you that you should be leaving as soon as may be."

"Has he hurt Miss Primrose?" Lucere demanded, his fury rising.

She shrugged. "Not unless she vexed him. He's like any man, really. Won't give you any trouble as long as you give him what he wants. Miss Primrose should consent to have him. She won't do any better here." She wrapped her arms about her. "Thank you for the money. I have two little ones." The sadness returned to her features.

"If there is anything—"

"I best return to my work." She stepped around him.

"Wait!" He dug into his pocket and retrieved a half-guinea. When he finally revealed his identity, he would give her more. He pressed the coin into her hand. "For your little ones."

She gave him a wavering smile. "Like I said, you seem like pleasant men." She hurried on.

* * *

Back at the boarding house, Lucere returned to the drawing room to find Estella curled on her side, asleep on the sofa. She still clutched the dusting rag. He watched her, wondering what anxieties wrinkled her sleeping brow. He nestled a blanket over her and then quietly pulled a chair close. There he remained, guarding her sleep, waving away her sisters when they tried to enter.

He was still watching over her when she awoke. A gentle, drowsy smile graced her lips when she saw him. "Mr. Stephens," she whispered. He slid from his chair and knelt before her. "My dear, Mr. Stephens."

He cupped her cheek in his hand. She leaned against it and closed her eyes again. He couldn't help but muse how it would be if every day she awoke so lovingly at his side.

Then a troubling thought darkened her face. She bolted up. "Oh dear, I should…" She gazed about, confused. "I should make dinner." She hurried to the door.

"Wait!"

She spun around so fast, her skirts flared about her ankles. "I'm sorry, Mr. Stephens, but we should never be alone again."

"But—"

She didn't let him finish but fled.

After that day, Estella withdrew from him more and more and, despite telling himself to keep a safe distance, the harder he chased her.

CHAPTER TEN

Estella was grateful that Mr. Todd was in York. She required all her strength to keep from falling further in love with Mr. Stephens.

On the ninth evening since her lodgers had arrived, Estella delivered her mother's dinner to her apartments. The gentlemen had forgone port, as they had every night since the first, to join the sisters in the drawing room. Estella desired to fly back downstairs so that she wouldn't miss a fascinating word that Mr. Stephens uttered or a beautiful song he sang. But she forced herself to stay upstairs, safe from his powers.

Although she struggled to conceal her true feelings for him, her senses were alive to every aspect of the man. The slight downturn of his lip caused her to panic that she had in some way offended him. That impish half smile especially kept her enthralled. She made a compromise with herself: If she managed to avoid him during the day, her imagination would be free to venture unchecked to any shocking fantasy about him. Thus her hours were passed with cleaning, cooking, mending, folding, ironing, and mentally making wild, passionate love to her handsome lodger.

"You look quite lovely tonight," her mother said between bites. "Something in your face and eyes. Has it to do with our special lodger? Hmm?"

Was Estella so obvious in her affections? She moved quickly to divert her mother from forming such an opinion. "Both lodgers are pleasant enough gentlemen."

Her mother continued to eye her, penetrating her daughter's breezy casualness. "Are they? The twins extol Mr. Stephens's handsome face and manners. He has made quite an impression on them, but you are not so moved. Perhaps this Mr. Harris is more to your liking?"

"Mr. Harris is a kind gentleman."

"Ah, look at you, your hands in your lap, your composed face. Butter wouldn't melt in your mouth." She pushed her plate away. "If you will not elucidate this mystery…" Her mother pulled the string to call a servant.

"Mama!"

Mrs. Primrose pushed herself up to her feet.

"Tonight, I shall go down and form my own opinion of our lodgers."

"No, no, Mama, it is too much. The physician said—"

"Pooh the physician," she said, straightening her gown. She glanced in the mirror. "Good heavens, I'm embarrassing myself. This cap is hideous! And you adorned me in this? We have handsome men about, and I'm in this cap. Quick, my girl, remedy!"

Estella smoothed her mother's hair with a brush and replaced her cap with a pretty lace one, all the while trying to talk her out of this folly. But Mama wouldn't relent. Lottie bounded from downstairs to help assist her mistress.

The two of them assisted her mother to the parlor. Estella could see her eyeing the house, no doubt noting how in disrepair it had fallen. Guilt weighted on her shoulders for not being able to maintain their home.

As she watched her mother shuffle along, shame racked Estella. She was making everyone suffer because she didn't want to marry a man she didn't love. She should admit that she couldn't care for this house, her mother, and siblings, as Mr. Todd said. She should stop believing she could improve her lot, thinking the Duke of Lucere could save her, and fantasizing about Mr. Stephens. She must marry Mr. Todd. She owed it to her family.

The drawing room door had been kept open, and she could hear the twins laughing and reading bombastic love poetry—no doubt from a vapid ladies' journal—to Mr. Stephens.

He protested the harsh treatment. "Good God, stop this cruelty! Have you no compassion for my pure artistic soul? No sympathy for my delicate ears? Don't tell me you fancy that silly rot."

Her mother glanced at Estella. "At least he possesses good sense, this lodger."

Estella waved off Lottie and escorted her mother into the drawing room. Mr. Stephens was comically hiding his head beneath a green brocade pillow as the twins continued their bombardment of his delicate senses. How he reminded her of her boisterous, playful grandpapa.

Meanwhile, Mr. Harris sat by a candle, quietly reading and sipping tea, unperturbed by the wild activity.

The twins fell silent upon their mother's entrance. Mr. Stephens removed the pillow from his face and then shot up to his feet.

"Mrs. Primrose, may I present Mr. Harris and Mr. Stephens," Estella said.

Mr. Stephens performed an eloquent bow. "Thank you for letting us apartments in your kind home. Allow me," he said, offering his arm. He gingerly led Mama to a chair and then wrapped blankets about her. "Do you require anything else for your comfort, ma'am?"

"You are a thoughtful gentleman," her mother remarked and gave Estella a furtive look that said, *I approve*.

"I am perfectly content," Mama continued. "My twins tell me that you are a tutor and have endeavored to help them with their studies. I hope my daughters haven't been making a May game of you and your friend. High-spirited ladies, they are."

"Your daughters, all of them, are well-mannered, gentle ladies."

Estella appreciated his willingness to lie to appease her mother.

Her mother sighed. "I'm afraid my dearest Estella has shouldered more burdens than a young lady her tender age should."

"Miss Primrose is an extraordinary lady," Mr. Stephens said. "A true noble Primrose. You are blessed to possess such a dutiful and intelligent daughter."

Although Mr. Stephens spoke in respectful tones, devoid of the usual playfulness, there was something intimate imbuing his voice that caused Estella's face to heat.

Her mother studied Estella, her eyes filled with motherly knowing, as when Estella had been young and promised her mother that she hadn't broken her favorite necklace. That she had wandered into the room to discover the beads everywhere and was trying desperately to fix it. And, yes, she'd thought she needed to try on her mother's gown and cap while repairing the necklace.

"She is a loving daughter," her mother said, and then shifted her gaze—still filled with that annoying knowing—to Mr. Stephens. "And whomever captures her heart will be a lucky man indeed. Wouldn't *you* agree, Mr. Stephens?"

Estella was embarrassed by her mother's transparent ambition. Everyone was in the process of coloring or shifting uncomfortably in their seats, except for her mother and Mr. Harris; nothing seemed to ruffle his placid countenance.

"Mr. Stephens, I am given to understand that you are a fine singer." Her mother continued her matchmaking. "Might I implore you for a song? Perhaps the one that Estella is always humming."

* * *

Lucere was tempted to laugh, until he glanced at Estella. He had been the target of many a scheming mama. He was wise to their designs and plots—the little offhand remarks to cause gossip and a sense of obligation by him. On the scale of shameless matchmaking, Mrs. Primrose's efforts hardly signified. Yet, Estella's eyes were hot agates, and her nostrils quivered, as if the very prospect of their marriage emitted a feculent odor in the room. She couldn't even look at him, but stared at her hands, which were balled in her lap.

Did she not want to marry him?

This made no sense. His wicked reputation aside, every young lady in London desired to be the Duchess of Lucere.

But then, he wasn't the duke here, but dull Mr. Stephens. He was himself.

He should rejoice that she didn't want to marry him. That he wouldn't break anyone's heart when he told her the truth and galloped off to his German princess. But that cool reason did nothing to stop his foolish despondence.

Wasn't her heart affected at all? Had their long conversations meant nothing to her? Did she bestow those warm smiles he thought so exclusively his own on other men?

He was furious. Or was he bereft? She didn't want him. The entire drama playing in his head, the struggle to contain his desire, was for nothing. He had lied against his principles, against the vow he made to his father, to be her friend. And that's all he was to her.

Now they expected him to perform like some Astley circus act. He was too broken. He struggled to come up with an excuse, because the only song he wanted to sing was, *I'm the Duke of Lucere. Do you love me now? Am I special in your eyes?*

Harris set down his book. "I believe Mr. Stephens complained of a sore throat this morning. Perhaps you should like to hear the twins sing the song they have been working on all week."

So it was decided. Lucere fumed as he played the keys. The twins sang their harmonies perfectly. Not a week ago, they'd sounded no better than cats mating. Now they were musical angels.

Meanwhile, Estella sat, scowling, all the beautiful words of Italian love falling like stones around her.

The evening quickly closed when Estella and Lottie returned the tiring Mrs. Primrose to her chamber. The twins tried reading their poetry again. Lucere barked at them to stop, then he felt instantly remorseful. They may have been insipid gigglers, but they worshiped him—unlike their older sister—and didn't deserve his ire.

"I'm sorry," he whispered.

He stalked to his room, ready to tell Harris to pack the bags. Forget about Mowne and his wounded arse. Lucere wanted his German princess. He would have his man of business give Estella whatever money she required. He would continue his transformation, putting this episode behind him.

He strode down the corridor past Mrs. Primrose's door. It was slightly ajar, a slant of gold light bleeding into the corridor. "Dearest, Mr. Stephens cares for you a great deal. He loves you. He looks at you like your father looked at me."

Lucere paused. Were the emotions he struggled to conceal apparent to everyone? He shouldn't listen. It was ungentlemanly. But he remained rooted to the spot, his breath bated as he awaited Estella's response.

"He is so very kind, but a poor tutor," Estella said.

"My dear," responded her mother, "if he has truly captured your heart, then you should marry him. You said the lodging house is running well. Amelia and Cecelia are so lovely, I'm sure they will be established in a year or two. Do not sacrifice your happiness."

"He has not asked for my hand," Estella stated flatly.

"Perhaps had you shown him a little encouragement. You didn't give him a smile or tiny flirtation. And the poor besotted gentleman couldn't stop looking at you, searching for one little sign of affection. Men are scared creatures beneath their bravado, my dear. They need encouragement and love."

Lucere felt no older than the toddler clinging to Catherine's hand. *I love my little boy most in the entirety of England.*

"Alas, I have no opinion of him," he heard Estella say. "The truth is, I do not love him."

Those words weren't heard but felt. They had jagged edges and brutal force.

He had shown Estella his true self, albeit under the guise of Mr. Stephens. And he wasn't good enough for her. She didn't love him. How could she? Her heart, so like Catherine's, brimmed with love and kindness. His was filled with cowardliness, years of terrible mistakes, and darkness.

The door opened fully, and Estella stepped out. "Mr. Stephens!"

He hadn't the power to compose himself. Whatever look he gave her caused her to reach for him in alarm. "Oh no!"

He couldn't even muster the pretense of merely passing by, of not hearing her and her mother's conversation. "Good night, Miss Primrose," he whispered.

He hadn't felt so bereft since Catherine died. He turned away from her and walked to his chamber. He shouldn't feel so dejected, but should rejoice that he was free of her with so little effort. After all, no marriage could exist between them.

Yet, this knowledge gave him no consolation. Her rejection of him before her mother only further proved his worthlessness. Without his title, he possessed nothing to recommend himself.

His days of Mr. Stephens would end tomorrow. He couldn't bear being the man a moment longer.

CHAPTER ELEVEN

That night Lucere dreamed of the horses. He was a boy again, holding his jellies as the runaway cart turned the corner. Minutes and minutes elapsed in the unreal world of his dreams. The horses galloped, their mouths foaming. Powdery dirt sprayed from where their hooves pounded the earth. But the faster they ran, the farther they seemed away. He leisurely ate his orange jelly and then the lemon one.

"Oh no, Mr. Stephens!" Estella cried. But when he turned to the sound of her voice, he found Catherine standing on the pavement, wildly waving her arms. Then time sped up. The horses were inches from his face now. "Lord Stephen!" Catherine cried. Her hands shoved him, and he sailed in the air to fall onto the hard cobbles. He rolled and rolled, his jellies decorating the air around him. Although only two horses drove the cart, it seemed like a thousand hooves ran over Catherine, bouncing her broken body against the stones.

He screamed but couldn't make a sound. Then the horses were gone. Catherine lay still in a gleaming, unstained white gown, red blood gushing from her temple. Lucere rose from the street, no longer a boy but a grown man. As he approached his nurse, he realized that the woman lying in the road had blond hair. It wasn't Catherine at all, but—

Lucere bolted up in bed, his cry echoing around him. He gulped for air as he reassured himself it was just a dream of a horrible memory. He slid from his bed and strolled across the frigid floor to the window. He opened it and let the night air cool his face. The night sky was velvet blue against the black outline of Lesser Puddlebury. No lights burned from the buildings; there was no noise but crickets and wind. In sleepless London, he would have reached for a courtesan or become lushy in a gaming hell to distract his mind. Now he had to stay with the memory, reliving each detail until the pain slowly receded.

* * *

His hands were shaking as he arranged the utensils on the breakfast table. Harris was silent. He seemed to know this was the day that Lucere would make his fateful pronouncement. Lucere's dream had broken any anger or resentment. Now, only sadness remained. He would mourn the loss of his and Estella's easy, equal friendship, as well as hundreds of other things about her.

Lottie entered with a platter of fried eggs. She didn't put them on the table, but hurried to him and threw her arms around him. "I love you, Mr. Stephens."

"I love you too," he whispered. How like a little family the inhabitants of the lodging house had become to him. He removed the platter from Lottie's hand and was carefully restoring the eggs that slid near the edges when he realized that Estella was present. She leaned against the threshold, her face swollen and her eyes red-rimmed. His own concerns petered away. He dropped the dish on the table with a clatter.

"Good God, Estella, are you well?"

"W-would you care to join me on a stroll after breakfast, Mr. Stephens? I know a place that you would enjoy."

* * *

The morning air was crisp on Estella's cheeks. She and Mr. Stephens silently strolled through the back garden, neither touching the other. She racked her mind for something casual to say to break the miserable, raw silence. But it was the clever Mr. Stephens who spoke first.

"I greatly admire your jungle, Miss Primrose," he said, surveying the garden that had been given up on years ago. In older times, it had been a lovely labyrinth. Now the bordering shrubbery had grown to the size of small trees.

"Have you ever lost a lodger in here?" he inquired.

"Five or six. I've lost count."

He chuckled nervously. She gazed up at him and smiled. In a twinkling, all the awkward tension that had ruined breakfast fell away. Her dear friend had returned.

"Oh, Mr. Stephens." She took his hand, interlacing their fingers. It was improper, but she needed the reassurance of his touch. She had wept through the night, believing she had hurt his feelings.

"Ah, you said house parties and such drew away your guests for the summer," he reminded her, "but perhaps they are merely lost, wandering around your jungle."

How she and he rubbed so perfectly along. She could imagine years of side-by-side strolls and laughter. But it could never be.

This sad thought caused her to quicken her pace until they reached the edge of the forest. Brambles had grown over the old path. She eased into the tangle, glad she had thought to wear her apron, else her gown would be snagged beyond saving.

"I'm getting rather nervous now," Mr. Stephens said, pulling aside tree limbs as he and she progressed into the wood. "Luckily, I told Mr. Harris that I was walking with you should you have nefarious intentions."

In the effort to make a quick rejoinder, the wrong words burst from Estella. "Should I calm your fears, or leave you to your own dark imaginings?"

His head jerked back as though she had slapped him.

"I'm sorry!" she cried. "I didn't mean… let me show you the secret place. You will enjoy it."

They wove around trees and brush until they reached the ancient spreading oak where she had carved the letters.

"Ah, a mysterious code." He feigned a shadowy voice.

"It's my initials," she explained. She glanced about, seeing no trace of the old door. She walked forward, listening to the sound of her feet striking the earth. When a solid *thud* became a hollow *thump*, she knelt down and dug her gloved fingers into the ground.

He joined her. "The suspense! Are we digging for a hidden treasure?"

"Of sorts." She smiled. His happiness spilled into her.

She had cleared enough of the soil that she could grip the old door. Together they tugged, lifting the wood, ripping apart roots. The sunlight filtering through the tree leaves lit a small, squat room that sparkled hues of luminous greens and blues.

"What in heavens?" He lowered himself down and gingerly brushed the dirt away from the ancient art with his hand. "This… this is a Roman mosaic."

"I found it when I was eight. My grandfather believes it's the floor of an old villa."

"It's amazing." He carefully revealed more of the geometric pattern.

"I thought it would please you."

He lifted his gaze to meet hers. "Oh, Estella," he whispered. He reached up and touched her face. "You know me so well."

She leaned into his touch, drawing strength to say what she needed him to know.

"I wanted to tell you"—her voice cracked—"that I lied to my mother last night. I think you heard the conversation."

"Don't, I shouldn't have—"

"My mother doesn't know the extent of our financial troubles. I've protected her. The physician said she shouldn't become excited because of her weak heart. I told her that I had no affections for you. But the truth is…" She forged on, despite her tightening throat. "As a lady of good conscience, I cannot trifle with the affections of a gentleman of modest means, no matter how respectable or kind he is, or how much I care for him." She paused, her eyes growing wet.

"Please don't be upset. Know that you are the most wonderful gentleman I have ever met. And if I've seemed indifferent..." Tears threaded down her cheeks.

"No," he whispered and tried to brush them away with his thumb.

"It's because I've fallen in love with you. I'm sorry."

"Oh God, Estella."

He combed his fingers into her hair, cupping the back of her head, and drawing her close. She should stop him. Didn't she hurt enough? She closed her eyes, surrendering to him and the damage she would do to her heart.

His mouth caressed hers, lulling away her reserve. His tongue licked her lips and then surprised her by slowly entering her mouth. Was this how true lovers kissed when they were alone?

She followed his tutorage, stroke for stroke. He moaned and brought her closer, widening her mouth, his pace quickening. Her mind quieted as her body awakened with a powerful yearning. She knew how infants were created between a man and a woman. The act sounded so undignified that she believed it to be another chore a wife must perform to keep a husband. But Mr. Stephens was rapidly changing her mind. Her nipples were straining for his touch. Her insides throbbed, ready to welcome his sex inside.

She released a high whimper. He withdrew from her mouth and gazed at her. His eyes were filled with such tenderness. He lightly touched her face, drawing his fingers along its contours. "You are truly beautiful," he whispered. "But your face pales to the exquisiteness of your heart."

"I love you," she cried. "I love you very much indeed." And then she burst into embarrassing sobs. Their force shocked her, years and years of tension erupting forth like volcanic tears.

"No, no." He tried to bring her back to him. "Tell me, what is the matter? How much money do you owe? Who is this Mr. Todd? Tell me, everything. I can help you."

Poor Mr. Stephens. He didn't deserve to be entangled in the wreck that was her life.

"I'm sorry." She came to her feet. "Please enjoy the mosaic. I knew you would like it." She rushed toward her home. She wished she hadn't been so weak.

He called behind her, "Estella, wait for me. There is something you must know."

She couldn't stop. She wouldn't let him become further entwined in her problems. Branches whipped her legs and arms as she ran. She could hear him calling her name as he pushed through the bramble. She quickened her step, skirting the back garden, and hurrying along the side of the house. As she entered through the front door, she almost collided with Mr. Todd, who was coming out of the parlor.

"She is here, after all," he said affably to his male companion.

Beside Mr. Todd stood a slight, graying man with limp whiskers growing beneath his cheekbones. He was dressed in somber clothes and sported a gold watch chain. She recognized him as Mr. Jenkins, a local landowner and the justice of the peace.

The realization of what was about to occur sank in.

Dear Lord, not today. She wasn't strong enough.

Mr. Jenkins had the power to send her to debtors' prison. The edge of Mr. Todd's mouth was raised in triumph. He had finally pulled his trump card. The future she had worked so hard to outwit was descending.

"What are you doing here?" she asked Mr. Todd. "I thought... I thought you were in York."

"I found reason to cut my stay short," he said.

The front door flew open again. "Estella!" cried Mr. Stephens. He stopped in his progress, taking in the other men.

"Who are you?" Mr. Todd rudely inquired, not waiting for an introduction.

Mr. Stephens must have sensed something amiss. His eyes glittered with menace. Estella saw a nasty retort forming on his lips and quickly interceded. She had witnessed Mr. Todd's vicious underside too many times and feared the man. "This is my lodger, Mr. Stephens. He's a tutor."

Mr. Todd raked Mr. Stephens up and down. "Collect your belongings and leave," he hissed.

"This is my home, Mr. Todd!" she cried.

"No, it's mine." Mr. Todd grabbed her wrist. "I told you, no more of this lodging-house madness. Now, you will go to the parlor this instant."

"You don't speak to her that way," Mr. Stephens growled.

The cold hate on Mr. Todd's face terrified her. She placed herself between the angry men to protect her lodger.

"I say," Mr. Jenkins remarked, taken aback by his friend's hostility. Mr. Todd showed his false colors to his neighbors.

Mr. Todd collected himself. "I'm sorry, Miss Primrose. I fear greatly for your reputation. It has been damaged enough. I've come to help you. Let us go to the parlor and talk."

"Please—please, excuse me, Mr. Stephens," Estella said, keeping her eyes low. She was embarrassed to have him witness this scene.

"Do you want to speak to these men?" Mr. Stephens's neck tendons corded. She could feel his pent-up fury and feared he would lash out before the justice of the peace.

"Yes," she whispered. "Come, Mr. Todd."

She allowed the banker to escort her to the parlor with Mr. Jenkins trailing behind.

CHAPTER TWELVE

"Won't you sit down?" Mr. Todd led Estella to the sofa. He performed the pretty for the sake of the justice of the peace.

Mr. Jenkins didn't take the offered wing chair across from her, but knelt down until they were at eye level. He spoke in a discreet whisper. "Mr. Todd has come to me regarding your significant debt to him."

"I have more money now. I can pay him."

"Do you have the 3,120 pounds you owe?" Mr. Jenkins responded.

"No. Enough for an installment. I mean, the installment that I am late paying."

"Miss Primrose, the state of your finances is no secret," Mr. Jenkins said, shaking his head. "You owe many merchants in this town." He rose, hooked his thumbs into his waistband, and leaned back onto his heels. "Now, I know how you ladies are. You like to assume airs you don't have and think a prince will save you like in the fairy tales you so love." He chuckled.

Estella dug her nails into the upholstery, trying hard to hold back a retort to such patronizing words.

"Mr. Todd has been most patient with you, young lady," Mr. Jenkins continued. "He is rightly concerned that if you persist in your folly, you will irrevocably damage the prospects of your sisters and worsen your mother's delicate health. Now, I don't want to be the one to take your mother to debtors' prison."

"What?" Her head turned to Mr. Todd, who waited by the window, pretending he had no responsibility in this matter. He was here merely to be her hero. "You would send my mother to debtors' prison?"

"It is your mother's home," Mr. Jenkins answered for him, resuming his discreet whispering. What strangers in the room would hear him? "Mr. Todd tells me that it is her lodging house on paper."

She shook her head, disbelieving how low a man would crawl.

"I'm going to tell you what I would tell my own daughters," Mr. Jenkins said. "You need to let go of your fancies and marry a man who will provide for you and be your wise master. Mr. Todd is a generous gentleman. His patience towards you speaks of his goodness."

Mr. Jenkins strode to Mr. Todd and placed his hand on the banker's shoulder, as though he were anointing him. "If you marry Mr. Todd, he can restore your reputation and your sisters', which have suffered by merely being your relation. For in truth, it is oft acknowledged that a child or sister be dead than bring dishonor to her family."

Estella sucked in her breath at such an offensive statement. It burned to her core that she must sit and accept such hatefulness.

"You are obligated to Mr. Todd in every sense, and yet, you neglect your female responsibility, instead carelessly allowing your virtue to be sullied."

Estella could stand no more. If she must marry Mr. Todd, she needn't suffer any more of these gentlemen's smug self-righteousness. "Thank you, I believe…" She struggled for the words. "I believe I would like to be alone with Mr. Todd now."

"Very good." Mr. Jenkins shook Mr. Todd's hand in congratulations and left the room.

Mr. Todd wasted no time in making his proposal. He knelt before her. "Miss Primrose, let me assure you of my devotion and—"

"I shall marry you." She spoke the words in haste, preferring the swift cut of the blade rather than suffering the long, drawn-out process.

"My Estella." He came to sit beside her. "You have led me on such a chase, but I would not be deterred." His lips descended on hers. For all Mr. Stephens's gentleness, Mr. Todd was rough—his skin, his hold, his kiss. He gave her no time to learn or trust in his love, but thrust his tongue into her mouth. She felt sickeningly violated.

She slowly untangled herself, feigning shyness.

"My sweet love, you are ignorant to the desires of man," Mr. Todd said. "I'm sorry I frightened you, but you drive me to such wildness. I shall be tender on our wedding night. I promise."

Estella didn't know if she could bear sharing a bed with this man, but she must learn.

"Let us speak of practical matters," he said. "You should know your husband is a practical man."

He told her that he had procured a license in anticipation of the event. He would have his home made ready for his bride. He had a well-appointed chamber that would be made into a lovely, feminine sitting room for her. He had already purchased paper and carpets. All the while he spoke, she said nothing, nor did he solicit her opinion. He had once accused her of thinking she lived in a dollhouse, but now she felt like some grownup doll to be played with.

"Come, walk me to the door, my love," he said.

In the hall, Mr. Stephens prowled like a tiger, back and forth in its cage.

"Wish me well," Mr. Todd told him. "Miss Primrose has consented to make me the happiest man. Now collect your belongings and leave. This lodging house is closed."

Estella couldn't bring herself to look at Mr. Stephens, but she could feel his blazing stare on her skin. At the door, Mr. Todd kissed her cheek and murmured, "Tomorrow I shall return."

She watched him stroll out. He stopped at the boarding house sign and kicked it over.

Mr. Stephens grasped her elbow. "Did that man coerce you into marriage?"

Estella winced at his thundering voice. Shouting and anger would not help her now. Her struggle was over. Nothing could be done. "No, I willingly accepted him. It has been a long understanding between us. That's what I tried to tell you."

"You don't love him! You said you loved me."

"This is best for my family! I can't... I can't take care of this home anymore. I can't take care of... anyone." The tears were coming again. She covered her face. "Please leave me."

"Estella, there is something you don't know—"

"Please, I need a moment, Mr. Stephens," she cried into her hands. "It has been a trying morning. I can bear no more."

The twins rushed through the door.

"The mail's come!" Cecelia said. "There's a letter from the duke." She paused, becoming aware of the tension around her. "Is something amiss?"

"May I see the letter?" Estella said.

She opened it and read the contents. "You were right about the duke, Cecelia," she said slowly. "He is a horrid man, as is his secretary. I'm happy that Mr. Todd kicked down the sign. The duke is nothing like our grandpapa. I'm glad I will no longer be a Primrose."

She dropped the letter and walked to her chamber. She curled onto her covers and finally cried in peace. She couldn't stop thinking of how rough Mr. Todd's touch had felt, so different from Mr. Stephens's tenderness.

Lucere picked the letter from the floor and read.

Dear Miss Primrose,

I assure you that I have spoken at length with the duke. He does not recognize your family relation. Please desist your correspondence.

Damn it. No.

CHAPTER THIRTEEN

Lucere waited for Estella to come, pacing the drawing room and cursing himself. Outside the window, the sunlight shone on the tree leaves. Conversing birds flitted between branches. The natural world didn't care that Estella was being forced into an unwanted marriage, or that Lucere was stuck, like the terrified child, watching the oncoming horses.

He should have known about her letters, her very existence. He should have belted Mr. Todd in the face. He should have been a better son. He should have jumped out of the way of the horses.

The things he should have done were interminable.

Across the room waited the pianoforte where he had sung to Estella and she had gazed at him with such unaffected admiration. None that he deserved.

He slumped on the sofa cushion and hung his head in his hands. His father's words echoed around him. *You're a disgrace.*

Estella never came down. She sent a message through Lottie that she would be unable to attend dinner and gave Lottie instructions for an easy, cold offering.

At four, Harris joined Lucere in the drawing room, closing the door behind him. The man quietly pulled up a worn, scraped wing chair until he was sitting just a few feet across from Lucere. Lucere picked up his secretary's letter from the side table and handed it to Harris. He watched his manservant read it.

"I've failed her," Lucere said as Harris refolded the missive.

"Were you ever given her letters?"

"No, but I can't blame it on my secretary." He rose and began to pace on the carpet. "I should have known. No telling what other vital matters have slipped through my notice because I chose to be distracted by a luscious morsel or a game of cards. I keep hearing my father's admonishments ringing." He bumped his fist on the top of the pianoforte. "I... I know what I need to do to be a better man, but I can't seem to do it. I fail over and over. I... damn it." He couldn't continue down this cowardly road of self-pity before stoic Harris.

Harris sat back in his chair and studied Lucere, his index finger on his temple, thumb under his chin. His penetrating, unblinking gaze was unnerving.

"Speak, man," Lucere said. "Don't look at me so and say nothing."

"May I be forthright, Your Grace?"

Lucere flung up his arms. "For the love of God, never be anything but forthright with me."

"Very well." Harris nodded. "I have been under the employment of both you and your father. Your father, though a fine gentleman, was severely limited by his intelligence. He had adequate enough wits, but not in the quantity to give him any profundity or true insight. Coupled with his rather coarse sensibilities, he performed his station in a manner that none would find wanting." Harris paused to give weight to his next words. "Nor any would find great."

Lucere stared at Harris. The man had vocalized something Lucere had felt for years but dared not say of his late father.

"Your Grace," Harris continued, "has all the elements to be the greatest Duke of Lucere, should he choose to exercise them."

Lucere gave a bark of derisive laughter, walked to the window, and gazed through the wavy leaded glass. Outside, the sun winked from the treetops. "You don't know the truth, Harris."

"You should not disagree with me!" Harris snapped.

Lucere spun around, shocked at the man's temper that had flashed from nowhere.

Harris rose. "You made a vow on your father's deathbed to be a better man. And you told yourself that to keep this vow you have to refuse the love of a lady who possesses the strong, valiant heart required of the Duchess of Lucere only because she was not born to the right parents and circumstances."

"You make me sound crass and cold."

"But if you care to look closely, you will clearly see that she has made you the better man. She will let you keep your vow."

Lucere could see the faint lines of smugness around the man's mouth. It angered him. The man knew nothing.

"How profound of you, Harris!" Lucere mocked. "How well you know me! A fine lesson, indeed. Now I see clearly my errors."

"Sarcasm is unbecoming, Your Grace."

"Then let me be in earnest," Lucere retorted, his voice breaking. He crossed to the pianoforte and played a quiet F chord. "There are secrets that I have kept all these years. Secrets that may change your view of matters. You say that I'm worthy of Estella and my title. Well, let me tell you why I am not."

He began to play a broken chord in the bass clef. The story that had haunted his life wanted to stay locked inside. But Harris needed to understand why his faith was so poorly bestowed. "The morning that Catherine—your Catherine—was killed, I ordered her to take me to the confectionary store for jellies. I was a child and adamant to have my way, even if I no longer wanted the damn jellies. 'I am a lord,' I told her, and that she, being a simple nurse, must obey me. Charming little boy, I was. You know how patient Catherine was. How loving. How gentle. How perfect. She said I was in such a state not to be worked on until I had a jelly."

Lucere changed his chord to a minor.

"After I got my prized jellies that I no longer wanted, Catherine left me on the pavement with strict instructions to stay out of the road while she popped into a store to buy some sewing notions. Well, I was not to be told what to do. I was a lord with his jellies. I played a little game of stepping onto the road and off. Tiny rebellions. Each time going a little farther, until I had built up my courage to stand in the street. That's how I wanted Catherine to find me."

He quietly played, coming to the part that dominated his life.

"I heard a loud noise like a powerful crash of thunder. People were shouting. Around the corner thundered a wagon with two massive horses and no driver. And I couldn't move. I was stuck there on the cobbles, holding my prized jellies. I remember clearly telling myself to move. I had all the time in the world to get away. But I couldn't. I was paralyzed, staring at the horses coming directly at me. Time seemed to slow down to a drip. I kept thinking, 'I'm going to die.' Then I heard Catherine scream my name, and I was shoved."

Lucere quit playing. He had to tell the last seconds of Catherine's life to her lover's face. The deep lines of Harris's visage were drawn down. Little red veins appeared around his irises. The cool façade he usually wore was stripped away, revealing his raw depths and intelligence.

"I was lying on the road," Lucere continued. "I remember the horses pounding the jellies, brown dusty hooves on yellow and orange confections and red blood. Catherine struggled to escape, but then I saw the wheel strike her head. She became still. The wagon clattered on, leaving her inert on the stones. Her limbs were twisted in unnatural positions. Her head lay in blood. People were rushing onto the street. I... I could not move."

Lucere gazed down at his hands. "I killed her, Harris. I killed your Catherine. I destroyed your loving, gentle creature. I wish it had been me who died. But that gives you little solace. It doesn't bring her back."

Harris swallowed. He pounded his fist on the armrest, then bolted up and stalked toward the door.

"I'm sorry," Lucere said. The word *sorry* was so impotent.

Harris's enormous shoulders rose and fell with his breath. "You were only a child."

"I've tried to tell myself that for decades. It does nothing to stop the memories or lessen the guilt. That horrible moment has led me down a path of destruction. For years and years, I have amassed more sin just trying to forget about that moment." Lucere rose, catching his reflection in the mirror on the chimneypiece. He knew he was a handsome man. He had heard that said to him enough times. But unlike Estella, he had nothing beautiful beneath his skin.

"So you see, I am not the man you thought. When Miss Primrose returns, I must tell her the truth of my identity. I will give her money—anything she requires. Then I will leave for my German princess. Estella will be able to live and marry as she pleases."

Harris whirled around. "She pleases to marry you and you her!"

"I'm not... not good enough for her. How can she forgive me? I have deceived and disappointed her in the deepest ways."

"Have you no faith in her?"

"I have every faith in her, but little in me."

"Miss Primrose is stranded on a street," Harris barked. "The horses are beating upon her. She can't move because she is terrified, exhausted from caring for her family and this home and fending off a man who she knows will destroy her, heart and soul. The horses are steaming. They are but inches from her now. What will you do? You can push her to safety and into the life she deserves. Will you redeem yourself?"

"I can't be redeemed!" Lucere shouted.

Harris's huge shoulders sagged. He regarded his master with tired, sad eyes that were filled with compassion.

"Yes, you can," he said quietly. "You can show all the love and kindness that Catherine gave you to someone who desperately needs you. You can learn from every mistake in your past to make you the wise and strong husband that Miss Primrose deserves. Don't hurt her out of your own fears. And don't dishonor my dear Catherine's memory by not giving the love she gave you to another."

Lucere's eyes burned.

"Don't think about your redemption or past failings or your vow to be a better man," Harris counseled. "Think only of Miss Primrose. If you leave, you will break her heart. You will hurt her. Give her your total love, and the rest will fall in line."

Lucere rubbed his finger where his signet ring had made an indention. Could he entrust anyone else to her care? Most gentlemen would never see past her beauty to her lovely character. He thought of Estella with no one to sing in Italian to her or converse with her about the customs of China or the architecture of Spain. And who could keep watch over her sleep? Who would make her laugh? Who would take her to Italy and walk with her amid the Coliseum? If she truly wanted his love—the broken, worn-out thing that it was—he would offer it all to her. He would give her everything Catherine taught him.

"Harris, please send an express to my man of business and solicitor in London," he whispered. "I will require money and… and a special marriage license."

CHAPTER FOURTEEN

Estella turned back from Mr. Stephens's door for the third time and hurried to her room with shaking legs. She had almost reached her chamber when she thought, *No!* She spun around and strode purposely to her boarder's door.

If she were giving her life away to Mr. Todd to save her family, she wanted to know again how a true kiss felt. Yet, as she held her hand up to rap on the door, her resolve petered away.

This is not how a proper lady behaves, a harsh voice rang in her head.

How those useless lessons still kept her in chains.

This is your last chance. She had to make memories to cherish for the rest of her life that would be spent in a loveless marital bed.

Her knuckles struck the wood. She paused for a beat and then began to back away, when the door swung open. Mr. Stephens was dressed in fine clothes—a deep blue coat, white trousers, and boots. Her breath left her body in one rush. He was as handsome as a London gentleman in his finery. How could he afford such clothes? Maybe they were castoffs from an employer.

Then Mr. Harris stepped around him. Estella's cheeks burned.

"Good day." Mr. Harris bowed curtly. "I shall take care of the business," he said to Mr. Stephens and continued down the corridor.

Mr. Stephens fingered the edge of his coat. He appeared nervous.

"Would it be an imposition…" she began, and then the rest of her words stuck in her mouth. She hadn't envisioned making her speech in the hall, or how Mr. Stephens's yearning eyes would set her emotions awry.

She boldly stepped inside his room and closed the door. His leather bag was open and set upon a chair, waiting to be packed. He was leaving her. He had been in her life only a short time, yet figured so largely in her mind now. All her thoughts flowed to him. The idea of his imminent departure hurt like a death.

Perhaps she was making a mistake coming to him, but she didn't care anymore.

"Mr. Stephens, you know I love you. And although I'm promised to another, would it be an imposition if I…" Tears swelled, choking her words. "If I kissed you again, so that I always have it to remember? Of course, you may decline—"

His lips were on hers in a flash. All the shock from the morning was gone. There was no fumbling or tentativeness, as before. The pressure of his mouth opened her lips, allowing his tongue inside. She caressed him as she explored. She loved the taste of him and the sensation of his muscled chest against her softness. For all that Mr. Todd repulsed her, Mr. Stephens drew her near.

His hands tangled in her hair. She could feel her pins falling away, her hair tumbling onto her shoulders.

His urgency deepened. His tongue lashed against hers. What had been sweet transformed into something primitive. She had come seeking a kiss, but now she pressed her body against him, begging for something, she knew not what. Sensations that she had never experienced with such violence were breaking over her. Her nipples ached and pressed against her shift. Her sex swelled and wetted with want of him inside of her. He filled her every sense.

He groaned and pulled back. Could he feel her raw yearning? Did she frighten him?

"I'm sorry," she cried. "Please don't turn me away." How humiliatingly plaintive she sounded.

"No," he whispered, lifting his gaze to hers. "I love you," he said. The words were ragged and worn, as if he had carried them for years, unable to give them to anyone. "I love you so dearly. I can't deny you anything." He embraced her, drawing her snug against him. His heart thrummed in her ear.

Today she had consented to marry a harsh man. The idea of giving her virtue to him was almost sacrilegious. Mr. Todd would never be her true husband, despite what vows she said. Her true husband now held her and kissed her hair.

This would be her wedding night. Her eyes wandered to the bed. It had been hers once. As a girl, her mother and grandmother had helped her embroider the white vines and leaves into the ivory-colored covers. Now it would enshroud her like a wedding dress.

She took his hand and slowly lifted it to her breast. "Love me."

"Estella," he whispered. "My beautiful star." She adored how he said her name, the gusts and stops of his musical voice.

He kept his eyes fixed on hers as his fingers delved into her bodice, finding a nipple straining to be known. He gently moved his finger across the bud until she shuddered and cried out. His lips were on hers again, taking in her whimpers. She pushed against him, trying to relieve the pressure building inside her.

He tore his mouth from hers. In a fast motion, she was off the ground and then falling onto the mattress.

"Tell me you love me again," he cried. "Let me hear you say it. Please." He rested his knee on the bed as he yanked off his coat and waistcoat.

"I love you," she whispered and kissed his forehead. "I love you." She kissed his cheekbone. "I love you." She kissed his ear. "I've imagined you and what it would be like."

His hands were shaking as he reached for the buttons of her dress. She didn't feel ashamed. She wanted him to see her. To let her body be a gift to him.

"Tell me everything you think, Estella. Everything you imagine. Tell me your dreams. You fascinate me. I want to know every part of your mind and body."

Her dress fell away. He began working on her stays.

"I imagine us in Italy, in piazzas and gondolas." She smiled. "Doing what husband and wives do. Although, I'm not quite sure of the actual details."

"*Ti insegno io,*" he said, then translated, "I shall teach you."

"Speak to me in Italian."

"*Ti sposerò. Viaggeremo in Italia e faremo l'amore a Venezia.*"

"What does that mean?" She slipped from her stays.

"A secret." He kissed her shoulder.

She undid the knot of her drawstring. She pulled, and the thin cotton tumbled to her waist, her breasts bared for him.

He sucked in his breath. "Oh God." He studied her. She felt no bashfulness, but loved how she could use her body to please him. He bent down and slowly circled his tongue around a nipple.

She gasped. The sensation elicited an acute pleasure. It was a lovely torture. His tongue flicked across the hardened tip. She clenched his arm and arched her back, pushing herself into his mouth. Her body began undulating against him. She wanted to cry out, but instead bit on her thumb. His body changed beneath his trousers. His sex grew hard and pressed on her belly.

Instinctually, she knew that it belonged in her. He wouldn't satisfy her on that score, but rubbed against her, their bodies in a complementary dance of sorts. He yanked off his shirt. His chest and belly was a network of muscles. She hadn't realized how strong he was until they were skin upon skin. He lay atop her, his body shielding her from the fears beyond this bed. They couldn't hurt her for now.

The throb in her core grew painful. She moved at a frantic pace, her body pleading with his. "Help me!" she cried and pressed her thighs against him.

"It shouldn't happen this way," he hissed through clenched teeth.

No, this *was* the way it would be. She knew it so surely now. She would give her maidenhood to her true husband.

He yanked her gown and shift away. Every part of her was exposed to him now. He released a ragged exhale and murmured, "My dear, trusting love." He squeezed his eyes closed, and his fingers pressed the bridge of his nose.

"Is something wrong?" she asked. "What is the matter?"

"Just let me kiss you," he whispered.

She rose to her elbows to meet his lips. He kept his eyes open, watching her as their tongues caressed. His hand moved slowly up her thigh until he found her wet folds waiting for his touch. She experienced no shyness. As he had made her feel safe to express her dreams and opinions, now she was safe to show her desire without reserve.

His fingers moved along her contours, exploring her as he kept her locked in his kiss.

Then he found that small peak above her entrance. He flicked his finger across it, and she jumped as if hit by a strange, pleasurable electricity. He chuckled in her mouth, letting his finger dance. Her head fell back on the pillow. She had never conceived of such pleasure. Her knees shook. She was wide open to him. His finger lowered, finding her source and sliding inside. She whimpered. "I love you."

But something was wrong. A coldness came over him. "I must stop," he growled and withdrew. "What I'm doing is wrong."

"No!" she protested. "I want to give you my virtue. Please."

He rose from the bed and put several paces of distance between them. He dropped his head in his hands.

"Will it cause you too much pain?" she asked. "That I can't marry you?"

"You misunderstand." He returned to her and began brushing the strands of hair from her cheeks. "I have to tell you the truth."

She shook her head. "What do you mean?"

"I love you," he whispered, trailing his thumb along her lip. "I hunger to see you abandoned in happiness and all the worry gone from your face." His fingers brushed her forehead. "But I cannot continue until you consent to marry me. To allow me to love you for the rest of your life and whatever world exists beyond this one." His lips hiked to a half smile. "To do otherwise would violate the Primrose code."

She saw nothing amusing. "I would marry you a thousand times over, but I refuse to destroy you. That is not how to love someone."

"No, it is not. Nor is concealing one's identity."

Estella shot up. "I told you everything! I have no secrets. My conscience is as bared as my body before you."

He kissed her lips, her chin. "I know, my love. I know. It is…" Fear imbued his eyes. "I have deceived you."

"Deceived?" She shook her head. "You are a tutor, no? You are Mr. Stephens? Why are you staying at my boarding house?"

He gave a wry laugh. "Because you run the Duke of Lucere's Boarding House. Where else would I stay?"

She felt suddenly vulnerable and tugged at the covers to conceal herself.

"No," he said, his hand meeting hers at her chest, halting her progress. "Don't be afraid. Please. You will break my heart." He twined a strand of hair around his finger as he peered into her face, searching. "Years ago, I met a girl with a lovely smile in Hyde Park. An azure blue ribbon, which matched her cloak, tied her pale blond hair. She held the hand of a kindly, old gentleman. His wild white hair bushed beneath his hat, and crinkles radiated from the corners of his eyes." He caressed the edges of her lids. "'He must laugh a great deal,' I thought, because I hadn't laughed in a year. My beloved nurse, whom I loved like a mother, had died in an accident I caused. Do you not remember me? I held a yellow and white kite."

Estella sucked in her breath. He kissed the edge of her mouth, his fingers caressing her cheek. "You asked if I could fly it, and I wanted so much to do so. I was greedy for your happiness and that beautiful light that surrounds you to this day. My mother seized my hand and mentioned something about returning home to receive callers. We walked on without acknowledging you or your grandfather. And I was ashamed."

Mr. Stephens was the Duke of Lucere? How could that be? It couldn't. This was one of Mr. Stephens's merry games.

He studied her, gauging her reaction. She stared at him. "You're... you're the Duke of Lucere?"

"The Duke of Lucere who loves you."

"Did y-you receive my letters after all? Is that your game? Did you come to check on me?"

"I never received your letters. I wish I had. It was mere coincidence, or perhaps divine intervention, that led me to your door."

She sank her head. She had experienced enough unwanted news in her life that she expected the hollow shock, followed by the true realization. She experienced none of this, but sadness. All her lovely memories of this week were poisoned. Mr. Stephens, whom she held in such pure esteem, shattered something sacred inside her. She didn't have time to consider the deeper significance. There would be hours and hours in the coming days to ponder the day her life fell apart.

"You don't need to marry me," she said at length. "I wrote to ask for ten pounds to make payments to Mr. Todd. But it is no matter now."

She tried to rise, but he seized her shoulders.

"But I *need* to marry you," he said.

"Because we kissed, because we..." She gestured to the bed.

"Because I love you. I need you."

"I love Mr. Stephens!" she cried, digging her nails into her chest. Fury now flooded in. "He is who I want. Kind, patient, beautiful Mr. Stephens, who sings lovely songs to me, teaches me about exotic lands, and makes me so happy inside. I don't know you. I don't know your world. How could you do this?"

"I am Mr. Stephens!" The desperation on his face arrested her anger.

The Duke of Lucere had loomed for so long in her mind that he had reached god-like proportions. Yet the man before her was flesh and blood and in pain.

"My name *is* Stephen," he pleaded. He seized her hand and rested it on his heart. Its beat thundered under her palm. "You know me. The man inside. The others—society, my family, even my friends, to some degree—don't know me, but a clever shell I put over myself. But there has been nothing between us."

"Except the truth."

His throat contracted with his swallow.

"Why did you not tell me?" Tears swelled in her eyes.

"My explanation may cause you pain."

"I assure you that I'm in great pain at this moment."

He muttered something and slicked his hands down his crumpled face. She thought he might cry too. She leaned in and kissed him before she realized she had done it. How easily her love swelled for him. "Just tell me."

He began his tale of the death of his nurse that had triggered years spent lost in dissipation. He jumped, in time, to a deathbed vow made to his father. He spoke about a duel that ended with his friend being shot in the arse. Having ascertained that the friend was recovering quite nicely, she could not contain her giggles. Even the part where he mistook her for a light-skirts was rather funny in the mellowing of hindsight. But the conversation quickly turned serious again when he spoke of finding his true nature under the guise of Mr. Stephens and falling in love with the most worthy and beautiful lady in the world. And the fear that by telling the truth of his identity he would lose the love of this extraordinary woman.

As he ended, lines of tears trailed down her cheeks.

He rose, crossed to his bag, and collected something from within. When he returned, a gold signet ring shone on his finger. He rested an elegant diamond necklace and ring before her on the mattress, as well as an ancestry chart bearing his and her grandfathers' names.

The diamonds sparkled in the light. A gift for her, no doubt. But she didn't dare touch them. They were from a man she didn't know, who dwelled in great homes and mingled among the *ton*.

"I take your silence as your rejection." Pain cracked his voice. "I will not continue to Scotland. There will be no woman after you. My heart will always be yours. Keep the diamonds as payment for my cruel deception. I am sorry. Mr. Todd will be paid off. I will repair your home. Your sisters will be educated.

Your mother will be attended by a physician. And you need not see me ever again if that is your desire. But I want you to know that all I've learned here from you—how you love, how selflessly you care for others—I will keep inside me. You have shown me how to be a better man. And I love you."

She took in his words and fingered the necklace and ring. "I do not know how to be a duchess."

"If that is your decision, I will abide by it," he said. He gently withdrew the necklace from her fingers and placed it around her neck. "But you are a true Primrose. Far more than myself. Look no further than the night you threw me out for besmirching your honor." He slid the ring on her finger. "And... and I can tutor you."

Something in his plaintive voice broke her. She smiled, tears dripping down her cheeks onto her chest. He wiped them away. "I need you, Estella. You are my North Star to navigate by."

The duke had hurt her, but she had hurt deeply before and survived. She studied him now, letting her fingers drift along the planes of his face. He felt like Mr. Stephens. The intense, pained eyes belonged to the same man who sang her lovely Italian songs. Enough people whom she loved had slipped from her life. Would she let this one go? Or would she forgive and take a risk?

All the while, he awaited her judgment.

"I require something more if I am to consent to your hand," she said.

He closed his eyes, joy and relief breaking over his face. "I have more jewels. I have estates. I can drape you in silks and satins. Feed you grapes and peaches from my orchards." He gestured around him. "And if that doesn't please, I supposedly have a lodging house in Lesser Puddlebury. What more could you want?"

She laughed. He *was* Mr. Stephens.

"A loving family again, ringing with laughter and beautiful music. Will you provide that?"

"My love." He answered her question with a kiss.

After indulging in his embrace, she drew back. "And I require the services of a certain Mr. Stephens, the Italian master and musician, to sing to me and teach me Italian."

"I don't know about that rascal," the duke protested sternly. "I'm quite jealous of him. I see how you look at him."

She tilted her head and smiled. "Full of love."

"Yes. I fear you may run off to Italy with him. I might just have to show you who is the better man." He kissed her deeply.

She could feel his emotions flowing into her.

She trailed her fingers along his chest. Men and their bodies were a mystery to her—their confident stride, strength, and aggressive forms of play. The male contours both intimidated and fascinated her. Her knowledge of what happened between a husband and his wife in the bedchamber was rudimentary and, as Stephen had shown her, quite misguided. Now her lover let her intimately study him. He released her lips, but continued to kiss her forehead and cheeks as her fingers feathered over the rise of his chest with its coarse hairs, to the straps of hard muscles over his ribs, to the solid plane of his belly. He was built for power.

She enjoyed the rush of his sighs and quiet moans as she caressed him. He cupped her breast again and flicked his thumb over its nipple, sending a hot shudder to her feminine core. But then he paused, his finger waiting atop her peak. She realized he wanted her to let him know if she was comfortable.

She raised her head, their gazes locking. Though his eyes were dark coffee, she could see through them like clear water to the sensitive man underneath the muscle, intimidating title, ironic humor, and cynical barbs. She could peer deep into the source of his music, born of love and pain. He shivered. How vulnerable he must feel to have his heart so bared.

She didn't speak, but used her lips to assure him that his secrets would always be safe with her. Then she intertwined their fingers atop her breast. He began his magic, gently circling and squeezing her nipple. She hummed, her sex aching for his touch again. She could feel the heat of his gaze on her, watching her bite her lip and lower her head. He played her like an instrument, each touch a building crescendo.

She shouldn't allow this intimacy to happen so quickly, given his revelation. But her body wasn't being rational. She was greedy to see what strained against his trousers. His body should be as revealed as she was. Skin to skin. Nothing between them.

She shoved him, sending him tumbling onto the mattress.

"Estella," he cried at her burst of violence.

She reached for his trousers, undoing them and ripping them down. His sex rose up.

"Oh, Stephen," she whispered.

His chest rose and fell with hoarse breath as he studied her expression, searching for something. She realized he was nervous. He wanted his body to please her.

"You're handsome," she said. "Every aspect of you is beautiful."

She had never seen a penis before, except in illustrations in medical books where they appeared to be silly-looking, dangling members. Those pictures in no way resembled Stephen's thick, erect shaft.

Did she touch him? Did she play upon him? Would she hurt him?

Her fingers tentatively hovered over him. He must have sensed her unspoken questions. He closed his hand over hers and showed her how to give him pleasure.

Up and down, she glided over his contours. He had been watching her, but now he closed his eyes and dropped open his mouth, lost in the ecstasy of her motion.

His penis was a thing of contrasts, much like the man—the hard shaft and the fragile sacks beneath. She learned how to please him by noting the subtle changes on his face. The tensing of his lids, the widening of his mouth, or the low stream of breath calibrated her tempo and the pressure of her touch.

"Estella, you make me wild, but I should please you."

She kissed his belly, dragging her tongue over his skin. "I enjoy your happiness. Your joy is my joy."

He found her breast again, this time the neglected one that had not received his lovely care. He quickly made up for the lack of attention, rolling its peak between his fingers, flicking across the top, giving it the gentlest squeeze. Her wet feminine parts throbbed as her body began to undulate. Her hand flew along him, all to the maddening pace of his finger. A deep pressure built from her core.

What would sate this rapacious hunger needed no articulation. It was as tacit as breathing.

Never mind that she had just learned he was the Duke of Lucere. In fact, never mind that they had truly known each other a little over a week or that she wasn't being a proper lady. She released his penis, rose onto her knees, and placed her face inches from his, letting her hair fall around him.

"I want to feel you inside of me," she whispered and kissed his lower lip.

She hadn't expected his jaw to tense or for panic to darken his eyes.

"What's wrong?" she asked.

"I'm scared I might hurt you, or you won't enjoy it. Or—"

"Hush," she whispered and let her mouth and tongue allay his fears.

His hand eased up her thigh, his strong, hot palm soothing her soft skin. She paused in their kiss when his fingers reached her wet folds. She shivered with anticipation. His tongue lapped hers as his finger slowly penetrated her. Inch by inch, he progressed, allowing her time to accommodate his presence. She released a low hum in deep satisfaction. He had ventured into a place no other person had known. She gave him the most sacred parts of her heart and body. His finger started to move, in and out, pushing and pressing.

The sensation resonated, deep and intense. Her body pressed against his hand, begging for more. Then his thumb found that small mound again. She tore her lips from his, tossed her head, and cried out as his thumb caressed her. His mouth found her hardened nipple, and his tongue lapped it.

She had no will anymore. She was completely at his mercy. He slid another finger inside, thrusting quickly as he pressed against her inner walls. The sensation of widening to him only intensified the sweet pressure that had grown so acute and powerful, she felt she might break apart from it.

He continued to stroke, whispering her name, telling her of his love. She couldn't respond. Her mind had turned dark, her lungs stopped. She teetered on some thin blade that cut with pleasure, not pain.

Then one touch more—the softest graze across her mound. Her body exploded beneath her skin. Tension flowed out in wild, cresting waves. She pushed frantically against him, grinding him deep into her, until she calmed like waters after a storm.

Then she collapsed onto him, her body spent.

* * *

Now she rested, her soft contours molding to his hard ones, her breath as gentle as lapping waves. He tried to think calming thoughts to relieve his burning erection. He told himself that he had given her pleasure, and that was all that mattered. His own needs could be ignored for the evening. There would be a lifetime of other nights.

And in truth, he was terrified of truly taking her innocence.

His gaze swept down her body. One of her breasts, nipple erect, was flattened against his chest. "My beautiful wife," he whispered.

"We are not married yet."

He touched the tip of her nose. "In my mind we are. We only need to say a few vows and sign our names. Trifling matters."

"My husband," she whispered, trying out the words. They sounded like gentle rain on his ears. He snuggled her closer. After all his sins and mistakes, what merciful God in heaven allowed him to have her? He remembered Harris's words to endeavor to be worthy of her.

"I love you," he said. "I love you so very much."

He received a stunning smile in reply. She wrote on his chest with her finger, *I love you too*, and then let that finger trail down his body, coming to his problem.

"Your p-penis," she stammered from shyness.

He chuckled and guided her hand away. "It's a little late to blush, Mrs. Stephens. But it is well. Do not be concerned about my penis."

"I'm very concerned about it, husband. We never, that is to say, I don't think we performed the proper act as I understand it. I think. I'm not so certain of these things."

"Would you like to?" he asked in somber tones.

"Will it give you the same pleasure that you gave me?"

"I would hope it would give us both pleasure, my love." But he was frightened that she wouldn't enjoy it. He had tried his hardest to prepare her so she wouldn't feel any pain. What if his efforts weren't enough? What if he hurt her? What if he broke her burgeoning confidence?

She drew her arm around his shoulder and kissed him. "Yes, then."

He eased between her legs. His back was quaking as he drew up her knees. Then he interlaced their fingers and raised her arms above her head. Her body was wet and softened, ready for him.

He watched her as he slowly pressed. Her body rose to accept him, snugly holding him within.

"My love," he choked, feeling her walls press around him. "Have I hurt you?"

"Of course not," she replied, clearly unsure why he would ask. "I feel absolutely perfect. As if I've been waiting for you all my life."

As I've been waiting for you. He closed his eyes and began to gently stroke, showing her what a good husband he could be.

Outside, dusk had deepened into night. Lucere and Estella lay in the darkness, cocooned in peace. Her cheek rested on his chest, their bodies exhausted from making love again and again. "Talk to me, Estella," he whispered. "Tell me everything about yourself. Start from your first memory."

"I think it is *you* who should tell me about *your* life."

He considered and then chuckled. "It began today."

CHAPTER FIFTEEN

Estella quietly left Lucere's chamber a little before dawn. How different she felt from the nervous woman who had tiptoed down that corridor the day before, so sure her life was over. Now she was almost stuffed with happiness, as if she had gorged upon it like a starving woman.

She dressed carefully, donning her ball gown for the occasion, simply because it was her best dress—the only one without a discreet patch or stain. Soon, the ambers and oranges of dawn glowed behind the trees. A rooster heralded the fresh morning. Estella heard a tap on the door, and she opened it to find Stephen dressed in his handsome blue coat again.

"Good morning, Mrs. Stephens," he said and then kissed her forehead. "How did you contrive to become more beautiful since I last saw you?"

"I'm not beautiful."

"My dear, you are welcome to squabble with me over any topic—I adore a lively debate—but upon the subject of your beauty and my steadfast affections for you, I shall suffer no opposition."

He held out his arm for her to take, and then he led her out of the house, through the back garden, and into the woods. By the Roman mosaic ruins, he knelt down and asked her formally to marry him. Estella wasn't one to believe in specters, but she had the sensation that her grandfather was there, his lovely spirit around them.

Later, she dressed her mother and set her in her invalid chair. Her mother remarked that her daughter's eyes were uncommonly brilliant. And why was she wearing her best gown in the morning? Had this something to do with the handsome lodger? Estella kept her secret until Stephen joined her. Holding her fiancé's hand, Estella told her mother her news in soothing tones, trying to keep her calm.

"You are the Duke of Lucere and not the tutor?" her mother asked him, even after Estella had explained. He affirmed. Estella expected her mother to carry on in transports that her daughter was marrying a duke, and not any everyday duke, but the great Duke of Lucere.

Mama surprised her. She leaned toward Stephen. "I'm sure you realize that you have won the hand of an incomparable lady."

He glanced at Estella. "I am humbled that she would consent to have me."

Her mother's face turned serious. "Promise me that you will take excellent care of her. As she has taken of me."

"I promise," he said soberly.

The twins were not so moved by deep love. Upon being given the news at breakfast, which Mr. Harris and Lottie had cooked, the twins stared, the truth rapidly sinking in.

"We're going to London!"

They burst from their chairs and began dancing in wild circles, giggling and babbling about plays, balls, shopping, and fashionable gentlemen.

Estella was mortified. "My dears, this is not what is important! We shall be happy again. A close, loving family. Dresses and balls are no matter!"

The twins didn't hear this. They were deaf to words concerning proper behavior.

"May we have an India shawl?" Cecelia shamelessly asked Stephen.

Estella wanted to slide under the table and hide. What must Stephen think of his new sisters? He only gave them a bemused smile and winked at Estella.

"If," he said sternly, holding up a finger, "you do not giggle for six months—not one little peep—devote yourself to your studies, and assist your sister in managing our home, I shall give you each one."

The twins were overwhelmed and almost sank into the forbidden giggles before catching themselves. Instead, they clasped each other's hands and made painful, high humming sounds through tight lips to prevent the prohibited twitters from escaping.

Estella should have felt exhausted—she hadn't slept at all—but near Stephen she felt more awake than she had in years and years. She wanted to pass the morning with him, just touching him and talking and marveling that she would spend the rest of her life with this wonderful man.

But he dashed her hopes. He had business to attend in town, he told her. But he kissed her and promised to return shortly.

"What if Mr. Todd calls?" She panicked.

"I believe you will be out."

* * *

Feeling unmoored with Stephen's absence, Estella headed out of habit to the kitchens and found Lottie scrubbing the pots. The woman turned around, still holding the plate she was washing, dripping water on herself and the floor.

"Is it true, miss? Mr. Harris said you are going to be a princess and that we will all live in a castle where a Frenchie man makes cakes for us." Her hopeful face crumbled. She shook her head. "But that can't be true. Can it? He is making jest of me like the townsfolk. Because I'm not smart like everyone."

Estella smiled. "Lottie, it's true. It's all true."

* * *

The happy, one-toothed pig herder pointed Lucere and Harris to Todd's home. It was a newly built home, boasting numerous gabled windows and heavy cornices. The greed for elegance only created the opposite effect.

A housekeeper opened the door, and Lucere announced himself as "the Duke of Lucere" and asked for an audience with Mr. Todd. Lucere and Harris were led to a drawing room that was an assault to good taste. The walls were covered in a mustard-colored paper and dotted with parakeets of all hues. The elaborate chimneypiece could have come from Versailles. Turquoise sofas and gray marble tables were gathered around a pastel carpet. Lucere already wanted to punch the man, and his drawing room did little to quell his aggression.

Harris was not so perturbed. He merely mentioned that he had never seen a red parakeet before and wondered if they existed.

Finally, Todd entered. A suspicious look furrowed his brow. He spotted Lucere and snarled, "What is this?" Only after this gracious greeting did Todd seem to register Lucere's fine clothes and the gold ring glinting on his finger.

Lucere smiled, enjoying himself. He ambled over to a side table and picked up an ivory box, turned it in his hand, and set it down. "I came to spare my fiancée, Miss Primrose, a scene that would prove unpleasant to her should you wait upon her today. Miss Primrose has consented to marry me, and therefore, I ask that you no longer press her with your unwanted affections."

"Marry you? You're the Duke of Lucere, are you?" Todd barked a laugh. "What were you yesterday? Mr. Stephens, the tutor. No doubt, the courts of England have another name for you. I thought Estella was unstable, but this is utter madness."

Lucere waved to Mr. Harris, who brought forward a pouch. Lucere handed it to Todd. "I believe the mortgage, as well as the other debts you had taken upon yourself to pay without Miss Primrose's consent, totals 3,120 pounds. Inside are 200 pounds. I can pay you the rest by a cheque from the Bank of England at this moment, or if you doubt my identity, you may wait for my man of business, who will be arriving in three days' time with a special marriage license."

Todd gazed at him and then the money. His upper lip quivered. "She is promised to me," he growled. "By accepting you—whoever you are—she has breached her promise, and I shall act accordingly."

"Why?" Lucere shrugged in the face of the man's fury. "Will it win her affections? Will hurting her be the only way you assuage your damaged pride? I do not understand your reasoning, unless you mean to win at all costs."

"She is mine!" he thundered. "I own her. Her mother would have been in debtors' prison years ago if it weren't for me. And if you are the true Duke of Lucere, you should thank me. For you did nothing for her but let her sink further and further down."

Todd landed an emotional punch to Lucere's gut. Lucere staggered under its blow.

The banker continued. "So you've won her faithless heart. Congratulations. She'll use you like she used me. Only, I'm not blind to her true grasping, whorish nature."

Lucere's fist smashed Todd's chin, knocking his head back. Todd stumbled, then righted himself on a marble table.

"You disrespect me in my own home." Todd wiped his bloodied mouth and charged.

Lucere deflected the man's coming punch and used Todd's momentum to throw him down. "You will not insult or belittle my fiancée," he said, pressing Todd's face into the carpet. "You will not intimidate or threaten her ever again. Yes, I admit I should have known about Miss Primrose's straits and taken her away long ago. That is a regret, among many, that I will harbor for the rest of my life. But I know enough of your character to give no consequence to your insults. And in your heart, you know Miss Primrose is loving and kind, to her very bones. Her outer beauty is but a glimmer of the treasures in her heart. That is why she would never willingly have you and why you so desperately desire her."

"She is no such thing," Todd spat.

"I tell you this, if you continue in your harassment of her, I shall have no scruple denouncing your bank throughout England. I will ruin you as you attempted to ruin her."

Lucere released the man and rose to his feet. "Come, Harris, I think we have concluded our business here, unless Todd requires further proof of my devotion to my wife and the lengths I will go to defend her honor."

Todd did not.

* * *

Outside, Lucere gazed up at the clear sky hanging over the fields and lodgings of Puddlebury. "I used my title to threaten Todd," he told Harris. "He would not have succumbed so easily had I been rich John Smith. You say I am worthy of the title, and I contend that I am not."

He held up his palm, halting the words waiting on Harris's lips.

"It is no matter. The title has been a gift bestowed on me, and I must use its powers wisely and justly." He chuckled. "How ironical. I'm getting 'shackled,' as they say, in a week's time. I'm a duke of vast responsibility, but I've never felt so liberated in my life."

Harris had no commentary on this great moment of epiphany, except a practical suggestion. "Let us buy something lovely for Miss Primrose so she will not ask questions concerning your whereabouts and receive answers that will distress her."

"You are always three steps ahead. Why do I think my father merely wore the title Duke of Lucere, but you filled the true office?" He held out his hand. "Thank you, Harris. You didn't give up on me when you should have."

Harris didn't shake his hand or respond to Lucere's earnest gratitude, but Lucere knew the man appreciated it. They ambled along the street until they reached a grocer, where a young girl stood among the cabbages and turnips selling flowers. Lucere requested the pale pink geraniums.

"Catherine's favorite," Harris remarked. "I think she would have adored Miss Primrose. They are a great deal alike."

"They are," Lucere agreed. And then his throat tightened. He hurriedly paid for the flowers. "Come, Harris, let's make haste home." Time was precious and shouldn't be idly wasted away from the people he loved.

He found Estella sitting on the drawing room sofa, her head bent over her sewing.

She lifted her gaze to meet his. "My love, I've missed you."

Her smile warmed him like the Italian summer sun. One day very soon, he would take his duchess of light to Rome so she could experience that sun and its glorious shine.

The End

Gentle Reader,

Once upon a time at a RWA conference, Grace Burrowes, Emily Greenwood, and I were chilling out and sipping wine at the hotel bar when Grace suggested that we should write an anthology. I had to think about her proposal for a whole two seconds before eagerly agreeing. However, I had never written a novella and was rather intimidated after the first shine of inspiration (and wine) had worn off. Luckily, Grace and Emily were amazing mentors and made the entire process a true joy. Best of all, I was able to work with these talented, smart, and fabulous women. I hope you garner as much happiness from these stories as we had brainstorming and writing them.

If you would like to read more of my work, please check out my Victorian comedies **Wicked Little Secrets** and **Wicked, My Love**.

Sign up for my newsletter at http://eepurl.com/bO51hv to receive information about my exciting upcoming releases.

My website contains excerpts of all my works, as well as interesting historical tidbits. Please stop by!

http://susannaives.com

Susanna Ives

KISS ME, YOUR GRACE

EMILY GREENWOOD

CHAPTER ONE

"Louisa, I do not *need* any wine," Claire Beckett said to her friend Louisa Firth as they sat before a cozy fire. It was late in the evening, and the hearth around which they were relaxing was in the handsome sitting room at Foxtail, the Duke of Starlingham's hunting box.

About once an hour since arriving three days before, Claire had reflected on the outrageousness of being at the lodge. Louisa, whose position as Foxtail's housekeeper would be in danger should it ever become known that she'd invited Claire to stay, had dismissed Claire's worries, insisting that no one would ever know since they were as good as alone there. But Claire couldn't help being concerned.

"Everyone needs wine sometimes," Louisa said. "Even Grainger."

"Grainger, like you, is an employee here, and his needs are being provided for by the Duke of Starlingham. *I* have no business being here at all, so I must in all conscience pay for anything I use here on my illicit holiday. Wine would not be a sensible use of my limited funds."

Claire had had quite a bit more money when she'd set out on her journey, but that was before she decided that she urgently needed to see Louisa.

Louisa, whose handsome features looked eminently respectable in her housekeeper's attire of plain dark frock and white cap, grinned cheekily and poured wine in a glass, then pushed it toward Claire. "Grainger and I, being the only staff living in, are allowed two glasses of wine on Sunday, and I only want one, so you must have my second glass."

"It'll be wasted on me—I never drink more than a sip or two."

"That's because your father has ridiculous notions about women being frail and foolish that he imposes on you."

It was true that Mr. Beckett always said that ladies should never drink more than a thimbleful of wine, lest they risk looking coarse. But Claire knew her father *meant* well. Or at least, that was what she'd always told herself until a few days ago.

Louisa nudged the glass closer. "Go on. It's really good wine."

Oh, why not, Claire thought. A glass of wine was nothing to telling lies and pretending to be what she was not. Claire took the wine and sipped. It was delicious, and she relaxed back against the high, upholstered sides of her chair in a comfortably unladylike slump.

The room was decorated in manly shades of chocolate and midnight, with the obligatory stags' heads mounted on the walls, though, happily as far as Claire was concerned, only three. As the fire crackled merrily, its light danced amid the mischief in Louisa's eyes. Though she was unfailingly hardworking and practical, Louisa was also prone to outrageousness. As the daughter of Claire's father's estate manager, Louisa had always been able to get away with more than Claire, the daughter of a gentleman. They'd been friends since girlhood, despite the difference in their stations.

"Imagine if your father could see you here," Louisa said.

Claire groaned. "I'm trying not to think of him, or my mother, or any of my brothers, discovering me here. Any moment now, one of the locals is surely going to realize I'm not the Duke of Starlingham's second cousin and expose me."

"Nonsense," Louisa said, leaning forward to select a biscuit from the plate she'd put on the small table between them. "No one around here has seen the man—or a single person from his family—for a good dozen years or more. The duke's man of affairs is the only person who ever comes here, and he only comes once a year to check on the place. Besides, the neighbors all think it's wonderful that the duke's cousin has come to stay."

"I never would have dreamed that one day I'd be a fraud," Claire said morosely.

"Have a biscuit," Louisa urged. "I hear almond biscuits are the very thing to relieve feelings of being a fraud."

"You are the most outrageous friend," Claire said, but she took two.

"I simply believe in the value of indulgence in times of uncertainty. From the slim look of you, I expect you've hardly enjoyed yourself at all in recent times."

Maybe, Claire thought, and felt instantly disloyal toward her family. But the biscuits were good, and she sipped her wine, which helped her mind less that she was disloyal and a fraud. "But what if someone *does* find out?"

"Phoo," Louisa scoffed. "You're a gentleman's daughter and just the sort of young lady who belongs at Foxtail, and I'd wager, if the old duke ever deigned to grace us with his presence, he'd agree."

"The poor old duke, who has no idea that a wicked woman is taking advantage of his hospitality in his very own hunting box."

"Stop worrying about the duke! The man has so many estates he can't even be bothered to visit them all, even if he does pay to have Foxtail ever at the ready should he decide to appear. You spend too much time being concerned about other people, Claire. Honestly, I don't know what's happened to you in recent years—you've become so horribly *nice*. Do you realize that 'I'm sorry' was the first thing you said to me when you arrived the other night?"

Claire only just managed to stop herself from apologizing for that.

"And clearly you've become accustomed to doing more than your fair share of tasks—I'm certain you were going to volunteer to wash the dishes for Sally this morning!"

"She's so busy, and surely my coming here has made more work for her."

"She's paid—and quite a bit more than she would make anywhere else in the county—to wash dishes here. You're not supposed to do her work for her."

"I'm sorry."

Louisa glared at her meaningfully, and Claire dropped her head into her hands and moaned. "You're right. I've just become so used to being accommodating. I hate disappointing people or making them angry."

"In the name of all that's sensible, Claire, you can't go through life making everybody else's wishes your command." Louisa shook her head with affectionate exasperation. "Coming here was the best thing you could have done for yourself."

Maybe that was true, even if Claire did still feel guilty about the deception she'd perpetrated on her family and the deception she was currently perpetrating at Foxtail. She had become so used to doing whatever it took to forestall one of her father's tirades that she'd hardly noticed when she'd begun to push her own needs and opinions aside. Until four days before, when her father had told her what her future was going to be, and something in her had snapped. She'd done the only thing she could think to do: escape.

"But I lied," Claire said. "My whole family thinks I'm at Loxford with Great-Aunt Mary. And you'll be sent packing if anyone discovers we knew each other before I arrived."

"Desperate times call for desperate measures. I've been urging you to visit for months, knowing full well that a housekeeper isn't supposed to invite guests." Louisa pulled off her housekeeper's cap and dropped it on the table next to her, muttering dark things about its dowdiness and about having to call herself "Mrs.," as was the custom for housekeepers, whether they were married or not. "I'll admit I didn't believe that you'd come. But I'm so glad you did."

Claire reached out and squeezed Louisa's hand. "Me too." Claire knew she couldn't stay at Foxtail longer than two weeks—her family would be expecting her home by then, and they'd worry if she didn't return. Despite everything, she didn't want to hurt them. But she *needed* this time with Louisa—especially if these two weeks were going to be the last happy days of her life.

"Say, how old do you suppose the dear old duke is, anyway?" Claire mused.

"The only person here who's ever met Starlingham is Grainger, but Grainger's as old as the hills and not good with anything that doesn't involve animals, trees, or streams. He always says the duke is 'but a wee lad,' which, considering Grainger's ancientness, could mean Starlingham's fifty. And I could hardly ask the duke's age when I was hired by that employment agency."

"I suppose not."

"Though I would dearly love to meet the man." Louisa nibbled a biscuit thoughtfully. "I've never seen a duke. I'll wager he has the most amazing clothes."

"His *clothes*? That's what you want to see?"

"If he's fifty or so, his clothes will likely be the most spectacular thing about him."

Claire laughed. "We *are* rather bad, you know." The fire was dying down, and she took the poker and stirred up the flames. "Lying to everyone."

"It's harmless," Louisa said firmly. "Besides, I hardly ever see a soul from one month to the next, aside from Grainger, Cook, and the two maids. You being here is helping to keep me sane, and since you're paying for your own food and firewood, it's not costing the duke a thing."

By the time they'd both finished their wine, Claire felt more relaxed than she had in days. Their companionable quiet was shattered, however, by an entirely unexpected and, considering the circumstances, unwanted sound.

"Heavens! Was that a knock at the front door?" Claire asked, sitting forward.

Louisa cocked her head, listening—and there it was again, a definite knocking. "A foreign sound at Foxtail, to be sure." She snatched up her cap and put it back on. Taking the candelabrum, she started for the door.

"I'll come with you," Claire said, reaching for the fireplace poker.

Louisa raised an eyebrow, but Claire said, "Grainger's surely retired to his little gardener's cottage with his wine, so there won't be anyone to protect us."

Louisa nodded and turned down the corridor leading to the front door.

The knocking, which had paused briefly, started again as they reached the door. It was a heavy, bold knocking, and it made Claire think of highwaymen shouting demands at terrified travelers. Clearly, she read too many Gothic novels, she thought, smiling to herself, but nonetheless she steadied her grip on the poker.

Louisa opened the door. The light from the candelabrum illuminated only an expanse of dark coat until Louisa raised it higher to reveal the face of a man.

Claire's first impression was of the squareness of his jaw, then of a mouth set in a firm line. Her eyes moved upward, taking in features that had been made with bold strokes. In the shadowy light, it was easy to decide his eyes were black, but she had a feeling they'd look that way in the daytime too. His hair was dark and longish, its spiky waves brushing the top of his dark coat and slashing across his forehead.

He was moderately tall and rather hulking. His shoulders were unfashionably brawny, and his finely tailored coat looked as though it must have needed an entire bolt of fabric. And what kind of gentleman had arm muscles that strained against his sleeves? This man might be a gentleman—and there was little doubt of that from the cut of his clothes—but the assertive jut of his chin and the leashed strength of his body spoke not of drawing rooms and dance floors, but sweat and force.

With a little shiver of something she couldn't have named, Claire thought that he would not have looked out of place swinging a hammer in a blacksmith's forge, and she imagined fire reflected in those intense black orbs while sweat trickled down the rough angles of his cheeks… the Roman god Vulcan at his work.

Clearly, she needed to stop reading those mythology books as well.

"Good evening," the man said in deep, cultured tones. "I am Mr. Fitzwilliam, cousin to His Grace, the Duke of Starlingham."

Claire and Louisa gasped at the same time.

* * *

Rowan MacKenzie Fitzwilliam, eighth Duke of Starlingham, barely restrained himself from rolling his eyes at the responses of the two women to his arrival at what was, in fact, his own hunting box. He knew that he could look like a brute, and truth be told, he liked that his appearance and his gruff manners kept most people at bay. But he wanted a hot bath and a meal in short order.

However, no one was meant to know that Foxtail's master had arrived. As Rowan had told his friends the Duke of Mowne and the Duke of Lucere when they'd agreed on the charade that had brought them to the town of Lesser Puddlebury, it was actually fortunate for him that Mowne had been shot in the backside, necessitating this stop so he could recuperate. Since they meant to disguise their ducal identities while rusticating at various locations in the area—lest Mowne's powerful Uncle Leo get wind of the circumstances of his wounding—Rowan would have a chance to visit his property unobserved. Mowne had not found Rowan's references to his "happy accident" amusing, but then, Mowne's rump had apparently yet to stop throbbing.

"Might I come in?" Rowan asked when neither of the women made any reply. Because of the position of the candelabrum one of them was holding, he couldn't see their eyes, though he supposed from their gasping that they were filled with trepidation.

"Of course," said the one holding the candelabrum in a surprisingly steady voice, and both women stepped back to let him in. "I am Mrs. Firth, housekeeper here," she continued. "Forgive me, but I had not expected visitors this evening."

In the better light of the corridor, he could see that his housekeeper was a handsome brunette, and tall for a woman. She was wearing a tidy, sober frock and looked exactly as a housekeeper ought, if rather young.

"I've just arrived in the area," he said, "and I require lodging for the night—and, in fact, for the next two weeks. My cousin the duke assured me I would be welcome to stay here, and he has asked me to inspect the property with an eye toward any needed improvements. I trust my arrival is not inconvenient for the staff."

In truth, Rowan did not expect to do improvements but planned to have a look around before he approved the sale of the property, though he didn't intend for his staff to know of this yet. Rowan's business manager, Forsythe, had been insisting for some time that Foxtail was nothing but a drain on the dukedom's finances, since no one in the family used it, and that it ought to be sold as soon as possible and the money used for repairs needed at the ducal seat. Forsythe even had a buyer already.

Rowan, whose only memories of Foxtail were the hazy snippets of the occasional visits made there during his youth (the last time when he was thirteen), was delaying in agreeing to the sale of Foxtail only because of his mother. She insisted they must keep the place because Rowan's father, dead these fifteen years, had had such happy memories of it. When Rowan pointed out that neither his mother nor any of his siblings ever visited it, she would always say, with an affecting moistness in her eyes, "It would make me sad to visit a place where my darling John was so happy. But you can't *sell* it."

His mother's nostalgia for Foxtail was the reason it was kept in immaculate condition and ready for guests, as a sort of shrine to the happy days she'd spent there with her husband in the early years of their marriage. A duke's coffers could easily afford such indulgences—but that didn't mean they were a sensible use of funds.

Rowan felt honor-bound to tell his mother before he gave his approval for the sale of Foxtail, though he hadn't yet been able to make himself have that conversation. He expected that this visit would allow him to gather evidence of Foxtail's general unworthiness. Surely his mother would rather see the place sold than allow it to simply molder away.

"Your arrival, while unexpected, is no inconvenience," the housekeeper said. Despite that initial gasp, she did not seem cowed by him, and he liked her the better for it. He abhorred obsequious or fearful servants and found brusqueness to be an effective way to weed out unsuitable people. "We keep all the rooms at the ready, should His Grace or any of the family arrive."

As, of course, the staff had been doing, pointlessly, for years. Rowan didn't want to think of the sum such daily preparing of unused rooms had amounted to.

His eyes traveled to the other woman, a blonde wearing a rose-colored gown. She was holding a fireplace poker at her side, apparently having armed herself against the possibility of an intruder at the door. He repressed the wicked curl that teased the edge of his mouth at the idea of this slip of a woman taking him on. But who was she? Her gown was far too fine to be that of a servant, never mind the fetching style of her hair and the soft beauty of her features.

And then their eyes met, and the oddest thing happened: An electric shiver of what felt like recognition went through him. There was something about her, something familiar, even though he was certain they'd never met before. No... it was more as if he already knew and understood her on some inexpressible level.

Even as he told himself he'd merely been struck by her looks, he felt it wasn't that. Whatever it was had nothing to do with how she looked; it came from within. Within her and within him.

Ridiculous.

Shaking his head to clear it, he focused his attention on the housekeeper. "I took the liberty of directing my carriage to the stable," he said, "and I trust my coachman can be accommodated. Though my valet was detained by a matter of some urgency."

His trunk—with his valet—had already gone on to Scotland before he and his friends had had to separate because of the incident involving Mowne's rump. Since neither Lucere nor Mowne had needed the carriage, which belonged to Rowan but did not bear his ducal crest, he'd taken it. He gestured toward his large valise. "I have just the one bag."

He could have sworn his words brought the light of suspicion to the blonde's eyes.

"Who are you?" he demanded of her.

"I'm sorry," she said, inexplicably. And then she shifted abruptly, as though Mrs. Firth had knocked into her.

"Pardon?" he said.

She seemed to draw herself up. "I mean," she said firmly, "I am Miss Beckett, also cousin to His Grace, the Duke of Starlingham, and a guest here. I'm sorry if you're surprised to find Foxtail already occupied."

What?

Rowan had the usual large complement of cousins, some of whom, it was true, he didn't know terribly well. But he was not so very shabby a head of family that he did not at least know *who* his cousins were, never mind that anyone related to a duke made certain to claim the connection as often as possible. That weird spark of recognition aside, this pretty woman was not his cousin, and indeed, there were no Becketts whatsoever in the family.

So who was she, and why was she pretending to be related to him?

"On His Grace's father's side?" he asked, deciding to play along for a bit to see what he could discover.

She drew herself up even straighter, achieving the sort of primness that would have done credit to a governess but was at odds with her delicate beauty. "Mother's."

Whatever she was up to, she clearly meant to brazen it out, and though he ought to have been outraged that this woman was taking advantage of Foxtail's hospitality, he found himself slightly amused by her. Not that he would let her see as much.

"And what are you doing here?" he demanded. He could feel the housekeeper watching him.

"I am..."—Miss Beckett cleared her throat—"on holiday. His Grace's mother told my mother that the lodge was unused and I might spend a little time here."

"Beckett," he mused, toying with her. "I didn't know there was anyone named Beckett in the family."

She colored, and he repressed the smugness that tugged at his lips.

"I am a second cousin," she said.

"Are you." Before he could quiz her further, the housekeeper broke in.

"You must be fatigued from your journey, Mr. Fitzwilliam. Have you eaten?"

"No. In fact, I require something hot as soon as possible."

"I'll have a tray brought up to your chamber."

Did she mean to ensure that he didn't linger downstairs? He thought of demanding to eat in the dining room just to thwart her, but in truth it had been a long day and he did just want to retire.

"Is the red velvet bedchamber available? I've been told I ought to experience it." His mother still spoke of staying there when the family used to visit. Apparently the red velvet room was the perfect example of what a comfortable hunting box bedchamber should be—or at least it had been years ago. Having been a boy at the time, Rowan had paid no attention whatsoever to such things as furnishings.

The two women shared a look.

"I could—" began the blonde, but the housekeeper cut her off.

"Miss Beckett is already occupying that room," the housekeeper informed him. "But I'm certain you'll be very comfortable in one of the other bedchambers."

Interesting. He'd wager anything that Miss Beckett had been about to offer to surrender her bedchamber to him, an entirely unnecessary offer that no gentleman would have accepted.

"If you would follow me?" the housekeeper said.

So he was to have an expedited journey from doorstep to bedchamber. Was the housekeeper eager to get rid of him so she could discuss him with his "cousin"? For now, he would oblige her.

CHAPTER TWO

"What on earth am I going to do?" Claire said to Louisa an hour later as they stood in Claire's bedchamber. Beautifully decorated in tones of wine and gold with velvet hangings around the bed and a large, distinctive golden clock on the wall, it was the nicest bedchamber in the lodge. Claire had initially balked at taking it, but Louisa had insisted.

Also, it was the only room in the lodge whose walls didn't display at least one animal's head. Most of the bedchambers had several, which both Claire and Louisa thought spoiled the coziness somewhat, though Louisa, out of boredom and a desire for companionship, however mute, had given all the mounted heads names and personalities; the ones in the breakfast room she called Tristan and Isolde, and the sitting room stag was Max.

At least Claire's bedchamber was at the other end of the corridor from the room Mr. Fitzwilliam had been given. Claire covered her eyes with her hand. "I ought to leave right this minute. What if he suspects I'm a fraud?"

"You're not leaving! Besides, why should he suspect anything? It's often the case that cousins from one side of a family don't know the other. I, for one, have never met any of my second cousins, since they live in the north. Anyway, he seemed to accept your presence here."

"Maybe." Claire let her hand fall. "But he certainly seemed surprised, and he was scrutinizing me."

"Actually," Louisa said, a smile curling the edges of her lips, "I thought he looked rather taken with you."

"Don't be ridiculous. He was even ruder to me than he was to you."

Louisa laughed. "He is a gruff character, isn't he? But I like a plain-speaking man."

"Plain-speaking? He grunted at me!"

"Isn't it always the girls the boys like best that they torment the most?" Louisa moved toward the wardrobe and began inspecting Claire's gowns.

"That doesn't go for men," Claire said. "He clearly dislikes me. What are you doing?"

"Just looking to see what you have to wear, now that we have a gentleman staying here." Louisa plucked a cream-colored gown from among those hanging in the wardrobe and held it out, fluffing the skirts. "You haven't worn this one yet, but it would look divine with your coloring. You should wear it tomorrow."

Claire made a face, took the gown from her, and put it back. "I hardly think a haughty, fine gentleman like Mr. Fitzwilliam would notice what I wear," she said, recalling the way he'd glowered at her. Though she also remembered how overwhelmingly—and fascinatingly—male he'd been. "I think he was testing me with his questions about my relationship to the duke."

Louisa waved a hand dismissively. "You're just nervous because you've become too used to telling people what they want to hear, so you've lost the capacity to lie when necessary. You always were a little too considerate of other people's feelings for your own good, but honestly, what *happened* to you in the last few years? You didn't used to be so revoltingly agreeable."

Claire dropped down onto the bed and Louisa joined her, and they settled back against the headboard as companionably as they used to on Claire's bed when they were girls.

"I don't know. Once Mama decided I was a young lady and thus couldn't run about as I liked anymore, I had to absorb all her lessons about being feminine and yielding to the guidance of men. I suppose it seemed right to discount my own opinions. That is, until the moment Papa told me I was to marry Lord Haight."

"Your mouth contorts hideously every time you say the baron's name. Do you remember that rhyme we made up about him when we were nine? 'Lord Haight, Lord Haight, can't get through the garden gate.'"

"If I'd guessed that he might one day be destined to be my husband, I think I would have run away from home right then. Which would have saved me from having to do it now that I'm twenty-one." Claire sighed. "I suppose Papa just wants me to be provided for."

"There are better ways of providing for his only daughter," Louisa said. "The baron must be almost sixty."

Claire nodded gloomily. "Everything about him sags, and his breath smells awful."

"If you marry that man, you will have to kiss that mouth."

Revulsion crawled down Claire's spine. "I know. The thought of his breath was what spurred me to run away."

Louisa sat forward and twisted to grab Claire's shoulders as if she were going to shake her. "Claire, you *can't* marry him!"

"But what choice do I have? Papa won't brook my refusal. I'd be cast out—he's already talking of disowning Robert."

"Maybe it's just bluster," Louisa said, releasing Claire and leaning back against the headboard again as she pondered. "How could your father really want to disown his son?"

The corners of Claire's mouth tipped down. "You've never seen Papa in high dudgeon. It's terrible. And if I'm cast out, where would I go and what would I do? I suppose I'll have to become a governess."

Louisa gave a hum of disapproval. "Unless you find a very good situation, you'd likely be expected to civilize impossibly spoiled children for terribly meager pay, and you'd no longer be looked upon as eligible by gentlemen." Louisa's expression turned serious. "Really, the best thing would be for you to simply find a husband on your own."

Claire slid off the bed, moved to the wardrobe, and began to look through the gowns herself. Except for her violet satin gown, which she'd originally packed in case Aunt Mary had a party, they were nothing very special, just the simple muslins she favored. They certainly hadn't helped her find a husband during her one Season, last year in London.

"I have thought of that, you know," she said dryly. "But it's hardly easy to meet a decent man and marry him quickly."

"Nonsense. Ladies do it all the time," Louisa said, leaping from the bed with one of her customary gusts of energy. "What about Mr. Rutledge? You've met him in town twice already. He's kind, pleasant-looking, and nowhere near sixty."

"Perhaps," Claire said in a tentative tone. "He *is* very... nice. And there is that assembly coming up. But maybe I'm exaggerating and Lord Haight isn't so very horrible. Perhaps I'm just being selfish."

"Claire Beckett! Do you want to be married to The Haight and his breath?"

"*The Haight?*" Claire shook her head at Louisa's irreverence, but then she straightened her shoulders. "No. No, I don't!"

Louisa cackled triumphantly. "You said no, Claire! And you said what you thought. There, was that so hard?"

"Yes," Claire said, then laughed. "Very well, it wasn't, but it's easy to say no when I'm talking to you. It will be impossible to say no to Papa and The Haight."

Her three brothers didn't mind saying no to Papa. Two of them were still at home—Robert was at university—and they all ran up debts and drank too much, which meant yelling and strife that Claire hated. It was far better to be pleasing.

Making people happy felt good, and all Claire needed to do to achieve that was to be agreeable. But now she had to admit that she'd become so accustomed to ignoring what she really wanted that she'd forgotten she had opinions and wishes of her own.

Her father telling her she was going to marry Lord Haight had awoken something willful in her, and refusal had stirred from some deeply hidden place. He'd delivered the news the day before Claire was to leave for a few weeks' stay with her great-aunt.

"You'll have a nice holiday with Aunt Mary, and when you return, we'll post the banns," Papa had said. *"Haight will make you the perfect husband."*

The shock of his words had been instant. She knew it was her duty to marry, but at twenty-one, she'd thought she'd have time to find a husband who suited her.

Claire had somehow managed to speak. *"Papa, I don't want to marry Lord Haight. I couldn't."*

His face had darkened, and her stomach had dropped at the realization that his anger would be turned on her. But then his face had softened into a smile.

"Of course it's a surprise, my dear. But you'll see, once you have a few moments to think, that you very much do want to marry Haight. Anyway, it's all settled, so there's no sense in fussing about it. There's a good girl." And he'd given her a cheery hug.

She'd gone to bed in despair and awoken knowing she had to find her way to the one person who would really listen to her—Louisa. And so Claire had left that morning pretending she was going to meet Aunt Mary's coach in town. Instead, she'd left a note with the innkeeper to be given to her aunt's coachman, announcing a change of plans, and bought a ticket on the mail coach that would take her to Foxtail.

"Well, now I'm deceiving the town of Lesser Puddlebury, the staff of Foxtail, and the cousin of the Duke of Starlingham. Is that enough of a sign for you that I've departed from my obliging ways?"

"No. For goodness's sake, the first thing you said to Fitzwilliam was 'I'm sorry.' And you would certainly have offered to give up your bedchamber to him if I hadn't kicked you!"

"I feel guilty about being here."

"Don't. For all we know, Fitzwilliam isn't really the duke's cousin either."

Claire treated her friend to a withering look. "Why would he be masquerading as the duke's cousin, never mind the impossible coincidence of two people here at Foxtail masquerading as the duke's cousins at the same time?"

"Stranger things have happened," Louisa said loftily. "But you know," she continued, as if an idea had just occurred to her, "it's really quite perfect that he's come. What you need is practice in saying no and not being so agreeable. Fitzwilliam is the perfect person to practice on, since *he's* certainly not agreeable, and after you leave here, you'll never see him again."

Claire snorted. "What on earth are you proposing—a campaign of being rude to the duke's cousin?"

"Not rude, just not so endlessly obliging. Although, it wouldn't hurt to be a little rude."

"That's the silliest idea I've ever heard," Claire said. "What I should really do is leave. What if Mr. Fitzwilliam discovers I'm no relation to the duke? And that you knew as much?"

"He won't. We've been careful to be sure that no one would think you were anything but a stranger to me when you arrived. Since none of the servants sleep here, and Grainger has his own little house out back, there's been no one here to notice our late-night chats."

"Mr. Fitzwilliam might have heard us talking and laughing tonight," Claire pointed out.

"If he mentions anything, we'll say it must have been the dogs."

Claire shook her head at Louisa's brazenness, but in truth she yearned to be more daring, as she once had been. "Maybe you're a *little* bit right that I need practice being bold."

"Certainly I'm right," Louisa said.

"And it does seem," Claire said slowly, testing out the idea, "that the gruff Mr. Fitzwilliam might not even notice or care whether I'm nice."

"Exactly," Louisa said enthusiastically. "You can start tomorrow."

A rising swell of sass made Claire grin. "And if he doesn't like it, I'll say something rude."

"That's the spirit!"

* * *

In his bedchamber early the next morning, Rowan stood before the looking glass with a freshly stropped razor poised to meet his cheek. It had been years since he'd shaved himself. Or stropped a razor, for that matter. He could almost feel the eyes of the stag's head mounted on the wall to his right observing his hesitation with disgust.

"Getting on with it," he muttered and drew the razor down his cheek, happily managing not to slice himself to ribbons. When had he become such a damned fancy fellow that he quaked to shave himself?

Fifteen minutes later he was done, with only one small cut that would be noticeable above his cravat and a couple of nicks on his neck, but he didn't think they'd show once he was dressed. He resolved there and then that, once he was returned to the ministrations of his valet, he would shave himself once a week to keep in practice.

He intended to make his way downstairs for breakfast before Miss Beckett arose so he could discreetly quiz the servants about his "cousin's" presence there. As he was sliding his foot into his boot, though, he heard someone greet her by name outside his room.

He jerked on his boot. The night before, as he was lying in bed, he'd heard the repeated sounds of female laughter, which had surely been Miss Beckett and the housekeeper, since she'd mentioned that the maids did not live in. Did Mrs. Firth know Miss Beckett was a fraud? The mystery of her presence had only deepened.

As he made his way downstairs, he recalled that strange feeling of familiarity—that veritable thunderbolt—he'd experienced at his first sight of Miss Beckett, as though she was someone very special. How ridiculous. Had the air of Lesser Puddlebury done something to his head? He'd spent the hours since parting from Mowne and Lucere touring the surrounding countryside, and perhaps he'd become more tired than he'd realized—tired to the point of imbecility, if he was imagining thunderbolts.

As he entered the breakfast room, he found his fake cousin seated at the table with a plate of toast and a cup of tea. She looked up at his entrance. She was still very pretty by the clear light of day. Even lovelier, actually, than he remembered from the night before.

Her eyes were blue, he saw now—the soft blue gray of lavender. Her fair, shining hair was dressed simply in a tidy knot ornamented with a few slim plaits, and she was wearing a stamped blue gown with a wide sash of darker blue under her bosom. Her skin was exceptionally lovely, creamy and tinged with peach at her cheeks, and an absurd desire to touch her made him curl his fingers inward.

"Good day to you, sir," she said, looking at him over the top of her teacup. He grunted at her and went to the sideboard to fill his plate.

He took a seat across from her and prepared to begin his interrogation. Lest he reveal his suspicions, though, he meant to proceed in an oblique manner.

"So, Miss Beckett, what do you plan to do during your stay here?"

"Oh… this and that. I find the Foxtail grounds very pretty."

If she was up to no good, she betrayed no anxiety about discovery, appearing collected and cool. He tested out the idea that she had come to Foxtail to escape the consequences of some sort of crime. Perhaps she'd stolen a lady's jewels, or tricked an old fellow into parting with his blunt.

But he couldn't see it. She looked perfectly suited to her surroundings, as though she would have been completely at ease having tea with his sisters or sailing gracefully around a London dance floor. There was a dignity about her that argued strongly against criminal behavior. And the way she brought her teacup to her lips—surely no nefarious woman could have done so with such artless grace.

He thought of how she'd been on the verge of offering him her bedchamber the night before and decided that, were she truly wicked, she would have brazened out the charade and insisted she was owed every bit of consequence due to a duke's cousin.

All of which evidence left him to conclude that whatever was prompting her to pass herself off as his cousin was most likely something harmless but reputation-ruining. Perhaps she was a governess who'd drawn the gaze of the master or been pursued by an eldest son. She was pretty enough to cause quite a bit of trouble in such a household.

"So you've been wandering the grounds, have you?" he asked.

"Mmm," she said vaguely, employing, to his annoyance, one of his own cherished techniques of avoidance.

He addressed himself to a bit of ham while Miss Beckett drank her tea and nibbled a corner of toast, apparently uninterested in him because she made no attempt to converse.

After several minutes of silence, he tried again. "And where do you reside when you are not availing yourself of the duke's hospitality?"

That caused her to pause in her toast-nibbling. Was she about to offer some tidbit that would reveal her identity? If she'd known Mrs. Firth beforehand, which he suspected, given the laughter of the night before, that might explain Miss Beckett's presence here.

"My family resides a few hours north of here," she said.

"And no one accompanied you on your holiday here? No sister, aunt, or maid?"

A pause. Was she going to apologize again?

"Like you, I found myself traveling alone for unforeseen reasons." She returned to sipping her tea in that graceful way.

She'd given him nothing. He could press her more specifically to provide the kind of information any relative of the duke would surely know, such as the names of his siblings, but he realized that he didn't want the mystery of who she was solved so bluntly.

She was, for some reason he could not understand, the most interesting woman he'd encountered in a very long time.

He frowned as he recalled a conversation he'd had a few days before with his mother, of whom he was extremely fond, though she *would* continue to introduce topics he did not wish to discuss.

"*Rowan, I suspect you of putting off marriage indefinitely, as though you have all the time in the world.*"

"*Expecting my imminent demise, Mother?*" he'd said with a grin. "*There is always Henry.*"

She'd given him a reproving look. "*Your brother is fifteen and far from ready to be a duke, should your demise turn out to be imminent. Which, as your mother, I refuse to consider.*" Her intelligent brown eyes had softened. "*I want to see you happily settled with a good woman.*"

"*Hmm,*" he'd said. He'd found with his mother that it was best not to offer actual words in such cases, or she would pounce shrewdly on them and attempt to change his mind.

"*Rowan,*" she'd said quietly. "*Most women are not like Maria. She was simply… a mistake.*"

He'd wanted to laugh, though it would have been a nasty sound, so he'd restrained himself. But truer words had never been spoken. He thought it baffling that he hadn't understood Maria's true nature until it was too late, because he'd known her all his life.

He and Maria had been childhood playmates, brought together frequently because of the friendship of their parents. His attachment to her had formed over time as they grew up—and wasn't that just the sort of attachment everyone said was the best foundation for a life together?

Everyone, it turned out, had been wrong. It seemed that people you thought you knew quite well, you might in fact not know at all.

It wasn't until the week before the wedding that Rowan had found the letter Maria had written to her lover, speaking of the babe she already carried and looking forward to the moment she would meet her lover again, once she was "safely married."

Rowan supposed he ought at least to have been happy that she'd broken off their engagement when he'd confronted her. What he'd felt, though, was nothing but relief—and a resolution never to get into a similar situation.

* * *

Mr. Fitzwilliam was frowning at the remaining sausage on his plate, and Claire was having a great deal of trouble resisting the urge to be cordial and try to cheer him, despite his blunt manners. Well, really, because of them, considering how she'd grown accustomed to averting others' displeasure by being warm and accommodating.

But now that she had gained some distance from home and given herself a chance to think, she was annoyed that she was tempted to smile at him. What she ought to do was get up and leave. She had, actually, had the cowardly urge to bolt when he'd first come into the breakfast room and turned those glaring dark eyes on her. He seemed to occupy an inordinate amount of space in the room, and even as she dabbed composedly at her lips with her napkin, the breadth of his shoulders made something inside her unfurl.

However disagreeable he might be—he was surely the haughtiest person she'd ever met, and she'd once met an earl—Fitzwilliam was also… manly. And she felt that there was more to him than just his blunt demeanor. She couldn't have said what exactly, though, and she told herself sternly that it had nothing to do with the visions she kept having of him in his shirtsleeves wielding a blacksmith's hammer.

He lifted his eyes and scowled at her, and unexpected warmth crept up the back of her neck. As he reached for a piece of toast, his sleeve strained against his arm, defining the heavy curves of his muscles, and she made herself look down at her plate.

She was absurdly, considering his scowling and that fact that he seemed to think a grunt was an acceptable conversational response, fascinated by him.

His eyes really were dark, as they'd looked the night before—not black, but a sharp chocolate brown. His hair was truly black, though—black as Vulcan's would be, she thought before she could catch herself.

Stealing a glance at him as he spooned sugar into his coffee, she noticed a small cut on his neck, the kind that her brothers sometimes got from shaving, and she supposed he must be missing his valet. Of course—he was the cousin of a duke and clearly a wealthy gentleman, even if he looked like he could forge a neat horseshoe.

Louisa entered the room at that moment carrying a fresh pot of coffee, which she put on the table. On her way to the sideboard, she caught Claire's eye and winked. Claire glared at her. Did Louisa *want* her to burst into inappropriate laughter, or say the wrong thing and expose their charade?

"Mrs. Firth," Fitzwilliam said, not turning to face her as he continued stirring, just as if he were a lofty duke himself, "I should like you to send a message to the local vicar, asking him to find someone suitable to stay here at Foxtail as a chaperone now that I've come. It's not appropriate for Miss Beckett and myself to be here alone."

"Of course," Louisa said, catching Claire's eye. Fitzwilliam was right about the impropriety of them being there alone. But Claire hardly wanted yet another person living in the house—someone else she'd have to fool as well.

Louisa finished fiddling with the sideboard and left, but not before giving Claire a meaningful look that she took to mean, "Don't be nice!"

"It's odd," Mr. Fitzwilliam growled, cutting into the last sausage on his plate—he'd already made three disappear, not that she was counting, "but I heard laughter late into the evening. It was loud enough to keep me awake."

Claire busied herself with taking a spoonful of strawberry jam to avoid his gaze. "Laughter? Surely not. Doubtless it was just the dogs. In the stables. One hears them sometimes."

"The *dogs*?" he scoffed. "It was surely women laughing, the way they do at a party."

"A party? Here, last night? You were evidently imagining things, sir. Perhaps it was a dream." Claire was practically squirming with the need to apologize that she and Louisa had kept him awake, but she resisted. Even if she hadn't been trying to undertake the plan to be not-nice to him, she couldn't afford to let on that she and Louisa were friendly enough to be laughing together late into the night.

"I don't dream," he said.

"I don't believe you," she replied, experiencing an immediate thrill at being contrary. It was quite exhilarating, actually, not to care about his feelings! "None of us can avoid them, whether we want to dream or not."

"Then it must have been you and Mrs. Firth laughing."

She nearly choked on her toast, but she somehow managed to force it down. "What an idea."

"Is it so preposterous?"

She just smiled and left his words hanging there.

"The butter," he said a few moments later, motioning with his chin as he took some more toast from the platter between them. It was ridiculous how much she liked the deep sound of his voice, especially when he was being so boorish. "Please," he tacked on as she hesitated.

"No," she began, then laughed as his eyebrows slammed downward. "I mean, of course." She passed him the dish of butter, and he accepted with a cocked eyebrow.

"It seems strange, Miss Beckett, that no one in my family has ever mentioned yours."

"Well, no one in my family has ever mentioned yours either." That was even true!

"Hmmph. My mother is quite interested in family," he growled, "and she ought to have mentioned you."

"Perhaps she did, and you forgot." She gestured at his neck, where a small spot of blood had appeared on his crisp white cravat. "I think you may have cut yourself a little."

His brows drew together, as if he was annoyed that his neck had dared to bleed. "It's nothing. Tell me, have you seen the duke lately?"

Pasting a sincere look on her face, she tried not to think about the wages of lying. "Not for some time. And you?"

"Oh... not since I was a child," he said. "Precisely how long do you mean by 'some time'?"

Clearly he was on to her vagueness. But by his own admission, he hadn't seen the duke for years, so surely she could make up something to give substance to her claim to having met the duke? "Oh, a year or so."

"And how did you find him? Is he very handsome?"

In for a penny, in for a pound. "Well, honestly, he's a thin, fragile, bald man—you know the type. Probably eats kippers for breakfast."

"What's wrong with kippers?" he growled. Didn't he ever get tired of growling? "I like them for breakfast."

"They smell terrible. And they give you kipper breath. I'll wager no one can stand you when you eat them."

He blinked, as though no one had ever suggested to him that he might be unappealing in any way. "I always brush my teeth. And no one has ever objected to my kipper consumption."

She laughed. "Not that you *know* of."

He cleared his throat. "You will accompany me today on a tour of the estate, Miss Beckett. Our cousin has charged me to look into the old model village in the woods, which was built years ago for some ladies of the family and has been neglected all this time. It's called Trethillin. I'm certain our cousin would wish to have your opinion on... any improvements needed there."

She almost wanted to say yes, but that would be a foolish thing to do for so many reasons, starting with the foolishness of being attracted to such a powerful man. Because she was. Her fingers itched to explore his unruly black hair, to smooth over the hard lines of his mouth and ramble over the muscles that bunched under his coat sleeves.

A jumble of unmaidenly thoughts assailed her, of naked bodies and rumpled sheets—surely the result of those wayward ideas about the sweating god Vulcan at his work. Had she lost her mind? A powerful, commanding man like Fitzwilliam was the last kind of man she ought to spend time with.

Maybe she did need to be looking for a husband—and in truth she had to agree with Louisa that it was probably her best plan for the future—but she needed a reasonable man like Mr. Rutledge, not some rough god who bent mortals to his will.

"No," she said. Her reflex was to add "thank you," but his words hadn't been an invitation.

"No?" he repeated, obviously taken aback by her bluntness.

"Exactly," she said, though she was actually a little curious about this Trethillin place. But she couldn't acquiesce to his attempt to dominate her. He stared, as though waiting for her to provide an excuse for her refusal, or to soften it, but she managed not to do so. Instead, she took a sip of her tea, replaced the cup in the saucer, and stood.

"Is it your policy, Miss Beckett, to answer 'no' whenever you are asked anything?"

"No." She smiled, quite enjoying herself. "Good day, Mr. Fitzwilliam. I hope you have a pleasant time touring the estate. It is quite fine."

"Just a minute, Miss Beckett," he said, standing as well and moving closer. "What are your plans for the day?"

"Fortunately, I don't need your permission to go about my own business, Mr. Fitzwilliam. I can't imagine what's given you the impression that I do."

As she turned to go, she thought she caught a glimpse of his lips twitching in begrudging amusement, but surely she was wrong.

In the corridor at the top of the stairs, Louisa intercepted her. They both glanced around to make certain no one was about, since they couldn't afford for anyone to notice that they were especially friendly with each other.

With a grim expression, Louisa handed Claire an envelope that was addressed to Louisa in a familiar hand. "This came for me a few minutes ago."

Claire recognized her brother Stephen's handwriting, and her stomach dropped. "How could he know I'm here? Oh God, does the whole family know?"

"He writes that he knows you didn't go to Aunt Mary's because he stopped by there on his way home from a trip, and she said there'd been a change of plans. He thought it odd, but when he later stopped at the Loxford village inn, the innkeeper asked after you, saying how you'd taken the mail coach south. When Stephen heard that your father had announced his plans for you to marry the baron, he guessed you'd found it a bit of a shock and might have come to me."

"Stephen always was my favorite brother," Claire said.

"You may feel less charitable toward him after you finish reading." Louisa pointed to a section of the letter.

If Claire is with you—well, I can suppose that she's nervous about marrying Haight. I haven't said anything to the family yet about her not being at Aunt Mary's, but the thing is, the baron means to pay for the wedding and take Claire on without a dowry. So Papa has already begun spending the money he set aside for her dowry on repairs to the manor.

Claire gasped. "Papa is all but selling me to The Haight!"

Horror and disgust and a profound sense of betrayal washed over Claire, and she sank against the wall behind her. Apparently she was nothing to her family but a bargaining chip.

"I could wish Stephen hadn't written this, clearly urging you to come home and marry The Haight," Louisa said, her voice tight with emotion. "I could wish that he'd told your father that you were not to be bargained away to a disgusting old man."

"Yes," Claire said, still reeling. "Though I suppose Stephen thinks he wouldn't be able to do any good. Papa and my brothers never agree on anything anymore."

"Still, if they all insisted together on what a mistake it'd be—"

Claire shook her head slowly, forcing herself to accept the full truth of her situation. "Papa would just dig his heels in. The more anyone opposes him, the more he resists. No, I must simply do as you and I discussed: I must find my own husband as soon as possible."

"Ah," Louisa said slowly. "So you will set your sights on Mr. Rutledge, then?"

Claire nodded once, firmly, and straightened her spine. "Mr. Rutledge. Now, if you could find me a pen and paper, I'll send a note back to Stephen."

"What if I wrote and said I haven't seen you?"

"Stephen would just worry and tell Papa I'm missing, and there'd be a grand hunt for me. They'd be bound to find me."

"But how will you keep Stephen from telling them that you're here? Or coming to fetch you?"

A crafty tilt pulled at the edges of Claire's mouth. "I didn't say I'd tell him *everything*. I'll write and tell him not to worry, and that I came to you because I needed a last time with my dearest friend before marrying. All of which is true."

Louisa quickly found writing supplies, and Claire penned her note.

Reading over Claire's shoulder, Louisa said, "He might not find that an entirely satisfying reply."

Claire added, *I'll be home in good time.*

"Which could mean anything," Louisa said approvingly as she rang for a maid to take the note.

"It will buy me some time, because he won't expect me not to cooperate as I always have."

As Louisa watched Claire seal the envelope, a calculating look came over her face. "What about Fitzwilliam? Just think how wonderful it would be if you married a duke's cousin! And you can't deny there's something excitingly potent about the man."

Claire treated Louisa to a look of profound incredulity, even though the suggestion gave her an excited shiver. "Have you taken leave of your senses? I've done nothing but lie to the man since I met him. What would happen when he found out I'm not the duke's cousin? Besides, he's the most grouchy gentleman I've ever met."

"Is he, though? I know he's been gruff—"

"Gruff? He keeps trying to order me about! Clearly the man expects to be obeyed."

Louisa cocked her head. "And have you cooperated at all?"

"No," Claire said, and then smiled, pleased with herself. "I've done rather well with the contrariness plan, haven't I?"

Louisa nodded, but she seemed distracted. "How does he respond when you say no?"

"When I declined to go to the model village with him, he demanded to know what I was doing with my day!" Claire reported, enjoying her outrage. "Of course I refused to say."

"And quite rightly," Louisa said. "Did he seem very angry?"

Claire considered. "No. But he was annoyed that I'd thwarted him."

"Ah," Louisa said.

"What do you mean, 'Ah'?" Claire demanded as a smug expression curled Louisa's lips.

"You had a dispute, and there was no disaster, right? He didn't do anything that scared you, right?"

"Well… no."

"See?" Louisa said, as though she was making sense. "You both expressed your opinions, even if the other one didn't like it."

"I thought the plan was simply for me to be difficult."

"And you have apparently excelled at that. And advanced nicely toward a proper argument."

Claire uttered an indelicate snort. "Do you hear yourself congratulating me for participating in a dispute?"

"People need to argue sometimes." Louisa tapped her chin thoughtfully. "Maybe Fitzwilliam would make you a fine husband after all."

Claire's eyes lofted toward the ceiling. "It was *one* interaction. And he *growled* half the time."

But Louisa didn't look like she was listening. "I think it would be very, very interesting to know what's behind Fitzwilliam's growling."

Claire silently agreed, thinking of how his lips seemed to twitch as she'd departed the breakfast room. But she made herself stop. Fitzwilliam was simply too much. Too powerful, too commanding, too manly, and she couldn't afford to think of him at all.

A spirited breakfast conversation was not much of anything. She didn't know Mr. Fitzwilliam, but she knew herself, and she'd seen how weak she could be. She wouldn't put her future happiness in the hands of a man who, once any attraction had worn off, would almost certainly run roughshod over her.

"Mr. Fitzwilliam is not a good idea as a husband," Claire said firmly. "He's… just not for me. But Mr. Rutledge, now, is all that's agreeable. And he'll be at the assembly tomorrow night."

The note dispatched, Claire left on foot for the town two miles away to buy some ribbons with which to trim her hair for the assembly.

CHAPTER THREE

Rowan finished his breakfast minus the distracting company of Miss Beckett, who seemed strangely inclined to be more contrary with him than he could remember any female being since he was in leading strings. Anyone at all, actually.

He wondered how Mowne and Lucere were doing in their respective lodgings. Lucere, the devil, had probably already secured the affections of some lovely female—he invariably had a nearly instantaneous effect on women. Not that Mowne was at all shabby in that respect, though being injured, he ought to be enjoying a calming respite at the home of his dull old cousin Jules. Rowan supposed he'd eventually have something of a story to tell the fellows about his own "cousin," once he discovered her secrets.

Well, he *had* figured out this much about Miss Beckett: She meant to avoid him, either because she didn't wish to make any mistake that would give away her ruse, or because she simply didn't like the way he was.

If she didn't want to spend any time in his company, he ought to be glad. What could he possibly want from her?

And yet, as he departed the breakfast room, he couldn't erase from his mind the way her eyes had sparkled when she'd said no to him, as though disagreeing with him offered her some private thrill.

He dearly wanted to know why.

And there was this: When he was in her presence, the very air around him seemed hot and alive, as if suddenly everything was different. Which was... silly, he told himself. But it was also intoxicating.

He made his way to his room, where he removed his bloodstained cravat. But as he tossed it over the back of the chair in his bedchamber, he recalled how much his valet bemoaned stains. Though Rowan had never in his life given any thought to such trifling concerns, he'd also never had to contend with them, and now that he had only a few things with him, he found he disliked the idea of a perfectly good cravat being ruined because of a small spot of blood.

He put the cloth in the washbasin and poured cold water on it. Leaving it to soak for a few minutes, he surveyed his bedchamber, which had made little impression on him earlier in his haste to get to breakfast.

Though simply decorated, the room was pleasing. Of course, he was accustomed to rooms being pleasing—he was a duke, and the staffs of several large manors had it as their life's work to ensure that his living quarters were luxurious and immaculate. But this room, and what he'd seen of the lodge so far, was different from his other homes. Unlike those grand, ostentatious places, Foxtail was sparsely decorated and happily devoid of the sorts of gilt flourishes that adorned far too many of his homes. It was properly manly, he thought with satisfaction as his eyes passed over the mounted stag's head.

The furnishings were simple: sturdy furniture, thick draperies. The windows were smallish, giving the room the feeling of a retreat instead of making him feel on display, as he sometimes did with tall windows all around.

A duke was always on display, always of interest to everyone around him. People wanted things from a duke: influence, money, alliance, favors. To most people, a duke was as distant from the average human as a star, and just as unlikely to be affected by the things that touched other mortals.

"*I didn't think you'd notice,*" Maria had said when he'd demanded to know how she could have engaged herself to him when she was in love with another man. "*You're not like me—your world is grander.*"

"*I'm just a man,*" Rowan had said, the words torn from him by hurt and fury over her betrayal.

"No, *you're not,*" she'd said. "*You're a duke.*"

He would never complain that it was an affliction to be born a duke; he was wealthy, powerful, and respected, and he liked exercising the responsibility of overseeing his estates.

But being a duke limited him too, he acknowledged as he tied a fresh cravat. And it made him aware of how little he could trust anyone who wasn't in his immediate family or among his few old, tried and true friends—which pretty much meant Lucere and Mowne. His unwelcoming manner allowed him to keep others from trying to curry favor, or thinking they knew him when all they knew was that he was wealthy and titled.

It occurred to him then, with bone-deep relief, that here at Foxtail he wouldn't have to go to the trouble of keeping people at arm's length, because there was hardly anyone here, and no one knew who he was anyway.

What would it be like to have such a refuge permanently, a place where no grand parties would be thrown and where he might laze about in old clothes, unshaved and unpolished? His mother always said of Foxtail that it had been the place where Rowan's father was most relaxed.

Rowan frowned. He wasn't supposed to be finding things to like about Foxtail. His goal for the day must be to explore his property to assess its state—and to find out more about the mystery of Miss Beckett.

He poked his finger at the fading spot on his soaking cravat and was pleased to watch the stain disappear. After hanging it over the back of the chair to dry, he asked Mrs. Firth for a packet of sandwiches and spent the rest of the morning roaming.

It was afternoon by the time he was making his way back to the lodge. His ramblings had shown him that the grounds were wild in places, that one of the stone bridges was gone and another crumbling, and that wildflowers and weeds had taken over paths he dimly remembered from his youth.

As he emerged from the edge of the woods onto the path that led toward Foxtail from the main road, he saw someone perhaps a hundred paces in front of him. It was Miss Beckett.

He called her name, and she stopped and turned. He caught up to her.

"Are you coming from town, Miss Beckett?"

"I am." She looked prettily flushed from her exertions. And there was that thrilling rushing sensation within him again, and the feeling that he knew her, that he'd always known her.

It's just attraction, he told himself. *An unusually powerful attraction.*

But he knew there was more to it. He itched to know more about her. He wanted to discover what she liked and what she didn't, and what made her laugh and what made her cry, along with all sorts of ridiculously trivial things, like whether she preferred dogs or cats.

He was a little infatuated with her. And at risk, apparently, of turning into an idiot. *For heaven's sake*, he told himself sternly, *Beckett might not even be her real name.* Though the naturalness of her manner when addressed made him inclined to think the name was hers.

"I was just about to visit Trethillin," he said untruthfully. "Join me."

He had been about to visit the little mock village earlier, but the poignant stirrings of nostalgia had stopped him. He had dim but happy memories of the place, tinged with the golden hues of youth, but he'd long ago learned that such enchanted places were never the same when visited as an adult. Everything would seem smaller and shabbier, containing none of the remembered magic of secret corners and spaces made sacred by the workings of childhood imagination.

Something flickered in her eyes, but it was quickly extinguished.

"No, thank you."

He frowned. "Miss Beckett, do you realize that you haven't said the word *yes* to me once since I met you?"

"And do you know, Mr. Fitzwilliam, that you've done nothing but frown at me and attempt to order me about since we met?"

His frown deepened, and she laughed. "There, you're doing it now. Frowning."

It had become second nature in recent years for him to frown and look severe toward anyone he didn't know well. No one expected a duke to laugh and caper about, and no one would gainsay him if he scowled.

Well, his mother and brother and sisters did, and Mowne and Lucere often teased him about his "lord of the manor" look and how it struck onlookers dumb. But they of all people understood how a duke was constantly under scrutiny, how a duke was expected to be wise and all-knowing and commanding. A duke didn't make mistakes. He wasn't vulnerable, and he would never allow himself to be tricked by a woman.

Except that Rowan had. Maria had tricked him quite thoroughly.

He tried arranging his features into a more welcoming expression, and Miss Beckett laughed again. "I'm afraid that's worse."

He growled at her.

"You're also prone to growling. I suppose all your dark looks and beastly ways intimidate everyone into doing your will."

"Usually."

"Is that so?"

"Yes." He paused. "It's a small thing, Miss Beckett, this little word *yes*—why don't you try it? I'll give you another chance. Would you visit Trethillin with me?"

"I can't. I have some things I need to do."

"You're on holiday at someone else's home. What could you possibly have to do besides letter writing, an activity that in my opinion can always wait?"

"If you must know, there's an assembly in town tomorrow tonight, and I need time to make some adjustments to my gown."

"An assembly? Why wasn't I told about this?"

"Because no one would think you'd want to do such a silly thing as dance?" she proposed.

He sniffed. "I happen to like assemblies. I shall certainly go." He paused. "And you must—er, will you save me a dance, Miss Beckett?"

She hesitated, and he thought, with more disappointment than he ought to feel, that she would say no, but she surprised him. "Very well, yes, I shall. Now, if you will excuse me, I ought to get back to the lodge."

"What you ought to do is come to Trethillin with me."

"Not this again…"

He shouldn't be asking her. Shouldn't be fascinated by her. The women who interested him—sexually, at least—were widows. He preferred smart, experienced women who knew what they wanted—and what they would get—from an affair with him. Despite the confidence that allowed her to hold her own against his bluster, this woman was young, and an innocent—he felt sure of it. The wisest thing would be for him to let her continue on her way and take himself off to Trethillin alone.

But he did not want to be wise.

"Come, Miss Beckett, surely it's a small thing the duke our cousin asks of us? As we are here enjoying his hospitality, don't we owe it to him to do this?"

She looked as though she was weakening. "How are we even to find it, since we are both strangers here?"

"Not to worry," he said. "I glimpsed the buildings through the trees earlier when I was walking."

"So you might have gone and looked then and gained impressions to give the duke."

"But I wouldn't have had your opinion, and as you are his cousin as well…"

She made a small sound of exasperation. "Oh, very well. Lead on, then, Mr. Fitzwilliam."

As they picked their way along an overgrown path, Rowan wondered if she would have been so begrudging about coming with him if she'd known he was the duke. Somehow, he felt that it would make no difference to her. He wanted to believe that, anyway.

* * *

"You do realize this assembly will be full of country people," Mr. Fitzwilliam said as he held a low-hanging branch aside for Claire to pass. She still couldn't think why she'd agreed to visit this Trethillin place with him—for one thing, it was contrary to her plan to be disobliging—but she would have been lying to herself if she insisted her acquiescence had had nothing to do with the appeal this haughty man held for her.

It was purely physical, she told herself firmly. Something pulled her toward him like the irresistible force that drew magnets together.

But there was something more to it than just a physical pull, something she couldn't have named, probably because she'd never felt anything like it before.

"I *am* a country person, Mr. Fitzwilliam. I rarely go to London."

"Is that so? I confess myself surprised; you have a certain polish."

"It's not Town polish, I assure you. I've been to London only once, and that was last year."

"For your Season? I'm surprised we didn't meet, with so many relatives in common." She thought he paused meaningfully before mentioning their relatives, as though mocking the idea that they were truly related, and her eyes skittered sideways, but his neutral expression did not suggest anything amiss.

She was being anxious over nothing, she told herself. If he truly suspected she wasn't the duke's cousin, why wouldn't he simply say so? He was hardly shy.

She quietly released the breath she hadn't realized she was holding. "We didn't stay for the full Season."

"And will you go again this year?"

"No."

"No? Not going shopping again for a husband?"

Claire coughed. "Really, must you be so blunt?"

He looked at her, those bittersweet chocolate eyes settling on her as a passing breeze ruffled his overlong black hair. Perhaps one of the reasons for all those blacksmith-and-hammer thoughts she had in his presence was that she couldn't imagine this brawny man being overmastered by anything, whether it was a forceful word, a wily foe, or a fierce blow.

"I find being straightforward cuts through a great deal of nonsense," he said. "Plain speaking lets people know where they stand."

He was right, actually. Why had it taken her so long to realize that refusing to speak of her own wishes and needs was a recipe for never letting anyone see who she really was?

Maybe because she'd believed that no one wanted to know who she was, or what she thought or hoped. Certainly no one in her family invited such discussions, though her brothers spent a great deal of time shouting about what *they* wanted, however much good it did. But ever fearful of causing conflict, she'd allowed herself to become incredibly bland.

Until she'd come to Foxtail and, in a way, gained the space to think about what she wanted and what she was willing to do to get it.

She shouldn't care if Fitzwilliam sought her company... but she did. She was *glad* he'd pressed her to come.

"Besides, you can hardly accuse me of being blunt," he continued, "when you've been saying *no* all the time."

It was funny, but their plain speaking made her feel more comfortable around him than she usually felt around gentlemen. In London, she'd been so concerned with not offending people and with being pleasing that she'd spent all her time and effort trying to appeal to others. Refreshingly, she didn't have to do that with Fitzwilliam, and it left her free to speak her mind. Even though so much of what she'd told him thus far was a lie, she felt, oddly, that she could be herself around him.

"In truth, I was meant to be finding a husband in London, but I was unsuccessful."

"I confess myself astonished," he said.

"There's no need to be polite."

Warmth touched the edges of his mouth. "The two of us haven't been very polite to each other, have we? But I wasn't being polite."

The implication behind his words was that he'd been thinking about her—just as she'd been thinking about him. A shiver of excitement tripped along her shoulders.

"I didn't really like any of the gentlemen either," she admitted, "so I wasn't particularly disappointed. And since none of them liked me enough to propose, I suppose you could count it even."

His snort of laughter made her laugh too. Who would have thought she would be laughing about her failure to attract a husband?

At that moment, a pair of hounds emerged from the woods ahead of them. Barking excitedly, the dogs bounded toward Claire and Fitzwilliam, but it was soon apparent that she wasn't of as much interest to them as he was. The dogs stopped before Fitzwilliam with their tongues lolling happily, and he crouched down to pet them, all traces of his customary rough hauteur replaced by an endearingly boyish enthusiasm.

"Who are you fellows?" he said as he ruffled the fur on their shining brown heads. "Some neighbor's beasts, I suppose?"

"They certainly seem taken with you," she said, petting one of the dogs and receiving a canine kiss in return.

"I like dogs," he said. "Perhaps they can tell."

"I can imagine you and dogs getting on quite well," she said. "No need for polite conversation."

He glanced up at her with a smile tugging at his lips, and Claire's heart thumped in response. From what she knew of him, his smiles must be rare. But how very, very handsome he was when he did smile. With a final ear ruffle, he stood up and sent the dogs on their way.

"So," he said, "you don't mean to go back to London next year to try the Marriage Mart again?"

She thought they'd moved on from that topic. "Perhaps I'll be married by then." If she was lucky, she'd be married before the month was out, and not to Lord Haight. She'd been invited to dine with the Clarke sisters that evening, and the guests would include Mr. Rutledge, so with any luck, they would have a chance to deepen their acquaintance. It was a sensible plan, even if it didn't fill her with enthusiasm.

"Oh?" His voice sounded different. Tight. "Are you engaged?"

She blushed. How had she come to be talking of such things with him? And yet, despite his capacity for growling, he was not judgmental, and he listened well. It was foolish to want to tell him much of anything about herself, but she did want to. And as long as she didn't give too many details, would it really matter?

"The thing is that my father has chosen someone for me to marry—a friend of his—but he's quite old and full of his own opinions and not a bit interested in what anyone else has to say. And his breath smells like a crypt."

"Sniffed many crypts, have you?"

She chuckled, though he didn't, as though the idea of her marrying a man like the baron could not really be amusing. Which it wasn't.

He'd told her almost nothing about himself, she realized, and indeed, he seemed like a man with an invisible hedge of thorns around him. And yet, she felt a constant pull toward him. She found herself wondering what it would be like to marry Fitzwilliam.

Stop building a fantasy! she told herself sternly. She knew what such men were like, and just because Fitzwilliam had a sense of humor didn't mean he wouldn't assert his powerful nature. She would be overwhelmed by him.

* * *

Rowan could easily imagine the sort of disgusting old oaf Miss Beckett's father meant her to marry, and the idea of her liveliness being extinguished by a loveless marriage made his blood boil.

Never mind that he himself was already falling under her spell.

He supposed this unwanted suitor was the reason she was at Foxtail. She must have left home to avoid the pressure to marry the man. And if she went against the wishes of her family, he guessed she would likely have to find her own way—which could be a lonely, dangerous path for a young woman.

"Can't you find a man who actually does appeal to you and marry him?"

He was being rude, but he didn't care. There was something about this woman.

He kept telling himself that it was ridiculous to feel such a connection to a person he'd just met, let alone a woman. But he did feel it, and the more he knew her, the more he liked her. The very fact that she'd had the pluck to resist her family's plans to sentence her to an untenable life spoke volumes about her strength of character.

"Well, yes," she said dryly, "that idea had occurred to me."

"Ah," he said. "The assembly." Hence the trip into town for the ribbons that were peeking out of her reticule. Did she already have some local man in mind? Rowan's mouth twisted. Clearly, considering her reluctance to spend time with *him,* he wasn't being considered as a potential suitor.

"Yes."

"Perhaps you already have someone in mind," he said, keeping his voice carefully neutral.

"Perhaps. Oh look, I think I see some kind of shack through those trees ahead."

She'd changed the subject, but likely that was for the best. After all, what could he possibly intend toward this woman who was little more than a mystery to him?

"It must be the hut folly." He'd forgotten about it. He had only vague memories of the hut folly, mostly because it had been reserved for his parents, a place the children could go only on rare occasions. The children had hardly cared, because they'd had the cottages to sleep in.

"A *hut* folly? I thought follies were supposed to be models of grand buildings."

"I think this one is a little different."

They passed through the trees, and there, in the large clearing before them, was Trethillin. Sunlight glittered on the small lake at its center.

"Oh," she breathed.

The little mock village had been designed as a sort of rustic retreat, as if Foxtail's lodge wasn't retreat enough. But the scale of the lodge was that of something belonging to a dukedom. Trethillin was entirely different.

CHAPTER FOUR

Claire was enchanted. Before them stood a scene of unexpected and gentle charm, as if the best parts of a hamlet had been scaled down and brought together in an intimate space.

The little village consisted of a semicircle of small stone buildings framing a modest lake. There were thatched cottages, a petite barn, a square shop-like building with a sign hanging from it, and something that looked like a grotto. In the middle of the lake, on a tiny island, stood the hut folly, pathetic-looking and battered, though there was something proud about it, too, that called to her.

"Is there a boat?" she asked. "We have to go out to the hut folly."

"There ought to be," he said as they moved into the clearing, "though whether it would be lake-worthy is questionable. I don't suppose anyone's used this place for years. Why don't we inspect the cottages first?"

The three little stone cottages were each surrounded by a garden, or rather, what had once been a garden. As they approached the closest dwelling, Claire said, "Oh look, a little statue of a…" She leaned closer to the small sculpture sitting amid some delphiniums growing in a mess under one of the cottage's windows. "Dog?"

Fitzwilliam bent down and pushed away tall dried grasses and flower husks. "I think it's a satyr, actually, with the head and arms missing."

"Grisly," Claire said. "I like it."

"You must surely enjoy the lodge, then, with all the mounted animal heads."

She glanced at him. Was Fitzwilliam *teasing* her?

"Ugh, no. That's completely different. Those creatures were once alive. I feel them staring accusatorily at me whenever I'm in the sitting room. Thankfully, there are none in my bedchamber."

"Ah, I see why you chose it," he said. "I enjoy the animal heads. They're like quiet company."

"Either you share your home with utterly disagreeable people, or you simply don't like people in general," Claire said. "My money is on the latter."

"How can you say I don't like people when I've invited you out here?"

"I don't think 'invited' is the right word."

He laughed.

She stared at him in surprise. "You laughed."

His eyes narrowed. "Is there some reason I shouldn't?"

"I just didn't think you would. You've hardly been lighthearted since I met you."

He leaned closer to the statue and began pulling out the surrounding weeds. "It's sometimes easier to be brusque with people."

"To keep them at arm's length?"

He was making a tidy pile of debris to the side of the statue. "Yes," he said, focusing on his task.

"Why?"

He ripped out a few more clumps so that the statue was now plainly visible amid a few sparse but pretty blue stalks of delphiniums. "Let's just say that in general I am endowed with resources."

As he crouched to gain better purchase on a sturdy weed, she shamelessly noted the flexing of his thigh muscles in his buff breeches. "You mean that you are quite wealthy and well positioned, and people want things from you."

"You could say that."

"Then perhaps you feel less free around other people." She moved closer to the door. The remains of a spider web lay across the handle, and she picked up a stick and cleared it away. "In which case, your money and power sound like burdens."

He stood up and brushed himself off. "If I felt that way, I should be pathetic indeed, when those very things offer great opportunities for myself and my family."

"Even if they lead others to believe you have endless favors to supply, or that you are not, in essence, the same as they are?"

"Am I the same?" He stepped closer and leaned over her shoulder to remove a long stick that was dangling from the eaves, where it must have been lodged by a strong wind. His height, his heat, and the scent of his soap filled her senses as he took his time. She repressed the urge to lean into him, and after her heart had nearly thumped giddily out of her chest several times, he finally stepped back.

"Well," she said, her voice a little husky, "perhaps you are not. Perhaps you have no desire for silly things like laughter and foolishness. Perhaps you don't make mistakes like the rest of us. Perhaps, as someone who may already have everything, there is nothing left for you to want."

"You presume to know me quite well," he said.

She took hold of the door handle and pushed, but the mechanism was stiff and wouldn't yield to her efforts. She glanced around to see him watching her with his arms crossed.

"On the contrary, I don't know you at all. How could I? We've practically just met."

He looked at her steadily for a few moments, and she thought he would say something further, but he pressed his lips together and stepped forward. "Allow me," he said. The handle surrendered to him, and the door opened inward with a heavy whine.

A thick layer of dust coated everything inside, but even with that, Claire could see the cottage was charming, the sort of place one might imagine a family of rabbits living, if they wore clothes and cooked meals and liked to curl up by the fire with a book.

The room was painted a pale yellow, and the square windows were hung with red toile curtains bearing scenes of laughing shepherdesses. Two sturdy chairs sat on either side of the small hearth, over which hung a still life of apples and pears. A group of prettily painted candleholders graced the mantel, along with what looked like someone's motley collection of favorite bits and pieces.

Beyond the chairs was a settee with a table in front of it, and Claire saw, as she moved closer, that a puzzle sat half-finished on it, as though it had been abandoned in the middle of some long-ago holiday. Through the doorway she glimpsed a modest kitchen.

"It's utterly charming," she said. Surely, if she could only come and live here for a few months every year, her life would always be peaceful and balanced.

"It's completely disreputable," he said.

"It just needs cleaning," she insisted.

A mouse skittered across the floor near their feet, and she gasped. He arched an eyebrow at her.

"And a cat," she added. "It only needs to be lived in by people who appreciate it."

They moved upstairs to inspect the bedrooms, which were, like the first floor, extremely dusty. The bedding had clearly been popular with the mice.

"I'm sure the duke can afford new linens," she said, not wanting to get too close to a pillow that looked suspiciously as though it had been used as a nest.

"Doubtless he can."

They inspected the two other cottages, which were in similar condition, then poked around in the grotto, which seemed to have something to do with fairies. The little shop turned out to be a "bookseller" that was clearly meant to be a small, freestanding library. Behind the diminutive barn, they found a rowboat.

"I don't know that we ought to use this," Fitzwilliam said, prodding the wood with his foot. "It might be worm-eaten. We could end up at the bottom of the lake."

"I can swim," she said. "Can you?"

His eyebrow cocked in devilish reply to her challenge. They dragged the boat down to the water's edge.

Fitzwilliam held the boat steady for her, then stepped nimbly in after her and took the oars. He handled them with ease. As they moved quietly across the still lake in the close space of the boat, she let her eyes linger on his bent head. She told herself there was something seriously wrong with her if she was fascinated by the sight of sunlight on black hair.

The spot of blood was gone from his cravat, and she guessed he must have changed it. Her gaze slid downward to the muscles bunching under his coat as he pulled the oars through the water, and she swallowed and made herself close her eyes. She lifted her face to the sun, but though its rays were gently warm on her cheeks, she knew sunlight wasn't all that was heating her skin.

They made it to the little island without sinking, though a fair amount of water had seeped into the boat by the time they pulled it onto the tiny shore.

"This boat is none the better for being left to the elements for years," Fitzwilliam remarked as he secured it. But Claire had already alighted and was moving toward the hut.

Hardly more than a narrow box with a slanted roof, the folly was made of unpainted wood, and several loosened slats leaned away from the roof just under its eaves. At least half the windowpanes were broken. The roof, which was missing a number of shingles, swayed ominously downward.

Claire stepped close to the window and peered in.

"There's a curtain blocking the view inside," she said, moving toward the door.

He caught her arm. "Wait. Perhaps we should ascertain that it's not going to fall over before we go in."

She turned to him, and he dropped her arm. "I thought you said the decrepitude was meant to be an illusion."

"That was the idea, as far as I understand it. But after all these years of neglect, it may not be an illusion anymore. This thing looks far too hastily constructed to be sound, and the whole place seems to have been forgotten for a good dozen years. That represents a great deal of wind and rain, with the potential for structural damage."

"I'm sure it's fine," she said, gripping the door handle. Unlike the cottage door, this one opened easily with nary a sound. She stepped inside and breathed out a sigh of awe.

"It's a wonder," she whispered reverently as he stepped inside next to her and pushed aside the window curtains. "And it's not decrepit at all."

"There's water damage from rain coming in the broken windows," he pointed out.

"A mere detail." Her eyes roved greedily about the diminutive room.

To her right was a bed that had clearly been designed exactly to fit its small space, with a quilt that looked like something a country granny had sewn with love. In a pretty blue glass-fronted cabinet were a small collection of dishes and an old packet of tea. Next to the petite fireplace hung two cooking pans, and on the floor stood a basin.

"It's a place to come when you want to utterly escape from the world," she said.

Across from the bed and against the wall—a journey of only a few feet in the small space—stood a slim table and a chair, a little spot that would be perfect for writing letters while a summer breeze floated in through the little windows.

On the wall above the table were shelves containing shells and what looked like doll furniture constructed of twigs. She stepped closer and picked up a polished stone even as her eyes were drawn upward to the collection of miniature portraits in round frames that hung in a row above the shelf.

"It's quite amazing," she said as she examined a portrait of a young man in the dated style of a few decades before, "how much of a family resemblance you have. Or, at least, I assume these are people in the duke's immediate family—it just says 'John.'" Each of the portraits had a little plate underneath it with only a first name, giving them an intimate feel, as though the family wished to be simply themselves here.

She realized with a start that she might just have given herself away—perhaps even a second cousin would be expected to recognize whichever members of Starlingham's family these people were. But Fitzwilliam simply peered closer at the pictures and said, "Mmm." He lingered briefly over the portraits, then strode toward the back of the hut and pushed aside more curtains. The little windows stood on either side of a door, and when he opened it outward, Claire sighed.

Through the doorway was a perfect view of the sun-dappled lake and, beyond it, the large overgrown garden to the side of the last cottage. None of the buildings were caught in the frame of the doorway, though—the view was of nature only. She moved to stand next to him.

"It's so peaceful here," she said. "I don't think I would ever want to leave. Do you suppose the duke really will fix this place up and use it?"

* * *

Rowan was struggling not to look at Miss Beckett, because whenever he did, that electric feeling her presence sparked became so strong it nearly overpowered him. And her joy in this place, her open pleasure in its faded charms, was doing something to him, too. It was working upon the bindings he kept on himself. Whispering that his life might hold things he hadn't even known he was missing. It wasn't as if he'd been unhappy, but he'd forgotten about joy.

Why the devil had he thought it would be a good idea to invite her out to this deserted place with him?

The hut had been the domain of his parents during the family's holidays there, and hadn't been of much interest to him as a boy, when most of his energy had been focused on the intricacies of learning to hunt with bow and arrow, an obsession he'd developed after reading numerous adventure stories about the natives of America.

"Actually, I think the duke means to sell Foxtail," he said. "I'm meant not to let the servants know. But he wants to know what kind of shape the place is in."

She drew in a shocked breath and turned to him with a look of dismay. "Sell Foxtail? Why would he want to do that?"

"I believe he has a number of properties to maintain, and some of them require great infusions of funds for their upkeep. The sale of Foxtail would provide such funds."

Her lips drew down in a fierce frown. "Clearly he doesn't appreciate Foxtail since he never visits. But surely someone in the family would enjoy it. And Trethillin ought to be fixed up."

That wasn't what the prospective owners wished to do with Trethillin—they apparently meant to raze the village and put in a manicured sculpture garden. He'd been prepared to find Trethillin in bad shape, which would have made it easier to convince his mother of the wisdom of selling Foxtail. But it wasn't in bad condition—a modest amount of money would restore it to its former glory.

"And someone should live at Foxtail year-round and use Trethillin," she said rather fiercely. "A caretaker's family. And the duke should offer it to his friends for holidays. A place like this should be enjoyed."

"I suppose." Rowan's business manager would disagree, and Rowan himself couldn't see how it would be a responsible choice for him to advocate retaining Foxtail. Starwood was the ducal seat, and it needed major repairs. No one used Foxtail, though it might have its charms, and Lesser Puddlebury was so far from civilization that he couldn't imagine his family ever wanting to come there, even just for holidays.

Or would they, if he fixed it up? They certainly never had before.

"No supposing about it," she said. "It's a waste for such a place to be unused."

A small, oval leaf fluttering past in the breeze landed in her hair, and he itched to brush it away.

Something gave a slide within him, perhaps the ducal pride that had created the distance he'd preferred for so long. He was completely and utterly charmed by this woman—by her enthusiasm for this decrepit place, by the sound of her laughter and the way she never let him get the upper hand. He wanted—no, he needed—to touch her.

"Mmm," he said noncommittally.

She turned on him. "You're not going to recommend he sell it, surely?"

"I'll be certain he's aware of its charms." He paused, smiling a little. "And of *your* partiality for it. I'm certain he'd value your opinion."

"Oh—er, perhaps," she said, her eyebrows drawing down a bit. "He should ask his mother what she thinks."

"The duke?"

"Yes. Or you could ask your mother. Any woman could imagine a family here. And don't you suppose that a duke might grow tired of being ducal and just want to relax somewhere away from the *ton*?"

Yes, he did.

The picture she was painting ought to have sounded like a sugar-sweet, fake dream of the future, but somehow it didn't. He'd ceased dreaming of the future since his failed engagement to Maria, and why should he have concerned himself with it when there were friends and whiskey and willing widows to occupy him, in addition to any number of ducal duties? But the future was suddenly beginning to feel like something very good—something he might begin to build on right now.

He hardly knew this woman. And yet, he did. He couldn't have expressed it to himself any better than this: Being with her made him want more of her.

He touched the back of her hand, a mere brushing of his fingers against her skin. Her expression turned quizzical, but there was something more to it that gave him hope.

"Thank you for coming here with me," he said.

"I... I'm glad I did."

"Might I know your first name, Miss Beckett?"

"Claire," she said quietly. He took her hand in his, and she didn't resist as he interlaced his fingers with hers.

"I am Rowan."

Her scent teased him, a little floral, a little musky, and so very appealing.

"I like you, Claire Beckett." Had he really just said such a thing? He could tell from her startled expression that he had.

A blush rose in her cheeks. "I... don't know what to say."

"That you like me too?"

She smiled a little. "I like a number of things about you."

"Such as?"

"You are kind to dogs."

He gave her a speaking glance. "What else? Something more personal."

"Goodness, Fitzwilliam!" she said, looking flustered.

"Rowan," he reminded her.

"It's quite outrageous, *Rowan*, to demand that people tell you what they like about you."

"I'll tell you what *I* like about *you*, Claire," he said. "You are strong."

He'd meant to compliment her, but the way her brows lowered did not suggest she was pleased. "I don't know why you would say that."

He laughed softly. "Come, Claire. I've growled at you and ordered you about, and you've spent not a moment quaking."

"It's easy to dismiss the bad habits of strangers."

"Ah, but we are not strangers. We have talked and even teased each other. I would argue that because we haven't bothered to dance around each other out of the cool reserve of politeness, but instead been direct with each other, we have come to know each other more than a little."

Her mouth drew into a serious line. "You don't know me."

"I know enough to believe that I want to know you more."

He read puzzlement in her eyes, but he was almost certain longing was there too. The space between them crackled with something hot and alive.

He stepped closer to her. "I want to kiss you." She didn't move away. The light touch of her breath whispered against his skin.

Quietly, she said, "You may."

Dipping his head, he drew closer until their lips were nearly touching. He lingered there a moment with his eyes closed and something like gratitude welling up within him.

Until a most unwelcome sound split the silence.

"Halloo! Halloo! Mr. Fitzwilliam?"

They stepped apart.

"Who the devil is that?" Rowan demanded as they turned and moved toward the opposite door. On the far bank of the little lake stood a short, white-haired man with his hands cupped around his mouth to amplify the sound, turning this way and that as he shouted.

"It's Mr. Dixon, the vicar," Claire said.

Rowan vaguely remembered having met the man, but considering that he'd been only thirteen at the time, it seemed unlikely the vicar would recognize him. "I don't suppose we can hide."

"Hardly. Anyway, he seems to expect you to be here."

With a grimace, Rowan stepped through the doorway into the sunshine.

"There you are, sir," shouted the vicar. He waved, his pink face split in an enormous grim. "Oh! And Miss Beckett as well," he continued in surprise as Claire stepped out from behind Rowan. They waved back to him in greeting.

"Mrs. Firth told me Fitzwilliam might be here," Mr. Dixon shouted, "but I hadn't thought to meet you as well. I've come to act as a chaperone."

Rowan growled a little.

"You did ask for one," Claire pointed out.

"I was expecting a sober spinster, not an imp."

Claire made for the boat with the alacrity of one glad to depart, and Rowan followed her. He supposed he ought to be grateful that Dixon's arrival had stopped him from kissing her, but his feelings were closer to murderous.

For pity's sake, he thought, what was happening to him? This woman he barely knew had some power over him. Surely that stirred-up, buzzing, entirely new feeling he had whenever she was near was nothing but an extremely potent physical attraction. The idea was more palatable than the one trying to breach the borders of his will: that he'd been struck by Cupid's arrow.

Love at first sight.

Just the sort of nonsense in which he'd never believed.

Though it was perhaps more accurate to say that he'd *ceased* believing much in that vaunted love between men and women after his experience with Maria. If he couldn't trust his choice of a woman he'd known all his life, why would he trust his capacity to choose at all?

"Fancy that," the vicar said once they'd reached the shore and performed the introductions. "Two cousins of the duke's here at the same time. And you both strangers to each other."

"A wonderful coincidence, isn't it?" Rowan said.

"I met His Grace when he was a child," Dixon said, "and I knew his father. You have the look of the family about you, sir." The vicar cocked his head. "In fact, I'd say that you are almost the very image of Starlingham's father."

"I've been told that once or twice before." Quite a few times, actually. Rowan's father had died when Rowan was fourteen, but there had never been a man Rowan had respected more, and any comparison always felt like a compliment.

They set off through the woods toward Foxtail.

"It's an interesting time for Lesser Puddlebury, Mr. Fitzwilliam," Dixon said. "We are a small, close community, and it's not often that a stranger comes to stay among us—let alone three. The three being yourself, Miss Beckett, and a gentleman lately come to the area, a Mr. Stephens," he said, which was the name Lucere meant to use while in Lesser Puddlebury. Apparently the vicar knew nothing of Mowne's presence. "Perhaps you are familiar with Mr. Stephens?"

"Wouldn't it be something if I were?" Rowan said, even as he wondered how his friends were faring.

"I haven't met him myself," Mr. Dixon said. "Well"—he rubbed his hands together with apparent glee—"so many young people visiting can only be a boon for the neighborhood."

CHAPTER FIVE

Once back at Foxtail, Claire went in search of Louisa. She found her friend in the cellar, looking at wine bottles.

"Do you suppose Foxtail should offer Fitzwilliam decent wine while he's here, or good wine, or *very* good wine?" Louisa asked, holding up a couple of bottles. "What if the duke has some plan for all this wine? Maybe he'll write any day, saying he's coming with a party of lords and ladies, and then he might be annoyed to find when he arrives that a special bottle is missing."

Or, Claire thought with a stab of worry for her friend, he'd soon sell Foxtail, and Louisa might no longer be needed. But maybe Claire could encourage Rowan to dissuade the duke from selling. She decided not to say anything to Louisa about her concerns just yet.

"I'm sure no matter what, Starlingham won't miss a bottle or two. Besides, Fitzwilliam is his cousin—surely the duke would want you to offer him the best hospitality possible."

"Still…" Louisa mused, but Claire cut her off.

"I just spent the afternoon with him."

"The duke?"

Claire groaned. "Fitzwilliam."

Louisa put down the bottles. "You did?"

Claire nodded. "I ran into him on the way back from town, and he cajoled me into visiting the model village with him."

"Oh! Isn't it the most charming, funny little place? I've wandered over there a few times, though it always felt too lonely there to linger." Louisa grinned. "Apparently what I needed was a manly fellow to accompany me."

She peered at Claire. "Are you blushing? You like him, don't you!"

Claire's gaze dropped to the shelf next to her arm, and she used her fingertip to make a curlicue in the dust on a bottle of burgundy. "Don't be ridiculous," she said, but it was a half-hearted effort.

"I'm not the one being ridiculous. Why not just admit you like the man?"

Claire traced a heart shape on the neighboring bottle. "I think he just causes some sort of temporary madness in me. At Trethillin, before Mr. Dixon arrived, Fitzwilliam was going to kiss me. I'm sure he would have if Mr. Dixon hadn't started hallooing."

"And were you going to let him?"

She rubbed away her tracings and brushed the dust off her fingertips. "Yes. Foolishly."

"Foolishly?" Louisa's eyes sparkled. "Nonsense! Why should a kiss with such a fantastically manly gentleman be a bad thing? Only, I wish Mr. Dixon hadn't arrived at just the wrong time."

"Louisa, I shouldn't be kissing Fitzwilliam!"

"I don't see why not." A dreamy look came over Louisa's face. "I haven't kissed a man for two years, since I came to this remote outpost. Mrs. Firth has to be the soul of propriety."

"I've never kissed anyone," Claire admitted.

Louisa's eyes widened as though Claire had said something dire. "Dearest, I hadn't realized. That is a tragedy."

"It's *not* a tragedy. And I can't be kissing the duke's cousin."

"But you wanted to kiss him!"

Claire sighed heavily. How had she come to feel so much already for a man she barely knew? "He makes my heart thump. That's not the same as *liking* him."

Louisa's look told her she didn't believe her. And she was right not to, because Claire did like him, very much. And though he'd claimed that the duke wanted her opinion about Trethillin, she knew there was more to his insistence that she accompany him.

"I like you," he'd said. So directly.

She liked his directness. She knew where she stood with him. That directness seemed to reach across all the half-truths and polite prevarications that good manners demanded and establish something that felt real.

"I wish he hadn't come," Claire said, "because he makes me feel less enthusiastic about trying to secure Mr. Rutledge."

"You should tell Fitzwilliam the truth about who you are and see what happens. He's already trying to court you. Maybe he will marry you."

Claire shook her head. "How can I tell him I'm not the duke's cousin and admit that I'm nothing but an interloper here? I'd lose any shred of good will he might have toward me. Besides, he'd certainly suspect you of helping me. I can't risk it."

Never mind that the far greater risk would be to her heart. But what she felt for Rowan was too new—and it left her too vulnerable—to say anything of that to Louisa. And nothing could come of their attraction, because he was wrong for her. It was only proximity and the heady excitement of desire that was tempting her to believe they might have any sort of future.

"I'd risk anything for love," Louisa said.

"No, you wouldn't. You're the most practical woman I know. Who else would have come to this deserted outpost of a lodge to work just to save enough money to travel? You're a woman with a plan, just like me. And right now my plan must be to charm Mr. Rutledge. I really did quite like him until Fitzwilliam showed up."

* * *

"Well," Rowan said as he, Claire, and Mr. Dixon paused at the entrance to the assembly the following night. The smallish room was nearly overflowing with people prancing about with the kind of unabashed glee that no one in Rowan's circle would have dreamed of displaying.

Rowan had spent most of his recent years avoiding dancing, because the young unmarried ladies tended to be terribly excited about the idea of dancing with a duke, and the less-innocent, widowed ladies tended to want to offer him things... like themselves.

"Isn't it lovely?" Claire said as she looked around the room.

Rowan smiled at the delight in her voice and cast a sideways glance at her, catching the sparkle in her eyes, though he hardly needed to look again to know that she was stunning in her violet satin gown. Its bodice, tasteful but lower than those of her other gowns, had left him behaving like a schoolboy in the coach, sneaking glances at her. He hadn't seen her all day—she'd apparently been visiting some neighbors—and he'd been struck almost stupid by the sight of her when she had appeared in the Foxtail foyer in her evening finery.

He'd just barely managed to say that she looked quite fine without tripping over his words, completely disgusted with himself even as her answering smile made him feel like a king.

"It's splendid, simply splendid," Mr. Dixon said. "Don't you think, Fitzwilliam, that even your cousin the duke would not be able to resist a turn around the room in the company of one of our lovely ladies? Certainly," he continued, his eyes dancing with what Rowan suspected was mischief, "the duke would be enchanted by his cousin Miss Beckett's loveliness."

The rosy color in her cheeks deepened as she blushed.

"I'm certain he would," Rowan said, capturing her eyes. Could she read in his own the effect she was having on him? Just looking at her made him ache, and he kept trying to tell himself that this crackling, alive thing between them was only attraction. But it was far more than that, and far beyond the physical.

She made him feel… split open. It was something to do with her joy and her liveliness, and oh, he couldn't even name all the whats and whys of it. What she did to him was mysterious and irresistible, and he wanted terribly to know what might develop between them, given a chance.

He was just about to invite her to join him in the next dance when a gentleman approached their party. A Mr. Rutledge, already known to the vicar and Claire, was introduced to Rowan. The man promptly claimed her for the dance.

Rowan stood with the vicar, watching them take their place among the couples on the floor. He cast a glance about for any sign of Lucere or Mowne, but he saw neither of his friends.

"Your cousin is a charming creature," the older man said, tapping his toes in time to the music. "I imagine you've been pleased to make her acquaintance."

"One always enjoys knowing one's relations better."

The vicar gave him a look. "It's really quite interesting that you'd never met before. Or, apparently, heard of each other."

"Not really. We are very distant cousins." Rowan paused, not liking the way Rutledge was leaning in to chat with Claire every time the dance brought them close. Rutledge looked to be younger than Rowan by a few years, a tall, slim fellow who moved as gracefully as a dancing master.

Claire smiled at Rutledge, and Rowan clenched his teeth. She'd as good as told him that she needed to find a husband soon, and despite the kiss the two of them had nearly shared yesterday afternoon, it was looking like Rutledge was a prime candidate for suitor.

Rowan had still not forgiven Dixon for interrupting that almost-kiss.

"Have you known Mr. Rutledge a long time?" Rowan asked.

The vicar nodded. "All his life. A fine family, the Rutledges. He has a very nice estate to share with some lucky woman." Dixon cast a sidelong glance at Rowan. "Though none of us has known Miss Beckett long, she's already a favorite in the neighborhood."

Rowan silently gnashed his teeth as he watched Claire laugh at something Rutledge had said. Rowan had a very nice estate or two—or ten, actually—to share as well, and he was beginning to think that maybe he wanted to share them with Claire. But he needed more time with her to find out—time he wouldn't have if she managed to ensnare the already clearly enchanted Rutledge.

The music came to an end, but before Rowan could make his way to Claire's side, another gentleman got there first, and Rowan lost his chance. Rowan was forced to return to his place near the vicar, who presented him to a young lady named Miss Dunlop.

Reading the vicar's expression, Rowan could see that if he didn't want to be considered an utter boor by the locals, he needed to dance with the young ladies of the neighborhood. Another thing that wouldn't have happened to the Duke of Starlingham. As a duke, his choosing to dance with a woman was generally looked on as a mark of great and unexpected favor.

In the end, it was hardly torture to dance with the ladies of Lesser Puddlebury. Miss Dunlop was sweet and quiet, Miss Cathcart was serious, and Miss Flint was curious about the duke and whether Rowan thought he would ever come to Foxtail.

"I shall certainly advise him to do so," Rowan told her seriously.

The whole time, his gaze sought Claire.

The last dance of the night was a waltz, and Rowan simply shut out the other men approaching her with an assertive movement that would have caused jaws to drop had the duke done it.

"Miss Beckett," he said, "I believe this is my dance."

She gave him a look. "I think you know perfectly well that Mr. Parker was already on his way to claim this dance." Parker was limping away from the dance floor with a dark expression. "Did you step on his *foot?*"

Rowan barely shrugged. "He was in my way."

* * *

Claire wasn't certain what Rowan was up to, but it *looked* like courtship. His singling her out would appear to everyone present as though he had intentions toward her. But though she was more than a little smitten with him, he couldn't court her.

Rowan pulled her closer. Wickedness gleamed in his dark eyes, and Claire's heart fluttered in excited reply. No man had ever looked at her like Rowan did.

He placed a hand on her waist, and she surrendered to the moment and put her hand on his shoulder. It was what she dearly wanted to do—how was she to resist? Beneath her hand was hard muscle, leashed power.

"You are the most outrageous man," she said. She could smell his soap, which she'd caught hints of in the carriage. It was *very* nice, expensive-smelling soap. "You always do just as you wish, don't you, with no concern for others."

"I don't give a fig about your other suitors," he said, and something flickered in his eyes, "but I do care very much what *you* think, Claire."

Her *other* suitors. So he did want to court her. Her foolish heart leaped at the knowledge, and a little voice tried to tempt her, insisting that Rowan could be kind and thoughtful and funny, and that she desperately wanted to know him better. She ignored it.

"What I think is that you will have a very nice holiday at Foxtail, sir, and return to London ready for much more exciting society." She made herself smile, determined to keep this light.

"I'm not looking for more exciting society than I have right here in my arms."

His words, spoken in that deep, masculine voice, made her forget to breathe. His eyes held hers as the two of them glided around the room, and a feeling of enchantment settled over her, as though they were on the cusp of something magical.

It was only an illusion, she told herself. Simply attraction and desire. Lust.

She did want Rowan; she wanted to touch him, and she wanted to kiss him as they'd almost done in the hut folly. And she wanted to explore… whatever else there might be with him. She'd lived a sheltered, circumscribed life, and in just the short time since she'd met him, he'd made her feel as though she was coming alive.

But she couldn't allow this attraction. Desire might dazzle them both now, but eventually his forcefulness would overwhelm her.

"Rowan," she began, knowing she must discourage him.

The music was coming to an end, the dancers completing the final steps. And then everything else fell away as Rowan's dark eyes pierced hers. "Just give me a chance," he said.

Something shifted within her in mute reply.

She was saved from having to speak by the sudden applause of the guests acknowledging the musicians who'd played so well all night. But Claire was alight inside with the knowledge that Rowan wanted her, and she wanted him.

Their attraction was utterly foolish. She needed a man like Mr. Rutledge. She would consider herself very, very lucky if Mr. Rutledge, who was infinitely preferable to Lord Haight, liked her enough to propose. What she dreamed of for her future was contentment and peace, a cooperative union of two people who wished always to be considerate toward each other. The kind of union she'd never have with a commanding man like Rowan.

His eyes burned into hers as if willing her to respond.

Just give me a chance.

"I can't," she whispered.

A dark look came over his face, but Mr. Dixon appeared then, his cheeks rosy and his white hair damp with perspiration.

"Why, I haven't danced so much in years!" he said, dabbing his flushed face with his handkerchief. "And if only the duke could have seen how well his cousins look together."

She felt Rowan's eyes on her as she excused herself to collect her wrap. She joined the men outside.

A coach stood in front of the assembly rooms, waiting for several slowly moving elderly ladies who were approaching it. Behind that was another coach, which left Rowan's coach far to the back, out of the circle of light from the building. As the vicar stopped to assist one of the older ladies into her coach, Rowan silently took Claire's elbow and led her toward his.

He opened the coach's door and they moved into its shadow, but instead of handing her up, he put his hands on her shoulders. She looked up at him, and his head lowered to hers.

It was a stolen kiss, full of heat and urgency and claiming, a physical riposte to those two words she'd just spoken: *I can't*.

He was insisting she *could*.

Nearly breathless, she responded as she had so dearly wished to do, lifting her arms to the sturdy breadth of his shoulders and welcoming the heat of his mouth on hers.

It was over too soon. They heard the sounds of someone approaching and quickly stepped apart. But as Rowan handed Claire into the coach, his gaze fell on her like the heat of a furnace.

* * *

Rowan was wishing propriety to the devil as he sat across from the vicar and Claire in the carriage. Dixon was an imp; Rowan guessed he'd sat next to Claire purely to tweak Rowan.

Never mind that Rowan was better off not sitting next to her, since after that kiss he wanted nothing more than to pull her into his arms.

"*I can't*," she'd said when he asked her to give him a chance. Why, damn it? She was looking for a husband, so why was he so objectionable? He knew he'd been overbearing and brusque with her, but she'd held her own and more. Between them already was desire and mutual respect and enjoyment in each other, so why didn't she want him to court her? He had to hope her resistance had to do with the lie she'd told about being the duke's cousin.

It was time to put their charades aside.

"I suppose," Dixon said, "as you are often in London, Mr. Fitzwilliam, this is a much earlier night than you're accustomed to."

"It is. When a ball ends near dawn, the next day is mostly lost."

"Would you agree, Miss Beckett?" the vicar asked.

"I've never attended an event that ended at dawn, so I couldn't say."

"Surely every young lady ought to attend a ball that continues into the dawn hours at least once in her life," Rowan said, his gaze seeking hers. "Perhaps even once a year."

She returned his gaze unflinchingly, not dropping her eyes meekly to her lap as so many young ladies would have likely done after being kissed soundly. But then, he would have expected no less of her. Her inner strength was one of the things he so admired about her, along with the joy that seemed to be always bubbling just beneath her calm surface.

The vicar chuckled. "A ball like that would be unlikely to occur in Lesser Puddlebury, where tongues would wag at such outrageous doings." He paused. "Miss Beckett, I hope you will not think it indiscreet if I share something made known to me this evening. But as you and Mr. Fitzwilliam are family in a manner of speaking, it seems appropriate to speak now."

"She doesn't mind," Rowan said.

Claire shot him an annoyed look. "I'm sure that will be fine, if you deem it appropriate, Mr. Dixon."

"It concerns Mr. Rutledge. He spoke to me this evening of his wish to make you an offer of marriage."

"Oh," Claire said. "He did?"

"Rutledge has asked," the vicar continued as Rowan ground his teeth, "that I act as a go-between and gauge your interest. He would not wish to intrude upon your sensibilities."

Rowan barely managed to stifle the curse that rose to his lips. What kind of shabby fellow employed a go-between with a woman instead of taking the risk of being rejected like a man?

"That was thoughtful of Mr. Rutledge," Claire said. "I... er..."

The vicar held up a staying hand. "Take some time to consider. You can let me know what you think of Mr. Rutledge's interest in the next day or so."

She nodded slowly.

So Rowan had little time. He could see that Claire was affected by what the vicar had said, but he was almost certain it wasn't happiness he saw on her face but relief. He had to believe he was right. And there was no time to lose.

CHAPTER SIX

In her bedchamber late that evening, Claire took down her hair. She knew she should be savoring what the vicar had said about Mr. Rutledge's intentions, but she couldn't stop thinking about Rowan's words.

"Just give me a chance."

If only she could.

There had been a reply from Stephen awaiting Claire on her return, assuring her that he wouldn't tell the family she'd decided to take a holiday with Louisa and telling her that he looked forward to her imminent return home.

You'll be excited to know that Papa talks of nothing, Stephen wrote, *but plans for your wedding. This marriage will be such a good thing for you, dear Claire—and for all the family.*

It hurt to think that her family cared so little about what her own wishes might be for her future, but how could she truly fault them when she'd never spoken of any hopes, or even acknowledged to herself that she had them?

She must guard against ever finding herself in another situation wherein she'd be tempted to make herself into a mouse to please others. A situation like allowing herself to be courted by an overpowering man such as Rowan.

She must not even allow herself to think of him, and how the time they'd spent together had stirred feelings she'd never known before. Of how he'd kissed her as though it was urgent, and something within her had agreed profoundly and kissed him back. It was not just *something*, though, she admitted now to herself. It was her heart. Her heart, somehow, knew him.

The moment that she found herself wishing she could give him a chance to see if they might suit, though, she told herself sternly to stop being fanciful, blew out the candle, and climbed into bed. He might be the perfect daydream of a strong man to sweep her off her feet, but that was only a fantasy.

Some minutes later, a soft click jolted her upright in the darkness, her heart racing. The door to her bedchamber had opened!

"Who's there?" she demanded.

"Shh, it's me."

"Rowan?" she asked in a loud whisper. "What's going on?"

Another click as the door closed. She heard the rustle of his footsteps as he approached the bed. "You can't come in here!" she hissed. "Have you taken leave of your senses?"

"Don't worry," he said in a low voice. "Dixon's asleep. I heard him snoring on the way here. And Mrs. Firth's gone to bed as well."

Since Louisa would probably think it a great thing that Rowan was apparently intent on compromising Claire, whether Louisa was awake or asleep hardly mattered. But it wasn't just propriety Claire was worried about.

"You really can't be in here."

There was a fumbling sound, as though he was putting something on the vanity by the hearth. "And yet I am."

If he had been closer, she didn't know whether she would have wanted to kiss him or shake him. Probably both.

She heard him walk over to the hearth. The fire had burned down to a low flame, and the next moment a candle brightened the darkness. He stood by the vanity, where he'd set a tray with a wine bottle and a plate of biscuits.

He put the candle next to the wine and looked at her. The firelight cast him in bronze, glowing on the bare skin of his forearms—his coat was gone and he'd rolled his sleeves to his elbows—and casting a giant's shadow from the breadth of his shoulders and chest.

"I know it's appallingly inappropriate for me to be in here, Claire, but I had to talk to you privately."

He poured a glass of wine and lifted it. "Won't you join me on the settee?"

For a private tête-à-tête complete with wine? Of course she should do no such thing. No good could come of his being there, and she ought to speak up firmly and order him to leave. She knew he would go if he understood that was her wish.

And yet, she very much didn't want him to leave. That was the truth, whatever sense or propriety would dictate. How had he become so important to her so quickly?

She reached for her robe, which she'd laid across the empty side of the bed, and pulled it on. "*Just* talking," she said.

"Of course," he said meekly, which she didn't credit at all. This man didn't have a meek bone in his body.

She took a seat on the settee and accepted a glass of wine from him. He held out the plate of biscuits, whose batter she had sampled earlier in the day while talking to Louisa, and she took one. They'd come out well, but then, Louisa's cooking skills were legendary, and she liked to make biscuits on Cook's half-day.

The fire crackled quietly—a peaceful sound, though her heart was beginning to thud. Rowan took up so much of the settee that there was barely room for any empty space between them.

He demolished several biscuits and a good half-glass of wine, then put his glass on the vanity. He draped an arm over the back of the sofa, as relaxed as a lord in his manor, and said, "You can't marry Rutledge, you know."

"I can't conceive what's given you the idea you might speak to me this way."

"That kiss, for one thing."

Her lips burned at the memory. As if she'd forgotten a second of it. "We shouldn't have done that."

"You don't really believe that. We both felt the attraction that's between us."

He was right, but she couldn't let him speak for her. "We shouldn't have done it," she insisted.

"What is it with you, Claire?" he asked softly. "Why are you so determined to say no to everything I propose?"

"Because I must make my own decisions and be responsible for them."

He shifted, leaning forward to rest his forearms on his thighs. "I know you're not the Duke of Starlingham's cousin."

Her breath died in her throat.

"I—" she began, utterly lost as to what she could say. Her heart thundered with the knowledge of certain disaster, but he seemed remarkably calm. He still rested on his forearms, and his expression held no signs of outrage or censure. Surely he was angry—so why didn't he seem so?

"I know you're not the duke's cousin," he continued, "because I'm not his cousin either." He paused. "I *am* the Duke of Starlingham."

She simply gaped at him for several moments. "*You're* the Duke of Starlingham?"

And yet, it would explain so much. But why on earth would he pretend to be a relation?

He smiled a little at her skeptical tone. "I really am. It's why I looked so much like the man in the painting at the hut—he was my father, John Mackenzie Fitzwilliam, seventh Duke of Starlingham. I have the signet ring in my valise if you'd like to see it."

"No," she whispered, reeling. But she knew it must be true. No wonder he'd seemed so potent and domineering and haughty, so inclined to order her about. He was a duke, a man possessed of vast estates and accustomed to commanding armies of servants. He was the Duke of Starlingham. The *eighth* one, apparently.

But why had he come to her room tonight, and why was he sitting here talking calmly to her? Why didn't he seem angry about her deception? Her face flushed as she realized that she'd *kissed* the Duke of Starlingham.

"It was something of an accident that I came to Foxtail," he said. "My coming here was due to a friend needing to lie low for a while, so I felt it best not to reveal my identity. No one knows me here because I haven't visited since I was thirteen." He chuckled. "And actually, I've discovered that it's quite pleasant not to be the duke for a while."

Anger stirred in her. "How you must have wanted to laugh when I declared myself to be your cousin."

She felt nearly ill. Of course she was anxious that, however relaxed he seemed, she was doomed to imminent disaster because of her deception. But there was more to the emotions washing over her.

His dark eyes glimmered with what looked like mirth, and this seemed like yet another shock, that he might be mirthful. "I was quite surprised at first to find that I had a 'cousin' here of whom I'd never heard, but I soon decided that, given your manner and person, you were not up to anything terribly dubious. I suspected you of being a governess fleeing a bad situation or some such, until you revealed that your family expected you to marry an objectionable suitor. That gave you a very good reason for needing to hide at Foxtail, even if I didn't know why you'd chosen my hunting box to do so. Though I suspect your arrival here had something to do with Mrs. Firth."

"We are old friends," she admitted. What was the point in keeping it secret now? "I'm sure you've enjoyed a great deal of private amusement over the idea of me being your cousin."

His eyes danced with glee, but the sight just made her feel worse. "Can you blame me? I arrive at my perennially deserted hunting box to find a lovely stranger staying here and claiming to be my cousin."

"Why didn't you expose me right away?"

"Because I was intrigued by you, of course." He paused. "More than intrigued."

She realized that she was clutching her glass far too tightly and put it on the table and stood up, needing to put space between them. And to think that only minutes before, she'd been trying not to hope he'd steal another kiss. With his seductive manner and the wine, she guessed that he'd intended to entice her into doing something far more foolish than kissing.

This was all a game to him. She had no right to object, considering how she'd tricked him, but she'd thought she knew him better.

She moved to the hearth and leaned a little on the mantel. Her charade was exposed. She would have to leave and accept whatever future could be scrabbled together, which might mean marrying the baron after all. Though even as the idea formed, she knew that she would not. She would never go back to being a woman who could accept such a thing.

But it had been foolish to believe that she might change her future into something wonderful.

"Please accept my apologies for imposing myself on your household. It was unforgivable of me. I'll be gone first thing in the morning."

He stood and drew closer. "Claire, I didn't bring all this out in the open to drive you away. I spoke because I want honesty between us. I want nothing but what's real between us, and what's real is that I'm *glad* you came to Foxtail—I would never have met you otherwise."

Her brows drew down. "How could you possibly be glad that I tricked you?"

"Because," he said quietly, "I don't feel tricked." He glanced down and reached for her hand, and she let him take it, though surely it was a mistake to do so. And yet, his manner and words were not at all what she would have expected, and she couldn't stop herself from wanting to know what he would say.

His fingers were strong and masculine, and despite knowing that they must routinely wield a quill to sign important documents and hold the most costly of crystal glasses, they still made her think of the blacksmith's hammer. Rowan was a physically powerful man, and he was also a duke. Everything about him was strength and power.

"From the first moment I saw you, Claire Beckett, you've done something to me."

She had not expected such words, nor the huskiness coloring his deep voice. For the first time since he'd exposed her ruse, she felt a glimmer of hope. "I have?" Could it really be possible that he felt as powerfully drawn to her as she did to him?

He leaned closer, his dark eyes holding hers. "I need to touch you, and everything in me has been burning with one question: Do you need to touch me too?"

He fascinated her, he made her heart beat faster, she felt things with him that she'd never felt before. *Of course* she needed to touch him.

How could she, in this moment, say anything but the truth? "Yes."

"I want you," he said.

Just like that, in his direct way. He was stating his desire to lie with her. He knew that she'd lied about her identity, and he'd doubtless guessed that she was of the kind of minor gentry with whom the Duke of Starlingham would never normally consort.

He was the Duke of Starlingham.

But he'd been Rowan to her first, and he was still Rowan. She'd known him as a man first and not a duke, and that man had made her feel things she'd never felt before. He'd made her want things.

Wanting wasn't love. He wasn't speaking to her of love, but of physical desire. She desired him too.

He was a man from a world vastly above her own, and after she left Foxtail—as she must surely do the following day—she would never see him again.

But would she ever have the chance again to experience what was between them, to explore their inexpressible connection and this potent desire?

Now would be her only chance.

For years she'd refused to acknowledge that she had needs and wants, but she'd come to understand that to ignore her deepest feelings was to chip away at the full unfolding of the person she was meant to be.

Now was her chance to take what she wanted, and she wanted him.

* * *

Rowan whispered a silent prayer of gratitude that Claire hadn't yet thrown him out. He'd gambled, coming to her room as he'd done, and revealing that he knew her secret. If she was indifferent to him, surely she would have sent him away by now, and his chances would have been finished. Or at least that was what he was telling himself.

How had she become so dear to him in such a short time? He was utterly infatuated with her. But no, that wasn't the whole truth. He wanted far more than some sort of affair. It was funny: He'd been attracted to Maria—a woman he'd known, or thought he'd known, for his whole life—but what he felt for Claire, whom he'd known only for days, was entirely different. It was wilder, messier, and more real. And impossible to resist.

He stroked her cheek with the backs of his fingers. Her skin was nearly unbearably soft. Her eyes regarded him steadily.

"Yes," she whispered, and his heart soared.

Leaning closer, he brushed her lips with his own, gently tasting her, coaxing her lips to part, and when they did, tasting her more deeply as he'd longed to do. Her mouth welcomed him with heat and moist skin, and their breaths mingled in the closeness.

One of her hands settled against the bare skin of his neck, and his own came on top of it, pressing her closer still. He slipped her robe off her shoulders and untied the strings at the neck of her night rail. She looked at him, her eyes never wavering, as she stepped out of it. She stood naked to him in the firelight, which shone in her golden hair and paid homage to the loveliness of her slender, feminine body.

"I have never seen anything more beautiful, Claire, than you are right now."

Her eyelids dropped lower for a moment as though she was suddenly shy, but then she lifted her chin and smiled pertly up at him, and his heart thrilled with that joy only she could bring.

She loosened his shirt, and he drew it over his head and removed his trousers.

They stood before each other completely naked. Her eyes traveled down his body and widened a little as they took in the evidence of his desire. He'd been naked with women many times before, but this was different. He'd never before wanted a woman to *see* him.

"Have you ever—" he began, but she stopped him with a finger against his lips.

"It is my choice," she said. "Let's not talk about practicalities. We are together here now, only for this. For what is between us."

He touched the elegant curve of her shoulder, his hand moving along the warm silk of her skin to cup her breast. Heat rose in him, and she quivered as he stroked his thumb over her nipple.

"Rowan," she whispered. He kissed her, their mouths meeting in tenderness and desire.

She was likely a virgin, and he would take her virginity tonight if she wanted to give it to him. But he would allow himself this only because he wanted to offer her everything. She was the woman he wanted to marry.

He took her hand and led her to the bed, and they lay down facing each other. He traced the lush mount of her hips and the valley of her waist and kissed her breasts, and she moaned, a quiet, husky sound that made him feel at once deeply carnal and also tenderly protective of what she was entrusting to him. She explored his chest, his shoulders, his hips. Her touch gained sureness, and her hand lingered over his erection. He burned for her.

Gently he urged her onto her back and slid his hand along the smooth skin between her thighs to touch that most secret part of her body. She was wet and hot, and he pleasured her until the shiver in her breathing told him she was ready.

He nudged her legs wider and moved between them. At her entrance, he paused to look in her eyes.

"Oh," she whispered. Her eyes were liquid and vulnerable, her skin glowing with a light that was more than fire glow. "Please come to me, Rowan."

He pushed into her steadily, met the resistance of her maidenhood, and thrust through it. He paused, but she made no indication that the moment had brought her pain and instead drew her legs up against him to urge him on.

He stroked into her, the bliss unimaginable yet made only more exquisite as she responded to him, her breath quickening and her legs tightening around him.

She found her release with a little cry that caught in her throat. He thrust into her a few final times until, overcome with a radical new pleasure—a pleasure that was far more than simple enjoyment but an opening to a territory beyond—he jerked himself from her body to spend his release on her belly.

A few moments later, he rolled to the side and located his handkerchief, which he handed to Claire before settling back under the sheets. After she had tidied herself, he slid his arm under her shoulders and kissed her cheek.

* * *

Almost as soon as her skin began to cool, regret settled over Claire like a blanket of snow. What had she done?

"I guessed it would be amazing between us, but my imagination has been put to shame, sweet." He kissed her forehead. "I'll have to move out of Foxtail now, so I can court you properly. And I'll have to figure out some way to explain why I've been concealing my identity from everyone here."

Claire's stomach dropped. He was talking about the future, about courting her. About the reality that he was a powerful duke whose movements were of great interest to many. The heat of the moment had allowed her to forget who she was, but the very idea of being courted by a duke—a title that allowed a man to ignore the word *no*—was a splash of much-needed icy water.

She pushed herself up against the headboard, pulling the blanket up to cover herself.

"You don't need to court me. There is no need."

"No need?" he said in a puzzled voice, moving to sit next to her. He rested his head lazily against the headboard and smiled. "Of course there's a need. Never mind that it's exactly what I want to do."

She wished it didn't have to be this way—that he could just leave now and they wouldn't have to say another word to each other. That they wouldn't have to discuss any of what they'd done. It would have been the easiest thing, though even as she told herself that, she knew it was a lie. Nothing about this entanglement of emotions was going to be easy.

"This was very nice—" she began, meaning to frame what they'd done in a way that would let them move past this moment, but he interrupted her.

"*Nice?*" he said, something dark creeping into his voice.

"It was very pleasurable," she tried again, feeling off-kilter. She drew her legs up and leaned forward, hugging them to herself, needing to close herself off from the powerful pull he exerted over her. "But it was still a mistake. A foolish mistake on my part. Could... could you leave now, please?"

Nothing from him but silence for long moments. She didn't turn to look at him.

"Do you mean to suggest that I seduced you? Is this the moment when you regret that you didn't say no?"

"Of course not. I wanted to do what we did. But it was just momentary lust, and there is no need for there to be anything further." It hurt to say such words—it hadn't been only desire that had made her step into his arms. But she couldn't afford to listen to the foolish, vulnerable part of her that wanted a man who was wrong for her. Did she need any more evidence of her own weakness than what she'd done tonight?

When he didn't reply, she finally glanced over her shoulder. He looked dangerous.

"I don't believe you," he said roughly, crossing his arms. "This is just you being contrary."

"That's just it, Rowan. I'm not contrary at all." Needing whatever distance she could claim, she turned away from him again. Her eyes settled on the outline of her toes pushing up the blanket where she'd pulled it across her feet. She'd never even taken off her shoes in the presence of a man who was not a relative before, and this man had seen and touched all of her. And it had all started because of that game she and Louisa had dreamed up.

"I'm not bold, and I never do things like I just did tonight. It was out of character for me, just as it was out of character for me to be contrary toward you, as I was almost as soon as I met you."

Though she wasn't looking at him, she could feel, in the heaviness of the silence he allowed to drag out, the ducal disapproval rolling off him. "You're not making any sense, Claire." His voice was firm. "I like you, you like me—I don't see a problem with our being together. In fact, I think our mutual liking means we ought to be together."

She needed to put more space between them, so she got up and pulled on her dressing gown. He watched her from the bed with an unreadable expression. "That's because you're a duke and you're used to ordering people around. If I spent any more time with you, I'd soon be just one more person you were dominating."

His brow plummeted toward dark eyes that had turned stormy. "That's the most ridiculous thing I've ever heard."

"No, it isn't. You've done nothing but order me about since you arrived."

"And you resisted me at every turn!"

"It was a game."

"A game?" He sounded genuinely confused.

"Something Louisa and I devised to cure me of a tendency I had developed of being too agreeable."

"An unusual undertaking," he bit off. "Yet, considering the difficulty I've had getting you to agree even to pass me the butter at breakfast, I'd say the game was a success."

She shook her head. "That's just it—it was only a game. I know myself, and I know my weaknesses. If you and I spent more time together, things between us would only become unbalanced."

He stood and drew near her. "You're not giving yourself enough credit, Claire." His tone was reasonable but firm, as though he believed that she was just about to see things his way. "You claim to know yourself, but you don't seem to have much faith in yourself. Do you really think I would have been so drawn to you if you were as weak-willed as you seem to think you are?"

She sighed, wishing he would just accept what she'd said. "Have you considered that the very reason you wanted me is that men love the chase? I have three brothers, Rowan. I know how men are."

Haughtiness settled over his features. He was a man accustomed to ordering things exactly as he wished, and she reminded herself that that quality would make him want to order her life as well, even though she knew she was being a little unfair to him. He *was* a good man. But he was also a man who didn't know what it was like to be powerless.

"You're unfamiliar with how *I* am," he ground out, "if you think I can't make up my own mind about what I want." He reached for her hand, enclosing it in his much larger one.

"What's between us is just attraction, Rowan. It's powerful, but it's not the stuff of everyday life. People can be attracted to each other—very attracted—but also be a bad match." Though she loved the strength and comfort of his touch, she reclaimed her hand and crossed her arms, needing to seal herself off from him and what he wanted her to accept.

A growl slipped past his lips. "What is it about me that makes you think we're a bad match?"

"It's not you…"

He gave her a dark look.

"Very well, it *is* you—and me. Rowan, I've spent the last few years of my life living like a ghost, meekly making myself into a woman who did just as she was asked. Coming here to Foxtail has given me the space to think a little, and what I've discovered is that I don't want to tie my life to a man who might overwhelm me."

He shoved a hand in his hair. "What are you talking about? Why would I overwhelm you? I care for you."

She could feel his frustration, feel how much he wanted things to be other than the way they were, and maybe that *feeling*—that capacity for empathy—was one of the reasons she'd come to ignore her own needs in favor of what other people wanted. Even now, with all she'd learned, she had to force herself not to give in to what he wanted from her—but then, was it surprising that because she cared for him so much, she was at the greatest risk of all with him? Capitulating to what someone else wanted from her would be the death of her hopes for herself, though, and she couldn't do it.

"I'm sure my father cares for me too. But I've seen how ready I am to diminish myself in the company of fierce people, and I know it's sensible not to put myself in such a situation."

"This is nonsense," he said, his voice hard with anger. "Look at yourself:

You've stood up to me just now, even though I'm trying to press you into marrying me. Which you want to do anyway."

"I'm not going to change my mind, Rowan."

She heard the sound of teeth grinding. "Am I to understand that despite what just happened between us, you want nothing further from me?"

"Yes."

His eyes held hers for long moments, dark eyes that seemed to penetrate to her very soul. When he spoke, the anger was gone from his voice, leaving only the deep tones she'd come to cherish, and now that was worse. "I'm not looking for a mistress, Claire, if that's what you think. I have far more serious intentions."

He meant marriage. She had to push down a nearly hysterical laugh at the idea of being married to the Duke of Starlingham. "You're a gentleman, and I understand that you feel constrained by a sense of honor. But I just need you to go."

He didn't say another word, and she looked away as he collected his things and left, closing the door quietly after himself.

CHAPTER SEVEN

Claire awoke to the bright daylight of midmorning and the sight of Louisa slipping into her room.

"Are you just waking up now?" Louisa said incredulously as she closed the door behind her.

"Yes," Claire said, struggling to throw off the fatigue of a bad night's sleep. She'd had trouble falling asleep after Rowan left, and memories of what had happened between them assailed her afresh now.

She sat up and pushed a few strands of hair out of her face. "I overslept." She would have to sort herself out to leave Foxtail as soon as possible, but she didn't know how she would explain her abrupt departure to Louisa. What had happened felt far too raw and private to discuss.

Louisa sat down on the bed. She was smiling. "You missed the excitement, such as it was. Fitzwilliam and Dixon moved out this morning."

"*What?*"

"They've gone to stay at the vicarage."

"Both of them? But why?"

Louisa's smiled deepened, and Claire detected a hint of smugness at the corners. "I thought perhaps *you* might be able to shed some light on that. I overheard Fitzwilliam telling Dixon that since he has decided to court you, it wouldn't be appropriate for him to stay in the house."

"But—that's ridiculous!"

Louisa laughed, but she also looked puzzled. "Goodness, you are making things hard for the man. Why should it be ridiculous that he wants to move out and court you, especially when you've already admitted to me that he makes your heart thump?"

"Because it's *his* hunting box," Claire said. "He's not the duke's cousin—he *is* the Duke of Starlingham. He told me so last night."

Louisa's eyebrows shot upward. "That must have been some assembly. You don't think he was joking, or hoaxing you?"

"I'm certain he wasn't."

"Well, well. Now we know that the dear old duke isn't old after all. But why is he pretending to be his own cousin?" She crossed her arms in playful vexation. "And where is his ducal finery? My one chance to see a duke, and there hasn't been a gaudy waistcoat or golden quizzing glass in sight."

"He's here in hiding because of something to do with a friend. Though I think it's also that he likes not being a duke for a change."

"You know," Louisa said slowly, "it makes sense now that I think of it, him being a duke. He's so commanding."

Claire nodded.

Louisa's eyes narrowed. "So why aren't you celebrating? He wants to court you! You've snared a duke!"

Outside the window, the sky was a perfect blue. Claire gazed at its vastness, which looked like freedom, while she felt trapped by her desires and circumstances. But she still had choices. "I don't want to marry a duke."

"What?" Louisa, sitting behind Claire, poked her, and Claire turned. "What can you possibly be thinking? Why not marry a duke?"

"Can you see me, quiet Claire Beckett, as a duchess?"

"You're not quiet," Louisa said fiercely. "You're thoughtful and good-hearted. The world needs more duchesses like you."

"I don't want him to court me."

"But you like him. He wants to make you his duchess. This is everything you need!"

It was so tempting to believe that, but Claire knew she'd already allowed herself to need Rowan far more than she should have. "We're not a good match. And I don't want to be a duchess."

Louisa treated Claire to a stern look. "I can't understand why you won't give him a chance. But if you don't find some man to marry soon, you'll end up a baroness."

"Or I won't marry anyone at all." Claire threw off the covers and swung her legs off the bed. "I have to get up and start packing."

"You can't leave now—nothing's sorted out yet. And clearly Fitzwilliam doesn't want you to go, since he's left you his whole estate for you to enjoy without him." Louisa paused, and her face melted into a satisfied grin, for she could never be stern for long. "And all this because you started saying no. Amazing, the power of two little letters."

"Amazing, the trouble caused by two little letters."

Louisa chuckled and made for the door. "This is too much serious talk before breakfast. I'll get you a nice cup of chocolate, and then everything will make more sense."

* * *

The vicarage was without a doubt the smallest dwelling in which Rowan had ever installed himself.

He'd awoken the morning after making love to Claire knowing that he was going to court her and that he needed to leave Foxtail to do so properly.

He'd botched the encounter in her room. He was so enchanted by her, and he'd been so certain enchantment was enough, that he'd rushed heedlessly forward. Until now, he'd been allowing what had happened with Maria to close him off to anything that might make him vulnerable, but he was suddenly ready for feelings he hadn't wanted in so long.

What was between him and Claire was different—*he* was different. Making love with her had broken open something in him that he didn't want to seal up again.

Rowan had needed to take Dixon into his confidence and had revealed his identity to him, to which Dixon had said triumphantly, "I suspected as much! I was a frequent guest when your father used to come to Foxtail, and you look exactly like him." He'd paused, the light of suspicion in his eyes. "But I wonder at you and Miss Beckett not knowing each other, being related."

Rowan didn't feel it was his place to reveal Claire's information. "Let's just say she's a *very* distant cousin."

Dixon, the imp, seemed quite amused by the whole thing. "And so you're going to court her properly," he said with a glee-filled smirk. "I wonder how a duke will do at courting?"

* * *

Rowan appeared the next morning at Foxtail with a bouquet of wildflowers. He was standing by the hearth when Claire came into the sitting room, having been alerted to his presence by an exuberant Louisa. Claire realized now that it was likely one of his relatives who had once dispatched the stag mounted on the wall behind him.

"Good morning, Claire. You are looking quite wonderful today."

He looked wonderful too. He was wearing an exquisite, ducal-looking coat of bright blue, though clearly he was still suffering from the lack of a valet, because there was a new, small nick on his jaw. She longed to feather her fingertips over it, as if her touch might soothe it, but she curled her fingers inward instead. She remained standing, resolved to be brisk and firm with him.

"This is your house, Rowan," she said. "If one of us is to leave, it should be me. I can pack my things and be gone in a matter of hours."

"I don't want you to leave," he said, the barest hint of his customary growl in his words. Why hadn't she realized before that his growling was half composed of haughtiness?

"But—"

"Foxtail is at your disposal for as long as you wish to stay," he said firmly.

And then he bowed and left, leaving Claire puzzled, frustrated, and ridiculously disappointed, never mind that she hadn't wanted him to come at all.

When he appeared the following morning, Claire didn't come down, despite Louisa's urging.

But Claire did send a note to Mr. Dixon that afternoon, letting him know that though Mr. Rutledge's interest had been flattering, she wouldn't be able to accept any proposal from him.

Her time at Foxtail had been meant as an escape from her looming engagement to Lord Haight and a last chance for a holiday with Louisa, but it had turned into so much more. She'd come to see that she did have choices for her future. Even if they were not terribly appealing, they were her own choices, and she would make them. At the end of the week, when her family would expect her return from Aunt Mary's, she would make her way home to let them know that instead of marrying Haight, she would be accepting a position as governess for a family Louisa knew.

Her family would doubtless be furious with her, but Claire knew she couldn't accept a future of misery for herself just to please her father. It would be wrong. But she would go home to say what she had to say in person. If there was going to be a permanent break with her family—and she very much feared there would be—she wanted to say goodbye. They might be difficult, but they were still her family.

When Rowan stopped by again on the third morning after leaving Foxtail, Louisa attempted to drag Claire to the sitting room. "He's being so sweet! How can you ignore him?"

"It's better not to encourage someone if the answer's going to be no," Claire said. After which statement, Louisa threw up her hands.

The fourth day, Rowan brought a puppy. This, Claire couldn't ignore. She came into the sitting room and found Rowan crouching down by the little brown dog whose barks she'd heard from upstairs. He was rubbing its stomach.

"Rowan, this is ridiculous. You can't purchase my cooperation by giving me a puppy."

He looked up, a hint of wickedness playing about the strong lines of his mouth. "I'm not giving Prince to you—I've borrowed him from Dixon's neighbor. But I did hope you would at least find him irresistible enough to emerge from your tower, or wherever it is you've been hiding."

She made an exasperated sound, but it tapered off into a laugh. "You're impossible," she said even as Prince sprang up and ran over to bury his head amid her skirts. She knelt down to pet the puppy's soft fur.

Rowan was quiet as Claire played with the dog.

"I've decided not to sell Foxtail," he said after a few moments. "I've already sent word to my man of affairs to arrange for repairs and refurbishments for the lodge and for Trethillin as well."

She straightened up and looked at him. Though his features might be too strong to be considered conventionally attractive, to her he was irresistibly handsome. "I'm glad to hear that. Foxtail is a unique and wonderful property that deserves to be maintained and enjoyed."

But it was terribly tempting to imagine herself there with him, lazing about in a boat on the lake, or reading in the little hut as a soft breeze wafted through its open doors. His eyes told her that he wanted to share this place with her, and she knew herself to be weakening toward him.

Because she cared for him.

No, it was more than just caring. She was very much afraid that she loved him.

What if he loves me too? an inner voice prodded.

She couldn't listen to it. She'd learned so much about herself in her time at Foxtail, and she couldn't afford to go back to the way she'd once been. Change wasn't easy, and it could be hard to maintain resolution in the face of pressure. Going home to tell her family about her decision to be a governess would be a true test of the direction she'd set for herself.

She was about to make some excuse and leave, but before she could, he said, "I just thought you'd like to know about Foxtail." He whistled for the puppy and took his leave.

Standing there alone again in the sitting room, she was very much tempted to stamp her foot.

On the fifth day, he didn't even ask for Claire, but instead invited Louisa to join him for a cup of tea, which she did. Claire, who could hear them laughing from her bedchamber, resolutely took up a book, but she had to force her eyes to stay on the words so she wouldn't be tempted to go downstairs and join them. Thank God, she thought, that she was leaving tomorrow, even though the idea of parting from Rowan and leaving Foxtail made her chest squeeze.

Late that afternoon, she strolled about the property as a sort of leave-taking. The sunlight fell like gold coins on the path through the wood, and she found her feet guiding her to the edge of the clearing by Trethillin. Gardeners were already at work clearing the weeds from the cottage gardens, and a workman was nailing down some loose shingles on the hut. The sight left her both happy and depressed.

She set out on the way back to Foxtail, resolved to be glad for the decisions she'd made for herself. She had nearly passed through the woods by the lodge when she met Rowan on the path.

* * *

"Louisa told me you might be here," Rowan said as he approached Claire. She was wearing a pale blue gown, and she looked almost unbearably lovely, familiar and mysterious at the same time.

She'd become utterly important to him.

He wanted to touch her, but he didn't know how she would receive it if he did, and so he didn't.

She smiled a little. "Trethillin looks much better already," she said. "It will be beautiful. Though I admit I loved the battered, wild look it had when I first saw it."

He could ask her right then if she would marry him. He wanted to ask her again. But how would she respond?

God, he was beginning to sound like Rutledge. What the devil was wrong with him? He'd never wanted for decisiveness before.

"I wouldn't have put any thought into keeping Foxtail and refreshing the village if it hadn't been for you."

"Then I'm glad, on Foxtail's behalf, that I came here and imposed on you."

A silence stretched between them. "Claire," he said, "I've come to care deeply for you." These were pallid words; in truth, he loved her. He wanted to tell her, but it seemed like too much in that moment. Hadn't she said she didn't want to be overwhelmed by him?

He chose to play down his emotions and appeal to her sense. "We are good together. Stay with me. Be my wife. Will you marry me?"

She turned her face away. "Rowan"—her voice sounded thick—"I thank you for the honor you do me, but I cannot accept."

He wanted to kick the mighty oak tree that stood next to him. "Damn it, Claire, why are you refusing to see what's real? It's true that we haven't known each other for very long, but there's something very good between us. It's a spark that's crackled from our first meeting, and it's grown into a flame, one that could light a lifetime."

She looked back at him, as though his words had touched on something significant. "Rowan, I'm not made to be a duchess. You would see this if only you would think."

"Do you think I've always liked being a duke?" he said fiercely. "That I wanted to be responsible for so much from an early age? To be always of interest to people because of my position and not because of the person I am?"

Though he might need to woo her with sweet, gentle words, he wasn't the sweetest of men, and he could only speak his truth to her. "I didn't get to choose. We're all born into a particular time and place and position, and there's not a thing any of us can do about that fact. But we do have a say over how we respond to what life brings us."

Her eyes darkened with some emotion, and he thought for a moment that he'd pierced the armor of polite reserve she'd drawn around herself, but when she spoke, her voice betrayed nothing. "Then you'll understand why I must honor the choices I've made for myself. I need to go home, to tell my family that I won't marry the baron."

She began walking, and he fell into step with her in silence. Shortly they emerged from the woods near the lodge.

"And then you wish to go and be a governess," he said, hating the words as he formed them.

"Yes."

He was so frustrated that she wouldn't honor what was between them. But he was not a beast. He sighed. "Then let me take you to your family."

She turned to him in surprise. "No, I couldn't. But thank you."

"I don't make the offer with a view to changing your mind. I'm offering because you'll be traveling alone otherwise, won't you?"

"It's no matter."

"Yes, it is. It's not sensible for a young lady to travel unaccompanied, as you well know. If you're going to be a governess, you'll have to set a good example." He paused. "I will ride outside the coach, of course. It's a journey of but a few hours, I believe?"

"Five," she said. "But I can't inconvenience you in this way, and the mail coach will be fine."

"Just let me do this, Claire. I don't like the idea of you traveling unaccompanied when I have the means to help. That's all my wealth and power are to me: the means to help those I care about be safe and happy."

She looked troubled, but she agreed.

They'd reached the front of Foxtail, and he bowed and took his leave.

CHAPTER EIGHT

As Claire prepared to leave Foxtail the next morning, she had to drag herself through each step. The place had become a second home to her, even though the very idea was ridiculous. It belonged to the Duke of Starlingham.

"I wish you wouldn't go," Louisa said as they stood in the front drive by Rowan's coach. He was there too, waiting for her on a tall chestnut horse. He'd merely nodded at her when she'd come out. It was better if he didn't talk to her, she told herself, but it didn't *feel* better.

"You know I have to leave. But we can't let years go by before we meet again."

Louisa pulled her into a fierce embrace. "You just save those governess pennies, and we'll go to the Continent together and have the most wonderful, audacious time touring about. We'll meet unsuitable people, drink more than ladies should, and see everything there is to see."

"That sounds wonderful," Claire said in a voice growing rapidly husky. They stepped apart, and she climbed into the carriage.

They set off with a crunching of wheels on gravel, and that was it, the end of the most magical time of her life.

As the journey was but five hours, there would be no need to stop. Claire settled into the seat and looked out the window and tried very hard not to dwell on what she was leaving behind.

And there was Rowan, framed in the small coach window as he rode alongside. He was looking ahead, perhaps lost in thought, but accompanying her. Not asking anything of her.

She watched him for a long time. He looked very good on horseback, and the sight of his broad shoulders in his dark coat brought memories of those moments when their bodies had expressed what words could not. But it wasn't only these thoughts that preoccupied her. It was the knowledge that he was simply there.

Eventually she drew the curtain to cover the window and forced herself to move to the other side of the coach and read a book. When that didn't work to distract her flitting thoughts, she took out some tatting. She thought about her family, and how good it would be to see them, and how they would likely be angry when she told them her news. She returned to her book, reading pages at a time without having any sense of what the words meant.

It began to rain. Rowan was outside, assuredly growing wet and uncomfortable on her account. She wanted to insist that he give this up, that he deposit her at the next town, but she didn't. She knew the commanding Duke of Starlingham would never agree to such a thing, and it would diminish what he wanted to offer her if she would not accept it. And so she accepted it.

Five hours in a coach alone gave her a great deal of time to think. And all she could seem to think about was the man riding steadfastly alongside her coach in the rain. Asking nothing of her. Demanding nothing of her. Though she was denying him what he wanted very much—and he'd made his feelings about this known—he hadn't tried to force her to accept his proposal. Though she'd feared her own capacity for weakness before his strength and the power he wielded as both a man and a duke, he'd never once tried to overwhelm her. And he might easily have tried.

She understood now that he would never seek to overpower her, just as she would never again allow herself to discount her own needs and wishes. He respected her, just as she respected him.

As the coach finally drew near the crossroad that would lead to the last three miles of her journey, Claire signaled to the driver to stop.

It was still raining, but she hardly noticed as she hurried to get out of the coach. Rowan was just circling back, having noticed that they'd stopped.

"What's going on, Claire?" he called as he rode closer.

"I need to talk to you," she shouted over the drumming of the rain.

He dismounted and strode toward Claire, who was growing rapidly wet.

He, though, was drenched, water running in streams off his hat and wetting his cheeks. He looked closed-off and unreachable, but she had to trust that was because he wasn't happy with the way things stood.

"Are you well?" he asked in those familiar gruff tones.

"I think I will be," she said, then felt suddenly shy. She dearly hoped she hadn't ruined everything between them. "That is, if you haven't changed your mind."

His shuttered expression slowly softened as her meaning penetrated. He leaned closer, his eyes now searching hers. "Do you mean… have you changed your mind?"

"I have, Rowan."

She had the very great privilege to see hope dawning in his eyes, to feel it reaching forward to touch the hope rising in her own breast. "Dare I hope that you love me as I love you, Claire?"

"Yes, Rowan. I do love you, so very dearly."

He closed his eyes for a moment, as though some great weight had been lifted. When he opened them, they were shining. "Then you will you marry me, Claire?"

His voice was hoarse and so dear to her. She threw her arms around him. "Yes, yes, yes! A thousand times yes!"

And then they were kissing and speaking broken phrases, the words tumbling over each other.

When they finally broke apart, Claire noticed that the rain had eased to a drizzle, and the coachman had wisely turned his attention to the horses. Rowan leaned his forehead against hers. "What changed your mind?"

"You," she said. "You helped me see how strong I am."

He shook his head, as though he couldn't understand such words from her. "Would you even have left home to begin with if you weren't strong? Or said no to me all those times when you wanted to say yes? You've made your own decisions and stuck to them, even when it didn't please me."

"I know," she said. She grinned. "Seeing you out in the rain, riding along just to see me safely home, made me realize that I can trust you. That I can trust myself to both give *and* take with you."

He looked down his nose at her with a deliciously excessive amount of haughtiness. "So what you're saying, Miss Beckett, is that you are very comfortable with me being uncomfortable?"

She laughed, and he chuckled, drawing her close again. "Who ever would have guessed that I would fall in love so quickly and so hard, and with a woman determined to hide all the sweetest parts of herself?"

"I suppose I'm lucky that you're not easily discouraged." She felt as though her smile would never stop.

"From the moment I first saw you, dearest Claire, I felt that there was something between us that had existed before we even met. Something eternal. Fate." He shook his head, laughing. "If my friends ever hear me talking like this, they'll never let me hear the end of it. I'll be getting gifts of tarot cards at Christmas, and encouraged to predict the outcome of every horse race, and teased until I want to plant them all facers."

"It does all sound ridiculous," she said.

"And yet it's true."

"And it's wonderful."

With Rowan's horse now tied to the coach, the two of them climbed inside for the last few miles.

"You've made all this quite moot," she said, "my coming home to announce I won't marry the baron. A duke is a far better catch than a baron, so I'm very unlikely to make any of them unhappy now."

"They might not like me," he pointed out.

Her lips quivered as her eyes lofted heavenward.

"Why don't you go in first," he suggested, threading his fingers through hers, "and confess that you went to Louisa instead of your aunt. I suspect that will give them adequate reason to be upset. And it will give you an opening to explain that you mean to proceed differently from now on. They will, after all, always be your family. You will want to be on good terms with them."

"That, my dear duke, is an extremely sensible idea." She kissed his cheek, lingering there simply to breathe him in. "I really have chosen exceedingly well."

He kissed her again, and she knew she'd never grow tired of his kisses, or of him. "You have, haven't you," he said, laughter rumbling through him. "And so have I."

THE END

Dear Reader,

I hope you enjoyed our dukes' adventures in Lesser Puddlebury. It was an absolute delight working on this story collection with Grace Burrowes and Susanna Ives, who are two of the most creative, talented, and generous writers I know.

March is an exciting month for me because this novella is releasing at nearly the same time as *How To Handle A Scandal*, the second book in my Scandalous Sisters series. This is the sequel to *The Beautiful One*, and I've included an excerpt of *How To Handle A Scandal* that I hope you'll enjoy.

You can keep up with all my releases and author events, and also sign up for my newsletter, on my website at **http://emilygreenwood.net**. I only send out newsletters two or three times a year, and I will never share your email.

Happy reading!
Emily

HOW TO HANDLE A SCANDAL

Seventeen-year-old Elizabeth Tarryton is having the time of her life being the talk —and maybe the scandal—of her first Season, and she has no intention of ending the fun any time soon by marrying. Tommy Halifax, who's a few years older, is the brother of Eliza's beloved guardian, Will, Viscount Grandville.

Tommy Halifax had the perfect solution to the little problem of Miss Lizzie Tarryton's adorable outrageousness: he was going to marry her.

The idea still made him a bit light-headed, because he hadn't thought to marry for years. He was not yet twenty-two, and if asked even the year before whether he might marry soon, he would have roared with laughter. But then he'd met Lizzie.

A twinge of conscience prodded him; he should probably have discussed his plans with Will first. But that was a conversation he didn't want to have yet. And they were brothers—there was nothing but respect and affection between them, so Will had no reason to object to Tommy's suitability.

The dance was over, and Andrew was leading Lizzie to where Will and Anna were talking. Before Lizzie could go off with anyone else, Tommy made his way to her, pleased that her face lit up when she saw him.

"There you are!" she said, coming close to give him a quick embrace. She smelled of that soft rose scent that was uniquely hers.

Andrew clapped Tommy on the back jovially, Anna embraced him, and Will asked after Longmount. After all the pleasantries had been tended to, Tommy, his heart beginning to race, looked toward the open terrace doors, where few people seemed to have gone despite the warmth of the summer night. He held out an arm to Lizzie.

"Let's go outside and cool off. You can tell me about everything I missed."

She agreed and chattered happily as they walked, telling him about what had happened while he was away. When they stepped through the doors and onto the terrace, she looked up at the dark summer sky and sighed. Her capacity to be nearly always joyous was one of the things he loved best about her.

"Isn't it the most splendid night?" she asked.

As Tommy watched the starlight mingle with the gold lights in her hair, he was pierced by her beauty. He murmured his assent as he led her away from the manor and into the quiet, deserted space of the garden, which was lit with torches.

"It *is* a splendid night," he said to the side of her face as she gazed at the stars. He took a deep breath. "But do you know what makes it truly splendid for me? Being here with you."

There was a longish pause, then she turned to look at him. He'd never said something so personal to her, and he was dying inside waiting to know how she would take it.

"You must be in the mood to flirt tonight," she said lightly.

"I'm not flirting. I'm serious."

She frowned. "I'm not good at being serious, Tommy."

"Nonsense," he said. "You can be serious when you choose."

"Er...thank you," she said, sounding puzzled.

He'd never once kissed her, though he'd wanted to desperately, countless times. But now that he had such serious intentions toward her, and considering how well they knew each other—surely it wouldn't be inappropriate now?

"Lizzie," he said, huskiness creeping into his voice, "I want to kiss you. May I?"

She seemed surprised by his request, as though all the days and nights they'd spent talking and flirting hadn't been leading in any particular direction. But there was a bond between them, built of affection and friendship. And attraction—he felt as certain of it as of his own breathing. They were meant to be together.

"Erhm." And then she smiled. "Yes. I'd like that." The words, breathy wisps that hinted at awakening emotions, inflamed him.

She tipped her head up and his heart thundered. When his lips finally— finally!—met hers, he *felt* it: she was going to be the love of his life.

Her mouth opened to him, and her tongue gently sought his, which gave him the unwelcome awareness that he wasn't the first man she'd kissed. How many of the gentlemen of the *ton* had tasted her? he wondered with a surge of jealousy.

He pushed the thought away. It didn't matter, because he meant to be the last.

A little whimper escaped her, and she hugged him closer as though she needed him. The awareness touched him in the most welcome way. She *needed* him, just as he needed her. He forced himself to break the kiss.

"Lizzie," he murmured, "we can't go on like this."

"Like what?" She sounded adorably dazed.

He smiled a little. "Stealing kisses in the garden."

"Who would know if we did?"

"Trust me, we can't. I won't survive the experience."

"What do you mean?"

"I mean, dearest Lizzie, that you make my head spin."

"Do I?" She laughed. "Will said the same thing yesterday when I told him I loved champagne."

"You make my head spin in a *different* way."

An inscrutable emotion flitted across her face. "Er…" She mumbled something that sounded like, "Me too." But it might also have been something that ended in "you."

Then she smiled brightly, as if they'd been talking about any old thing, and said, "Do you know, I should quite like a lemonade."

And before he could say a word, she'd stepped away from him toward the ballroom.

He stood blinking for a moment at her abrupt departure. That kiss…it had been amazing, but it hadn't been amazing just for him. He'd felt the thrill pulsing between them, heard the wonder in her voice.

He moved to the doorway. She'd found her way to Will and Anna, who were standing with the rest of his cousins near the edge of the ballroom. It occurred to Tommy that this was perfect: most of the people they loved best were right here. What better moment could there be to declare their love for each other?

* * *

Lizzie swept into the ballroom wondering if she had a silly smile on her face. But Tommy had just kissed her! And it had been a little wonderful.

He was a *much* better kisser than Lord Hewett, who'd stolen a kiss in an alcove at a house party last month, or young Mr. Fletcher, who'd quickly pressed his lips to hers under the mistletoe at a Christmas party. She wasn't even going to count the lieutenant she'd kissed in the garden at the Rosewood School the year before, because that had really been about something besides kissing.

Her smile slipped a little as she thought of what Tommy had said afterward. He *had* made her head spin a little, but she didn't want to talk about it. Talking made things too fixed, like they were all decided, when really she just wanted everything to be *possible.*

She hoped the kiss wasn't going to make it impossible to go back to the way they'd always been, because she needed Tommy to be her friend.

She hoped… No, surely it wasn't necessary to hope anything. Surely *Tommy* wasn't going to be like the other gentlemen who'd wanted to be serious. This was Tommy, with whom she always laughed and teased with no consequences. Surely it had only been a kiss, even if it had been a little amazing. But she decided right then that they mustn't do it again.

"And what have you been up to, Lizzie?" asked Will's cousin, Louie Halifax, who only months before, on the shocking death of both his uncle and his cousin, had become the Earl of Gildenhall.

Lizzie thought "Gildenhall" was the perfect title for him, since, with his dark blond hair and extremely handsome looks, he seemed gilded. And since he'd been a commoner his entire life, he was not at all stuffy—which wasn't to say that he didn't have quite a bit of presence. He was certainly considered the catch of the season by all the mamas of the *ton*, even if despite being over thirty, he seemed in no hurry to be caught.

"Oh, nothing," Lizzie said. "Are there any cakes left?" She strained to see beyond Louie's shoulders.

He chuckled. "There were three left last I saw, unless Andrew ate them."

His brother rolled his eyes. "Why would I do such an uncouth thing?"

Emerald, their younger sister, cocked her head. "Have you ever noticed how we say people are uncouth, but we never say they are 'couth'?"

Emerald was the same age as Lizzie, and, with eyes as purely green as Tommy's, perfectly named. Thanks to the dramatic reversal in her family's fortunes, Emerald and her older sister Ruby were enjoying the kind of lavish season they could never have had with the burden of debt that had once pressed on them all.

"Or 'ept,'" Ruby pointed out. "People are inept, but never 'ept.' Maybe we should make it a word. This could go down in history as the 'ept' season."

"You can't just sprinkle your conversation with made-up words and think everyone will start using them," Andrew said.

"Can't I?" Ruby said with the light of challenge in her eyes. Ruby Halifax might look haughty, but she had a competitive streak when it came to her brothers, and Lizzie found their squabbles entertaining.

From the moment she'd met them, Louie and his brothers and sisters had treated Lizzie like one of the family, and getting to know them had been one of the best parts of becoming Will's ward.

Someone tapped her on the shoulder. She turned, and there was Tommy. He looked funny, but not in a humorous way. Something fizzed unpleasantly inside her.

"You left so suddenly, Lizzie. I had an important question to ask you."

She'd heard that kind of thing before, and it wasn't good. *Oh no. Oh no, no, no, no.* He wasn't going to do the very thing she desperately didn't want him of all men to do--he mustn't.

She had to lighten the tone immediately and keep him from speaking serious words he would regret. But before she could speak, Will said, "What's going on, Tommy?"

Oh please, she thought desperately, *don't let this be what it sounds like.*

Tommy's green eyes pinned her. He had black hair with a rogue blade of white slashing through at his forehead, and she'd seen more than one young lady swoon over his striking good looks. But to Lizzie he was simply Tommy. And he wasn't supposed to say momentous things to her.

"I'm sure Tommy doesn't have anything to say to me that can't be said in front of all of you," she said, giving him a smile meant to encourage him to keep things light.

But his face was serious.

"You're right, Lizzie. The words I have to say, while especially for you, will mean something for all of the family. Because what I want to ask, dearest Lizzie," he said, taking her hand and dropping fluidly to one knee as his eyes held hers and her stomach plummeted, "is if you will do me the very great honor of becoming my wife."

All the breath rushed out of her. She could feel that Will had gone still next to her, and she heard Anna's quick intake of breath and knew that the others were watching as well. Behind them, people were glancing curiously their way, doubtless drawn by the sight of Tommy Halifax on bended knee.

Panic rushed through her, making her light-headed and off-balance. She felt startled and also a little angry that he was ruining the friendship they'd shared. No—he was ruining everything, because how would his family ever look on her the same way again, now that he'd chosen her? Already excitement was beginning to brighten the beloved faces around her. She felt as if the parson's noose were already slipping over her neck—and everything within her revolted against it.

Which was how, unable to stop herself in that terrible, awkward, panicking moment, she did the one thing she should never have done.

She laughed.

In the stunned moment that followed, she heard Ruby gasp and saw a terrible dark look come over Tommy's face, changing it so she felt suddenly that she hardly knew him. He was still holding her hand as though frozen. She struggled to find something to say, but she couldn't say yes, and she couldn't disappoint him, so she said nothing.

His eyes turned into shards of sharp green glass that cut her, like a knife paring a rotten part from an apple. He dropped her hand and stood up, but now he would no longer look at her, and she understood with a terrible finality that nothing would ever be the same.

Without a word to her or anyone else, he turned and left the ball.

She wrote him two different letters that night and tore them both up before crawling into bed, desperately unhappy and confused and wishing she'd never even gone to the ball.

The failed proposal was the talk of Town, but Lizzie supposed Tommy didn't care or, more accurately, didn't notice, because three days later he boarded a ship for India.

**Find out more about How To Handle A Scandal at
emilygreenwood.net**

Made in the USA
Middletown, DE
16 March 2017